Over and over she told him, "I love you Philip. With all my heart." As they lay wrapped in each other's arms, she told him about falling in love with him when she was only fourteen. "I know some people would think that was impossible but it's true." She pulled his face down to hers and kissed him. "I've never told anyone about this before."

It was only as they rode back to town that she realized he hadn't proposed to her. But hadn't he said, "We belong together"? Didn't that mean that he was making plans for their future? Of course it did.

But a guilty feeling came over her. She had been wanton. Given herself to a man before marriage. Something she swore she would never do. But was it so terrible? They'd be married soon. Now they were one, mates in every sense of the word, so of course they should spend the rest of their lives together. . . .

GOLDEN FLAME

Dorothy Dowdell

FAWCETT GOLD MEDAL • NEW YORK

To my daughter and her husband,
Joan and William Moore

In memory of my uncle, Ward Lusk,
a mining engineer in the gold mines
of Mexico, South America, and Cuba

In memory of my brother-in-law, Arthur Dowdell,
who was on the staff of
the Empire Mine in Grass Valley,
one of the most famous gold mines in California

CHAPTER 1

It was one of those clear, mild evenings in January for which San Francisco was justly famed. As Dorcas Hamilton stepped out onto the balcony leading off the library, she draped a short ermine cape around her bare shoulders, but even that was too warm, so she pushed the soft fur away from her neck. Just the anticipation of the evening ahead made the blood race through her veins in excitement. How good to be young and alive in this new year of 1894.

Her diamond necklace, as well as the rhinestones that formed an intricate rose pattern on the full skirt of her yellow ballgown, sparkled in the faint light. She carefully smoothed the wrinkles from the fingers of her elbow-length white kid gloves. This was her family's first ball after six months of mourning for her father, and she felt she was emerging from a long, dark tunnel. A whole new phase of her life lay ahead.

As usual, she was the first one ready, but she was glad to have a few moments to savor the moonlit scene before her. The Hamilton mansion, situated on the crest of one of the city's forty-two hills, provided a breathtaking view. To her left, the long swells of the Pacific Ocean, silvered by the three-quarter moon, crashed against the shore. In front, two fingers of land, barely discernible in the darkness, almost met to form the Golden Gate, the entrance to San Francisco Bay. On her right, lights glowing from the small towns and cities around the bay outlined its shores. The great black hulk of a steamship cut slowly through the water.

The door opened behind her. "Oh, here you are, my dear." Dorcas's grandfather stepped out and joined her on the balcony. The light from the library glowed on his white hair and trim mustache. A tall, distinguished man in full-dress evening attire, he looked every inch a financier and civic leader. "How beautiful you are."

Dorcas stood on tiptoe and kissed him lightly on the cheek.

She had a special affection for her grandfather in spite of the awe he often inspired in her. "I feel beautiful tonight. And I don't always. Sometimes I seem quite plain." She opened her cape to show him the beaded bodice of her dress. "It's my new ball gown. Isn't it luscious?" The jonquil yellow enhanced her thick chestnut hair, biege-rose complexion and large brown eyes. She tucked her arm under his. "And this is your night of triumph."

There was a strange, sarcastic tone in Clyde Hamilton's voice as he answered, "Yes, the grand opening of the Hamilton Regency Hotel. The finest hostelry since the Palace was built nearly twenty years ago." His lip curled. "There's no fool like an old fool."

His attitude, so unlike him, shocked her. He always seemed so in command of every situation. Along with the Crockers, the Stanfords, and the Hearsts, Clyde Hamilton was one of the giants of California. There was nothing his great wealth and power couldn't accomplish.

"Grandpa, you mustn't call yourself an old fool for building that magnificent hotel. We're all so proud of you. It's just been so much bigger an undertaking than you anticipated."

"But I should have had more sense than to dive into a multimillion-dollar project at my age." He stared out at the flickering city lights.

Dorcas patted his arm. "But it's finished now and will be a great success. From now on you can take it easy."

This past year has been a difficult one for Grandpa, she thought in compassion. First, there was all that trouble when one of his trusted employees embezzled so much of his money. The worry over the trial and the anguish when the man was sent to prison had taken its toll on Clyde Hamilton. Of course, building the hotel, with all its problems, had meant endless conferences with the architect and contractor. Then, during the most crucial time in the construction, her father had been killed in a mining accident.

Losing his son, his only child, on whom he leaned so heavily to manage the Hamilton mining interests in California and Colorado, had been a devastating blow from which Clyde Hamilton had not recovered. Nor had Dorcas. She blinked back the tears that washed through her eyes. Even now, six months later, grief for her adored father was always close to the surface.

They heard the clip-clop of horses' hooves as the family coachman brought the carriage, a six-seat cabriolet pulled by matched bays, around the corner and to a halt in front of the mansion.

"There's Wilson with the carriage. We ought to be on our way." Dorcas's grandfather turned to the balcony door. "Do go find out what's keeping the others." When he stepped back inside the room, he took out his gold pocket watch. "Good lord, it's already half past eight."

"Now don't get nervous. I'm sure they're nearly ready. I'll tell them to come."

As she hurried across the dark Persian rug, she heard the leather chair swish as her grandfather sat down. Grandpa could be impatient and very difficult when he felt under too much stress, and it seemed unnecessary to upset him on such an important night. Why wasn't Judy down here and ready to go to the ball? Drat her, anyway. Dorcas was often tempted to give her sister a good shake. Hadn't Grandpa invited them all to come live in his mansion after Papa died? The least they could do was cooperate with him.

Of course Grandpa was on edge tonight. One could hardly blame him, she told herself, as this grand opening was the culmination of three frustrating years of effort. From the first, the whole project had been jinxed with complication after complication. Even so, when several business leaders had first talked about holding the San Francisco midwinter fair to stimulate business, Clyde Hamilton was determined to have his hotel finished in time. And at last, in spite of everything, it was all set to coincide with the opening of the fair, which had happened last night, January 27. Most of the important visitors at the fair were staying in the hotel in anticipation of tonight's ball.

As she ran up the stairs, holding the train of her ball gown high, she saw her brother coming down. In his tuxedo he looked much older than his sixteen years. When they met, she gave his arm a squeeze. "Oh, Keith, I'm so glad you're ready at least. Do go into the library to keep Grandpa happy. He's anxious to get started, and he'll be cross as a bear pretty soon. I'll get the others."

"You'd better prod Judy along. You know what a slow-poke she is," Keith said.

And a spoiled brat, Dorcas added to herself. Judy was even

3

more beautiful than their mother, with the same pale gold hair, dainty figure, and violet eyes. Now that they were out of mourning, her eighteen-year-old sister was primed to be the belle of sophisticated San Francisco society.

When Dorcas saw her mother in the hallway, looking stunning in her lavender ball gown, about to enter Judy's room, she sighed in relief. She'd been so afraid that Lenore would back out at the last minute and refuse to go. Not only would Grandfather be furious, but it was high time that her mother picked up the pieces of her life and got on with it, instead of languishing in such deep mourning.

Dorcas recalled how her father would often say, "You must be more patient with your mother. She's so frail and gets depressed easily." Sometimes Dorcas would bite her tongue to keep from saying that if her mother would quit thinking about herself and her health so much, she wouldn't get depressed at all.

Judy stood in the center of the chaotic room admiring herself in a long mirror framed in a wooden stand. Clothes were piled on the bed, shoes tossed in a corner, rice powder spilled on top of the bureau, and hairpins scattered across a silver tray.

Dorcas saw her glance at their mother. "Should I wear my pearls or this pink cameo with the black velvet ribbon?" Judy asked.

"I think the cameo would be just right," Mrs. Hamilton murmured as she gazed adoringly at her youngest daughter. "Doesn't she look like a picture?" Now that her own beauty was beginning to fade, the older woman seemed more and more to be living through her lovely child.

A tinge of envy ran through Dorcas as she looked at her sister. Judy was breathtaking. A true beauty. Her pale rose gown fit snugly over her hips, flaring to the floor in a bell shape, ending in a train. The bodice had inserts of handmade Chantilly lace. At the waist was an arrangement of deep pink satin roses in green leaves. The golden curls on top of her head were held in place by their mother's diamond hair-ornaments. Short white ostrich tips added the final touch. No doubt she would be the belle of the ball. In spite of being spoiled and thoughtless, she could be charming, and one couldn't help but love her.

Dorcas said impatiently, "Grandfather's all ready to go. He's getting into a state. So come on!"

"Just a minute. I have to try—"

Dorcas grabbed the black velvet ribbon and tied it around Judy's neck. Then she yanked a velvet cloak trimmed with mink out of the closet and flung it around her sister's shoulders. "I said, come on!"

Judy flushed. "You're the bossiest person I've ever known. Ever since Papa died, you've been impossible!" But she followed Dorcas and their mother out of the room and down the stairs.

As their carriage swung into the circular driveway of the Hamilton Regency, a shiver of excitement ran through Dorcas. This splendid, imposing structure, twelve stories high, took up a full city block in the heart of San Francisco. Lights glistened from the windows. Tall lamps on each side of the carved entrance doors cast yellow pools on the steps. A doorman in a red uniform with gold braid draped across his chest to his shoulder epaulets helped ladies alight from their carriages. He took special care that their feathered hair ornaments and elaborate gowns were undisturbed.

When the Hamiltons' carriage pulled up under the porte cochere, the doorman saluted. "The governor just arrived, Mr. Hamilton. He's gone to his suite, sir."

"Drat! I'd hoped to be here in time to greet him." Clyde Hamilton thumped his gold-headed cane in annoyance. His face flushed as he glared at his younger granddaughter.

But if Judy felt any remorse about making them late, she didn't show it. She alighted from the carriage, walked up the steps of the hotel, her head held high, well aware of the admiring glances coming her way.

"Judy thinks she's so smart," Keith muttered in Dorcas's ear. "Look at her, Queen of the May!"

"Well, she does look beautiful," Dorcas whispered. "But she'd better not push Grandpa too far."

"She thinks she can get by with anything just because she's pretty." Keith squeezed her arm. "You don't look bad yourself, Sis."

"Neither do you. The girls'll all think you're ages older than you really are." A rush of love for her brother came over Dorcas. Now that their father was gone, she felt particularly responsible for him, since he was the only male heir to the Hamilton fortune.

When they entered the splendid lobby with its rich red carpet, gilt and velvet furniture, and paintings of San Francisco on the walls, Dorcas caught her breath in admiration. Huge arrangements of flowers were placed on all the tables. It must be the most luxurious, elegant hotel in the world, she thought.

"As soon as you check your wraps, meet me at the door of the ballroom," Clyde Hamilton said as he slipped out of his topcoat. "I want us to form a receiving line at the foot of the steps."

Every important person in California must be here tonight, Dorcas told herself more than once as they received the guests. The governor and his lady, along with the other state officials and their wives, had come from Sacramento. Important landowners, many the descendants of great Spanish families, were here. Prominent business and professional men who lived in the area, as well as professors from the University of California in Berkeley across the bay, waited in line to greet the Hamiltons. What a gala evening, she thought.

While the mayor held up the receiving line as he spoke at length to Clyde Hamilton, Judy poked Dorcas in the ribs with her elbow. "Look at the man coming in the door," she whispered. "He's so good-looking."

Dorcas glanced up and saw a tall, handsome man of about thirty standing at the top of the steps leading down to the ballroom. Slowly he surveyed the crowd as if trying to decide whether to come in or not. He was the last person she ever expected to see.

"That's Philip Richmond." She fought to keep her voice sounding normal. "Surely you remember him. The Richmonds own the mine next to ours at Alpine Heights."

"Yes, I remember him now," Judy said. "But I was only ten when we left."

Dorcas hardly listened to her. The receiving line was moving again. Mechanically she greeted the guests, but her mind was on Philip Richmond. During the two years her family had lived in Alpine Heights in the Californian Trinity mountains near the Oregon border, she had worshipped him from afar, but he had paid little attention to her. Not that she'd blamed him. Why would a man in his twenties notice a scrawny fourteen-year-old? There had been little opportunity for them to meet socially, as there were bitter feelings between the two families over a long disputed mining claim. When the adults had been thrown together, they barely spoke.

But she had been aware of Philip Richmond—of his clothes, the way he combed his dark hair—the way he smiled. There was an air of mystery about him as he was not Elliott Richmond's son but a relative; however, no one seemed to know in just what way. How she had daydreamed about him. He was her knight on a white horse who would sweep her away someday. In the summer she'd often strolled by the Richmond house, situated well back on a large lot across from the Presbyterian Church, hoping to see him playing croquet or tennis. Even a fleeting glance of him made her day skyrocket with happiness.

Was it possible for a fourteen-year-old to truly fall in love? Sometimes she believed so, because after they'd moved to Colorado, where the other Hamilton mine was located, it had taken her a long time to recover from the sense of loss and the persistent ache in her heart.

Even now, eight years later, she was reacting strongly to him again. As she watched him come down the steps, her heart pounded wildly in her chest. She tried to tell herself not to be ridiculous. It had just been a schoolgirl crush. But had it been? Every man she had met since paled in comparison.

Was he married? If not, he must still be the most eligible bachelor in California. Not only was he incredibly good-looking and charming, but he came from a wealthy family as well. The Richmonds owned the Golden Star mine in Alpine Heights, which tapped into the legendary Andromeda Lode. And of course it was that fabulous lode that had caused the bitterness between the two families. Her grandfather and father had been convinced that one branch of it extended into their mining property, but they had never been able to find it. They were sure that the Richmonds had crossed the underground boundary lines and mined the Hamilton share.

What would Grandpa do when Philip Richmond joined the last of the guests in the receiving line? Would he tell him to leave? As Philip approached at the very end, her grandfather straightened himself to his full height and clenched his jaw. How cold and stern he looked. Dorcas shivered in fear of what he might say.

But Clyde Hamilton put out his hand and spoke stiffly. "Good evening, Mr. Richmond. This is a surprise."

After Philip shook hands, he held up an engraved card. "I'm registered here at the hotel and found this invitation in my room."

"That's correct. All of the hotel guests are invited to this ball." Clyde Hamilton gestured toward his family. "Surely you remember Mrs. Hamilton and my granddaughters, Dorcas and Judy. This is my grandson, Keith."

When the greetings were over, Philip glanced at the dance program dangling by a cord from Dorcas's wrist. "May I have the pleasure?"

Flustered and for once not caring what her grandfather would think, she slipped the card over her hand and gave it to him. While he signed it, she studied the chiseled planes of his face and the way his thick dark hair covered the tips of his ears and ended in a wave against the collar of his dinner jacket.

After Philip returned her dance program, he turned to Judy and asked for hers. He even stopped in front of Mrs. Hamilton, who shook her head. "Thank you, but I'm dancing very little this evening."

As Philip left their group, Dorcas's grandfather muttered, "Of all the nerve."

Dorcas patted his arm. "Well, Grandpa, you did invite all your hotel guests, so he had every right to come." She glanced down at her program and felt a tremor of delight when she noted that Philip had signed up for the supper dance. But she had little time to savor that fact, as she and Judy were immediately surrounded by young men also wanting to sign their programs.

Soon Dorcas's grandfather held his arm out to her, and they walked together to the platform at one end of the ballroom where the orchestra was seated. After a flourish of drums, Clyde Hamilton spoke. "Welcome to the Hamilton Regency. May the opening of this new hotel, as well as the midwinter fair, mark the beginning of a new, prosperous era in this great city. Now please find your partners for the grand march."

All evening, as she whirled through schottisches, reels, and polkas, Dorcas kept glancing at Philip Richmond. He certainly didn't lack partners. No doubt he was well-known in

San Francisco. In any case, all the matrons would make sure that such a dashing young man met their daughters.

If anything, Philip was more attractive than ever. Sometimes their eyes met; he'd nod, and her cheeks would flush in excitement. I'm being silly, told she herself. It's just a holdover from my girlhood. But no other man had ever had such a profound effect on her.

However, during an intermission, while her partner went to get her some champagne, all thoughts of Philip suddenly fled Dorcas's mind. As she stood half-hidden by a large flower arrangement in front of a pillar, two older men walked past her. One of them looked around at the crowd, his lip curling. "Do you think old Clyde invited all of his creditors to this ball? I see a lot of them here, including us."

The other man shook his head. "Good grief, no. They couldn't possibly fit into this ballroom. Why, it would take Portsmouth Square to hold them all."

"Do you think Hamilton's going to weather the storm?"

The other shrugged. "Who knows? Who cares if that old robber baron goes under? We're all waiting for the spoils. I suppose you heard . . ." His voice faded as the two men walked away.

Shocked, Dorcas peered around the edge of the floral arrangement at their departing backs. How very strange. Were they implying that her grandfather might go bankrupt? But that was impossible. Everyone knew how wealthy Clyde Hamilton was. That he had been one of the fortunate ones to strike it rich in the Gold Rush. Then, through investments and lucky real-estate deals, he had parlayed his original success into a vast fortune. So what did these men mean by "weathering the storm" and "going under"? That was impossible.

As she slumped against the pillar, a knot of worry formed inside of her. At first, after her father's death, she had thought that all she had to do was get her family to San Francisco and then her grandfather would take over. But it hadn't worked out that way at all. It had been up to her to wind up her father's affairs in Colorado. Her mother had been no help. Dorcas had had to close the mine, sell their house, and arrange to have their furniture moved to California.

Even after they'd arrived at the Hamilton mansion, there had been so many decisions to make, such as where to invest the insurance money, what school Keith should attend, and how to help her mother cope with her grief. Dorcas longed for someone more experienced then she was to advise her. But her grandfather had seemed too distracted to give her much help. And now it looked as if the poor man himself might also have to lean on her. But if he really were in financial straits, what could she do?

She tried to shrug off her despair. Of course, San Francisco had been going through a deep depression, just like the rest of the country. But everyone expected that conditions would soon improve. Naturally it would have taken a lot of creditors to finance a big project like this hotel. But the Hamilton Regency would soon be a success and the money would all be paid back. It was silly to get so upset over the conversation she had overheard. No doubt the men who had been talking were just jealous. She pushed her worry to the back of her mind; there was nothing she could do about the problem tonight. When her partner came back with the champagne, she greeted him with a determined smile.

Later, when Philip claimed her, all her radiance returned. She rejoiced that they would have not only the dance together but the whole supper hour as well. As he took her in his arms for the Merry Widow waltz, her hand trembled a little in his. Around and around they whirled until she felt as if she were floating on air. She could hardly contain the happiness that surged through her. He was a superb dancer, and for once she felt light, graceful, and not too tall.

Shaking his head in amazement, he looked at her. "I can't believe what I'm seeing. How could the coltish girl I knew in Alpine Heights have turned into such an alluring young lady?"

"Then I was all legs and too skinny." Her eyes danced with excitement. By far her best feature, they were large, widely spaced, and a dark, velvety brown. Most of all, her eyes were so expressive they showed every mood change.

"I remember that you had freckles across your nose and on top of your cheeks. Even those have disappeared." He smiled at her teasingly. "Metamorphosis must have taken place. A butterfly emerged from the chrysalis."

Dorcas laughed. "I think my poor mother despaired that I would ever turn out well. My sister didn't go through any ugly stages. She's always been a beauty."

"Now you don't have to play second fiddle to anyone. Even your lovely sister."

He looked at her with such genuine admiration that her blood quickened. His magic appeal was still there, only intensified. The intervening years had matured him, given him confidence and authority. As he gazed at her, she was conscious of the myriad of browns, greens, and blues in his dark eyes under their thick brows. How suave and charming he was. Even his clothes were in perfect taste. His white linen shirt, with a stiff bosom, high collar, and cuffs, was most becoming against his tanned skin. His evening attire, with a silk braid down the trousers, made him look even taller. She had met many men since she had left Alpine Heights, but none came up to his standard. There was only one Philip Richmond.

"Are you going to spend some time in San Francisco?" she asked.

He nodded. "About another month. I've been stuck here in an office since the middle of December. As you know, the roads in and out of the Trinity mountains are almost impassable during the stormy season, so we keep only a skeleton crew in the mine."

She hoped she would see more of him. Surely they were destined to meet again.

When the dance ended, her grandfather mounted the platform and invited them all to a buffet supper being served in the main dining room.

While they ate, Dorcas asked Philip about various people she had known in Alpine Heights. Shivers of joy ran through her as he spoke. She had never really forgotten him; she'd simply stored all her memories of him in the back of her mind. She wanted to reach out and touch his arm. She listened to him talk, relishing his nearness and wishing it could go on and on.

"I was sorry to hear about your father's death. Have you left Colorado?" he asked.

Dorcas told him about the move and added, "We're making our home with Grandfather now. Mother is slowly getting back to normal."

"She seems to be enjoying herself this evening." Philip glanced toward the Hamilton table.

Dorcas followed his gaze and was glad to see her mother throw her head back, laughing heartily. Clyde Hamilton was holding court, commanding the attention of his prominent guests. Of course everything would turn out all right for his enterprises, she told herself. How could it be otherwise? A man of his experience couldn't lose his entire fortune. It was impossible. But it was not so easy for her to dismiss a lingering sense of foreboding

Clyde Hamilton was sitting alone at the breakfast table when Dorcas joined him. She kissed him and said, "Grandpa, I'm surprised to see you. I thought you'd sleep late after our big night."

He shook his head. "I must go down to the office." His face was drained of color and his eyes looked haunted.

"To the office? But this is Sunday. Surely you're aware of that." It must be a real crisis to make him miss church, she thought.

He toyed with his scrambled eggs, then put down his fork. She had never seen him so discouraged. All of her life she had thought of him as being all powerful. So rich. So utterly in command. How his employees feared his wrath. Clyde Hamilton was a legend in the West. But this morning he looked old and helpless.

Trying to cheer him up, she patted his arm. "The ball last night was a triumph."

"Was it?" How indifferent he sounded.

"Everyone had a marvelous time." But he wasn't listening to her. Finally she leaned forward. "Grandpa, won't you tell me what's wrong? Perhaps I can help."

"You?" He looked her up and down in despair, then shook his head. "How can you help me? There's nothing you can do."

"How will you know if you won't let me try?"

"But you're just a female." His long bony fingers rumpled his napkin. "Oh, if only your father were alive."

Worry gathered like an aching ball inside of her. So it was true that her grandfather was in serious trouble. But how could that be when he owned so much? Once again she wished she were a man so she could take charge.

"Grandpa, please confide in me. You could train me so that I could take some of the responsibilities off your shoulders."

"If you only could," he whispered. He made a gesture of

dismissal. "Don't worry your pretty head about me. I'll manage somehow."

"But I want to help."

"There's nothing a young woman like you can do. Nothing at all."

Before she could say anything more, the doorbell rang, and soon a maid brought in a large basket of long-stemmed roses and placed them on the buffet. "They're for you, ma'am," the maid said.

Puzzled, Dorcas slipped the card out of its envelope. As soon as the maid was gone, she read the note aloud:

> *Dear Miss Hamilton:*
> *Will you and your sister do me the honor of accompanying me to the Midwinter Fair this coming Wednesday afternoon? I understand that it is a most interesting exhibition and well worthwhile. I will await your reply, which you may send here to the Hamilton Regency.*
>
> > *Your humble servant,*
> > *Philip Richmond.*

Clyde Hamilton slammed his fist down on the table. "How dare he? The nerve of that young man! The despicable cad!"

"Grandpa!" Dorcas slumped back in her chair and stared at him in shock. "Why do you say that?"

"I have my reasons." His jaws clamped shut.

"But what has Philip ever done to you? He had no part in that old trouble you had with the Richmonds."

"They're all out to ruin me. I know it."

"But that's ridiculous," she protested.

"Not at all. Why did they send young Richmond here to San Francisco?"

"The Richmond company has an office here."

"Philip opened that office just last month. Why? The company headquarters are in Sacramento. That's a hundred miles closer to their mining properties than San Francisco. He was sent here to bring me to my knees."

"I don't believe that for a minute."

The old man shook a long bony finger at her. "Sooner or later you'll find out the truth. They've smelled blood and they're in for the kill. You just write and tell him you're not going—now or ever."

"Grandpa, I can't do that." Her eyes filled with despair.

"Why not? Surely you don't want to go with him?"

"But I do. Very much."

His face purpled in rage. "Go, then." He pushed his chair back, rose to his feet, and pointed to the note. "But mark my words. There's some ulterior motive behind this."

"Perhaps I can find out what it is."

He snorted and stamped out of the room into the foyer. Her eyes brimmed with tears as she watched him take his heavy overcoat off the rack and put it on. He picked up his tall silk hat and gold-headed cane, then opened the front door. How she hated to upset him. But wasn't he getting a little senile? How could he harbor such thoughts about the Richmond Mining Company? It was almost paranoid.

At least Grandpa hadn't *forbidden* her to go with Philip. It was unthinkable for her to refuse. Excitement pulsed through her as she looked at the beautiful roses. Philip wanted to see her again. It was almost too wonderful to believe.

In a few minutes Dorcas's mother came downstairs. Her dark gray dressing gown made her skin look drab and sallow. When she entered the dining room she smiled wanly. "I couldn't sleep, so I thought I'd get up."

Dorcas patted her on the arm. "I'm glad you're joining me. I wanted to tell you how lovely you looked last night. That lavender dress is so becoming."

"Perhaps I should have worn my black velvet. It might have been more appropriate under the circumstances."

"Indeed not. Your lavender was perfect." Dorcas tapped the bell again.

After the maid came with fresh orange juice, coffee, and toast, Dorcas went on, "You looked as if you were having a wonderful time last night."

Her mother's face clouded. "I can't have a wonderful time anymore. You know that. My life has ended."

"Mama, don't talk like that! You're only forty-three; you have a long time ahead of you."

Her mother shook her head.

"But Mother, some of your relatives have lived until they reached their eighties. Perhaps you will, too."

"I hope not."

Fighting to keep the exasperation out of her voice, Dorcas continued. "But if you do live until your mid-eighties, it means you're only at the halfway point now."

Lenore sighed. "When I think of those years ahead, I wonder how I'll ever get through them. They'll be so meaningless."

"You just can't waste the rest of your life. There are so many things you can do."

"That's easy enough for you to say." Lenore threw her napkin down on the table. "What does the future hold for me? Nothing!"

Dorcas wanted to shake her mother. "You're the only one who can snap yourself out of this grief. You're giving way to it," she exploded.

"Exactly what do you expect me to do? You're young and have some reason for living, but I—"

"The first thing you can do is try to change your attitude. Remind yourself that you're out of mourning and ready to begin again. Start by getting rid of your mourning clothes. That horribly drab dressing gown, for example. Give it away. And wear something besides all those black dresses."

Lenore glared angrily at her daughter. "What else do you want me to do, since you're so set on rearranging my life?"

Dorcas tried to be patient as she answered, "Mama, you must make a fresh start. Write a list of everything you're at all interested in. Needlework. Clothes. Church work. Social functions. You should try to do one new thing a week until you're back in the swing of things."

"But I couldn't."

"Of course it'll be hard at first, but you must force yourself. You're just wallowing in your misery, and it's time to stop." Dorcas's voice rose in her impatience.

Lenore pushed back her chair and stood up, her chin trembling. "Now I'm all upset. I'm going back to my room." She raised a handkerchief to her eyes. "You don't understand me at all!"

After her mother left, Dorcas let out an exasperated sigh and poured herself another cup of coffee. No, she had never understood her mother, who had always been frail and delicate, with an air of helplessness. How much was genuine? Or was it just a role that she played? It was quite the fashion among women of her mother's generation to be fragile and overly interested in their health. They discussed at length their fainting spells, their childbearing experiences, and their headaches. Could anything be more boring?

In any case, Dorcas had little patience with dependent women. She admired people, male or female, who accomplished things. She had always felt closer to her father and grandfather than to her mother and Judy. And of course, Keith, who showed so much initiative and potential, was the joy of her life. How she adored him. Someday he would take over the big Hamilton company and put it back on track. Nothing must happen to the family corporation before then. With his whole life ahead of him, Keith would make the company prosper again.

It was as if her thoughts conjured up her brother out of thin air, because he came bounding down the stairs. A lock of dark brown hair, so like hers, flopped down over his forehead. His tall, lean body still needed to fill out. A few new pimples had broken out just under his jawbone.

When he came into the dining room, he tapped Dorcas on her shoulder and then pulled out his chair. "What's wrong with Mother? She sailed down the hall to her room in a dreadful snit. Didn't even speak to me."

"She's mad at me again." Dorcas repeated her conversation with her mother. "I'm trying to snap her out of the doldrums, but it's no use."

"You're right, Sis, but . . ."

"I get so out of patience with her. She thinks she's the only one who grieves. What about the rest of us? We lost Papa, too."

"I know you mean well, Dorcas, but you'd better forget it. You just make matters worse when you charge in so strong."

For a moment she felt resentful, then she shrugged. "This is a red-letter day. So far, I've managed to make both Mother and Grandpa angry at me." She handed Keith her note from Philip.

Her brother whistled as he read it. "Do you think Grandpa will let you go?" He looked over at the roses.

"I don't have to ask his permission. I'm of age and can make up my own mind." She rang the bell for the maid.

After he'd placed an order for a hearty breakfast, Keith gave Dorcas a searching look. "You can't wait to say yes, can you? You always were sweet on Philip."

Her cheeks flamed. "Why on earth would you say that? I hardly know him."

"I can remember how you'd take me on walks. We'd always end up outside the Richmond house. I was only eight years old, but even then I guessed."

"Oh, don't be silly." To distract her brother, she stood up and stepped to the buffet to count the roses. "There are eighteen of them. They must have cost a mint this time of year."

"If I had access to the Andromeda Lode, I could afford to send roses to a girl, too." His breakfast arrived and he began to eat. "If you want to answer your note, I'll take it to the hotel as soon as I finish breakfast. I've nothing else to do today. I'll go on the cable car."

"No, we'll have to wait until Judy gets up so I can ask her."

"You'd better forget about Judy. Don't say anything to her."

"I can't go alone with him on this first outing. Nice girls don't do that. It wouldn't be proper," Dorcas said.

Keith crossed his legs and swung his foot back and forth as he chewed on his toast. "Then find some old lady to take along as your chaperon." He pushed his fingers through his brown hair in a gesture that reminded her so much of their father, Edward. In his appearance and actions, her brother was growing to be more and more like him.

"You know your sister," Keith went on. "She's taken away from you every admirer you've ever had. Frank. Jim. Wallace. Just to name a few. They start out so interested in you and then, in no time, they're hers."

Hurt stabbed through her, and she looked away quickly. What he said was all too true. But she wished her brother would stop probing at the sensitive spot where she was so vulnerable. It had been part of her ever since her sister had matured.

Unaware of the fact that he was opening old wounds, Keith continued. "Philip Richmond will be the same way. Just let Judy loose and she'll grab him."

"What do you mean?" Judy demanded from the doorway. "Let me loose and I'll grab who?"

Dorcas tried to answer, but the words wouldn't come. She looked at her sister in her white negligee, her golden hair a shimmering cloud around her exquisite face, her violet eyes alluring and lovely.

A leaden ball of dread formed deep inside Dorcas.

CHAPTER 2

As Philip tucked her arm under his to keep them from being separated in the milling crowd, a surge of pure happiness flowed over Dorcas. What a wonderful, glorious day!

Never mind how furious Grandfather would be when he found out that she actually had come to the fair with a hated Richmond. Nor did it matter that Judy was pouting because she had to play second fiddle for once. Wasn't the sunlight sparkling on the buildings? Wasn't the sky an azure blue? And wasn't she with Philip, who looked at her with unabashed admiration? He wasn't paying any attention at all to Judy. Tremors of joy made her feel as if she were floating with her feet barely touching the ground. No, nothing could spoil this perfect day.

"Is it all right if we go to the Oriental exhibit next?" Philip asked.

"Of course. They're all wonderful. I didn't expect anything like this. Did you?"

"Yes, because all the international exhibits came from the Columbian Exhibition held in Chicago last year. When Michael de Young, who represented San Francisco, saw how outstanding those exhibits were, he got the idea of bringing them to the West Coast so all of us could see them."

"How lucky for us. They must have made an all-out effort to get these buildings finished in time." Dorcas looked at the large structures that formed a quadrangle around the Grand Court, a terraced open area planted with palms as well as camellias, gardenias, and azaleas, all in bloom. From the center rose the Electric Tower, a high massive steel framework outlined with lights.

From the large turnout, it looked as if the California Midwinter International Exposition was already a great success. Surely that would help fill the Hamilton Regency Hotel as well, Dorcas told herself as she matched her steps to Philip's. When they started to cross the Grand Court, she glanced back to make sure the others were following.

When Philip had called for them that afternoon, he had brought along another, somewhat younger man, saying, "This is Andy Woodard, a mining engineer for our company and my right-hand man. But his job today is to take care of Judy."

Before Andy had put his bowler hat back on, he'd run his fingers through his thick auburn hair. His dark blue eyes lit up with interest as he looked the girls over. Judy was particularly fetching in her new green woolen coat-dress, trimmed in black Russian lamb, with a matching fur toque. She'd acknowledged the introduction while glancing at him coquettishly.

Andy had taken Judy's arm to lead her down the steps to the waiting cab. He'd looked over his shoulder and grinned. "Boss, this sure beats mucking underground at the Golden Star."

Dorcas had watched him and thought what a delightful smile he had.

As always with a new man, Judy went out of her way to be charming and acted as if she enjoyed Andy's company. No one but Dorcas seemed to notice the jealous looks that Judy gave her when their eyes met. It was quite clear that her sister thought the prize escort should belong to her.

Philip took Dorcas's arm again. "I've been looking forward to today."

"Oh, so have I." But "looking forward" was too mild a term for her feelings. What would he think if she admitted that she had thought of him constantly since his basket of roses and note had arrived? That she'd relived their dance and supper hour together a hundred times? He'd think she'd taken leave of her senses. He had no way of knowing her secret yearnings when she had lived in Alpine Heights. Nor the months it had taken to get him out of her thoughts when she moved away. How easy it would be to fall deeply in love with him all over again.

"You look like a Gibson girl," he said, smiling at her.

That pleased her, too. Wasn't that exactly the effect she was trying to achieve? The navy-blue serge skirt with a white shirtwaist, decorated with a red bow at her throat, had been copied from a Gibson drawing that was all the rage. Flung over her shoulders was a navy-blue military cape, lined with red as shown in the picture. She had even combed her thick chestnut hair in a loose pompadour and put on a wide-brimmed sailor hat like a typical Gibson girl. The artist portrayed tall, athletic girls in simple clothes ready for the challenges of the twentieth century just ahead, which suited Dorcas perfectly. Today she felt not only up-to-date but appropriately dressed for a long afternoon and evening at the fair.

They stopped for refreshments in the Japanese tea garden, built as a gift from Japan. Dorcas thrilled to the artistry of the evergreen plantings around a pool and the graceful moonbridge that spanned it.

After they left the tea room, they stopped in front of an intricate mine model made from hundreds of pieces of bamboo. Miniature miners, animated by invisible machinery, dug at material representing ore and loaded it into cars that were drawn to the surface and pulled to a replica of a stamp mill. Men worked simultaneously in the different shafts. Dorcas had never seen anything so complex. Philip moved around to the other side to watch the amazing movements.

But Andy stayed by Dorcas's side and explained to her the steps involved. "Don't let me bore you, but mines fascinate me, of course," he said.

"I'm interested in them, too. After all, my father was a mining engineer like you."

He leaned on the railing surrounding the model and turned to her. "It's none of my business, but I've often wondered why your grandfather closed the mine at Alpine Heights."

"I suppose he thought the one in Colorado would be more productive." But she, too, had been puzzled by the sudden move. It was so unexpected. One night she had heard muffled voices from her parents' bedroom. Soon the children were taken out of school, and they moved to Colorado. She often wondered if there had been another quarrel between the Hamiltons and Richmonds. Had it been partly spite on her grandfather's part that made him close the mine and cut the revenue to all the businesses in town owned by the Richmonds?

"But your family's mine at Alpine Heights could pay if it were put into operation."

"Would it really?" She was impressed by this young engineer. He seemed so open and honest. "How do you know?"

"Perhaps I shouldn't admit it, but I persuaded the caretaker to let me go underground with him when he went on an inspection tour. The timbers seem to be in good shape. The water pumps have kept the tunnels reasonably dry. As far as I could tell, the machinery was in workable condition. Even the core samples looked promising. I'm sure there's enough gold in the quartz to make a good profit."

She smiled at him. "It's too bad you aren't mining it."

"If I could only raise the money, I'd offer to buy it. But with this depression on, money's so tight. No bank would finance me."

"Grandfather wouldn't sell it anyway. He's holding the property for my brother to operate someday."

"Is your brother going to train to be a mining engineer?"

"Oh, yes. As soon as he graduates from high school, he's going to the Colorado School of Mines."

"That's where I went. And so did Phil. In fact, we were roommates. It's an excellent school," Andy told her.

"Keith comes from a long line of mining men. I'm sure he'll reopen the Alpine."

"One thing about gold, it doesn't deteriorate. It'll still be there when your brother's ready." He smiled at her. "What about the mine in Colorado? Is it in operation?"

"No, it was closed after my father was killed in a cave-in. Grandfather can't face opening it again right now. I doubt that he will, until my brother's ready to take it over as well."

When Philip joined them again, he asked, "What happened to Judy? She's not here."

Startled, Dorcas glanced around. "But she must be."

"Wait here," Andy said. "I'll look for her. She can't be very far away."

In a few minutes he returned, looking distressed. "I don't see her anywhere."

Philip suggested, "We'd better start out and look for her." He took out his pocketwatch. "Let's separate and then come back here to this mining exhibit in half an hour." As Dorcas turned away, he added, "I suggest that you look in all the ladies' rooms you can find."

Annoyance rose in her as she started her search. Judy could

be so darned thoughtless. She'd probably gotten bored with the mining exhibit and had gone to look at something else without telling them. She must be someplace close by.

But at the end of the half hour, when they all reported back, there was still no sign of Judy.

Philip took charge. "Dorcas, you stay here and watch for Judy in case she returns. Otherwise she won't know what to do. Andy and I will carry on with the search."

Dorcas nodded, but as the minutes dragged by, her worry turned to fear.

Earlier, Judy had stepped to one side while the men and Dorcas exclaimed over the mine model. What could be more dull? She stamped her foot in disgust. They'd be here for hours looking at that blasted model. Even Andy, who was supposed to be looking after her, was talking to her sister, instead. Judy had hoped to get Philip interested in her, but he had been too enchanted with Dorcas in her Gibson girl outfit. What was so alluring about that plain old skirt and shirtwaist? In fact, the whole afternoon had been a disappointment.

Judy stood on one foot and then the other, seething with impatience. Finally, she decided to look around on her own. She'd be back long before they'd be ready to leave that precious exhibit. She walked out the side door and mingled with the crowds milling around the concessions. She wandered from one booth to another and watched demonstrations of potato peelers and special magnetic gadgets that would cure rheumatism, common colds, and female disorders. Perhaps she should buy one for Mama, who was always complaining about her health.

Reluctantly she went back to the mine model, only to find Philip, Andy, and Dorcas gone. They were probably looking for her, but it served them right for neglecting her. As she waited for them, an idea struck her. Why not give them a good scare? She could go far away from this building, to someplace where they weren't likely to find her for a long time. When they did, she could make up some excuse about getting confused.

After leaving the fair proper, she walked for blocks around the back of the buildings until she was at the opposite side of the quadrangle. When she sat down to catch her breath on a bench outside a temporary structure, she saw a large sign inviting everyone to enter and see an art exhibit sponsored by the Northern California Art Institute. This was more like it. The only interests she had outside of clothes, parties, and beaus were sketching and painting. They were her favorite hobby, and art had always been her best subject in school.

After she felt rested, she stepped inside and looked at the exhibit. A pamphlet she had picked up at the door said that the paintings and drawings displayed were the work of students at the Art Institute. She could hardly believe it; they looked so professional. Her interest grew when she read that visitors to the gallery were invited to take part in free art classes held every afternoon in the room at the back. What a good place to hide for an hour or so!

When she peered around the door to the back room, she saw people in a semicircle of chairs and easels facing a table with a still life arranged on it. They were working with pastels. She found an empty spot.

"Don't start until you study the still life carefully," someone said over her shoulder. Startled, she glanced up at a tall, thin man with a dark, pointed beard standing in back of her.

He smiled and went on. "I'm Courtland Burke, one of the Institute instructors. What do you see in the still life on the table?"

An impatient note crept into her voice. "A brass bowl with some fruit. A brass candlestick and a candle."

"I'm sure you can do better than that."

"There's a shawl underneath."

His startling white teeth contrasted with his dark beard as he smiled again. "What fruit do you see?"

She shrugged. "An orange, banana, grapes, a lemon, and three walnuts." What was this? Some kind of silly game? She was used to men groping for excuses to talk to her, but this was getting irritating.

"Why do you suppose I chose these?" He pointed with a long, slender hand. Dark hair grew between his knuckles.

What a pest! Why didn't he leave her alone? "I suppose because they were easily available."

"Indeed they weren't. As a matter of fact, the grapes came from cold storage."

"Then I'm sure I don't know why you chose them." She was tempted to add that she didn't care, either.

"Don't you see that I picked up the colors from the shawl? Notice the dark red of the grapes, and the green in the candle. You'll find them predominating in the embroidery."

Nodding, she twirled the chalk between her fingers. She wished he would let her begin. How irritating to have him hanging over her shoulder.

But he went on. "Have you noticed how the light reflects from the brass? Have you carefully observed the folds in the shawl that give a sense of movement to the composition? The first skill an artist should develop is a good eye."

When he finally moved on to the person next to her, she looked at the still life again. It was surprising how many details she saw as she studied the arrangement. Soon she began and became completely absorbed in the project. She paid little attention to the others. When she finished an hour later, she sat back and admired her work. It was the best she had ever done.

When Courtland Burke stopped by again, she waited for his praise. As he studied her piece, he tipped his head to one side and then the other. "Not too bad for a rank amateur."

Angrily, she looked up at him. "I think it's pretty good myself. May I pay for the materials, as I would like to take my picture home?"

"It's yours, of course, but you'd better apply a fixative so it won't smear. You're welcome to take it with you. There's no charge."

"I'd be glad to pay."

"No, the Institute is doing this to get the public interested in our work."

"What is your work?" she asked.

"For one thing, we're building a great art museum here in the city. It will be one of the major ones in the country when it is complete. A group of financiers have furnished the money for the building itself, but we need funds for acquisitions. We hope to have donations so we can buy important pieces of art throughout the world."

"I'll speak to my grandfather," Judy said thoughtfully.

"Who is he?"

"Clyde Hamilton. I'm sure you've heard of him."

Burke looked startled. "Of course. Who hasn't? He's already been approached, but said at the present he wouldn't make a contribution. It's seems he's too involved in the opening of the Hamilton Regency.''

"I'll tell him what you've told me. Perhaps later he'll send you some money.'' She rose to go.

The instructor helped her on with her coat, then reached in his pocket and pulled out a brochure. "We've already started an art school, to be run in connection with the museum when it's finished. In the meantime, we're renting a place. This will tell you all about it. Perhaps you'd be interested in enrolling. You do show some promise.''

She put the brochure in her purse and rolled up the piece of art paper. "I'll consider it.''

She was actually far more interested in lessons that she would admit to this irritating man. She had always wanted to study art with real professionals, but there had been little opportunity do so in their small mining town in Colorado. As she walked back through the gallery, she admired the exhibit again. Excitement ran through her. If she could only become as skilled as these students.

Her plan to take art lessons so absorbed her that she was hardly aware of leaving the gallery. When she walked outside and started down the steps, she stumbled and landed on her knees, her purse and drawing flying in the air.

An older man helped her to her feet and picked up her belongings for her. "Are you all right?''

"Well, I guess so.'' She brushed the dirt off her skirt. When she tried to take a step, however, a pain shot up her leg. "I'm afraid I hurt my ankle a little, but I'll manage.'' She thanked him and limped away, back into the quadrangle.

But the farther she walked, the more her ankle hurt. How was she ever going to make it back to the Oriental exhibit? She felt a little nauseated from the pain. It wasn't long before she saw a sign pointing to a first-aid station, so she headed in that direction.

Worry had turned to fear as Dorcas paced back and forth near the Asian exhibit. When Andy returned to the meeting place the second time, she greeted him with, "You wait here while I go look. I'm so frightened.''

"Don't be. Your sister isn't a child. If she can't find us, she can get home by herself.''

"But it'll be dark soon." She twisted her fingers together anxiously. "I can't imagine what happened to her."

"I'll bet you a dollar she deliberately walked away from us just to stir up some excitement."

"How can you say that?" Dorcas felt her neck redden in annoyance. "My sister wouldn't be that thoughtless."

"I'll apologize if I'm wrong." Andy's eyes twinkled with amusement. "If not, you owe me a dollar, or—better yet—permission to call on you."

"You are wrong, Mr. Woodard. Judy knows how I'd worry."

"Well, I have her sized up as a young lady who wants to be the center of attention."

"Naturally, with her beauty, she's always been admired." Furious, Dorcas whirled around and walked away. The nerve of him, a stranger, to criticize her sister. But as she retraced her steps through the exhibits, her indignation at Andrew Woodard was transferred to Judy, who had ruined their wonderful day.

She tried not to think of the splendid time she had been having with Philip, nor of the significant looks he had given her, nor the pressure of his hand on her elbow as he guided her through the crowd. The happy mood of the outing had been changed to one of anxiety and worry.

She thought longingly of the exhibits they hadn't seen yet, such as those from Russia, the Ottoman Empire, and Italy. Altogether, eighteen countries, four western states, and all the California counties were represented. They had only seen about a fourth of them. Drat that girl! She was spoiling everything.

Of course they could come back to the fair on their own, but she doubted that Philip would bring them. He must be provoked at Judy. Her behavior, along with her grandfather's coldness at the ball, would turn him away from the whole family. And Dorcas had been hoping against hope that he would start courting her in earnest. As she went on with her search, she blinked back tears of disappointment.

When she finally returned to their meeting place, Andy greeted her with a wave. "Philip found Judy. She twisted her ankle and is in a first-aid station. Otherwise she's fine."

Relief flooded through Dorcas. "I thought all along she must be hurt. Thank goodness it isn't more serious."

Andy took her arm. "Philip's getting a cab to take us all home. He told me where to meet them."

As she hurried along with him, she laughed and said, "I knew Judy wouldn't deliberately run away from us. So you lost the bet. You owe me a dollar."

"Now just a minute, my dear Miss Hamilton. You're the one who lost, not I."

"How can you possibly say that?"

"Because the first-aid station is about as far away from here as you can get. She'll tell us that she was lost and confused, but she went off on purpose. In fact, she took an art lesson."

Annoyance flared in Dorcas. "If that's true, I owe you an apology on her behalf. She ruined our day."

"Not at all. I've enjoyed your company, and I've won the privilege of calling on you."

He was nice, she had to admit. "You're a good sport," she told him. But how was Philip reacting? She could imagine his disgust with her hopelessly spoiled sister. The vixen. Dorcas wanted to shake her.

At last they approached the gate where Philip was waiting with a cab. When he saw them, he waved and walked hurriedly toward the first-aid tent. Soon he emerged carrying Judy, who was holding a rolled-up drawing. One arm was clasped around his neck as she gazed triumphantly up into his face. Smiling, he looked down at her. It was obvious from his expression that he was her latest conquest.

A stab of pain thrust through Dorcas. It was the same old story. Her admirers always lost interest in her and turned to Judy. Don't cry, she warned herself; keep under control. No one must know how utterly devastated you feel.

"I'm sorry to have caused all this trouble," Judy greeted them. "I just got so lost and confused. I had no idea where I was."

Andy turned away to hide a smile.

"Well, I was terribly worried," Dorcas put in crossly. "I was afraid something awful had happened to you."

"Only my poor ankle. It's still throbbing," Judy said prettily. "I can't possibly put my foot down."

"You won't have to," Philip reassured her. "I'll lay you across the seat and brace you against me. Andy, can you give me a hand?"

When her sister was finally settled, Dorcas numbly climbed

into the jump seat with Andy beside her. All the way home she had to watch Judy flirt with Philip, lying with her head cradled in his lap and her injured foot propped up on his folded overcoat. It was all Dorcas could do to hold back her tears.

After the men carried Judy up to her room and turned her over to the care of the maid, Dorcas walked with them to the front door. Andy went down the steps to the waiting cab, but Philip lingered behind.

"We only saw part of the fair. Would you care to go with me on Saturday so we can take in the rest?"

"I'd love to, Philip." Perhaps all was not lost after all.

"I'll call for you about ten in the morning. We can take our time and spend the whole day."

"I doubt that Judy will be recovered enough to go."

"Well, you and I can make it an outing anyway. There's nothing wrong with us. So I'll see you Saturday." He tipped his hat and ran down the steps.

Dorcas waved good-bye, hardly containing her relief and joy that she would see Philip again.

She thought of him all through the next two days and dressed with special care on Saturday morning. She wore one of her most becoming brown suits with leg-of-mutton sleeves. Her toque was trimmed with brown birds' wings. When the doorbell rang she picked up a brown fur muff and hurried down the stairs. Philip! Philip! her heart sang. They'd have a whole day together.

But when she flung the front door open, Andy stood there.

"Philip couldn't make it. He sends his apologies. A mining man has arrived from Nevada, and they had to meet today."

It was all Dorcas could do to keep her voice steady. "How kind of you to give up your day." But she ached with disappointment.

Andy watched the expression in Dorcas's large brown eyes change from eagerness to despair. He felt her hand tremble as she placed it in the crook of his arm. As they walked down the steps, he asked himself, Is she in love with Philip?

"Did you and Philip know each other before, in Alpine Heights?"

"Yes, but not very well. I was only fourteen when I left," Dorcas replied.

28

How strange, Andy thought. Yet she's half-sick with disappointment at having to settle for me. When did she get this feeling for his boss? Surely not since the ball. He had a hunch that it ran much deeper than a surface attraction.

By the time they reached the fair again, Dorcas was in a muddle of mixed emotions—anger, hurt, and disappointment, along with irritation at Andy. How could anyone take Philip's place? Why hadn't he himself telephoned to explain the situation and arrange for another time? It was as if this day hadn't been very important to him after all. Certainly he hadn't been counting the hours until it came, as she had done. Well, she'd see some of the exhibits and make an excuse to go home as soon as possible.

As they entered the Santa Barbara building, Andy looked at her with a knowing smile. "Right now you're telling yourself that soon you can pretend to have a headache so you must go home."

Her face turned scarlet as she looked at him in astonishment. Could he read her thoughts? She yanked her arm away from him.

"I'm warning you," he went on, his eyes sparkling with mischief. "I'm accepting no excuses. We're here for the day."

"Really, Mr. Woodard, you're—"

"The name is Andy. Yes, I'm impertinent. So just forget your disappointment, because you'll have a better time with me." He tucked her arm in his and grinned at her.

They looked at several exhibits, and then he said, "Come on, let's find something to eat. I'm starved."

In spite of herself, she had to smile back. It wasn't his fault that he had to take Philip's place. "I'm hungry, too," she agreed. "I saw a place that served crab cocktails."

Not only did they have crab cocktails, but Andy found another concessionaire who sold them big wrapped tamales from a steaming cart. They finished their lunch with double-dip ice cream cones.

"It'll serve us right if we get stomachaches." Dorcas giggled as she tried to lick the melting chocolate ice cream from the outside of her cone.

When they finished the last of their cones and had wiped

their faces, Andy suggested, "Let's go on the giant Ferris wheel. Just the thing for our digestion."

"Oh, Andy, we'll be sick."

"No we won't. Come on."

The rest of the day they moved from one carnival attraction to the next, throwing balls at bowling pins, trying to hit a clown's head or shooting at a moving target in the gallery. They rode the carousel and finished their outing at an Italian booth, eating spaghetti and meatballs. It was impossible to find a hack, so they got into a streetcar, transferred to a cable car, and rode the hills up and down. At last, they walked along the dark street to the mansion.

Andy had been delightful company. His charming smile, teasing, and laughter had made a day that she wouldn't soon forget. When they came to the front door, Dorcas put out her hand. "I've had a marvelous time, Andy. Thank you so much."

He leaned down and kissed her lips. "I'll always remember this day." He took her key and unlocked the door. "Good night, lovely Dorcas." He turned and went whistling down the steps.

Judy enjoyed the week's confinement while her sprained ankle healed. Her mother and all the servants pampered her, and Keith ran errands. Even though Dorcas was still cross, she'd resurrected a wheelchair from the attic and made it soft with pillows so it could be wheeled into their mother's sitting room, where Judy spent most of the time. Best of all, Philip and Andy called and brought candy, flowers, and books. It was great fun being the center of attention. She noted that Philip talked with her far more then he did with Dorcas.

All the time she was recuperating, she thought about the art school. Looking at the brochure, she found that one class started on February 15 and met just three mornings a week— Monday, Wednesday, and Friday. That would be best as a start. Besides, she was only interested in art work as a hobby.

"Unless you take this seriously, I don't want you in my class," Courtland Burke told his students. "Because we only meet three times a week, it's important to attend every class.

Be here not later than nine o'clock, and be able to stay until twelve.''

Judy listened with growing annoyance. What a shame that this irritating man was the instructor. She had hoped that someone else would be in charge.

"Today we're going to start with the basics of pencil sketching.'' He held up a pencil. ''You will all find a graphite pencil at your place. It has been sharpened with a knife, which is better than using a pencil sharpener. Before our next lesson you are to go to an art store and buy a supply of graphite pencils of varying degrees of hardness. You'll find a list of the supplies you'll need on the table. Now, rub the lead on a scrap of paper until it makes a broad, firm stroke. When you turn it over, it will produce a thin, sharp line.''

Judy's impatience grew as Burke had them draw cubes, cylinders, and spheres.

"These are simple, basic forms,'' he went on. "All other forms are composed of them or parts of them. You will soon discover that there are many forms that lie between the cube and cylinder, such as the egg. Now I want you to draw eggs.''

But even Judy became interested when Burke showed how they could create more complex figures by combining the basic forms. They drew a spoon near a cube, which became a lump of sugar. Another cube on top of a house became a chimney. The cylinder quickly turned into a neck beneath a head. By adding a stem and a leaf, the sphere turned into an apple. The next step was to draw the human figure. The flexor muscle of the arm was egg-shaped, while the tensor above the hip was a double-egg symbol.

"Now I want to try action figures,'' Burke said. "But learn to think of the torso in terms of two block forms that move independently of each other: the rib cage, or chest section, and the pelvis, or hip section. Draw your figures running, playing tennis, or sprawling on the floor—it doesn't matter, as long as they are doing something. Don't forget to put in a spinal column. Watch the slant of the shoulders and hips. Try to show the rotation of the body due to twisting of the vertebrae.''

When class was dismissed, Judy was the last to leave. As she put on her coat and gathered her materials together,

Courtland Burke came to her and asked, "Do you understand your homework assignment, Miss Hamilton?"

"I guess so. I just hope I can get it all done. I'm recovering from a sprained ankle." She told him about her fall.

"Then you'll have to be sedentary for a while. A perfect time to take an art course."

"Well, I have a lot of other things to do, too." She tossed her head.

"Such as going to tea parties, I suppose?" There was a note of sarcasm in his voice. "Don't expect me to feel sorry for you. Do you realize that most of our students here at the Institute work part-time? They scrub floors, wait on tables, or sweep the streets. One young man has to clean stables before he comes to class. They manage, and you'll have to as well."

She bristled. "Well, I can't help what other people have to do."

As he opened the door for her, he looked her up and down. "Let's get one thing understood right from the first—just because you're Clyde Hamilton's granddaughter and a very attractive girl, you don't have special privileges. More than once this morning, you were inattentive and I had to repeat my instructions just for you. That's not to happen again. Do you understand?"

Pouting, she started past him without answering, but he grabbed her arm. "I have no time for spoiled society girls. If you're willing to buckle down and work hard like everyone else, I'm glad to have you. If not, don't come back." His dark eyes pierced right through her.

She yanked her arm away. "Perhaps I won't return."

He shrugged. "That's entirely up to you. But if you have talent, Miss Hamilton—and I'm far from convinced that you do—you owe it to yourself to develop it."

Still seething, she limped down the stairs of the huge old house that served as the temporary headquarters for the Institute. She had half a mind to stop at the office and ask for her money back. She hesitated at the door, but finally walked on. She'd show that horrible man something. She'd prove to him she had real talent. A new, strange emotion stirred deep inside her: a desire to achieve.

CHAPTER 3

Dorcas opened the heavy, brocaded draperies in her mother's room and looked out. The cold, overcast February day held little promise of good weather to come.

She crossed the flowered carpet and touched Lenore's shoulder. "Time to wake up, Mama. I brought your breakfast."

"I don't want anything." Her mother snuggled into her pillow and pulled her down comforter up over her shoulders.

But Dorcas picked up a pink satin bed jacket from the chaise lounge and brought it to the bed. "Now sit up, Mother, and put this on. Then you must eat. Remember, this is Thursday, the servants' day off, so it's our day to go downtown shopping."

"I don't think I'll bother to go today. I'm tired, so I'll just stay in bed. I can make myself a cup of tea later."

Annoyance flared in Dorcas, but she tried to keep her voice light. "No, darling, I have our day all planned. We're going to look for Easter outfits. I want you to have the prettiest bonnet in all of San Francisco. We'll get material for a lovely new suit to go with it. Something gay and cheerful."

Lenore shook her head as tears gathered in her violet eyes. "I'll wear one of my old outfits on Easter. What difference does it make now?"

"It makes all the difference in the world! You're going to begin a new life starting now. No more mourning clothes. No more doom and gloom. You're going to buy a lovely wardrobe so you can go out and make new friends. Today we'll go to all the finest shops and have lunch at Pierre's."

"But I don't want to."

Dorcas held up the bed jacket. "Mother, I insist."

The carriage swayed as Wilson pulled on the reins to guide the horses around the corner from the mansion and enter a street leading down the hill to the center of the city. Dorcas gripped the hand strap and braced herself to keep from sliding against her sister, who sat in the middle between her and their mother.

Only half listening to the others discuss where they should go first, Dorcas stared out at the carriages climbing the hill in the opposite direction. For once, she felt real enthusiasm for the shopping day ahead. Unlike her mother and Judy, who could spend hours wandering through the department stores aimlessly looking at gloves, hats, or laces, Dorcas was bored by such shopping, as it seemed like a waste of time. But today was different. It was crucial that she get her mother outfitted and ready for the social events to come.

She wished she were a man who had an office to go to each day. If she could only work and spend her time purposefully, how she would love it. But it was unthinkable for a young lady in her position to be in trade. She was supposed to take her place in society, find a suitable husband, and get married as soon as possible.

The only man she had ever cared for in that way was Philip, but she could not interpret their recent friendship as his courting of her. In fact, it was Judy who now seemed to interest him the most. It was her sister who was the center of attention whenever he and Andy called to pay their respects. They talked mainly about Judy's art studies; Philip praised the drawings lavishly. It was Judy's dance program he signed first at the balls they all attended. Of course, Dorcas hadn't let anyone know how hurt she felt.

No matter how she longed to be alone with him, he made no move in that direction. It was Andy who took her outside to get a breath of fresh air, who pressed her hand to his lips, who whispered, "You look so beautiful tonight." And all the time she wished it were Philip by her side.

Her thoughts turned once more to a career. How she would love to be a lawyer, but women weren't even admitted to professional schools, let alone to the Bar. Or if Grandfather would only take her into his office. Surely there were clerical duties she could perform. If she were with him, she might be able to help him. He seemed to be getting thinner and acting more and more distraught. Every evening he worked in the library with his papers spread across his desk. One time she had gone in and put her hand on his shoulder. He muttered,

"Just leave me alone. There's nothing a girl like you can do." His bleak expression, utterly devoid of hope, had twisted her heart.

The carriage jolted into a pothole, and she grabbed the strap again. Idly she watched a Chinese man push a vegetable cart up the hill, his long pigtail swinging across the back of his padded jacket, his face distorted, and his neck muscles bulging with strain. Suddenly, a hack, its driver seated on a high perch, swung recklessly around the cart, crossed the center of the street, and narrowly missed scraping the side of their carriage. They were only inches apart.

As she stared at the elderly passenger in the cab, Dorcas gasped, "Grandfather!" She turned and looked out the rear window at the hack, now back in its proper lane. "I'm sure it was he."

They all looked back, watching the cab turn the corner and disappear from sight.

"He must be going home. Why would he do that?" Judy asked.

Dorcas grabbed her sister's arm. "Do you suppose he's sick? Nobody's there to help him."

"Don't worry." Judy pulled her arm away. "He probably went home to get something."

"I think I should go and see." Fear gripped Dorcas. "I'll walk back."

"No you won't!" Lenore turned to her and scowled. "It was your idea that I come today. The least you can do is stay with me."

But Dorcas leaned forward and opened the glass. "Stop as soon as you can, Wilson." Every instinct told her that her grandfather needed her.

"You have your nerve!" her mother cried angrily. "I didn't want to come, but you insisted. I'll be very cross with you if you go back."

"Mama, I'm sorry, but I must," Dorcas cried. "Judy, you help Mother shop."

She climbed out of the carriage and started up the hill, shivering in the cold wind. A newspaper blew across the street against her skirt. Was she foolish to be so apprehensive? Grandfather had probably just gone home to get something from his files. But he'd known they would be going shopping today. Why hadn't he just called to ask her to bring to his office whatever document he wanted?

Would he be angry at her for following him? In a way it must be hard on her grandfather to have all of them at the mansion, since he was so used to his privacy. Still, he had insisted that they come. He'd said that he was lonely in his big house and wanted them. No doubt he was grateful now that all the household expenses were paid from her mother's insurance money.

Had he become ill at work? Dorcas doubted it, because he hadn't been slumped against the back seat. He was sitting erect in the cab, staring straight ahead, almost as if he were in a trance. He hadn't seemed to notice that the vehicle had swung dangerously close to their carriage.

She walked faster and faster. Something seemed to urge her to hurry. When she came to the alley in back of the mansion she decided to go through the servants' entrance to save time. Holding her skirt high to keep the hem out of the dust, she ran past the bins of trash. She gasped for breath as she came to the rear gate and opened it. At last she was at the back door. Frantically she rummaged through a cabinet to find the hidden emergency key. When she had it in her hand and jammed it in the lock, it bounced out and fell to the landing.

Now she was in a panic. Her hand shook as she reached down and picked up the key again. Hurry! Hurry! At last the door opened and she ran across the dimly lighted cellar. Odors of coal dust, stored apples, and onions assailed her. A cat rubbed up against her leg and she brushed it gently aside. She crept up the back stairs silently and walked through the kitchen into the back hall.

First she must check the library, because if Grandpa did feel ill he might have lain down on the couch there, rather than climbing the stairs to his bedroom. The thick carpet muffled her footsteps as she rushed down the hall.

Should she call out and tell him she was home? But if he were just getting one of his documents, he might be annoyed that she would interfere in his affairs. If that was what he was doing, she could go back quietly the way she had come, and he wouldn't even know the difference.

When she reached the library, she stopped in the doorway. Clyde Hamilton sat at his desk, his back to her, his shoulders slumped as he wrote something. He dipped the pen in the inkwell and scratched at the paper. Should she speak? Should she tiptoe away?

For a long moment she waited, uncertain what to do. Finally she started to speak, but the sound died in her throat as her grandfather stood up and reached over his desk to pick up something. Paralyzed with horror, she saw that it was a pistol. Slowly he raised it to his temple.

Terror catapulted her across the floor. Just as she reached him and hit his arm, he pulled the trigger. A deafening roar filled the room, reverberating from wall to wall. The bullet grazed his head, shot through the air, and struck the ceiling. An acrid odor enveloped them.

"Grandfather!" she screamed. "Oh, my God!"

In shock they stared at each other. A little stream of blood slowly trickled down his forehead and onto his ashen cheek. He slumped toward the desk and braced himself with his hands while the pistol skidded across the polished surface and bumped against a lamp.

"Dorcas!" he gasped. "Where did you—"

"I saw you coming home. I ran back to see if you were all right. Thank God I did!" It was an effort to form the words. This was unreal. A nightmare. It couldn't be happening. "You're bleeding."

For the first time, he seemed to be aware that he was wounded. He pulled a handkerchief from his pocket and wiped the blood away. He stared at the stained cloth in disbelief and then looked at her in despair. "Why did you stop me? I don't want to live."

"Oh, Grandpa!" Dorcas held out her arms and clasped his old thin frame to her. "Don't say that."

She looked over his shoulder at the pistol against the lamp and the suicide note on the blotter. Wave after wave of horror washed over her again. "Why did you—"

"I'm losing everything! All my fortune." The words were muffled against her neck. "Everything I ever worked for . . ."

She patted his thin shoulders through his dark suit coat.

"It will all be gone." He began to sob—dry, shuddering sobs that tore clear through him. They seemed to pull his body apart.

Tears ran down her cheeks as she rocked him back and forth. She made soft comforting noises and kissed the top of his white head. "I love you so much, Grandfather."

"I love you, too," he whispered.

"Don't you see that you'd be taking away the very person I need the most?"

"Need? You need me?" His old voice quavered. He started to cry again. "I didn't think anyone needed me now."

"But I do. Keith does. We all do."

"Your grandmother did. And your father. But they're gone—"

"That's why *we* need you so. We don't have them, so you're more precious than ever."

"But I'm losing everything."

"Oh, Grandpa, it's not your fortune or your power as a businessman. It's *you* that we need."

"I have nothing for you."

"But you do. Your love. Your caring for us the way you do. And we need your experience. Your wisdom. You can't take that away from us."

"Oh, Dorcas." His sobs started again. They were racking sobs that shook clear through him. His body trembled. His shoulders heaved.

She held him close while he cried. Let him get it all out, she told herself. The terrible worry. The desperation he must have felt as he saw his empire crumble. The anguish all these months. He had held it all within him for so long.

"Forgive me, Dorcas."

"But I want you to let go and rid yourself of all your despair. You've kept it in too long."

She stroked his back and held him while her heart ached for him. Think what he must have gone through today. Making his plans. Getting the cab. Entering the house and no doubt searching it to make sure he was alone. Taking out the pistol and loading it. Writing the note. Steeling himself to pull the trigger.

Another wave of horror hit her as she tried to imagine what he had gone through. Thank you, Lord, for sending me to him in time, she thought fervently.

Over and over she murmured, "I love you, Grandfather. I love you with all my heart."

His sobs began to subside.

She went on, "Surely life is worthwhile when someone cares for you as much as I do. We'll be able to work out something, as long as we have each other."

A final sob quivered through him. He slumped against her in exhaustion.

"Come on, Grandpa, I want you to lie down on the couch." She led him there, lowered him onto it, and put a pillow under his head. After she pulled off his shoes, putting them at the end of the couch, she covered him with an afghan.

Clyde reached out and took her hand. "Don't leave me."

"Of course I won't. Just let me light the fire." She found matches by the hearth, and as soon as the flames began dancing and the chill was gone from the room, she took off her coat and hat and put them on a chair. Next she poured him a small glass of brandy and held it to his lips. Then she looked at his wound.

"It's just superficial, but it's oozing again. Don't you think we should call Dr. Ellington?" she asked.

"No! Never! He'll get the police. You can dress it yourself later." As she knelt beside him, he grasped her arm with frantic fingers. "No one must know about this."

"Of course not. Don't worry."

Tears gathered in his eyes. "Promise me you won't tell anyone about this. No one. Not even your mother, Judy, or Keith."

She took one of his bony hands in hers. "I'll promise, if you'll swear to me on your honor that you'll never try to take your life again."

He nodded.

"I want to hear you say it," she insisted.

He closed his eyes. "I swear on my honor that I will never try to take my life again." He laid his head back in despair, as if he couldn't face the future.

Her heart ached with pity for him. "Do you want to talk, or would you rather rest?"

He gripped her arm. "Don't leave me. I want to talk."

"Then confide in me. Let me share your troubles."

"You're the only one I can trust."

"Tell me about it," she repeated softly.

"I'm at the end of my rope. I don't know what to do. I thought I couldn't go on." His voice trailed off weakly. A sigh shuddered through him. "How did you happen to come back and find me?" he asked.

She told him about seeing him in the cab. "I think the

good Lord intervened so I could recognize you." She put her hands to her face and started to cry. "Oh, I'm so thankful I was in time."

He caressed her arm. "I'm so sorry I've put you through all this, dear girl." A tear ran out of the corner of his eye.

When she got herself under control, she said, "Just talking about your problems will help, Grandpa."

Finally he began to speak, but she had to lean toward him to hear his quavering voice. "I'm sure you know about Frank Wells, who embezzled so much from me. Even worse, he led me to believe I was in better financial shape than I was. I overextended myself badly to build the hotel. It cost far more than I expected. I poured every cent I could raise into it. It was the most foolhardy thing I've ever done in my life. Your father tried to talk me out of it, and he was right. I should have known better."

"Surely it will be a success, though. You told me yourself that the hotel has been full nearly every night since the opening."

"But it takes two or three years to make much profit on such a big undertaking." A sigh of hopelessness escaped him. "Then it'll be too late."

He lay back and closed his eyes, clasping and unclasping his hands. Finally he went on. "When I started building the hotel, I soon got in so deep I couldn't stop. Got way over my head in debt. Everything I own is mortgaged to the hilt."

Dorcas sat back, appalled. "Surely not everything? Not this mansion?"

He nodded. "It and all its furnishings." A tear ran down his cheek. "Only one large foundry, which I might have a chance to sell, is free. We've been negotiating for over a year."

"But won't that help?"

"If the deal goes through, I'll be able to make a payment to my various creditors. That'll hold them at bay until October first. But that date I have to make a payment of $125,000 on the loans. There's no way I can do it."

"Don't say that. Surely we can figure out some way to refinance your debts."

"Dorcas, I've tried over and over again. My lawyers have been working on it. But money is terribly tight. We've been going through a deep depression. Not only here but all over the country. No one wants to tie up that much money in these uncertain times. There are millions involved. Besides, the debt would still be there. A great monster ready to devour me."

She shifted to a more comfortable position. "Grandpa, can't you go to your various creditors and explain the situation?"

He laughed mirthlessly. "That's the last thing I want to do. Once my creditors get wind of how bad things really are with me, my house of cards will come tumbling down. Oh, they suspect. Don't think they don't! Rumors are flying everywhere. But they don't know for certain. That's the secret—to gain time."

She thought of the conversation she had overheard at the ball.

Clyde went on. "They're just waiting for the end and then they'll descend like vultures."

"But why would they do that?"

"That's just the way it is."

"Aren't most of them your friends?"

He shook his head. "Associates. Not friends."

"But you've known some of them so long," she persisted.

"When you deal in high stakes like I do, you trust no one. It's yourself pitted against the others. It's like a war. You attack. Take advantage. Withdraw. Go after the weak flank."

Shocked, she stared at him. "But that's so merciless."

He sneered. "Mercy? There's no such word in high finance. Most of the fortunes in this city have been made through foreclosures. The idea is to lend money on some venture that has prime collateral. If the borrower can't pay on the loan, you eventually foreclose and get a business with great potential or a valuable piece of property at a fraction of its worth. Hold it until the time is right, then sell it for a huge profit."

"But aren't there laws to protect people from that?"

"A lender has the legal right to foreclose if the borrower can't pay. Besides, most laws can be bent and officials persuaded to look the other way."

Frightened by what she had been hearing, she put her hand on his arm. "Grandfather, have you been part of this?"

He shrugged. "How do you suppose I accumulated my fortune? The mines were just the start."

"I heard some men at the opening night ball call you a robber baron. So that's what they meant."

His lip curled. "That's like the pot calling the kettle black. Any of those older men at the grand opening are doing the same thing. We're all in it together, and it can get rough."

"It must."

"It's dog eat dog, Dorcas. The strong after the weak. They wait for us to fall by the wayside." A sob shuddered through him. "That's where I am now. Old and helpless. Ready to fall and be devoured by the pack."

"Grandpa, we're not giving up hope yet." She laid her cheek against his.

"It's part of the game, Dorcas. You shouldn't get into it if you can't take the consequences."

"I don't remember Papa having such dealings."

"No, your father wanted no part of it. That's why he took charge of the mines. But for some of us it's the most challenging, exciting part of life. The risks. High stakes. Winning against all odds."

"I can't imagine Keith ever—" Dorcas began.

"We'll have to see. The boy's got starch in his spine. But it takes years of experience to hold your own in my world."

Tears sprang to her eyes as she thought of Keith and his dreams. "Grandfather, will you lose the mines?"

He shook his head. "I tried to borrow on them, but no one would take them as collateral. Closed mines are a dime a dozen, nowadays."

"Then at least we still have them."

"I'm not so sure." His fingers balled into a fist. "The Richmonds may get them."

"How could they, if you didn't use them for collateral?"

He opened his eyes and stared at her. "But I owe $100,000 to West Coast Mining Supply, which young Richmond just bought for his company. That was the final straw." He glanced toward the pistol. "That's why—" He couldn't go on.

"Oh, Grandpa!"

He shook his finger. "I knew Richmond was here for some reason. Didn't I tell you he had an ulterior purpose? I warned you, didn't I?"

"But I don't understand. How could the Richmonds get our mines?"

"If I can't pay West Coast Mining Supply, it could take them over. Some of West Coast's equipment is permanently installed in them."

"But the Alpine's been closed for years."

"When your father had some equipment installed in Colorado, he had pumps put into the Alpine as well, to keep the tunnels dry. But that was just before his death. The bill hasn't been paid. Now there's no money to take care of it."

He sank back on the pillow, his face ashen. For some time he didn't speak; finally, his voice flared with bitterness. "The Richmonds deliberately bought that company just to get the Alpine. They'll get it for a song. They sent that young scalawag here to San Francisco for that purpose."

"That's hard to believe," Dorcas protested.

"He came here to find out about my financial position as well. He's been sniffing around after me like a bloodhound. Going everywhere so he could hear all the rumors."

Her heart constricted in hurt. Could that be true? She cared more for Philip than any man she had ever known. Was he a friend to her face and deliberately scheming behind her back? Had he bought the mining supply company for the very purpose of taking possession of their mines? Of course he would hear the rumors about her grandfather's straits, since they would be passed around in the men's clubs, in offices, and at the stock exchange.

Was that why he was living in the Hamilton Regency? Why he was so friendly with Judy and herself?

"Grandpa, are you sure the Richmonds bought the mining supply house?"

As his eyes sparked with anger, he nodded. "My lawyer told me yesterday that the sale had gone through." Clyde Hamilton lay back and turned his face away to hide his tears. "I realized that I was at the end of the rope, so I made my plans. My creditors are waiting—just waiting. They're not even hounding me anymore."

Dorcas watched the flames leap in the fireplace and listened to logs crackle as they burned. Poor man. He must have suffered terribly all these months. He had always been so powerful. How it must hurt his pride to be at the mercy of others—now to be the object of their contempt.

"But you do have the foundry sale to put them off for the time being?" she prompted softly.

"Yes, if it goes through. But when it's gone, what then?"

If we could only open one of the Hamilton mines and get some gold to pay off the debts, Dorcas thought. The one in

Colorado? It had been prosperous. But that would be too painful after losing her father there. But what about the one in Trinity County here in California?

"Grandpa, couldn't we open the Alpine mine again?"

He shook his head. "It would take more capital than I've got to put it into operation. And even if I could afford to do it, it would still be a great risk; it might not pay."

"But would it cost so much?" She told her grandfather about her conversation with Andy Woodard. "He's very enthusiastic about the mine. Says the timber is good, the tunnels are dry, and the machinery is in reasonably fair condition. He's a mining engineer and should know."

"I wouldn't trust anyone connected with the Richmonds," Clyde Hamilton said flatly.

"Oh, Grandpa, I'm sure Andy is honorable. Why would he tell me things that aren't true? He'd have nothing to gain."

"I don't know. But that Richmond outfit can't be trusted."

"Please let's consider reopening the mine. We know the gold is there, so why not dig it out?"

"It's not that simple. It'd take enormous effort to get the mine back in operation after eight years." Clyde leaned his head back and closed his eyes. "I'm a broken old man now and I haven't the strength to try."

Dorcas persisted. "But couldn't you hire someone to go up there and operate the mine on a small scale?"

"I wouldn't know who to approach. I've been out of the mining part of our business for so long. Your father handled it, and the idea was that Keith could take it over in another five or six years."

"Perhaps Andy could recommend someone."

"I told you I don't trust him. Whoever he'd recommend would soon be playing right into the Richmonds' hands. Besides, quartz mining takes a lot of capital, and I don't have it." His thin jaw clamped. "You don't know anything about it, so just forget it."

She wanted to continue the discussion, but she knew how stubborn her grandfather could be.

He sighed and turned his head away. "I'm very tired, Dorcas. I have to rest now."

"Of course you do. I'll dress your wound right now, then perhaps you can sleep." Still feeling that she was living in a nightmare, she walked down the hall to the bathroom for first-aid supplies.

As she sterilized the superficial wound, preparing to put gauze around his head, Clyde whispered, "Throw the note in the fire and put the pistol in the drawer."

"I'll do that."

When she was through bandaging his wound, she added a log to the fire and tossed the note in, watching it burn. Shuddering, she picked up the pistol and hid it in the back of a drawer.

"Try to sleep now." She leaned over him, adjusting the afghan on his shoulders. "I'm going upstairs now to change my clothes, but I'll come right back. I'll be home with you all day."

He took her hand and held it to his lips. "You're a jewel. A rare one." Tears washed over his eyes. "Even if I lose everything, I'll still have you."

She kissed his thin, sunken cheek. "And best of all, I'll have you."

Numbly, Dorcas took off her hat, put it in its box, and stuck the long hatpins back into the porcelain holder on her dresser. She removed her suit and blouse, hung them up, and put on a printed cotton housedress. As she combed her hair into a pompadour and pinned the bun with tortoise shell combs, the enormity of what had happened slowly dawned on her. Yet, in spite of the horror, she could understand her grandfather's suicide attempt.

She couldn't imagine Clyde Hamilton without his power. He'd always been the ruler of a vast empire. Even her father had sometimes been in awe of him. Grandpa's word was law. They all knuckled under to his will. He could be dictatorial, stubborn, and difficult, yet tender and devoted. A remarkable man who had accumulated a great fortune. It seemed impossible that he could lose it all.

A terrible thought suddenly hit her. Their inheritance would be gone! She stared at herself in the mirror, her large dark eyes opened wide in shock, her arm still raised with the hairbrush in her hand. Slowly she brushed the stray locks into place. If her grandfather went bankrupt, there would, of course, be nothing for them to inherit. All their future security would be gone with the crash. It was more than she could grasp.

Ever since their father's death, she, Judy, and Keith had known they were the sole heirs to the Hamilton fortune. As a male and the one who would one day head the corporation, Keith was the principal heir, but she and Judy would be very wealthy. That is, if the fortune was still intact when the time came. But how easily it could be lost.

Feeling ill with dismay, she staggered to a slipper chair and slumped down into it. She looked around the luxurious room as if she were seeing it for the first time. They had all taken it for granted that this way of living would go on forever. But that wasn't true at all. If Grandpa lost this mansion, where would they go?

Actually, there was no such thing as security. It was all an illusion. Wars, disasters, financial reversals, could sweep all one's possessions away like the surf battering down a sand castle.

Of course, they wouldn't suffer as long as her mother's insurance money lasted. When her father had died, her mother had turned the responsibility of handling the family funds over to her. "Dorcas," Lenore said, "I've told the lawyer to give you the power of attorney. I want you to manage everything. I just can't."

For the first time, Dorcas realized what she had taken on. The money wasn't a great sum, but it could be all they would have. How unreal all of this seemed. From now on, they must economize.

Finally, she rose to her feet. It was time to go downstairs and stoke the furnace. And she should start some lunch. She wiped the tears from her eyes and dusted rice powder onto her blotched face.

As she descended the stairs, some hope returned. All was not lost yet. If the foundry sale went through, they still had some time. The final crash would be postponed for about seven months.

Squaring her shoulders, she told herself that she might be young and a female, but she had determination. She'd fight to save them all! Whatever was to be done was up to her. And she'd do it, too!

CHAPTER 4

The hall clock struck three.

"The others will be coming home soon, won't they?" Clyde Hamilton asked as he sat in his leather chair, staring at the fire.

Dorcas looked up from her embroidery. "Yes, anytime now."

"If you'll help me upstairs, I'll go to bed." A long sigh quivered through him. "I don't feel up to talking to them."

As they climbed the stairs, he stopped to rest and asked, "What are you going to tell them?"

"That you didn't feel well, so you came home. That's nothing but the truth."

His expression saddened. "Perhaps you'd better prepare them for what might come."

"I think so, too." She patted his back. "I'm sure they realize that you've been terribly worried."

"Our conversation today was strictly confidential."

"Of course, Grandpa."

"But they might as well know that I might not survive financially." He smiled ruefully. "The rest of the city knows it."

"We mustn't give up all hope."

"I'm afraid I have."

"You've been upset enough for one day. I hope you'll nap again, and I'll bring you some supper later."

When Dorcas returned downstairs, she glanced out the window and saw a hack stop in front of the mansion. Her mother and Judy climbed out and started for the door, carrying hat boxes. The cabby followed with other bundles piled high and had to return for a second load.

Rushing to open the door, Dorcas cried, "Well, it looks as if you had good luck."

"We had a marvelous day. Do come upstairs with us and

see what we found." Judy's voice was high-pitched in excitement.

Even her mother seemed to be in a happy mood. "What about your grandfather?"

"He's upstairs in bed. He doesn't feel well."

"Poor old man. Perhaps he's coming down with the grippe," Lenore murmured sympathetically.

"He's had a wretched day. I'm so glad I came home," Dorcas said.

Piling the boxes in her mother's room, the girls ran down for another load. By the time they returned, Lenore had changed into a dressing gown.

"I'm completely exhausted, so I'm going to lie down on my chaise. Judy, you show Dorcas what we bought."

Trying hard to disguise her growing dismay, Dorcas watched as box after box was opened. Soon the top of her bed was covered with taffeta petticoats, handmade chemises, and tea gowns from France, all trimmed with lace. Judy displayed the softest leather shoes with matching handbags. Suede gloves. Silk hosiery. Nightgowns and peignoirs. Elaborate hats. Dress goods formed a rainbow of silk, foulard, moire, figured satin, and voile on the counterpane. All Dorcas could think about were the bills that would come.

"You don't seem very enthusiastic," Lenore said from the chaise. "What's the matter? Don't you like them?"

"Of course. They're the most beautiful things I've ever seen. But I'm overwhelmed. It's so much."

Lenore sat up in annoyance. "Well, you told me to get a new wardrobe! It was all your idea, Dorcas."

"I know, Mama, and I'm happy for you. I wanted you to get out of your mourning clothes."

"I'm grateful that at least Judy stayed with me and helped me shop."

"Oh, so am I. That's just wonderful." Then Dorcas added lamely, "Everything you bought is in perfect taste."

Judy put her hands on her hips. "If you're jealous, why don't you admit it?"

"But I'm not jealous. Honestly, I'm not. I think it's just great," Dorcas protested weakly.

Lenore swung her feet over the edge of the chaise and sat up. "But your whole attitude has changed since this morning. I demand an explanation!"

"Grandpa's been talking to me all day. He's going through a real financial crisis. It's so frightening." Dorcas looked from her mother to her sister. "The hotel cost so much. He has a lot of debts to pay."

Lenore frowned. "What has that to do with me? He's not paying for these things. I am." Irritation showed in her face.

"I know, Mama. But from now on, I think we'd better take it easy. We'll have to economize."

Judy laughed. "Honestly, Dorcas, don't be such a spoil-sport. I have no intention of economizing. In fact, I'm going to enjoy the spring social season to the utmost."

Lenore settled back on the chaise. "That's just what you should do, honey. You're only young once, so make the most of it."

"I intend to." Judy tossed her head. "If Grandpa has debts, he can just pay them back. Nobody made him build that hotel."

"Your papa was opposed to it right from the first," Lenore put in. "More than once he said, 'Father has no damn business getting into that project. It'll ruin him.' So Clyde Hamilton needn't come running to me for sympathy."

"Me neither." Judy started to fold a satin nightgown. "Help me carry my things to my room, Dori."

When they were out in the hall, Judy turned to Dorcas and snapped angrily, "Why on earth did you act like that? It took me all morning to get Mama into a happy mood so she'd buy something. She was so mad at you for leaving us. But I finally won her over. It's the first time in months she's been willing to shop."

"I'm sorry, Judy."

"Now you've spoiled everything for her."

"I didn't mean to. But I'm terribly worried about Grand-father."

"If he has troubles, I don't want to hear about them. He's so quick to tell us what to do and what not to do. If he knows so darned much, let him solve his own problems."

"I won't talk to you about it again," Dorcas said. She couldn't make Judy understand.

Judy pushed open the door and placed her things on her bed. "Frankly, Mama and I are both getting awfully tired of living here under Grandpa's thumb. He's such a dictator. We'd like to move into a nice flat and be on our own."

"Oh, no. Not just yet. He needs us right now." What would Grandpa do without our household money? Dorcas thought worriedly.

Judy tossed her head. "I don't care."

Dorcas tried another tack. "Judy, you need this mansion as a backdrop for the social season. People are impressed with this big house. The staff of servants. The carriages. The Hamilton name."

"Perhaps."

"Grandfather's one of the most important men in the city, and that reflects on you. It wouldn't be the same if you weren't living here. Besides, let's remember this neighborhood is convenient for Keith to get to school."

Judy shrugged. "Well, I guess we can stay until summer."

Dorcas helped Judy put her new clothes away and returned to her mother's room to get it in order. Lenore dozed, looking serene and lovely. Dorcas gently laid a light coverlet over her and then turned to the bed, which was still covered with the luxurious garments. God help them when the bills pour in, she thought.

But her mother had made an enormous step forward toward recovery. If these things snapped her out of her grief, perhaps they were worth the staggering cost. Now Dorcas regretted her objection to them. She began to fold the undergarments, feeling the smooth satin and silk, and admiring the handmade lace.

Before she left the room, she saw her mother's opal and diamond bracelet with its matching earrings in a silver tray on top of the bureau. She held the bracelet to the light and watched the glittering fire inside the stones. As she put the pieces away in a velvet-lined box, she was reminded of her own exquisite jewelry that she had inherited from Grandmother Hamilton. It was a lifetime collection of magnificent birthday and holiday gifts.

Just thinking about her jewels made Dorcas gasp. What would they be worth? Enough to reopen the Alpine mine?

A shiver of apprehension ran through Dorcas as she pushed open the heavy, carved doors of Angliers' Jewelry, the most exclusive store of its kind in San Francisco. Dark-suited salesmen waited on customers seated at the display cases.

Velvet pads lay on top of cases filled with rings, brooches, and watches. The atmosphere in the elegant shop was leisurely. No one hurried a customer on the verge of purchasing an expensive jewel.

The head salesman walked quietly across the oriental rug. "Good morning, Miss Hamilton. May I be of service? I suppose you want to pick up one of your rings or necklaces?" As was the custom among the wealthy patrons, her jewels were stored in the firm's vault for safekeeping.

"No, not today, thank you." She smiled at him. "Would it be possible to speak to Mr. Jacques Angliers?"

"Please sit down and I'll see." He indicated a Louis XVI chair.

As she waited, her heart thumped against her chest. She had spent days agonizing over her decision. What excuse would she give for wanting to sell her collection? How could she admit her need without giving away her grandfather's plight? How could she avoid starting rumors? But she had to have money. A lot of it.

Their only hope was to reopen the Alpine mine and get at the gold; even try to find their part of the Andromeda Lode, if it existed. If they didn't succeed in that, surely there were lesser amounts of gold imbedded in quartz that could be mined to make the October payment.

How could opening the mine be as complicated as her grandfather had said? What seemed like an enormous undertaking to him might not be to her. If she could get her hands on some money, why not hire a mine manager, go to Alpine Heights herself, and get the mine in operation? She was the only one who could do it.

"Mr. Angliers can see you, miss," the head salesman said at her elbow. "Just follow me."

Jacques Angliers, an elderly Frenchman who had come with two brothers from Paris to San Francisco soon after the Gold Rush, rose from his chair, walked around his desk and held out both hands to grasp hers. His pink scalp showed through his snow-white hair. Long sideburns framed his plump face. "Miss Dorcas, it's always a pleasure to see you. Let's sit here on the sofa and chat. I've sent for a cup of coffee."

After he had inquired about her grandfather's health, the coffee arrived in a delicate Limoges china pot with matching cups and saucers. As he poured he asked, "To what do I owe this delightful call from such a beautiful young lady?"

"Well, Mr. Angliers, I hardly know how to begin." The color mounted in her cheeks. "I'm sure you'll be shocked." Her voice faltered. "But I would like to have you sell my grandmother's jewels for me."

As he stared at her, he put his cup down with shaking fingers. "I couldn't. That's a sacrilege. Those jewels are family heirlooms."

"I know. Just the thought of it distresses me." Sudden tears washed her eyes. "But I need money. A lot of it. Those jewels are my only recourse."

Instead of answering, he rose and pressed a button on his desk. When a clerk came, he said, "Bring me the Dorcas Hamilton container from the vault, please." Then he took his place beside her again. "I would like to tell you some of the stories behind those pieces. Perhaps you will change your mind."

Distress showed in her large, expressive eyes. "This is not something I want to do, you understand."

"Of course not." He leaned back, making a tent with his fingers.

When the clerk brought the container, Dorcas and the old jeweler moved to his desk. He untied the canvas covering and lovingly lifted the velvet boxes out. He lined them up in front of him.

"This is one of my favorites." He held a ruby pendant to the light. "I bought this stone in Paris twenty years ago. It was supposed to be part of Madame Pompadour's famous ruby necklace. When I brought it home, I put it aside for your grandfather until we could decide on a setting. As you no doubt know, your grandfather was deeply devoted to your grandmother. I had a standing order from him to provide a special gift for him to give her three times a year: Christmas; their anniversary, May fifteenth; and her birthday in September."

Dorcas tried to estimate what her grandfather had spent on jewelry each year.

The jeweler went on. "Always during my world travels I was on the lookout for something special for Mrs. Hamilton. Not only gems but rare porcelain, figurines, pieces of cloisonne from the Orient, antique snuffboxes. I understand that all those things are still in the mansion."

She nodded as she thought of the inlaid cabinet where the priceless bric-a-brac was displayed. "I look at them every day," she said. They would all go in the crash. Her heart sank in despair.

Mr. Angliers continued. "After Mrs. Hamilton's death, your grandfather instructed me to divide the jewelry into three parts. Two, made up of the most valuable pieces, were to go to you and Miss Judy. The third, of lesser worth, I sent to his nieces in Philadelphia, except for some that your mother received." He droned on about the stones he had found in Berlin or Rome or South Africa. Opals from Australia. Matching pearls from Tokyo.

Finally, Dorcas interrupted. "But what is this collection worth?"

He looked at her sadly. "Many more times what you can get right now during this depression. Fine jewels are flooding the market. There are desperate people all across the country trying to save their homes and businesses." He shook his head in dismay. "And it's hard to sell pieces of this value."

Dorcas fidgeted. How could she pin him down? Surely he knew how difficult this must be for her. "But if you were to put them on the market now?"

He pursed his lips. "A poor time to sell. One of the worst." He coughed and leaned toward her. "I can see how upset you are. If you have a personal problem and want to go away for a while, why don't you—"

Her cheeks flamed. He must think she was in the family way. "It's not that at all, Mr. Angliers. I want the money to open the mine in Alpine Heights. It's been closed for eight years. I want to take a mining man up there and—"

Gaping at her in surprise, he cried, "You? A young lady like you? That's unheard of! Your grandfather will be—"

"Outraged, of course." She smiled at him. "I hope I can persuade him to let me try. He's too old to do it himself, and my brother's only sixteen. If anyone takes on the project, it will be me."

"I see. I see." The jeweler rubbed his forehead. "I've heard rumors that Mr. Hamilton was pressed for money. That hotel must have cost millions. Of course, his affairs are none of my business."

"And I'm not free to discuss them. But I am anxious to raise some money. You still haven't told me what these jewels will sell for."

"I doubt that I could get more than ten thousand dollars right now."

It sounded like a great fortune to Dorcas. With ten thousand dollars, surely she could reopen the mine. Men were desperate for work and glad to get $2.50 a day, she had heard. And certainly for a couple of hundred a month, she could hire a mine manager.

Of course there were other expenses in operating a mine. But the tunnels were there and timbered. The portals all built. The machinery in place. Hadn't Andy told her of the mine's good condition? And once they were in operation, they would have the gold to fall back on. It was just a question of getting started. And now was the time. As slim as it was, there was always the chance of finding their branch of the Andromeda Lode.

Feeling sick over the agonizing decision, she braced herself, swallowed hard, and said, "Sell the collection."

Jacques Angliers slumped down in his chair. He seemed to be studying her. What is he thinking? she wondered. He glanced down at the Pompadour ruby, picked it up, and held it to the light.

"You know, Miss Dorcas, you remind me of this jewel. You seem to have the same depth, inner fire, and real worth. There's not one girl in a hundred who would have the courage to go way up to northern California and open a mine."

"I don't believe it will be as hard as you and Grandfather think. Anyway, I want to try."

"Good for you. Who knows? You might succeed." He shrugged. "Over the years, Mr. Hamilton has been my best and most loyal customer. He bought gifts here not only for his wife, but for his friends and employees as well. I have to confess that more than once his steady patronage pulled me through a crisis. So I think I owe his family something."

"What do you mean, Mr. Angliers?"

"Miss Dorcas, I'll tell you what I'll do. I'll buy this collection from you."

"Oh, good!" She sank back and sighed in relief.

"I'll write you a check for ten thousand dollars today. But I'm not going to put the jewels on the market right now. I'll place them back in the vault until the Christmas season. That's when we do the major share of our business. Anytime before that, if you want to buy the collection back from me, you can.''

Tears flooded her eyes. "Oh, Mr. Angliers, you're such a darling.''

He patted her hand. "Those terms will all be stated on the bill of sale, just to protect you.'' He smiled. "I'm an old man myself. I don't know how long I'll be here.''

Dorcas's grandfather was sitting in his big leather chair when she joined him that evening. "Sit down, my child. I'm glad to see you. I thought you had gone to the theater with the others.''

"No, Keith went with them. I wanted to stay home and talk to you.''

He reached out and patted her arm. "You're the joy of an old man's heart. What would I do without you?''

"You seem to be in much better spirits. Did the foundry sale go through?''

He nodded. "Finally. Thanks be to God.'' He drummed his fingers on the chair arm. "I sent a payment to all my creditors, including the Richmonds, and kept the sheriff from the door this time.''

"Grandpa, how marvelous!'' She jumped up and squeezed his shoulders, then planted a kiss on both his cheeks. "I'll pour us a glass of sherry for a toast.'' When they had their sherry in hand, she raised her glass. "Here's to your wonderful sale! Now things are going to be much better.''

"No, my dear.'' He shook his head and sipped his wine. "I've just postponed the inevitable. The next payment is due the first of October. There's no way I can meet it. No way at all.''

"I think there is, Grandpa.'' She hesitated so that her statement could sink in. "All I need is your permission.''

"What do you mean?''

"I want to reopen the Alpine. You don't have to do anything about it. I'll take charge.''

"You?'' He stared at her as if he couldn't believe his ears.

"Yes, me. Dorcas Lenore Hamilton. At your service. You're looking at the next general manager of the Alpine. I've been around mines all my life. And I've got molten gold for blood, just like you and Papa.''

His face purpled. "Forget this absurd idea at once," he shouted. "It's out of the question!"

"Why? Because I'm a woman?''

"Yes. And you're a Hamilton! It's unseemly for you to do such an outrageous thing!''

"What if you go bankrupt? Would it be unseemly if I taught school? Became a governess? A store clerk? That is, if I could get a job in these hard times.''

"Don't be ridiculous! You won't have to work. Your mother has her insurance money." He settled back.

"But it won't last forever, Grandpa. We have to use it to send Keith to mining school as well as live on it, and it's all mother's got. And Judy's spending it as if it were a fortune.''

"Well, a pretty girl like you will marry soon. You'll have a rich husband to take care of you.''

"Will I? Exactly how desirable will I be to men of our class without the prospects of the Hamilton money as a lure?''

"Humph!" He made a fist. "Let's not waste time arguing about this. It's impossible, anyway. I haven't the funds to open the mine.''

"Well, I have." She reached in her pocket and took out her check book. "See for yourself.''

He stared at the balance openmouthed and then at her, "Where did you get ten thousand dollars?''

She told him about her morning at the jewelers. "I have it all planned. I'm going to use some of the money to hire a manager, and he'll help me round up some miners. I know Andy will give him advice about the engineering side. I'll pay a consultation fee, of course. I'll get an older woman to go to Alpine Heights with me as a chaperon. Perhaps we can live at Widow Hendricks's. Andy told me she still takes in boarders.''

Clyde Hamilton half rose out of his leather chair. "How dare you go ahead with this without consulting me first? I'm surprised at you.''

She jumped to her feet. "You would have said no, without giving me a chance.''

His face reddened in fury. "Of course I would've said no. I forbid such a thing! Dorcas, you just march right down to Jacques Angliers tomorrow and give him his money back.'' His jaw clenched.

"No! Not until we talk this over when you're not angry!" She stuck out her chin.

He glared at her. "How dare you defy me!" She was one of the few people in San Francisco who would.

"Because I'm right and you're wrong!"

He slumped back in his chair in astonishment.

She sat down again and leaned toward him. "Now, don't be stubborn, Grandfather. I want you to consider this. There's no reason at all why we can't open the Alpine and use the gold to make the next payment on your debts."

"Impossible!"

"But we have seven months. What are we supposed to do? Sit back and do nothing to help ourselves? Go to parties and balls as if we had no problems? Well, I won't. I'm going to fight to the last!"

"But you're a female," he whispered.

"Didn't I take care of all our affairs back in Colorado after Papa's death? Didn't I sell the house? Close the mine? Hire caretakers? Move us all back here?" She pointed her finger at him. "You told me more than once that a man couldn't have done better. So why can't I do this? How can it be any harder?"

"But what will people think?" her grandfather demanded.

"That I have gone to Alpine Heights to take care of some of your affairs, accompanied by a chaperon."

"Who?"

"I'll get someone." She put her hand on his knee. "Grandpa, this is a crisis. A grave one. Is it any different from a war, when women have to run farms or manage businesses while the men are away fighting? You've read about Abigail Adams way back in Revolutionary times. Look what she did. This is almost the twentieth century. A new age! We women aren't helpless."

"But the gossip—" He looked away and muttered. "It's bad enough now."

"It'll be a lot worse if you go under. Then they'll really have something to chew over. Can't you see the headlines in the paper? The whole country will chortle with glee to see a tycoon like you collapse. A robber baron brought to his knees. It mustn't happen."

Clyde Hamilton cringed. "How can I face it?"

"You don't have to, Grandfather, if you'll just give me a

chance. I know I can make the mine pay. We'll have the money for the October payment.''

His voice softened. "You've got guts, Dorcas. I'll say that."

"Grandpa, it's not only your welfare that's at stake. We're all in this."

"I know. That's why it hurts me so much to lose everything. My life is about over, but the rest of you—"

"Keith should have the chance to take over the corporation when he's ready. We know his potential. He'll be a smart, powerful man like you and Papa. Your company has a great future if we can get through this bad time. Think of everything you and Papa worked for. Should it all be lost now?"

"You don't know what you're getting into," Clyde Hamilton warned her.

"Perhaps that's just as well. But I'll manage somehow." She dropped to her knees beside him. "Please, Grandpa, I beg you. Just let me try."

"But your money might all be lost. It's like pouring it down a rat hole." His chin quivered. "You'll lose your grandmother's jewels."

"I must take that risk. How do we know but what I'd lose them, anyway? What if we run out of insurance money and Mother is ill? I'd have to sell them then." She put her head against his leg. "Grandpa, no one cherishes those jewels more than I do. I want to pass them on to my daughters if I have them." Tears ran down her cheeks.

"I know, Dorcas. You're a good girl." His voice quivered. "How can I say no when you want so badly to try this?"

"Oh, Grandpa, I'll need all your help and advice."

"And my prayers." He shook his head. "I know far better than you what you're getting into. God help you."

The next day Dorcas tackled her mother and Judy in the upstairs living room. As she walked in, they were sitting near the window shortening petticoats they had bought on their shopping spree.

Dorcas went to stand beside her mother, running her hand over one of the garments. "Isn't this lovely? Look at the tiny embroidery above the flounce. It's exquisite."

Her mother smiled. How pretty she is, Dorcas thought.

"So you approve after all?" Lenore asked.

Dorcas leaned forward and kissed her mother. "Of course I do. I'm so proud of your making the effort to go out and buy these things."

Lenore patted her arm and said, "We're all invited to the Northern California Art Institute's Easter ball. It's to raise money for their fund. It'll be the biggest social event of the spring."

"My art teacher saw to it that we all got invitations," Judy put in. "Even Grandfather. Of course, they hope he'll make a contribution." She smiled at Lenore. "Mother's promised me that she'll dance this time."

"Marvelous!" Dorcas patted her mother's shoulders. "Mama, that makes me so happy."

"Judy can be very persuasive." Lenore's beautiful face looked serene and content for a change. "I feel I want to do things again. This is the first time I've had any energy since . . ." Her voice faded.

Dorcas turned to her sister. "I'm proud of you, too, Judy. You're taking good care of Mama. Doing more for her than anyone else could."

Judy looked up and flushed at the compliment.

Lenore put in, "I'm thinking of making a contribution to the Art Institute."

"Mother, I don't want to discourage your good intentions, but I think you'd better hang on to your money," Dorcas said.

"What do you mean?" Judy asked.

Dorcas pulled a chair up close to them. "I don't think either of you understands just how serious things are with Grandfather."

"That's his problem," Lenore snapped angrily.

"Is it entirely?" Dorcas asked. "What about Keith and his future? He's supposed to take charge of the corporation when he's ready."

"Well, he's going to, isn't he?" her mother said. "Surely Clyde hasn't made other arrangements. I'll never forgive him if he has."

"No, Grandfather's made no other arrangements."

"Stop talking in riddles," Judy ordered crossly. "Of course Keith will take over."

"Not if the corporation goes bankrupt. There'll be nothing left for him then."

"Oh, no!" Lenore whispered, in shock. "Your father predicted this would happen. He argued and argued with that stubborn old fool, trying to talk him out of it!"

"Our inheritance!" The color drained from Judy's face. She gripped Dorcas's arm. "What's going to happen to it?"

"Obviously if Grandpa goes bankrupt, there won't be any."

As tears gathered in Judy's eyes, she cried out angrily, "How could Grandpa do that? He must be the most stupid man in the world." She reached into her pocket for a handkerchief.

Dorcas sat up straight. "Before you call Grandpa stupid, you might remember who earned the fortune in the first place!"

Judy sniffed, "But he owes it to us."

"Where is it written that Grandfather owes us anything? All our lives we've benefited from his generosity. He told us we were his heirs, but that was before he got into this trouble."

Lenore put aside the petticoat she was working on. "This is just awful! Isn't there something that can be done?"

"Yes; that's what I came to discuss with you," Dorcas said, as she tried to think of how to begin. "I've considered every possibility—"

"Why doesn't he sell some property or a factory?" Judy asked, a frantic note in her voice.

"It isn't that simple." Dorcas explained how Clyde had tried and tried to sell some of his holdings, how all of his assets were mortgaged to the maximum. "We're in a deep depression, and few people are buying mills or factories or real estate. Besides, prices are at rock bottom."

Lenore sighed in despair. "If he does go under, will it be soon?"

"No, he just sold a foundry that he's been trying to unload for a long time. That property didn't have a mortgage on it, so he had money to make a payment to all his creditors."

"Then what's the emergency?" Lenore asked.

"The next payment is due the first of October and somehow it must be met. Grandpa says he has nothing else to fall back on. If he doesn't make it, his creditors will force him into bankruptcy. They're all powerful financiers and they want his property. They're just waiting to pounce on him.''

"It sounds so cruel," Judy whispered, her violet eyes round in astonishment.

"But at least we have almost seven months. I've finally figured out what to do."

"What? Tell us," Lenore urged.

"I'm going to open the Alpine mine. Surely there's gold—"

"What do you mean? *You?*" Judy interrupted, looking shocked.

"I mean I'm going to hire a mine manager and take him up there. I'll find some older woman to go along as chaperon."

"You can't!" Lenore shouted. "I absolutely forbid it!"

The girls looked at her in astonishment. Lenore stood up, her face white, her eyes haunted. "You'll never have my permission! Never!"

Dorcas reached up and put her hand on Lenore's arm. "Mother, calm yourself. I'm twenty-two years old and an adult, just as you are. I don't need your permission. I have the right to make my own decisions. I'm going to do this because it's our only hope. Don't you understand that?"

The wild expression in her mother's face frightened Dorcas. Lenore began to tremble, and she twisted her arm free. "That mine is cursed! It's an evil place! Stay away!"

Judy stood up and ran to her mother. "Mama, please—"

Lenore pointed to Dorcas with a shaking finger. "Don't go there! It'll destroy us all." She put her hands over her face and began to sob.

"Mama, dear." Judy took her in her arms. "Please don't get go upset." But Lenore was still sobbing hysterically.

"Come with me, Mama," Judy went on. "We'll go to your bedroom so you can lie down. Dorcas can tell us more about it later."

"No! She mustn't go there! Ever!" Lenore buried her face in Judy's shoulder.

"Mother, please don't go to pieces over this. Let me help—" Dorcas begged.

"No! Leave me alone! I don't want you near me!"

Judy urged, "Come, Mama. I'll help you." She led her mother toward her bedroom.

When they were gone, Dorcas slumped in her chair, hurt to the quick. Why would her mother get so upset over opening the mine? It was more than just the dread of gossip; she was terrified. Dorcas wondered for an instant if her mother had a streak of madness.

Judy returned, saying, "I've given her a sedative. She wants to be left alone."

"Why did she get so upset?" Dorcas asked.

"I suppose she's thinking of how tongues will wag about your going to Alpine Heights and trying to run a mine."

"I'll take a chaperon with me. If anyone asks where I am, tell them I've gone to Alpine Heights to take care of some business for my grandfather."

"They'll still gossip," Judy pointed out.

"We can't help what they say." Dorcas wondered if she should confide her fears in her sister. "Mama acted so—strange."

"You always upset her, Dorcas." Judy stamped her foot. "I get her into good spirits and then you spoil it, every time."

"I don't mean to, Judy—I really don't—but we've been going through a lot lately." Dorcas put her hand to her face. "I'm just trying to save us from losing everything."

Judy patted her on the shoulder. "I'm sorry, Dori. I shouldn't have said that, because you're the one who's kept us all going. Now you have to solve Grandpa's problems, too."

Dorcas looked at her sister through a blur of tears. "After I go to Alpine Heights, it'll be up to you to run the mansion and take care of Mother."

"I'll try. But I don't want to pay the bills. I don't want anything to do with finances."

Wearily, Dorcas leaned her head back. "Send them up to me."

"Let's finish this sewing while we talk." Judy handed Dorcas a petticoat and their mother's thimble. The hem was all pinned in place, with the needle and thread dangling from the garment. As they began to work, she asked, "Oh, Dori, what on earth are we going to do?" Her eyes flooded with tears and her chin trembled.

"We have Mother's insurance money, so we'll be able to go on just as we are for a while."

"But that's Mama's money. I was expecting that I'd have a lot of my very own someday." Tears spilled down Judy's cheeks. "It'd be mine and I could spend it any way I pleased." She put a handkerchief to her eyes.

"Without my scolding you." Dorcas smiled wanly as she wiped her own eyes.

"Or, even worse, having a husband telling me what I could and couldn't do. I would hate that. Remember how Mama always had to consult with Papa and ask his permission before she bought anything? How angry he got when he saw some of her bills. She even had to ask for grocery money. I want my own income so I can do what I please." Judy stamped her foot.

"So do I, of course. I suppose all women resent having to beg a man for funds. It's so degrading," Dorcas agreed.

"Oh, Sis, do you think you can save our inheritance?"

"I'm certainly going to try. For all our sake. Especially Keith's. He's so looking forward to taking over the family corporation. He should have that chance. It's what Grandfather and Papa dreamed of and worked for all these years."

Dorcas told Judy about Andy's enthusiasm for the mine. "I'm positive we can get enough gold to keep up the payments on the loans. If we can just do that, Grandpa won't go bankrupt. Later on, when times are better, he can sell some of his property at a profit and get himself out of this hole. Besides, the hotel should begin to pay by then. His other businesses also. The trouble is he doesn't have cash right now. His assets are all frozen."

"You'll miss all the fun this spring."

"I can't help that. Besides, I couldn't enjoy all the balls and parties with this awful disaster hanging over our heads the whole time."

"I suppose not. I'm going to try not to think about it," Judy said decisively.

"Anyway, in a few months I'll be home and can take part. I won't try to keep the mine open in the winter."

Judy looked at Dorcas slyly. "Philip and Andy will be in Alpine Heights this summer. Didn't that have something to do with your decision?"

"Don't be silly! Of course it didn't." Dorcas's face flushed. "My mind's been on a lot of things besides them."

"We saw them at the theater last night. They told me they'll be leaving for the mountains next week. They're going to call Sunday afternoon to say good-bye. Make sure you're home."

"I will. I want their advice. Especially Andy's." But it was Philip whom Dorcas looked forward to seeing.

* * *

As the week passed, the atmosphere in the house grew even more tense, because Lenore sank deeper and deeper into a depression. Only her young personal maid, Rosalie, could persuade her to eat.

Dorcas stayed away until she could stand it no longer. She had to see how her mother was doing for herself. One afternoon, she went up to her mother's bedroom and tapped lightly on the door.

When Rosalie opened it, the maid tiptoed over to her and whispered, "I think she's sleeping."

Dorcas gasped in shock as she gazed at her mother. Silently she crossed the room on the thick carpet. Lenore lay in the bed coiled up like a newborn baby with her knees drawn to her chest and her head bent forward. Her face looked haggard and gray, with dark circles outlining her closed, sunken eyes. The haunted expression on her face chilled Dorcas to the very marrow.

"Mother, it's Dorcas. I came to see you."

Lenore opened her eyes, gazed at her daughter, and screamed, "Go away! I don't want you here!" She began to tremble.

"I think you'd better leave, ma'am," Rosalie whispered. "I'll give her a sedative. Miss Judy never mentions your name, as it upsets her so."

Dorcas put her hands to her face and ran from the room. Was her mother going insane? Lenore had never been this deeply depressed. What could they do? She'd read about doctors in Europe who were working with nervous disorders. Was there anyone here who could help her?

She found Judy in her room getting ready to go out. When Dorcas told her about the incident, her sister turned on her. "Why did you go to Mama's room? You always make her feel worse, and then Rosalie and I have to work all day to get her relaxed again. Just leave her alone."

"Does she hate me? Is that why?" Dorcas had never felt so hurt.

"Of course she doesn't hate you. You just upset her because, I think, you remind her a lot of Papa."

"But it's Keith who looks like Papa, not me."

"But you're the one who's taken his place as head of the family. Mama senses that."

"I'm so frightened. I think she's losing her mind."

"Of course she isn't. She's perfectly rational when I'm with her. She's just depressed. She'll come out of it eventually. She always does. But don't go near her again."

With tears streaming down her face, Dorcas hurried to her room. She had never felt so rejected in her life. She could hardly wait to get away.

The last wisp of fog had disappeared at noon. Warm sunshine glowed from the bed of daffodils and crocuses. A huge camellia, each petal in perfect symmetry, seemed to be bursting with blooms.

Dorcas held her croquet mallet and tapped the ball through the wicket. She looked up at Philip and caught his eye as he took his turn. How handsome he looked in his buff jacket and brown pants. His hand brushed hers as they readied themselves for another turn. They were alone momentarily, as Andy and Judy were sitting in the lawn swing looking at her portfolio of drawings.

"Your eyes fascinate me, Dorcas. They're the most beautiful I've ever seen. So big and expressive," Philip said.

"Thank you." As her blood quickened, she looked away from him. She didn't want him to see how she felt. A tumult of emotions churned through her. Ecstasy. Sadness. Desire. She swallowed hard trying to get herself under control. It didn't matter what her grandfather had told her about the Richmond chicanery. She loved Philip. She loved him with all her heart. All these years she had cared for him. And she loved him now. She'd go to the ends of the earth with him. But did he truly care for her?

A maid crossed the lawn and put a tray with lemonade and cookies in the garden house.

Philip looked at Dorcas and smiled. "For a moment you looked so sad. Is something the matter?"

"Yes, I'm sure you're going to win." As she watched him make the last goal, she forced a laugh. "In fact you have. I'm soundly beaten. Now, do come and have some refreshments. Then you must see Judy's drawings. She's making excellent progress. We're so proud of her."

After they were settled around the table in the latticed garden house, Andy remarked. "We're going to miss you two girls while we're at Alpine Heights slaving away. Aren't we, Philip?''

"Of course we are." Philip looked at Judy. "You must write and tell us about all the exciting things you're doing. The parties. The theater.''

Judy giggled. "I'm a horrible correspondent. But you won't miss Dorcas. She's going to be up there, too.''

The two men turned to Dorcas in surprise. Drat Judy, she thought. Why did she blat it out like that? "Yes, I'm making arrangements to reopen the Alpine mine.''

"Good for you!" Andy cried enthusiastically. "That's marvelous!''

"As soon as I find a manager and an older woman to accompany me, I'll bring them up there. I'll need advice from both of you.''

"I'll do anything I can to help you," Andy assured her as he patted her arm. "Just call on me. You'll have two experts right on tap. Won't she, Philip?''

"Of course. I'll be glad to do anything." But there was an enigmatic expression in Philip's eyes.

CHAPTER 5

The next morning Dorcas sat in the library, working on the list of things she had to do before she left. She hoped to get away within a week. But there was shopping to do. Warm clothes to pack. Her fur-trimmed ankle-boots to have mended. Most important of all were the manager and chaperon she must find. The list grew as she made her plans.

It would be a relief to get away. Her mother's condition upset her. And Grandpa was beginning to get on her nerves.

"I think we're making a mistake reopening the Alpine. I'm not sure that's what you should do, Dorcas. I've been thinking it over and . . ." he'd say again and again.

"Grandpa, you just relax and leave everything to me.''

"But a young girl like you has no business—''

"I'm going. Just realize that once and for all. I've made up my mind, Grandpa. I don't want to discuss the pros and cons anymore." If I can just get away without losing my mind, she'd thought more than once.

The door to the library quietly opened and the housekeeper came in. "Miss Dorcas, may I have a word with you?" she asked hesitatingly.

Dorcas looked up at the older woman. "Of course, Mrs. Williams, come in and sit down." She had always liked their quiet, shy housekeeper, who had worked in the mansion for twenty years.

Mrs. Williams settled herself in a chair. "I was talking with Mr. Hamilton this morning, and he told me that you are looking for a chaperon to go with you to the mine."

"Yes, I am. Do you have someone in mind?"

"My sister Esther would appreciate it, Miss Dorcas, if you'd consider her."

What a stroke of luck it would be to have someone along who was related to this fine woman, Dorcas told herself. "Tell me about her."

"Her name is Esther Morrisey. She's fifty-four and was recently widowed." Mrs. Williams's chin quivered. "She needs work bad. Her sons try to help her, but they're only able to work part-time. They've got young ones to feed as well."

"I'm certainly willing to consider her. I've no one else in mind yet."

"She's a good Christian woman. Raised her family and took care of her husband."

"Do you think she'd be willing to go up into the mountains and live in a rooming house?" Dorcas asked.

"Of course she would, ma'am. She's desperate."

"She'd have to come to the mine with me every day, but I might find something for her to do."

"Esther'll do anything to help you. She's never worked outside her home before except for picking peaches on a fruit ranch when she was a girl."

"Send Wilson with a message for her. See if she can come tomorrow morning." Dorcas smiled. "I could interview her now, but it's Monday, and she's probably in the midst of her washing."

Mrs. Williams nodded. "Yes, ma'am, she is. She's quite a hand at sticking to a schedule. Esther's an excellent housekeeper.'' She rose. As she pulled her sleeves down and straightened her immaculately starched cuffs, she added, ''Thank you, Miss Dorcas. I think you'll like her. She's kind of jolly and more talkative than I am.''

Dorcas patted the woman's hand. ''Mrs. Williams, if she's as conscientious and sweet as you are, she'll do just fine.''

Mrs. Morrisey nervously tucked stray strands of iron-gray hair into the thick braid wound around her head. She was a tall woman with broad shoulders and a plump, sturdy figure, but she looked ill-at-ease sitting on the edge of her chair, her face flushed and her eyes glancing around the library.

Thank goodness for her size, Dorcas thought. A chaperon might have to stand up to an overaggressive man. Certainly the mountains were no place for a fragile person. But Esther Morrisey had her sister's sweet expression and pleasant manner. She'd do very well.

''You understand what I want, don't you?'' Dorcas asked.

''According to my sister's note, you'll be needing a chaperon. I'm willing to do other things, such as your washing, ma'am.''

''Good, because I may not have time to take care of my clothes myself. I've lived up there and I know what that red dirt will do to a skirt.''

''I'll cook or do any housework.''

''I expect to be staying in a boardinghouse. At least at first. There's a house up there on the grounds of the mine, but it's empty, so we can't live there at present.''

''If I go with you, I could give it a good sweeping and scrubbing. It's probably filled with cobwebs and rat droppings. The windows would need washing,'' Mrs. Morrisey said.

''I'm sure the house needs a good turning-out. But we won't worry about that at present. My chaperon will have to go to the mine each day so that the men working for me will know that I'm not out there alone. I don't want there to be any gossip or any chance a miner might think he could take advantage of me.''

''I'm big and strong. Sometimes my husband and his cronies took a mite too much to drink and I had to handle them.''

Dorcas laughed. "I'm glad you were able to. I don't know what we'll run into."

Mrs. Morrisey nodded. "You never can tell."

"I've lived in mining towns most of my life, but my father was always there to offer protection. I've never tried to get a mine into operation before, but I'm determined to do it."

"My sister says you've got real spunk, Miss Hamilton. She says you can handle your grandfather better than anyone."

"We'll both need real spunk if we tackle this job, Mrs. Morrisey. I'm going to hire you although you're the only one I've interviewed. I think we'll get along just fine."

The older woman's eyes filled with tears. "Thank you, ma'am. I need to work. You don't know what this means to me."

"It means a lot to me to have a good chaperon. But I'm warning you. You might get awfully bored."

As Mrs. Morrisey dabbed at her eyes, she smiled. "That's better than being hungry or out in the cold without a roof over my head."

"That's true. I'll pay all your expenses, of course, and a modest salary." Dorcas named a figure and saw her new chaperon start with pleasure. "I'm going to advance you twenty-five dollars so you can buy anything you might need to take with you." Dorcas went to the desk and got an envelope with the money.

"Thank you, Miss Hamilton."

"If we're going to work together, why don't you call me Miss Dorcas just like your sister does."

"And you call me Esther as all my friends do. I think we're going to be friends."

"I'm sure of that." As they shook hands, Dorcas suggested, "Why don't you have a cup of coffee with Mrs. Williams, and then the coachman will take you home. He has another errand to run anyway."

As her new chaperon left the room, Dorcas told herself, "Well, at least that job's filled. I hope I'm as fortunate in finding a manager."

That evening her grandfather greeted her. "I have a lead on a manager for you. For several years he was manager of the Wiley mine in the Mother Lode, but it's closed now."

"Oh, Grandpa, where did you find him?"

"I was out at the foundry, signing some final papers with the new owners. As I was leaving, this man approached and introduced himself as Wes Ferguson. He wanted to find a job at a mine and thought maybe I could help him."

"What did you think of him?" Dorcas settled herself on a footstool in front of the fire in the library. What a relief it would be if her grandfather chose the manager. That responsibility worried her more than anything.

"As far as I could tell, he looked like a reliable man. I told him to come here tomorrow night and talk to us."

"What is he doing at the foundry?"

"Common labor. But don't count that against him. A man has to earn a living any way he can these days. After Ferguson left me, the foreman at the foundry came out to say good-bye because he'd worked for me for years. I asked him about Ferguson and he said he's a reliable workman. Doesn't come to work drunk or anything like that." Clyde shrugged. "Dorcas, you'll have to take people on face value and hope for the best."

"I suppose it will be chancy no matter whom I hire. I'd feel better if you interviewed him, too."

"Of course." Clyde patted her arm. "My dear, you'll find that hiring good employees is the hardest job of all. We'll see what you think of Ferguson."

"It's what *you* think of Ferguson that's important. If he'll do, just hire him."

"No, Dorcas. If I approve, I'll get up and put another log in the fire. While I'm doing that, you look at me. If I nod, you go ahead and hire him."

"But why me? Wouldn't he be more impressed if Clyde Hamilton—"

Her grandfather chuckled. "Perhaps. But that's not important. You're going to be his boss. The figure of authority. Act like one." He thumped his fist on the table. "If you hire him, by God, you can fire him. And he'll realize that."

Dorcas served brandy to her grandfather and Wes Ferguson, then took a glass of sherry for herself. As she settled in her chair and sipped her wine, she studied the stranger in the glow the fire cast on his rugged features. What qualities

70

should she look for? Size was important, since he would be dealing with hard-rock miners. Ferguson was big, no doubt about that. Six feet three, she estimated. Broad shoulders and biceps that strained the sleeves of his blue serge suit coat. His square hands were large and callused. Age—early forties. Appearance—neat. Brown hair carefully combed and mustache trimmed. His high collar and dark red tie were clean. Shoes shined. Surely that indicated conscientiousness and a desire to get this job. Personality—she hesitated. She didn't particularly like him. Not the way she had warmed to Esther at once. But how important was that? Did it really matter whether she or the miners liked him? If he gained their respect, wasn't that all that was necessary?

Wes Ferguson took an envelope out of his vest pocket. "Here's a letter of recommendation from my former boss, Mr. Wiley." He handed it to Clyde Hamilton, who glanced at it and quickly passed it on to Dorcas.

To Whom It May Concern:
Wesley Ferguson worked for the Wiley mine in Placer
County, California, from April 1, 1878, to October 1,
1893, at which time the mine was closed. He served the
last seven years as manager. I recommend him as a
man of ability and experience.

Hubert L. Wiley, Pres.
Wiley Mining Co.

As she refolded the letter and slipped it back in the envelope, Dorcas half listened to the men discuss the famous mines of Placer County. Finally, Clyde rose from his leather chair, stepped to the brass hamper, and selected a piece of oak. After he added it to the blaze, he brushed his hands and nodded slightly. Now it was up to her, and she was scared.

"Mr. Hamilton," Wes Ferguson began. "I'm anxious to get back to the mountains. Now that spring is coming, the mines will be opening. I thought perhaps you would have an opening on one of your properties—"

Dorcas half rose from her chair and handed his letter back to him. Her heart thumped. "You may address your remarks to me, Mr. Ferguson. I am my grandfather's agent."

The mining man stared her way in shock. "You?"

Dorcas nodded. "I will be leaving shortly to open the Alpine mine in Trinity County, which belongs to the Hamilton company. It has been closed for eight years, so I will need an experienced man to hire miners and act as manager."

"But—but—you're—" Ferguson gasped.

"Young and a female." She sat up straight with her head held high and controlled her voice. "But I've been exposed to mining all my life. In northern California and Colorado. My father, a mining engineer, had charge of our properties there."

"I see," Ferguson mumbled as he glanced down at his hands.

Dorcas went on. "I am also a Hamilton and have been given complete authority to act as general manager. Isn't that correct, Grandfather?"

"Absolutely." Pride shone in Clyde Hamilton's eyes as he slumped back in his chair, as if to stay out of the picture.

Dorcas turned back to the miner. "Do you have any objections to working for a woman?"

His face flushed. "I never have worked for one before, ma'am, but I see no reason why I can't."

"Very well. Before we make any final decisions, let's have certain things understood right now. The manager will have authority to hire and fire the miners and direct their work. He will be responsible for the safety and well being of his men but must make sure they earn their money. I won't tolerate any laziness or inefficiency. In other words, the manager will carry out the actual underground operations of the mine, as well as supervise the stamp mill and other phases in the processing of the gold."

Ferguson nodded. "That's what I did at the Wiley mine."

"The manager must consult with me on a daily basis," Dorcas went on determinedly. "As general manager, I will buy supplies, order all the equipment, and be in charge of the payroll. After consulting with a mining engineer, I will plan where the miners will work."

"You'll have a mining engineer there?" Ferguson asked.

"Part-time. Andrew Woodard, from the mine adjacent to ours, has consented to help us." She tried not to think of her grandfather's objections. "You must let me do what I think best, Grandfather," she had said to Clyde the night before. "We can't afford to hire a full-time engineer at this time. Later, perhaps."

Now they discussed further the duties of a manager until she asked, "Are you a family man, Mr. Ferguson?"

He nodded. "Yes, but I don't expect to take my wife to the mountains this summer. She is caring for her elderly father, who had a stroke."

"I imagine we'll all be living in boardinghouses anyway. I have no idea what condition the buildings on the mine grounds are in."

Ferguson cleared his throat. "What salary do you expect to pay?"

"I need an experienced manager, and I'm willing to pay well." She named the sum and could tell from his expression that he felt it was generous.

"The miners will get standard wages for the area." Fortunately, she had had a chance to talk with Andy before he left and had found out what was paid at the Richmond mine. "Now that you have the details, I would like to offer you the position of manager of the Alpine, Mr. Ferguson."

As he rose from his chair, he laughed a little hollowly. "I accept, Miss Hamilton."

He doesn't seem very enthusiastic, Dorcas told herself. She put out her hand. "We'll take the train on Monday morning, March fifth. Could you meet me at the ferry building at eight?"

"Of course, ma'am. I'm at your service."

After Ferguson had left, Dorcas turned to her grandfather. "I'm afraid I don't like him very well."

"Humph!" Clyde held out his brandy glass for a refill. "That's the trouble with you women. You always react to everything in such an emotional way."

Dorcas poured the brandy. "What do you mean?"

He sipped his drink. "A man asks, Can he do the job? A woman, Do I like him? What in tarnation difference does it make whether you *like* him or not? Does your liking him make him more able?"

"No, I guess not." She shook her head. "And you think he'll be all right?"

"In my judgment—yes. I've met Hubert Wiley. You couldn't find a smarter man. Do you think he'd put up with Ferguson for fifteen years if the man didn't have ability? Of course he wouldn't. He'd boot him out in no time."

"I feel better." She sat on the footstool by her grandfather's feet and leaned her head against his bony knee. "I got kind of scared, Grandpa."

"Of course you did. But don't worry about that. A man would feel the same way." He patted her head. "But you conducted yourself like a real trooper. Always remember that you're the one in authority. You're the Hamilton."

Tears blurred her eyes. "And the one trying to save the family fortune. I pray that I can."

His voice held a tremor. "If you can't, it'll be lost. God knows, it's beyond me to save it."

They had been on their way for two hours. The wheels clickety-clacked over the rails. The first excitement of leaving the house and boarding the train was over. Mrs. Morrisey sat next to Dorcas, dressed in her Sunday best, with her eyes closed and clutching her purse. Their suitcases and box lunch had been stored overhead.

At least Mr. Ferguson had excused himself and gone to the smoker as soon as they got underway. Dorcas was thankful for that, because she liked him even less this morning. But she pushed her misgivings aside and thought about Judy and Keith, who had come to the ferry building to see them off.

Her sister had kissed her and said, "Don't you worry about us. And I'll take care of Mama."

"She just turned her head away when I went to say good-bye. Wouldn't answer me at all," Dorcas had told Judy. The hurt still stung.

"Leave her to me, Dori. I'll snap her out of it," Judy had promised.

Keith had patted Dorcas on the shoulder. "As soon as school's out, I'm coming up to spend the summer with you."

Dorcas had thrown her arms around him and given him a hug. "Please do. I'll need you."

Now she gazed out at the flat green Sacramento valley. Occasionally she saw men walking behind plows that cut through masses of yellow buttercups, wild mustard, and lavender brodiaea growing in the rich grass. It seemed a shame to spoil the fields of wildflowers, but of course they had to prepare the soil for planting.

The train headed east toward the Sierra Nevada range. It wouldn't be long before they would have to disembark and change to a train going north, straight up the heart of the valley to Redding, the closest railroad town to the mine.

Dread of what lay ahead gathered in Dorcas. What would she be facing? Where would they stay tonight? Was there still a stage they could take to Alpine Heights? She had forgotten to ask Andy about that. Or would she have to find a man with a horse and buggy who would be willing to take them the final thirty-five miles westward into the mountains? The little mining town of Alpine Heights lay along the banks of a river that snaked its way through the range. It was a rugged trip, and not every man was willing to risk his team.

It was one thing to talk about what she was going to accomplish while in the comfort and safety of the mansion in San Francisco; it was an entirely different matter to carry it out. But she pulled herself together and determined not to get discouraged.

When she arrived in Alpine Heights, she would at least be near Philip. Just thinking about him sent a warm glow through her. As the train swayed and chugged along, she passed the time by thinking about him. She tried to recall every occasion they had been together in San Francisco. What he had worn; what he had said. The expressions that had come and gone on his handsome face.

In midafternoon the northbound train stopped, and the conductor came through to announce, "They are working on the track up ahead, so there will be some delay. You may get off the train and walk around if you wish. But when you hear the whistle, get back on immediately."

As the cold wind bit through their clothing, Dorcas and Esther walked up and down the side of the track. How good it was to breathe fresh air and stretch their cramped muscles after sitting in that stuffy coach.

Dorcas looked up the track and saw Wes Ferguson walking toward her with a tall, dark-bearded man in tow. "Miss Hamilton, say howdy to Gus Ortmeyer. We got acquainted on the train. He's looking for work in the mines up our way, so I told him to come along with us."

A shiver of foreboding ran along her spine as she acknowledged the introduction. The stranger looked so disrespectful, his lip twisted into a slight sneer.

"I've heard of the Alpine mine," Ortmeyer said.

"Miss Hamilton says it's been closed for several years. We'll be reopening it," Ferguson put in.

"I figured to apply at the Richmond mine. The Golden Star."

"You still can, Mr. Ortmeyer," Dorcas said coldly. "Their property is adjacent to ours."

"Oh, Miss Hamilton, don't say that," Ferguson said. "I've just persuaded him to work for us."

The train whistle blew just then, so she didn't have to answer. When they were settled in their seats again, Dorcas turned to Esther. "I didn't like his looks, did you?"

"I didn't pay much attention to him. Likely you won't be seeing much of him, anyway."

"To be honest, I don't care much for Mr. Ferguson, either. Grandfather got quite disgusted with me. He said the important thing was whether or not the man could do the job, not how likeable he was."

"Perhaps. But it's good to feel confident in a mine manager, at least." Esther patted her hand. "You're a brave girl to take this on."

"The closer we get to the mine, the more misgivings I have. That's just between you and me, of course."

There was another delay along the way. By the time they pulled up to the small depot in Redding, it was dark. Ferguson and Gus Ortmeyer came to help them with the luggage, for which Dorcas was grateful. The big engine hissed steam as the passengers disembarked onto the platform. A few kerosene lanterns hung from the eaves of the little building and formed flickering pools of light. Now what should she do? Where should they go to find rooms for the night? It didn't help her uneasiness to have these two hulking strangers waiting for her to make up her mind.

"Dorcas!" Someone stepped out of the darkness, and she recognized Andy. "I thought you'd be on this train, so I came to meet you," he said.

"Oh, Andy." She took both his hands in hers. "I've never been so glad to see anyone in my life."

"I had to come into town for supplies, so I waited until today. Thought you might need a hand."

While her knees shook in relief, she introduced him to the others. How like Andy to be so thoughtful.

Andy nodded toward the street. "I have a horse and wagon

76

right over there. Let's load the suitcases onto it and I'll take us to the hotel. It's not much of a place, but it's the best one in town.''

''I hope they can put all of us up,'' Dorcas said.

''I reserved two rooms besides my own when I got here this afternoon.''

''You can bunk in with me, Gus,'' Ferguson said as he picked up two suitcases and headed for the wagon.

Andy and Dorcas lingered over their coffee in the dining room. Mrs. Morrisey had excused herself after she had eaten a bowl of thick soup and a slice or two of homemade bread. ''I'm too tuckered out to eat much,'' she had said. The two men had gone to the nearest saloon.

''Do you know when there's a stage going to the mine?'' Dorcas asked.

Andy smiled at her. ''I was planning to take you myself. That's why I brought the big wagon.''

''I thought you had a load of supplies.''

''Not such a big one that we can't all go, too. Actually, the supplies I purchased were just an excuse to come meet you,'' he admitted. ''You women can sit with me on the seat, and the two men can manage in the back of the wagon.''

''Do you suppose this hotel would put up box lunches for us?''

''That's a good idea.'' He motioned their waiter over and asked him.

''Yes, sir. We often fix box lunches for our guests,'' the waiter assured him as he added more hot coffee to their cups. ''Besides mining people, lots of hunters and fishermen come through here.''

When they were alone again, Dorcas murmured. ''I don't know how to thank you for meeting the train and reserving these rooms.'' A sigh shuddered through her. ''I'll admit I was nervous when I got off the train in the dark.''

''You looked kind of scared.''

''I had no idea you'd come along and solve all my problems.'' She smiled at him. ''Thank you, dear friend.''

''You don't have to thank me, Dorcas. Just knowing that I helped you out of a bad spot is reward enough.''

*   *   *

Andy gazed at her face, pale with weariness, dark circles under her huge brown eyes. How beautiful she is in spite of her fatigue, he thought to himself. Underneath her brave front, he could sense her apprehension. He wished he dared tell her that he was falling in love with her. But he was all too aware of her feeling for Philip. As long as she was infatuated by his boss, he had no chance. No, now was not the time to declare himself. It would just mean that she would avoid him—their friendship would be over, and he couldn't bear that. Besides, she needed him now.

Early the next morning, they started west from Redding, a railroad town on the banks of the Sacramento River. For a while the journey across the floor of the valley was comfortable except for a cold wind that penetrated their clothing and undulated the tall grass in long waves.

The road crossed the lush growth ablaze with orange poppies and yellow mustard. A mountain range lay ahead, between the coast and the great Sacramento valley. When the road began to climb a grade, the grassland gave way to a dense, moisture-loving forest with towering Douglas firs, coastal redwoods, and cedars, all nourished by the rains that swept in from the Pacific Ocean. The travelers were protected by trees from the worst of the wind, but they had to stop frequently to let the horses rest or to push the wagon out of the ruts.

As they rose, they could see in the distance the snow-covered mountains, incredibly beautiful and majestic.

At noon they stopped by a stream, where Andy built a little fire and brewed a pot of coffee. How good the hot brew tasted, with the thick beef sandwiches and pieces of applesauce cake that the hotel had provided for them.

It was slow going up the long grade, and by afternoon they had covered only twenty miles. "We'll have to stop at this stage station to spend the night," Andy said. "I made reservations for us on my way in."

The next day the road was even steeper, and rut-filled from the winter storms.

More than once Dorcas whispered to Andy, "I'm so glad you met us." As they plodded along, she felt so safe perched next to him.

They turned off the main toll road to Weaverville and headed north over another grade. It was late afternoon by the time they started down to Alpine Heights, which was situated in a beautiful bowllike valley in the midst of the mountains. A river wound its way through the high grass. Off in the distance, the snow-laden Trinity Alps towered in front of the setting sun.

Although they had only gone fifteen miles since their overnight stop at the stage station, Dorcas ached from weariness and the jolting of the wagon. As she looked at the small mining town spread before her, she thought how lonely and isolated it was, and so far from San Francisco. But her spirits lightened at the thought that Philip was here and she would see him again. Perhaps their friendship would deepen into something far more.

As they rode slowly through the town, she looked around at all the familiar landmarks. The drug store, the barber shop. The general store, which sold everything from washtubs to dry goods. Some of the people walking on the wooden sidewalks turned and waved to Andy.

A horse trotted up beside them and a voice called out, "Welcome to Alpine Heights." Dorcas turned and gazed up at Philip, her heart pounding wildly. "Hello, there," he said with a smile.

Philip followed them to Widow Hendricks's boardinghouse, where Dorcas and Mrs. Morrisey were to stay. As soon as he tethered his horse he came over to the wagon, where Dorcas introduced him to Esther and then to the miners, who were clambering out of the back.

First, Philip helped Mrs. Morrisey down from the wagon seat. After she was safely on the ground, he held up his arms for Dorcas. Her cheeks flushed, her eyes sparkled, and her whole body seemed to come alive as he lifted her down. Completely forgotten was her numbing weariness.

"It's so good to get here," Dorcas cried as she gazed up at Philip's face.

Feeling sick at heart, Andy watched them.

CHAPTER 6

Widow Hendricks, a stout, good-natured woman, stepped out onto the porch of her Victorian house and greeted them. "Good evening. Come right in. I was about to ring the dinner bell."

Dorcas called back hello, taking one of her cases from the back of the wagon. Andy and the two miners carried the rest of the women's luggage to the front door.

"I'll take the men to their boardinghouse and see you in the morning," Andy said. "I'll pick you up at about seven."

Dorcas squeezed his hand. "You're such a dear person, Andy. I can't thank you enough." She watched him return to the wagon, then waved good-bye to Philip as he mounted his horse.

"Land sakes, Dorcas Hamilton," Widow Hendricks began when her guest entered the house, "I haven't seen you in ages. You've grown into a fetchin' young miss."

Dorcas introduced Esther and protested as the landlady picked up the heaviest suitcase and led the way up the stairs. "You must have your dinner to look after. If you'll just tell us where to go, we can manage ourselves."

"I have a helper looking after the victuals. I want to show you to your room. You're in the front bedroom, Dorcas, with Mrs. Morrisey right next door. After you freshen up a bit, come right down, as everything is ready."

The rooms were comfortable and clean. Dorcas looked longingly at the high feather bed with its patchwork quilt. She could hardly wait to climb into it after their long journey.

Before Widow Hendricks left them, she said, "Mr. Richmond told me to take good care of you two, and I intend to do just that."

Dorcas's cheeks flushed. "Do you mean Mr. Richmond himself, or was it Mr. Woodard?"

"They came together, but it was Mr. Richmond who wanted

to make sure you'd be comfortable. He knows I ain't about to take anyone he doesn't approve of. He's an important man in this town."

"I'm sure of that," Dorcas murmured in reply, but her heart sang. It wasn't just Andy who was concerned for her welfare. It was Philip, too.

That night she dreamed about Philip. They were strolling in the woods with the sun slanting through the tall forest trees. He took her in his arms and kissed her and she told him over and over that she loved him. He pushed back the tendrils of hair from her face and kissed her again. As she woke up she heard herself crying, "Do you love me, too? Oh, Philip, please care for me as I do you."

That morning, Andy came with a horse and buggy. "I rented this at the livery stable for you. I thought you'd need some transportation back and forth to the mine."

Dorcas smiled at him. "Oh, Andy, you think of everything. Now I want to reimburse you."

He shook his head. "I just paid for one day. I thought you yourself could make arrangements with the liveryman if you want to rent this rig while you're here."

"I'm sure I will."

She climbed into the buggy and held out her hand for Esther. "What about Ferguson and Ortmeyer? Can they find the way?" she asked Andy.

"I'll go back and get them today, but after this they can walk."

It was about two miles out to the mine, which was situated on the side of a mountain. She had forgotten how beautiful the ride was between the town and the Alpine mine. The breeze ruffled the long, sweeping limbs of the sugar pine and shook its pendulous cones. The rising sunlight filtered through the thick forest and dried the dew that hung in sparkling drops. A red squirrel scurried out to the end of a white-fir limb, which buckled under the weight.

Andy's heart beat faster as he glanced at her. Her great dark eyes sparkled and her long lashes fanned against her high cheekbones. He loved to watch the color come and go in her pretty face. "You look as if you rested well," he said at last.

"Oh, I did. We're so fortunate to be able to stay at Mrs. Hendricks's house."

As they climbed a grade, the forest thinned. The ground leveled off somewhat before the cliff rose again. It was on this shelf that the mine buildings, surrounded by a stone wall, were located. When they arrived at the iron gate, the chain that kept it fastened hung loose and a big padlock was hooked around a loop in the wrought iron. A sign on the wall read: ALPINE MINE, HAMILTON MINING COMPANY.

"I told the caretaker that you'd probably be out here this morning," Andy explained. He pulled on the reins and handed them to Dorcas while he climbed out of the carriage to open the gate. She flipped the straps against the horse's rump, and they entered the mine grounds.

A stone building to the left held the offices. Ahead of her, Dorcas could see the familiar, weathered head-frame standing over the main shaft. Heavy steel cables ran from a huge spool in the hoist house, over the pulleys on top of the framework, and down into the mine. A truss bridge carried the tramway toward the stockpile of ore, near the corrugated-iron stamp mill. As she looked around, she felt a surge of grief for her father. She could almost see him in the doorway of the office or crossing the yard to the stamp mill.

Andy helped them out of the buggy, then pointed toward the caretaker's gray-shingled cottage in the distance. "Hank's coming now." He climbed back in the buggy, saying, "I'll drive back into town to get the others."

Hank Buckler hurried along the path toward them, his spare frame huddled against the chill. "Long time no see, Miss Hamilton," he exclaimed, and put out his hand as the wind stirred his gray hair. "I figured you folks would come today. I got the office opened up. I'm afraid you'll find things a mite dusty."

As they walked toward the office, Mrs. Morrisey said, "I can take care of the dirt in short order if you could spare some rags."

"I'll get them right away," the caretaker told her. "But first I'll touch a match to the fire I've laid in the wood stove and warm the place up a bit."

A blast of bitter-cold air hit them as they opened the office door. Dust lay thick on the rolltop desk, the chairs, and the wooden floor.

Hank removed the stove lid and struck a match. "I put fresh water in this teakettle in case you want to make tea."

Esther Morrisey sniffed. "I'd better use the water to give this place a good scrubbing. Goodness, it's filthy in here." As Hank walked out the door, she called after him, "Could you bring me soap and a bucket along with those rags? Ammonia, too."

As soon as the caretaker returned with the supplies, she started to wash the windows.

It wasn't long before Andy arrived with the two miners. He hitched the horse to a post near the office building and put a container of oats and a bucket of water near the animal. When he stepped inside the office, he said, "We're going to power up, and later I'll take the men down the shaft. Dorcas, you'd better come along with us. I'll explain things to you."

Eventually the whir of machinery starting up and the meshing of gears in the hoist house made her look up from the old files. In a little while, Andy tapped on the window and she went outside to join them. He held a large kerosene lantern and a box of dynamite sticks. The men wore miners' candles in their caps. Between them they carried a bulky, unwieldly compressed-air drill, as well as their lunch buckets. The heavy iron doors of the mine entrance stood open. A skip, an open-sided sledlike device where men could sit one above the other, waited for them.

"Watch your head. Keep it back," Andy warned her as the cable slowly lowered the skip to the shaft station at the five-hundred-foot level.

As they stopped, she could see a block and tackle attached to a circular rail above her. "That's to remove timbers or heavy objects from the skips," Andy explained. "But it won't be necessary to use it on you."

She smiled. "I hope I'm not that heavy." She climbed out of the skip with Andy's help.

Wes Ferguson looked her up and down as she straightened her skirt. "Have you ever been underground before?"

"In Colorado I went down into our mine with my father several times."

Ortmeyer's lips curled in derision. "Lots of miners think

it's bad luck for a female to come down into the mine. Spooks it for good."

Anger surged through her. "You men will just have to get used to me. I intend to keep close supervision on the whole operation, and I will come down often."

Andy squeezed her arm in approval. "I'll be here as much as possible myself," he added.

Thank goodness for Andy, Dorcas thought. His presence alone would bolster the respect the men had for her. And she sensed she would need every bit of support she could get.

As the miners unloaded the compressed-air drill, Dorcas looked around and noted the escape ladder, critical if the hoist should fail. There was a low-pressure pipe to blow in fresh air. Off to one side of the shaft station was an underground powder magazine with a heavy iron door to keep out the moisture.

She could hear water dripping from the roof of the tunnel and smelled the damp, musty odor of a mine that has been closed too long. However, it was much warmer here than on the surface. Her father had told her once that the underground temperature stayed at about sixty degrees, ideal for hard work. Even if it was snowing outside, the air below remained mild.

As Andy led the way along a tunnel that branched off from the main shaft, he waved his lantern at several ore cars standing on the narrow-gauge tracks. "Watch out for the rails. Mind your footing."

As they slushed through the mud, a shudder ran through Dorcas. How she would hate to be a miner and have to spend a long shift in such a dark, uninviting place. She knew only too well the dangers that always lurked in mines—falling rocks, gases, cave-ins. She felt the moisture seep through her leather shoes and decided to keep a pair of rubber boots in the office for these trips underground.

The lantern cast spooky, flickering shadows on the overhead timbers, which braced the walls and roof of the tunnel.

Finally, Andy stopped at a smaller opening about five feet above them. He turned to Dorcas. "This is a stope—a limited excavation following a vein. I'm sure this is where they were operating when the mine was closed. With your small crew, I would work here. Of course, the Alpine goes down to the fifteen-hundred-foot level, but we'd better leave all that until later. Be careful of the timbering overhead."

The miners hoisted themselves up, and Andy handed them the air drill. "Put your foot in this niche, Dorcas, while I help you. Wes'll give you a hand."

Soon all of them were in the smaller tunnel braced with square-set timbering that made a head injury a constant danger. But as Andy held up his lantern, she could see the vein, varying in width from three to five feet and running the length of the excavation. It glimmered in the light.

"Of course, Dorcas, as you know, this is quartz or crystallized silicon dioxide with both gold and silver scattered through it. But there are also deposits of pure jewelry gold." He spent the next half hour pointing out the larger amounts of the precious metal.

Along the wall of the stope next to the tunnel were inserts of wooden chutes. "Wes and Gus, you can shovel the ore down these chutes and it'll drop into the ore cars below." He gave more directions to the men before he helped Dorcas out of the stope.

As the two of them walked back toward the skip, Andy went on. "I ran tests on the quartz, and it's rich. Shows real color. That's why it's strange that this mine was closed."

"I've often wondered about it myself. I may find the answer to the puzzle in the records in the office."

"I know it will pay to put it back into operation. Later you may want to have a larger crew than the ten men Ferguson expects to hire."

As they rose to the surface, she asked, "Don't you have to go to work at the Golden Star?"

"Yes, I'm leaving right away."

"But you've spent so much time here this morning. Won't Philip object?"

"I arranged for the time off."

Andy vowed that he wouldn't tell her about his confrontation the week before with Philip, who had said, "When Dorcas gets up here, don't you forget that you're working for the Richmond Mining Company and not the Hamiltons. We're paying you a good salary and have the right to all your time."

"Not all of it, Philip. Ten hours a day. I'll guarantee that you'll get your full ten hours. If I spend any time helping Dorcas, I'll work overtime here to make up for it."

"See that you do." Philip had stalked away angrily.

Ever since they had returned from San Francisco, Andy had worked evenings and on Sunday to earn the hours it would take to get Dorcas started. Now he squeezed her hand. "Remember, I'll be behind you all the way. You're not to worry at all. I'll help."

"I know you will, Andy. You can't imagine what that means to me. And Ferguson has some respect for you, at least, if not for me."

"Once he gets his crew together and settles in, he'll be all right."

"I wish I felt as confident." At the surface, they climbed out of the skip. "How will Ferguson be able to hire men if he's down in the mine all day?"

"Miners looking for work are drifting in here all the time. They'll hang around the saloons. Ferguson will find them there in the evenings. You're letting him do all the hiring, aren't you?"

"Yes. I don't want that responsibility. Besides, I know he'd have no use for anyone I'd choose," she said sharply.

He sighed inwardly. She did have an uphill battle ahead of her. But he'd do everything in his power to help.

Dorcas walked Andy to the gate. As she thanked him again and told him good-bye, he gave her his endearing smile. His whole face came alive, his eyes twinkled, and tiny laugh wrinkles radiated above his cheekbones. How sweet and sincere he is, she thought. A prince of a fellow. As he headed down the road to the Golden Star, he turned and waved. The sun glinted in his auburn hair and turned it to flame.

When she entered the office again, the odor of wet wood, lye soap, and ammonia assailed her. Already the place looked better. While Esther scrubbed, Dorcas looked through the files.

Finally she found a logbook and read the reports for the last few months the mine had been open. When she unrolled the underground maps from a wall case and studied them, she realized that the stope where the men were digging now was the one her father had been working on just before he closed the mine.

She read a geologist's report on the Alpine:

The gold occurs in veins and fissures within a sedimentary Bragdon slate formation, which is of two distinct types—one hard, silicous, and blocky, and the other soft, black, and graphitic. These have been intruded by igneous materials, all of which have fissured and fracture extensively. The veins strike in various directions, but with a general east-west trend. The gold-bearing veins vary widely in size, direction and values, ranging from $10 to $1,000 per ton. The ore is primarily white quartz carrying 1 to 4% sulfide; pyrite and sphalerite; a little galena; and free gold.

The report certainly sounded favorable. She must show it to Andy. Her father must have expected to make a profit here at the Alpine, so why had he closed it so hastily? Their move to Colorado didn't make sense.

Puzzled, she put the logbook and reports away. She had reason to believe that even with their limited operation, they could recover enough gold to make her grandfather's October payment. Would it come to even more? There was real color showing in the quartz today. Was that the forerunner to finding the Hamilton branch of the Andromeda Lode—that elusive fortune that had always escaped them? For a moment she daydreamed of how all their problems would be solved if they could only find it.

What a fickle mistress gold was. No matter how many core samples were taken or how carefully the engineers planned and mapped, they could miss a big strike. More than one mine had been abandoned and sold for a few thousand dollars. Later the new owner would hit a rich vein within five or ten feet of the old diggings. There was no way of knowing what was locked in the heart of a mountain.

At the end of the day, Dorcas heard a muffled underground explosion; the building shook. Unconsciously she began to count. One. Two. Grief for her father almost overwhelmed her. How often she had stood in this very office and listened to him count the blasts when they were close enough to the surface to hear. With the tenth blast, he'd nod in approval.

*   *   *

In a few days, Ferguson had gotten his crew together. Besides Ortmeyer, he'd found eight more hard-rock miners with experience. Every morning, at the start of the shift, Andy would come by and go underground with the men. Soon the machinery was all tested and the ore cars were running.

The manager assigned half the crew to the mill to process the stockpiled ore, which was rich but had lain in the dump so long it had hardened. The men had to blast the ore to loosen it so it could be hauled to the stamp mill and crushed. All day long, Dorcas listened to the throb and pounding of the stamp mill, but it was an encouraging sound.

She wrote a long, enthusiastic letter to her mother and Judy. She also spent two hours on a report to her grandfather. She concluded her report by stating, "So you see, Grandpa, everything is going to be all right. You won't have to worry now."

Her euphoria lasted until Ferguson came to her the next morning. "We've got a problem. They told us at breakfast at the boardinghouse that they can't keep us after March twentieth."

She stared at him in shock. "But why?"

"Richmond's hiring more men. They gotta have a place to stay."

"But you men just moved in. Besides, you were there first."

Ferguson shrugged, took a bag of tobacco out of his pocket, and slowly rolled a cigarette. "So?"

"But it's not fair. March twentieth is just ten days away!"

"That's right."

"What are you going to do?"

He stuck his cigarette in his mouth and scratched a match on his pants to light it. As he cupped his hand to protect the flame, he answered, "You're the general manager. That's your problem."

She felt a little sick as she wondered what action she could take. "Well, I'll go talk to the person who runs your boardinghouse."

Ferguson's eyes mocked her. "Why don't you do that, ma'am."

How surly and impertinent he was. She felt like slapping his face. He acted as if he were glad they had this complication.

Angrily, she turned away. "I'll go right now and see what I can do."

His lip curled. "Good luck. You'll need it."

As she and Esther drove the buggy into town, Dorcas said, "I'm going to give whoever runs that place a piece of my mind."

But she wasn't prepared for the giant of a man who confronted her at the door. He wore dirty white pants and shirt and held a toothpick in his mouth.

"Are you the manager?" she demanded.

"Yes, ma'am."

"I would like to come in and discuss a matter with you."

He stepped back, held the door open, and nodded toward a simply furnished lounge. "Take a seat."

Dorcas and Esther walked in and sat down on a leather settee.

"I'm Miss Hamilton, and this is my assistant, Mrs. Morrisey." She sat back, wondering how to go on. "We represent the Hamilton Mining Company."

He laughed as he leaned against the door frame. "I heard tell there was a female out there at the Alpine."

Dorcas sat up straight and stuck out her chin. "Our mine manager informs me that you've given them notice to leave."

"That's right. They got until the twentieth to clear out."

"Now see here. They took rooms at this boardinghouse first, so why should they get out? They need a place to stay."

"Well, ma'am, you ain't been living here in some time, have you? Apparently you don't know that the Hamiltons don't count for much anymore. This is a Richmond town. When I get orders to make room for a new crew for the Golden Star, that's just what I do."

"But that's not fair!"

"Seems fair enough to me." He shoved his toothpick to the other side of his mouth. "The Richmonds'll be here long after your two-bit operation folds again."

Dorcas jumped to her feet. Her cheeks flushed and eyes snapped. "I intend—"

"I ain't interested in what you intend. Just get one thing straight, ma'am. Your men are to be out of here on the twentieth." He tightened his biceps as if to demonstrate that he could easily pitch them out on their ears. "That's final! So if you'll excuse me—"

Dorcas turned to Esther. "Come on." She walked to the door.

As they climbed into the buggy, Esther said, "No use wasting your time with him, or going anyplace else in town. It's all Richmond. Unless you want to talk to the mister himself."

"No!" Secretly it hurt Dorcas that Philip seemed so unconcerned about her welfare. It was always Andy who gave her support. Her pride kept her from running to Philip and begging for his cooperation. He had bunkhouses and mess halls on his mine grounds for his crew. Why couldn't he accommodate ten more men? Surely he knew where her miners were staying and that it would be very difficult for her to house them at the mine just now. But in all fairness, perhaps he hadn't thought that far.

It must be a great responsibility to run a mine as big as the Golden Star. They had three shifts going six days and nights a week. Andy had told her that when the mine was in full operation, they employed 150 men. How clever Philip must be to keep it all running smoothly. She was having trouble enough with just ten men. Imagine the complications when there were more than a hundred involved.

When Philip rode past the boardinghouse on his way to the Golden Star mine, he saw the manager sweeping the front porch. The big man looked up and hailed him down.

"I just want you to know that I took care of that matter," the manager said after walking out to the street. "The Alpine men will be out of here on the twentieth."

"Thanks. Ten of my crew will move in then."

"A little while ago, that Hamilton dame came to see me—madder than a wet hen. I told her that what she wanted cut no ice with me, that I catered to the Richmond Company."

"Fine. Thanks a lot." But as Philip rode away, a surge of loathing for his uncle swept over him. He hated doing Elliott Richmond's dirty work. The snooping around in San Francisco trying to find out the truth about Clyde Hamilton's financial condition and buying the mining supply company wasn't so bad. But being told that he had to make everything as difficult as possible for Dorcas really galled him.

"We want Hamilton to declare bankruptcy. Hit rock bottom! It'd serve the old fool right," his uncle had said when they'd had a private conference at the Richmond headquarters in Sacramento. "Then we'll get control of Alpine. He must be getting senile to send his granddaughter up there to reopen the mine. What does a female like her know about it?"

"You have to hand it to her for trying," Philip had put in.

"I'm not handing her anything. And I want you to make it as tough on her as you can. Throw every possible roadblock in her way. You're to report everything to me. No detail is too unimportant to tell me about. I want to know everything." Elliott had banged his fist on the table.

"The SOB," Philip muttered aloud as he slapped his horse on the flank. He'd always had a strange relationship with his uncle. Of course, he'd been grateful when Elliott had come to Salt Lake City to get him when his mother was dying of tuberculosis. He'd been only sixteen.

"Promise me, Elliott, that you'll look after Philip," his mother had said that last day.

"I promise, Sis. You can count on that. I'll send him to school and see that he gets trained for a profession. He'll always have a home with us."

Philip would never forget her gaunt face, so thin that her bones almost pushed through the skin. Tears had gathered in her eyes. "There's one more thing. Promise you'll take him to see Papa."

Elliott had turned to him and said, "Son, you'd better go outside and wait for me. I want to talk to your mother alone."

Philip had stood by the window out front, hoping to hear what his mother and uncle had to say, but sometimes their voices were too low to follow. But he had caught his mother begging, "Please take him. Perhaps Papa has had a change of heart. He's never seen Philip. He doesn't know that the boy looks just like him. Acts like him, too. His own kith and kin. You will take Philip, won't you? Promise me."

"Of course I will. I'm sure Father feels differently now. Grace and I will give Philip the best of care. He'll have a real home with us."

"I've never heard a word from Papa these last sixteen years. Not one word. He's never forgiven me."

Their voices had faded to murmurs. While Philip had fought back tears, he had wondered what had caused the terrible rift between his mother and grandfather.

Philip had adored his mother. She had been the only family he had ever known since his father had deserted them soon after his birth. "His name was Alan Washburn," she had told him one time. "But he's gone out of our lives, so we're going to use my maiden name—Richmond."

When Elliott had finally called for him to come back in the room he had whispered, "She's going fast."

Philip had fought to control himself, but when he had dropped by her bedside, he had sobbed heartbrokenly.

After the funeral, Elliott had taken him home and enrolled him in school in Alpine Heights, but no effort had been made to take him to San Francisco to meet his grandfather, who had started the mining company that had grown under his uncle's management.

As he rode along, Philip tried to put his mind on other things, instead of reliving all the old painful memories. But soon he was recalling that unforgettable time when his grandfather had died. All the other Richmonds had gone to the funeral. He was told he had to stay home with the housekeeper.

After the family returned, his cousin Matt kept hinting about the fine trust funds that he and his brother had inherited according to the terms of the will. When the younger boys were sent to bed, Philip sought out his uncle, who was working at his desk in the study.

"Uncle Elliott," he had begun, "why wasn't I remembered in Grandfather's will?"

"Because your grandfather never recognized your existence. Now run along, Philip. I'm busy."

But Philip had planted his feet on the rug and stared at his uncle. "I'm seventeen years old now. I demand to know the truth. What happened between my mother and my grandfather? Why was I always kept away from him? Surely he knew I was born!"

"Philip! I told you to leave!"

"I'm not going. I'm sick and tired of all these evasions. All these half-truths. I demand an explanation!"

Elliott had angrily slammed his pen down on his desk and stood up. "So you want to know the truth, do you? Dammit, you're going to get it then. Before you were born, your mother was disinherited. Father kicked her out of the house and told her he never wanted to see her again."

"But why?"

There was an evil glow in his uncle's eyes. "Because your mother was expecting you. And she wasn't married to your father. In other words, Philip Richmond, you're a bastard! My father didn't want to have anything to do with you."

Philip felt as if he had been struck right in the stomach. He staggered back. "My mother told me—"

"She probably made you think she was married to your father, but she never was. You see, he was already married. After he got your mother into trouble, he just left her. She moved to Salt Lake City near some friends who owned a hotel and restaurant. She worked for them."

"Yes, the Hendersons," Philip said, his voice cracking in his thick throat. He wanted to cry. It was all he could do to keep his composure. But he wouldn't let himself bawl in front of his sneering uncle.

His lip curling, Elliott looked him up and down. "I kept my promise to your mother. I took you into my home, and I'll see to it that you get an education. But you'll never inherit anything from your grandfather's estate, nor from mine."

"But you never gave my grandfather and me a chance to know each other."

"That's right."

"You promised my mother you'd take me to meet him."

"I didn't do that."

Philip leaned across the desk and looked his uncle straight in the eye. "Don't lie to me! I heard you promise her. Why didn't you take me?"

"Because I'm not a fool."

"What do you mean?"

"Never mind." His uncle refused to meet his eyes.

"Was it because I looked like him? I remember Mother saying I did."

Elliott Richmond stared at him without answering.

"Was it?" Philip shouted as he reached out and grabbed his uncle's arm.

Elliott shook him off. "Of course it was. My sons look just like their mother's side of the family—Vandovans, both of them. But you're a Richmond. Spitting image of the old man."

"That's why I should have known him. Why didn't you take me to him?"

"Why should I have given you a chance to make up with

your grandfather and jeopardize my inheritance and that of my sons? I'm not that stupid! Now, get out of here. I have work to do.''

Phllip whirled around and headed for the door. He looked over his shoulder. "I'm not the only one who's a bastard!"

His uncle's face turned an angry purple. "Watch it, kid, or you'll be out on your butt. You'll be digging ditches instead of going to college.''

From that time on, Philip had avoided his uncle as much as possible. Nor did he feel close to his aunt and cousins. They always made him feel that he was the outsider. An unwelcome intruder. All he had was himself. Something died in him. The capacity to love.

It was a great relief when he went to Colorado to mining school. By the time he graduated, times were hard and jobs difficult to find. When Elliott offered him the position as manager of the Golden Star, he'd gladly accepted it. It was a long way from Sacramento, where his uncle now lived, so Philip knew he would be on his own.

Here at Alpine Heights he had a taste of what it meant to be the one in power, and he gloried in it. He was the most important man in town. Actually, the village existed because of the mine. Everywhere he went, people paid him respect. It helped him forget that he was illegitimate.

There had been several girls in Philip's life. Each one, especially those who had succumbed to him, had satisfied some driving need in him to prove his worth in spite of being a bastard. How thankful he was for his fine appearance so he could attract the opposite sex. He needed the admiration of the ladies. The more the merrier. But none of them had been able to penetrate the barrier he had built around himself. Only he knew how insecure he felt inside his handsome facade.

Now there was Dorcas. An aristocrat from a noted family. No name in California meant more than Hamilton. And she was in love with him. Every instinct told him so. It bolstered his self-esteem to think about it.

Suddenly Philip threw his head back and laughed aloud. How hopping mad Elliott would be if he, his bastard nephew, got involved with Dorcas Hamilton! That'd spike his guns. It would serve him right.

CHAPTER 7

All the way back to the Alpine, Dorcas and Esther mulled over how best to solve the problem.

"Seems to me, Miss Dorcas, your only solution is to fix a place at the mine for the men to stay. Nobody in Alpine Heights is going to take them in."

"Actually, there aren't that many places in town. Just Widow Hendricks, and she's full, and then the boarding-house. I guess there are private families who take in one or two boarders as well. Andy lives with one."

"What do folks do when they don't find a hotel?" Esther asked.

"I suppose the important mining men stay with Philip, and the rest have to camp out. But if I'm going to keep a crew, I'll have to find someplace for them to live."

"What about that storage building near the stamp mill? Couldn't you fix it up?"

"I suppose so, but not in ten days." She slapped the reins on the horse's rump. "There's the manager's house, of course, but there's nothing in it. The family who lived there owned their furniture and moved it out when the mine closed. Besides, it's small. Just a couple of bedrooms."

"Let's look it over," Esther suggested, then sniffed. "If it's anything like your office was, it'll take a spell of cleaning."

"Even worse is getting it furnished." Dorcas's spirits sank as she thought of the beds, linen, dishes, pots, and dozens of other items needed to board ten men. Where would she get all those things? And the cost worried her. Her ten thousand dollars in capital didn't look so great now that she had a payroll to meet every week.

The manager's house sat in what had been a clearing in the woods but was now filled with a tangle of tall weeds and wild blackberries. A stand of pine trees screened it from the rest of the mine buildings. They followed an overgrown path around

95

to the front and stepped up onto a wide, covered porch. At least the redwood exterior of the dwelling was in good condition.

But when they went inside, Esther shook her head in dismay. "Land sakes, look at this. I don't think that caretaker ever stepped his foot in here."

Cobwebs hung from the ceiling; a layer of dust covered the sills and floor. The worn linoleum was as blotched as the dreary gray walls.

Dorcas shuddered as she looked around. "This place needs far more than cleaning."

"I'm quite a hand at painting. And I can't see any reason why that caretaker can't pitch in. Don't seem to me that he's earned his salt," Esther said tartly.

"We could hire a couple of other men, too. When they're finished inside, they could clear out the weeds around the place."

A big stone fireplace took up most of the wall next to the kitchen. Three dirty, rain-streaked windows would let in plenty of light if they were washed. Actually, with some fresh paint, new linoleum, and curtains, it would be a pleasant room, Dorcas told herself.

"We could put some easy chairs around this fireplace." She stepped off the space along the north wall. "A dining table with ten chairs would fit right here by this window."

Esther nodded in agreement. "That's right. The table would be right close to the kitchen door."

"Speaking of the kitchen—" Dorcas began. They found a medium-size room and a pantry with shelves. "At least it has a good cookstove and running water." She ran her fingers over the bleached wooden drainboards.

The front bedroom was somewhat larger than the one off a short back hall. Finally, they found a glassed-in porch, which was the most cheerful spot in the house.

"I don't remember this at all," Dorcas exclaimed excitedly, beginning to see how they could take care of their crew. "We could put six cots out here."

"And two more in each of the bedrooms," Esther added.

"No, Mr. Ferguson is the manager, so he should have the front bedroom to himself." Dorcas decided to buy a bed and a bureau for his room. "I can't stand him, but he has to be treated with respect and have special privileges. We can put three cots in the small bedroom.''

As they walked out into the weed-ridden backyard, they found a shed full of split logs and kindling. Nearby was a primitive washroom with a shower and a stove to heat the water. Farther back among the trees stood an outhouse.

''I think I'll get a fire going in the cookstove and heat some water,'' Esther said. ''I might as well get started. It's going to take some time to get this place ready to paint.''

After they carried wood into the house, they located the valve outside to turn on the water. They even found an old broom to sweep down the cobwebs.

While they worked, Dorcas said, ''If we're going to paint, we might as well make the color light and cheerful. I hate these gray walls. Let's paint the walls a very pale yellow and then put light green linoleum on the floor. With some pretty rag rugs, it should look really nice.''

''It might be a mite crowded with ten men in here, but it'll be a lot more attractive than that boardinghouse they're staying at.''

''That's true.'' As she washed a sill, Dorcas added, ''We'll have to do something about curtains.''

Esther nodded. ''Mrs. Hendricks has a sewing machine. If she'll let me use it, I could make some curtains. They'd look nice, and besides, it will give me something to do in the evenings.''

A wave of gratitude ran through Dorcas. What a jewel she had in Esther. ''I'll leave the cleaning, painting, and curtains up to you while I worry about the rest.'' She bit her lip. ''I'll have to hire a cook, for example. As soon as we get back to town, I'll send a telegram to Grandfather. We have a marvelous Chinese cook there at the mansion. I imagine he could find us a good one.''

''But where'll you put him?''

''I don't know. I guess he'll have to put up with a cot in the kitchen.''

The next week showed an amazing transformation in the manager's house and yard. Two hired workmen and Hank Buckler, the caretaker, cleaned and painted under Esther's supervision. Dorcas found linoleum she liked at the general store in Alpine Heights, and it was laid when the painting was completed. When the men were finished inside, they tackled the overgrown yard.

When it came time for the Chinese cook to arrive, Dorcas and Esther took the stagecoach to Redding to meet him.

In midafternoon they met the train. A cheerful young Chinese man carrying a small bamboo trunk stepped off the last car. As Dorcas approached, he asked, "Missy Hamilton?"

"Yes."

He put down his trunk, tucked his hands inside the sleeves of his black padded jacket, and bowed low while his neatly braided pigtail swung across his shoulders. When he straightened, his eyes lit up. "Name is Sing Lee. I come to cook."

After she introduced him to Esther, he pulled out a long paper from an inner pocket. "I bring list. Know what to buy. Okay?"

They spent the rest of the day supplying the kitchen with dishes, cooking utensils, coffee mugs and silverware. The next morning Dorcas gave him money to order food supplies while she and Esther went to the stores in Redding to buy bedding, braided oval rugs, and dozens of other items on her own list. They found some good used furniture for the living room and Ferguson's bedroom. She also arranged for a freight wagon and a driver for the journey home. She tried not to think about how much money she was spending.

By the time they got back to the mine, they had one day left before the men were to move in. Sing Lee helped the two women unpack the boxes, set up the cots, and place the other furniture.

As the men rose to the surface at the end of their shift, Dorcas met them. "Tomorrow you will move into a house here on the grounds," she told them. "I have arranged for a wagon to be outside the boarding house at six-thirty. Be ready with your gear. The driver will bring you out here for your shift and then you can take your things up to the house."

Ferguson leaned against one of the uprights supporting the headframe, his eyes mocking. "I looked that place over when I first came. It's just a dump. Doubt it'll hold us all anyway."

"I believe it will do. In any case, Mr. Ferguson, you can bring your men there when you're through tomorrow night." The miners started to leave. "Oh, one more thing. I'll be deducting from your wages two-thirds of what you've been paying to the boardinghouse."

"I hope it'll be worth it," Ortmeyer put in. "That was a regular boardinghouse."

"But they won't keep you. Remember?" She bit her tongue to keep from snapping at him.

As she walked away she told herself that he and Ferguson were in for a surprise. They had no idea how hard she and the others had been working to get ready. Anger flared in her. Not once had her manager offered to help solve the housing problem. Instead, the minute the shift was over, he was on the road back to town.

Dorcas gave the house one final inspection. The miners were due any minute. A big fire roared in the fireplace. Lamps cast a pleasant glow around the sparkling-clean room. The setting sun shone through the front windows framed with soft yellow-and-green-striped curtains. Outside on the porch she could see the new canvas chairs where the men could sit and look out on the freshly mowed grass and weeded beds of spring bulbs that had been planted years ago.

Here in the living room, an upholstered sofa and easy chairs were grouped around a big braided rug in front of the hearth. The dining table was covered with green oilcloth and set for ten places. In the center was a big bowl of yellow jonquils and Dutch irises.

From the kitchen came the appetizing fragrance of fricassee chicken, biscuits, and mashed potatoes and carrots warming at the back of the stove. Two big apple pies waited in the pantry. It hadn't taken Sing Lee much time to settle in and get to work.

How inviting Mr. Ferguson's room looked, with a white tufted spread, a scarf covering the top of the dresser, and a bowl of California poppies reflected in the mirror.

Even the crew's cots looked neat, with light green spreads covering the blankets and pillows. Along the wall of both the sunporch and small bedroom were shelves divided into sections, providing a space for each man's belongings, with hooks below for his clothes. In each area was a new towel, washcloth, and a soapbox with a bar of Ivory soap. A mirror hung on the wall.

When she heard the men scraping their feet on the mat, she

rushed to the front door and opened it. "Welcome to your new quarters, men."

As they crowded in, they gasped in pleased surprise. "Gosh, Miss Hamilton," one said, "this sure looks like the Ritz compared to what I'm used to."

Another let out a long whistle. "Look at the bouquet. How about that?"

A third miner reddened as he tried to express his thanks. "You sure must have worked hard to make it look like this."

"We wanted to make it as comfortable for you as possible." She opened the door to the main bedroom. "Mr. Ferguson, this is where you'll sleep. You'll find your suitcase right by the wardrobe." For once, the manager was too surprised to be mocking or sarcastic. The men inspected his room and kept telling him how nice it was, but he didn't answer.

The miners seemed delighted with their separate lockers and attractive quarters. "You'll find washrooms out in back," Dorcas said.

As they filed out the sunroom door, the young cook walked around to the back. Dorcas introduced him and said, "You take good care of Sing Lee and he'll cook anything you want. I sent to San Francisco for him, and he came with excellent recommendations. So I'll go now and leave you in his hands."

As she and Mrs. Morrisey left to a chorus of thank-you's, one young miner followed her. "I just want to say thanks, Miss Hamilton. I'm darn glad to get out of that boardinghouse. The manager made us feel like we didn't belong there."

This Russ McFarlane was her favorite. "I know just what you mean," Dorcas agreed. "He practically told me to leave when I went to see him."

"He kept saying that Mr. Richmond wanted us to quit working for you and join his crew." The miner scuffed his feet. "Some of the guys wanted to. Ortmeyer, especially, but I talked them out of it. I said you'd treated us right and we had no call to walk out on you."

Dorcas felt a little sick inside. "I think that was just a lot of talk on the part of the boardinghouse man. I'm sure Mr. Richmond had nothing to do with it."

"Maybe not. But every once in a while he'd come to the boardinghouse and talk to the manager. Well, I'd better go back and eat. Thanks again for the nice place here."

"Thank you, Russ." But she wished he hadn't spoken to her. Of course she didn't believe for a minute that Philip would deliberately try to get her men away.

As they hurried down the path to the horse and buggy, Esther squeezed her arm. "Land sakes, the men acted tickled to pieces. It was worth all the work just to see their faces light up. And did you notice that Ferguson had nothing to say? We sure surprised him."

But a lot of the pleasure over their triumph had gone out of Dorcas. Had Philip really tried to get her crew to quit? Of course not. Why would he? She tried to push her fears to the back of her mind and respond to Esther's enthusiasm. "I'm sure the men will like it a lot. They can sit around the fire in the evening or play cards. I'll get equipment for them to bowl on the lawn or play croquet. We could even fix a horseshoe lane and a hoop for basketball. As the weather warms up, they'll want to do things outdoors. It must be horrid to be cooped up in the mine all day."

On the way into town, they kept talking about the refurbished house. "I think Sing Lee likes it, too," Esther said. "He told me he'd keep the place clean and was going to plant a garden so he could grow vegetables."

Dorcas's worry over Philip still nagged at her, but when she ran into him on the street outside the general store the next day, all her doubts vanished.

"Dorcas, I'm so glad to see you. I've been intending to call on you, but I've been rushed at the mine, getting it back into full swing again."

She smiled at him. "I can appreciate that. Just my limited operation has kept me very busy."

"Andy told me that you're actually under way." He walked with her toward her buggy. "I'm inviting a few people for Easter dinner, and I'd like to have you and Mrs. Morrisey come."

Her big brown eyes glowed with happiness. "We'd love to. What time?"

"I've told the others five o'clock. But you come earlier—about four-fifteen. I ran across some pictures I'd like to show you." He helped her into the seat and tipped his hat. "I'll see you on Sunday."

Her heart pounded as she watched him walk down the wooden sidewalk. How tall and erect he stood, with his head held high, just like the dynamic leader he was. Everyone passing by spoke to him or gave him a pat on the shoulder. In spite of his importance, he seemed to be a popular man, and she had never known a more handsome or charming one. No doubt he captivated every woman he met. But she was far more than captivated; it was as if he possessed a part of her being.

When Mrs. Morrisey came out of the store, she handed her bundles to Dorcas and climbed into the seat. "My goodness, Miss Dorcas, I'd swear you swallowed a canary you look so pleased with yourself."

"We've had a very special invitation. I'll tell you all about it as soon as we get going."

"Do you remember when this picture was taken?" Philip handed her a photograph of a group of children posed in front of a two-room schoolhouse. A teacher stood at each end of the row. "This one is you, isn't it?" He pointed to a tall girl in the back row with a long dark braid on each side of her face.

Dorcas giggled as she looked at herself. "Yes. I was thirteen years old. One of the biggest kids in school. There's Judy. Oh, and here's your cousin next to Keith. They were in the same class."

They stood in the library in front of a tall walnut secretary. From the parlor she could hear Esther and a neighbor woman discussing a crochet pattern. She and Philip shouldn't stay away from the others too long. But it was such a magic moment to be entirely alone with him.

He opened a drawer and took out a photo album. "I found some pictures in this that should interest you." He led the way to the sofa. "Let's sit down here, where the light is better."

When they were seated side by side, he placed the album in her lap and she began to turn the pages. She pretended not to notice when he slid his arm across the top of her shoulders. She tried to keep her mind on the photos, but she was even more aware of the soft wool of his jacket sleeve against the back of her neck.

"Oh, look, here I am on horseback," she exclaimed. "Your cousin Matt is riding behind me. I don't remember anyone's taking our picture."

"Do you still ride, Dorcas?" She felt his breath on her neck.

She glanced up, her eyes sparkling with excitement at being so close to him. "I haven't ridden since I left Colorado. I had my own horse there, but we sold him."

"Would you like to ride with me sometime? I have a lively mare in my stable."

"I'd love to."

"Let's make it early next Sunday morning. I'll get you back in time to change before we have to go to church. My housekeeper is an excellent horsewoman. She can come along as chaperon."

Dorcas's cheeks flushed as she nodded. "About seven? I'll have to find a riding habit somewhere."

"I have some at the house. I keep them for guests. I'll send a couple over to Widow Hendricks and you can try them on." His fingers twisted around a curl that hung from her pompadour. "You're so beautiful, Dorcas," he murmured. His hand trailed around the side of her neck and traced the planes of her face.

I should slip away from him and sit at the end of the sofa, she told herself. What if someone came in and found us like this? But his dynamic personality seemed to mesmerize her. She felt spellbound, with no will of her own.

He spread his hand across her cheek and tipped her head up until his lips came down on hers. A strange, throbbing yearning for him swept over her as his arms held her close. Finally, he pressed his face against her burning cheek and whispered, "I've wanted to hold you in my arms for a long time—ever since the night of the ball."

She put her arm around his neck and cupped the back of his head with her hand until he kissed her again. She longed to tell him how deeply she loved him.

Out in the hallway, the doorbell rang and a maid hurried to answer it. Dorcas pushed him away from her. "Your guests are arriving. You must greet them."

He stood up and stretched out his hand to her. "No, you go ahead," she said. "I'll put the album away." Still shaken from the intensity of their time together, she had to have a few moments to compose herself. She stared at her reflection in a mirror. Never had she looked so radiant. Lovingly, she touched her lips and relived their kisses. Surely Philip must care for her the way she did for him. With one last glance at herself, she crossed the hall, slipped inconspicuously into the parlor, and found a chair at the back—in time to be introduced to the new arrivals.

Andy, carrying a paper bag, was the last to come. "I had to help with an Easter-egg hunt for the kids in the neighborhood," he explained. He pulled up a chair next to Dorcas and sat down.

Later, when the others were in the midst of a lively conversation, Andy turned to her and murmured, "I don't want the others to see, but I brought you something from the Easter bunny."

As his eyes danced with mischief, he pulled out of the bag a small box lined with fresh grass. Inside the nest were two colored eggs. Standing between them was a carved-wood figure of a woman. "I whittled it for you. It's called the Lady Miner." He pointed to the head. "She's wearing a miner's hat. See the lamp."

"Why, Andy! It's darling! I didn't know you could whittle like this." Actually, it was an exquisite carving. The folds of the skirt, the well-formed hands, the carefully chiseled face, must have taken hours of work. "Thank you so much. I'll keep it always."

"Better put it back in the bag before the others want to see it. It's just for you." His endearing, sweet smile showed how pleased he was with his gift.

Carefully, she put it away and tucked the bag behind her chair until she was ready to leave. "I love it, Andy. I really do." She wished she could love Andy as well. How she hoped that her dear friend wouldn't be dreadfully hurt someday.

At the end of the next day, when Dorcas and Esther arrived at their boardinghouse, Widow Hendricks met them at the door. "Mr. Richmond was just here asking for you." She chuckled. "Land sakes, he's enough to make even my old heart go pitter-pat. But if you think he's handsome, you ought to meet his uncle Elliott."

"I've met him. He lived here when I did," Dorcas said.

"That's right. He's now in Sacramento, running the company from the main office. But he should be on the stage, that one. Looks just like an actor. A real ladies' man. I can remember when he lived here; the women would almost swoon if he looked their way—"

"Did Philip bring a package for me?" Dorcas interrupted, knowing that her landlady would chatter on for an hour if they let her.

"Yes, he did. A big suitbox. I put it on your bed."

"He's lending me a riding habit. We're going riding next Sunday before church." Dorcas thought it was best to satisfy the widow's curiosity. Her landlady was as goodhearted as could be but very garrulous and inclined to stick her nose into everyone's business, especially her boarders.

"I'll send for my own riding clothes as soon as I can." She edged away from the talkative woman and headed for the stairs, thankful that Philip had remembered.

She found two riding habits in the suitbox, one black and the other a rich chocolate brown. The black one was too small, but the other fitted perfectly. It had a divided skirt that came to her ankles. She even found a pair of boots and a riding cap. Now she could ride astraddle, which was much more practical on mountain trails than sidesaddle.

The rest of the week dragged by as she waited for Sunday to come.

That morning she was ready at seven sharp and tiptoed down the stairs to wait outside. Soon she saw Philip riding his black stallion and leading a bay mare down the empty street. About a half-block behind, on a gray mare, came his housekeeper, Mrs. Austin.

Philip sat high in the saddle, his broad shoulders squared, looking as if he were completely in charge of himself, his mount, and everyone around him. He was a natural leader. How handsome he looked in his buff riding trousers and polished black boots. A heavy black turtleneck sweater completed his becoming outfit.

Her heart thudded with excitement as she returned his wave. Now, don't act too eager, she warned herself. No doubt every woman in the area fawned over him, just as they had done over his legendary uncle. She'd do well to use a little restraint.

He pulled up beside her. "Good morning. How lovely you look. The habit fits you very well."

In spite of herself, the blood rushed to her cheeks. "It's very much like my own. I'll return it as soon as mine comes." She felt flustered. That last statement implied that she expected him to ask her again. Perhaps that wasn't the case. "Actually, I could give it back as soon as we come home."

"Oh, no, keep it as long as you want. I hope we can ride often." He dismounted and stepped over to the mare. "This is Gypsy. She's just the color of your brown hair." He patted her affectionately.

Dorcas ran her hand over the horse's sleek coat. "What a beauty you are!"

The stallion turned his head and nuzzled Philip. "You have to pat Sultan, too. He gets jealous."

Dorcas laughed and patted the dark, noble head. "You're as handsome as can be, Sultan."

"We'd better get started."

Dorcas turned to the mare and put her foot in the stirrup. With Philip's help, she swung herself up on the saddle, put her leg over, and waited for him to mount. Soon they rode together down the main street, Mrs. Austin trailing behind.

"Is it all right to ride up Silver Falls?" he asked. "That's my favorite trail."

"I'd love to see the falls again. When we lived here, Keith, Judy, and I rode up there once, but Father found out and told us never to go again. It's on Richmond land, of course."

"And that made it verboten," Philip added. He smiled, showing his even white teeth. "I never did understand what the trouble between our families was all about."

"Nor did I." She tossed her head. "In any case, it's ancient history now and has nothing to do with us." She would never let some silly old family quarrel keep them apart.

As soon as they passed the outskirts of town, Sultan began to canter across the meadow, and her mare followed suit. The dew-laden trillium, fawn lily, and Indian paintbrush brought color to the sea of tall grass. As soon as they entered the forest, the morning sun, low in the horizon, filtered through the trees and cast long shafts of light across the trail. Never had the trees seemed so green, nor the wildflowers so beautiful. She wanted to cry out with joy! How glorious to be young and in love with the most exciting man in California. She listened to the clear, flutelike song of a hermit thrush that seemed to be expressing her own exaltation.

It wasn't long before their chaperon caught up with them and Philip led the way along a trail branching off from the road. As soon as they began to climb, the horses slowed to a walk. Dorcas remembered, from years before, the landmarks along the way. The rotting cart tipped on its side; the flat, pitted rock where Indians had ground their acorns long ago; the tall lodgepole pine with most of its trunk gutted and blacked by lightning. A stream by the side of the trail tumbled over massive rocks.

At last they emerged into a small clearing. At one end they could see the waterfall coming down in a graceful arc and sending spray over the ferns on each side.

"Do you feel like hiking up to the top?" Philip asked.

"Of course."

Mrs. Austin said she would wait with the horses.

With the roar of the tumbling water drowning out all possible conversation, they clambered up, using the rocks for footholds, and were soon gasping for breath.

Finally they reached the top where the stream crossed another meadow before it fell over the cliff. Not far from the banks was a log cabin. It was not a weatherbeaten old cabin but one in good condition. Shutters were closed across the windows. A picnic table and benches leaned against the side.

"My uncle had this built about twelve years ago. He loved to come up here. In fact, all of us did. My cousins and I pitched tents out here in the grass and the folks slept inside. We had lots of fun."

"But how did they ever get the building supplies up the face of the cliff?"

"There's a back road from our mine. Sometimes I use that way when I'm coming up here to stay a few days and fish."

A sad expression came over Dorcas's face. "My father and I went fly-fishing together in Colorado. I loved it."

"I have poles and all the equipment stored in the cabin. Next Sunday let's plan to fish and cook breakfast."

She looked up at him, her eyes glowing with excitement.

"Wonderful. But let's leave about six so we'll have plenty of time."

"Fine. We can either ride up the trail or take a horse and wagon around the back way."

"Let's ride."

Beads of perspiration stood out on his forehead. "Next time I won't wear such a hot sweater for that climb over the rocks." He took out a handkerchief and wiped his brow. His hair had the blue-black sheen of a crow's wing, very thick and wavy and following the fine shape of his head. How she longed to cup her hand around the back of it. He pushed up his sleeves and the dark hair of his arms clung moistly to his skin.

As she watched him out of the corner of her eye, she patted the moisture from her own face. Would he kiss her again? She longed for the pressure of his lips against hers. Glancing down, she saw that she was clenching and unclenching her left fist, for what reason she did not know, but it seemed to ease the rising tumult within her. But he didn't even seem to be aware of her as he gazed at the falling water and the mist that blew their way with a welcome coolness.

"Perhaps we'd better start back," she said at last.

Philip smiled at her, which melted away the annoyance she'd started to feel. "Not just yet." He put his arm around her and kissed the pulse that throbbed in her neck. "You're a lovely wood sprite."

All her resolve to be more controlled left her. He brought her arms up around his neck; soon his lips were against hers. She could smell the virile scent from his warm, moist skin. She felt weightless—almost floating—as he held her close. Her senses had a life of their own, as a throbbing longing for him engulfed her. For a long time he held her. She could feel the beating of his heart, the pressure of his body, the strength of his arms. Finally he let her go and murmured, "We'd better be on our way."

All the way back to town, she felt a wistfulness inside. She loved him with all her heart. Surely he must guess how she felt. Why didn't he indicate that he cared for her as well? Was she just someone to occupy his time while no one more alluring was around? She wanted him to court her. To ask her to marry him, eventually. Did she have any reason to hope at all?

All week, as Dorcas had to cope with the problems at the mine, the fact that she was going fishing with Philip sustained her. It was something to look forward to, a change of pace from the countless irritations that came up every day.

Apparently, Wes Ferguson took particular delight in bringing every minor problem to her. If he shrugged his shoulders one more time and said, "That's up to you. You're the general manager," she thought she'd slap him in the face. How she hated the sneer on his lips, the disdain in his eyes. No doubt it galled him to work for a woman, and he never let her forget it. He made no effort to be resourceful or to make do. She found herself driving into town to buy small items for him—bolts, special screws, or belts.

One morning she said to him, "Let's go through the storeroom and take an inventory of the supplies there."

"I'm too busy right now. You do it, Miss Hamilton. After all, you're the general manager."

Her temper snapped. "Yes, and don't you forget it! I said that we were going to take an inventory of the supplies, and that's just what we're going to do. You know as well as I do that I'm not familiar with what you need. I won't recognize what you can use." She took her keys out of the desk drawer and grabbed her coat. "Come with me, Mr. Ferguson."

His face turned red and ugly, but he followed her to the storeroom, where they worked all morning. "I'm going to make duplicate lists of the things we found here. One for you and one for me. Before anything new is purchased, we'll check to see if it's on hand. A lot of the items you asked me to buy in town are right here. So don't let that happen again."

Oh, how he irritated her. She could imagine how quickly her father would have dealt with his uncooperative attitude. His utter disrespect because she was a female spilled over to some of the other miners, too. She was well aware of the glances they exchanged and the sneers they barely hid when she made a mistake.

She worried over her finances as well. Her money was not going to last very long. It had been naive of her to think that ten thousand dollars was enough to get the mine opened and able to pay for itself. But she had Sunday to look forward to;

her heart sang every time she thought about it. A whole morning with Philip. She doubted that they would try to get back in time for church. And she didn't care, either. To be with Philip was all she wanted. Just the thought of him seemed to cheer her and wipe out all her troubles.

Philip opened the metal shutters and swung them back from the cabin windows. After he unlocked the door they stepped inside. They had sent Mrs. Austin back home when they'd started their climb up the cliff, promising to meet her later on.

"It's so nice!" Dorcas exclaimed as she looked around at how well the interior of the cabin had been finished—with varnished walls, a floor covered with linoleum, and clear glass in the windows. A double bed stood under one window. Taking up one corner, a woodburning stove heated the cabin and provided a place to cook. There was even a metal sink with wooden drainboards, but no running water. Instead, two buckets had been placed on the floor.

Against the wall stood a rack holding a selection of fishing rods. Philip took a tin box from a shelf. "This is what I do in the evenings when I'm up here; I tie flies." He opened the case and showed her a colorful selection."

"My father used to tie flies, too. These are beautiful." She looked up at him, her large, expressive eyes glowing. "Can I have my pick?"

"Of course. Any of these will do for our stream." He kissed her on the end of the nose. "It's fun being with you. You're not like some girls, who won't take part in any sports. You ride and fish and are willing to do things that men enjoy."

She glowed with pleasure. "Oh, I like to go sailing or hiking or 'most anything." Surely Philip would consider her love of outdoor activities an asset in a wife.

"I'll get a fire going and put on a pot of coffee so it'll be ready when we get back." Philip rummaged through his knapsack for the can of coffee. "I brought doughnuts, too."

After she chose her pole and flies, she followed him out of the cabin and along the banks of the stream.

"This is one of my favorite holes," Philip said. "Cast upstream and let your fly be carried down with the current. Don't slam it down on the water, but allow it to settle gently as if it were an egg-laying flying insect."

They began to fish, and Dorcas wondered how she could contain her happiness. The sun glittering on the stream, the cool breeze against her skin, and Philip standing a few feet away casting into the clear water made tremors of pure joy surge through her. What could be more wonderful than to be near him?

Soon they had enough trout for breakfast, and they carried their poles and catch back to the cabin. The smell of coffee reached them before they opened the door.

"I'll clean the fish while you set the table. You'll find everything in the cupboard." Philip leaned his pole against the side of the cabin.

It was fun getting ready for their breakfast. It made Dorcas dream of what it would be like if they were husband and wife. She found a clean rag, which she dampened, and then she wiped the green oilcloth. In the cupboard were tin plates and mugs and silverware. While she worked, she glanced more than once at the double bed covered with a heavy brown spread. Her cheeks flushed at her longings. If they could only get married!

"We really had good luck today," he said after he'd fried the fish and they had sat down to eat. "If we move right along we'll be able to get back in time to change and go to church."

"I don't care if we do." All she wanted was to spend more time with him. Church and the people in Alpine Heights seemed a million miles away. She wished they could prolong their day together.

"But I told Mrs. Austin to be at the foot of the falls at nine-thirty." He leaned over and kissed her cheek. "Besides, there's no use starting tongues to wag, my lovely Dorcas."

"You're right, of course." But that didn't ease her disappointment.

CHAPTER 8

Dorcas watched the last cleanup in the mill, her eyes glowing with excitement. She could see the wooden frames that held the amalgam plates, which had been treated with mercury. When the pulp, a mixture of ground ore and water, had flowed across the plates, the mercury had collected the gold. Now two men were scraping the amalgam from the plates and rolling the mixture into balls.

She turned to Wes Ferguson and asked, "Will we have enough this time?"

"Should have, and some left over."

Now came the final process. The balls would be placed in a retort and the mercury vaporized under intense heat. The result would be gold, called a sponge. As the sponges cooled, they would be weighed, along with the others they had been saving. Tomorrow, they would melt down the sponges, if there were enough. The final step was to pour the molten gold into a bullion mold. It would be their first bar.

Her excitement lasted all evening, and it was hard for her to sleep that night. She and Esther arrived at the mill early the next morning. Ferguson was there, taking the sponges from the retort. When they were weighed, he nodded at Dorcas. "Could you get the others from the safe? We have enough for a melt down." He turned to his assistant. "Fire up the furnace."

Dorcas ran to the office, opened the safe, and took out the container with the gold sponges they had prepared from previous cleanups. When she returned to the mill, Ferguson put them with the others.

Wearing masks, protective glasses, long asbestos gloves, and carrying tongs, the men busied themselves. Ferguson mumbled something about the chemicals that had to be added to the molten mass to purify it to the required percentage. A utensil shaped something like a bread pan stood waiting.

Finally, Ferguson pulled a long handle that tipped the container so that a slow flow of liquid gold came pouring out.

Dorcas gasped with delight as the molten fluid poured out of the channel. It was a beautiful color, more red than gold. The fluid filled the mold almost to the brim and then automatically stopped. The mass lay there smoking. Ferguson squirted cold water on it, and it hissed and steamed. Gradually, it faded from red to gold.

"I'll bring it over when it cools," Ferguson said. Dorcas walked back to the office.

Later in the day the mine manager came in with the bar and put it on her desk. Dorcas turned it over and looked at the underside, where it was stamped with the sign of legality and purity. Each bar they shipped had to be up to the exacting "good-delivery" standards of the London market by being at least 995 parts per thousand pure gold. It weighed 275 ounces and was worth $9,525. She rubbed the gold with her hands. How beautiful it was. And it was worth almost as much as she had gotten for her jewels. And this was just the beginning. There would be many more bars in the future, enough for her grandfather to make the October payment.

As soon as possible, she would send the gold by Wells Fargo Express to the mint in San Francisco. When it was received, the officials at the mint would send a payment to her grandfather.

She caressed the bar again. It was exciting to actually have something to show for all their effort. The mine had been in operation for a whole month. Even though they still had a long way to go to make a real profit, it was a good start.

At the end of the day, Andy stopped by. "I suppose you're pleased, Lady Miner." He crossed the office floor and took the chair across from her desk. When he picked up the gold bar, he rubbed his hands across its gleaming surface. "At least you've proved that the Alpine can be operated."

"I couldn't have done it without you, dear friend." She leaned across her desk and patted his arm.

Andy picked up the jar with the extra gold sponges and casting grains. "Is this all you have left?"

"Yes. What's the matter? Did you expect more?

"As a matter of fact, I did. I thought you'd have a good start on a second bar. I can't understand this." He frowned worriedly.

"You must have overestimated."

He shook his head. "No, I don't think so. I'm pretty good at sizing up yield. That ore showed color." He stared at the jar again, his expression puzzled. "Are you sure that Ferguson brought all the gold leavings in?"

"He said he did."

"Dorcas, you'd better keep your eye peeled. I don't like the looks of this at all."

She felt a growing sense of uneasiness. What did Andy mean? "Do you think the men are stealing?"

"Could be. You have some rich ore. It's awfully easy to dig out the pockets of pure gold with a penknife."

"Wouldn't Ferguson catch them? With so few men to watch, how could they get away with theft?"

"Easy enough if he's in on it. Maybe he looks the other way. I could be wrong, but just be on your guard after this." He rose from the chair. "I've got to be going."

After he left, she put the bar in a canvas container, wrote the address of the mint on the outside tag, and placed it, along with the leftover gold, in the safe. But much of her elation over the bar was gone. She remembered how her father searched the men every once in awhile. Sometimes he discovered a thief. Surely Ferguson was taking care of the searching. Wouldn't that be part of his job as manager?

For the rest of the week, Dorcas thought about the problem and it gnawed at her. When payday came, she got the envelopes ready with the miners' wages in cash and said to Esther, "You and I are going to have a little surprise ready for the men."

By the time the crew came up from underground and walked over from the stamp mill, she had made a makeshift table from two planks laid on sawhorses. "Put your lunch boxes on the table please," she told them.

They stared at her in surprise but obeyed, exchanging glances as they plopped their tin boxes on the top of the table.

No one spoke as Mrs. Morrisey opened the first lunch box and looked through it. "This is all right, Miss Hamilton." She read the name on the outside. "Evans."

"All right, Walt. Here's your envelope." Dorcas handed the sober-faced man his wages.

Mrs. Morrisey looked in the next one and found a few

nuggets of gold wrapped up in brown paper. "Ortmeyer," she read.

Dorcas picked up a prepared dismissal notice from a pile she had ready. "Ortmeyer, this is your last pay from me. Don't bother to come back on Monday morning."

Ortmeyer gave her an ugly look and grabbed his pay envelope. "I never did want to work here. A female boss!" He snorted. "I'm sorry I didn't take more."

"That's enough out of you. Just stand aside."

Mrs. Morrisey looked in the next lunch bucket and found small lumps of gold tied in a rag. "Al Berrotski."

Dorcas glared at him. "I'm surprised at you, Al. You should be ashamed of yourself. I suppose you were able to take more because you work in the stamp mill. But since the gold happens to belong to my grandfather and not to you, I'm afraid you're through." She handed him his pay envelope along with a dismissal notice.

She saved Ferguson for last. "Why didn't you check up on this, Mr. Ferguson?" Dorcas looked at her manager and saw him flush.

"I didn't know anything about it," he muttered.

"The hell you didn't," one of the dismissed men retorted.

Although Mrs. Morrisey looked in the manager's lunch bucket and found nothing except some apple peelings, Dorcas handed Ferguson a dismissal notice along with his pay. "It was your job to check up on the men. You didn't do it. I don't want you around here anymore."

"You can't do this to me." He glared at her with hate-filled eyes. "You got nothing on me."

"Well, I'm firing you anyway." She looked at the rest of the men. "Is there anyone who thinks that I am treating him unfairly? If so, speak up!"

No one said a word. "All of you with dismissal notices are to follow me up to the house. Pick up your gear and get out."

She led the procession to their quarters, the men following along behind, with Mrs. Morrisey bringing up the rear. Angrily, the dismissed miners went inside and got their things together while the others stayed on the porch.

As Ferguson came outside again he looked Dorcas up and down. "You just wait. I'll get even with you!"

Dorcas tried to shake off her apprehension at his threat. She turned to Russ McFarlane and smiled. "I'm glad to see you weren't among those who were given their walking papers. I want you to act as foreman and carry on the best you can until I get a new manager.''

One man, who didn't look much older than twenty in spite of his beard, spoke up, "You did the right thing, Miss Hamilton. They were robbing you blind. Whenever we hit a pocket of gold, those guys gouged it out with their knives. What you found today was nothing compared to what they usually took.''

"They thought we were crazy not to join in," another stated, "but my father is a parson, and I didn't want thievery on my conscience.''

Now they all were anxious to talk. "I'm sure glad to see the last of Ferguson. Didn't cotton to him at all.''

"Ortmeyer was the one who galled me. I wanted to report how they were stealing, but it was too dangerous. A guy like Ortmeyer would get revenge. He'd have a rock accidentally fall on you or something like that.''

"They were nothing but crooks. Ferguson included.''

"The four of us'll keep things going for you, Miss Hamilton," Russ put in. "From now on, you won't have to worry.''

"Well, I'm glad I still have you fellows. I think you should spread out while you have the chance. Russ, you move into Ferguson's room. I think there's room for a cot in there as well, so one of you move in with him. We'll put Sing Lee in the small bedroom and the other two on the sunporch. Is that all right?''

"We sure like our quarters, miss. We'll get reorganized," one miner agreed.

"I'll tell Sing Lee what to do," Russ said.

"You'd better clean up and have your dinner now. I'll see you on Monday," she told them.

As they rode back to town they caught up with Andy, who was walking alongside the road. Dorcas stopped the buggy. "Climb in. I want to talk to you.''

Esther moved over so Andy could sit between them. On the way back to town, Dorcas told him all about the incident. "So now I am down to four men and no manager. Do you have any suggestions?''

"I'll think about it and walk over tonight. We can talk it over then.''

*   *   *

Dorcas and Andy sat playing checkers at one end of the parlor, where they could talk without being overheard. "One man came to mind—Red Wallace," Andy told her. "He worked for us last summer, and he has the experience to be a mine manager. I heard that he was at a silver mine in Nevada."

"Do you know where?"

"Virginia City, I believe. His cousin is one of our foremen, so he probably knows how to get in touch with him. If we could get him, I'm sure he'd do a good job."

Dorcas sighed. "Now I'm wondering what Grandfather will say. I never even consulted him."

"How could you consult him? You had to act fast. Besides, he's given you full responsibility for the Alpine."

"I'm glad to get rid of Ferguson. I never liked or trusted him."

Andy grinned at her. "You should've paid more attention to your feminine intuition." With that he jumped over the remainder of her checkers. "I've beaten you this time!"

As he laid out the board for the next game, he went on, "Dorcas, you might as well face some facts and reevaluate your whole scheme of things. Your crew was too small even before you dumped more than half of them. You're not going to get very far with so few men. You need at least three or four men in the stamp mill. You ought to have someone able to run the chemical tests. And you need at least twelve to fifteen men underground. Of course, you also need a manager."

"Andy, I can't afford that."

"You can if you have an efficient operation. The way you're limping along, you're not going to succeed."

"But where can they live? I can't house any more than ten in the cottage. It's overcrowded at that.

"You'll have to build a bunkhouse. It doesn't need to be elaborate. Maybe the men in your crew could put up a building for you."

"Andy, I get a sick feeling when I think of all the money it would take. Besides the bunkhouse, we'd have to have a mess hall with a stove and all that."

"And a room for your cook." Andy shook his head. "I'm warning you. You can't go on the way you are now. Either do it right or close down the mine."

"I can't do that, either." She thought of how rapidly her capital was dwindling. Just the payroll for a big crew would take a lot of money each week. Of course, it was true that they would be getting gold out, right along.

As if he were reading her thoughts Andy said, "Now that you're rid of the thieves, your mine will be much more profitable. You can use some of your gold to pay your expenses. Old Jack at the general store will buy any extra gold you mine. He can't get his hands on enough of it. Probably has a fortune buried under his house."

"I've been paying my tab with checks, but if he'll take gold, that would help."

"He's got the finest gold scale in the country. All the old duffers that pan gold in the Trinity River bring it to him."

"If I built a bunkhouse, Esther and I could move into the manager's house. That would save some money."

"You told me that your brother wanted to come for the summer, anyway. He could stay out there with you."

"It would make a real change for Mother and Judy if I could get them to come as well."

Andy moved his checker. "If you'd like to, we could ride out to the mine tomorrow afternoon and see where you could build."

"All right. We have our main meal at one on Sundays, so we could start out about two."

It wasn't easy to find a level site on the mine grounds that didn't already hold buildings.

"You'll have to grade some land," Andy declared as he stepped off a good-size lot on an uneven parcel. "Better plan on a ball diamond, too."

Inwardly groaning, Dorcas tried to estimate how much the grading would add to the expense. "Do you know of anyone who could do the grading?"

"There are men here in Alpine Heights who are builders. They have the equipment. But you ought to get started as soon as possible. You want to make the most of the spring and summer."

She nodded in agreement, thinking of the October deadline ahead. This was already the middle of April.

As the horse trotted back to town, Andy flipped the reins and said, "Let's go talk to a man who's done some work for Philip. He might be free and able to get on the job."

* * *

The carpenter walked out to the buggy and stood with his hands in his pockets as he thought about the proposed bunkhouse and mess hall. "I was about to start on a house I promised to build."

"It's very important that we get our buildings up right away." Dorcas looked at him imploringly. She wished she had Judy's ability to influence a man.

"I don't know where I'd get any helpers. I'd have to go into Redding—"

"I have four able-bodied men who might be willing to work with you instead of going underground for a few days. They would just be utility buildings and wouldn't need skilled finishing. With you supervising the job, I'm sure my men could do the work."

"Well, ma'am, I'll come out to the Alpine tomorrow and we can look it over. Then I'll tell you if I'll take on the job."

The next morning Dorcas was at the mine by the time the men were ready to go underground. She told about the need to build a bunkhouse and asked if they would be willing to help the carpenter for a while instead of mining.

"A job's a job," one of them said. "Makes no difference to me what I do as long as I can earn a living."

"We'd get the same pay, wouldn't we?" Russ asked.

"Yes, of course."

After they all assured her they'd help, Dorcas went into the office feeling better. After consulting with Sing Lee about the kitchen, she even made several sketches of what she had in mind.

When the carpenter came, she tramped around the site with him and they found a storehouse that could be moved and converted into the mess hall. They also uncovered some stored lumber, which would help a little.

"Well, ma'am, I'll do the work. It won't take too long," the man finally agreed.

"You can do the grading as well?"

"Yes, ma'am, I have a team and a grader. I'll start tomorrow."

As soon as the building was under way, Dorcas and Esther planned to return to San Francisco to report to her grandfather and ask her mother if some of the furniture in storage could be moved to the mine.

CHAPTER 9

Courtland Burke helped the nine-year-old girl up onto the platform and settled her in the model's chair. He arranged the thick braid on each side of her face and fluffed the bows on the ends. Then he handed her a long loop of string. "Make a cat's cradle with the string. Look down toward it, but keep your chin tipped up so we can see your face." He turned to the class. "You've had several lessons in sketching and have learned the proportions of the human figure. Now take out your sketch pads and see what you can do with Priscilla."

While they worked, he pinned up lengths of black sateen over part of the studio window. "We want to redistribute the light to get a good strong shadow on one side of her face. This will enhance her cheekbones, cause her eyes to sparkle, and brighten the color of her hair. Too much light flattens the features, especially with children." He continued to explain the importance of regulating the light. "As soon as I check your sketch, you can begin your portrait using larger paper and either pastels or charcoal."

He moved from student to student and corrected their work until they were able to go on to the next step. As he stood behind Judy, his blood quickened. It was all he could do to keep himself from touching her. How incredibly lovely she was. She wore a soft violet smock that matched her eyes. He could smell the faint fragrance of her rose toilet water. Damn her, anyway. She wasn't part of his future plans. Yet she had gradually gotten under his skin. He eagerly greeted those mornings when she took her lesson. He always leaped out of bed early, bathed, and trimmed his beard with special care. He made sure his shirt was clean and his cravat spotless. Damn her, anyway, he told himself again. She enchanted him.

She glanced up at him. "How am I doing?"

"All right, I guess. We'll have a critique the last hour."

But she had talent, he admitted to himself. A lot of it. Her sketch was far superior to anyone else's. It wasn't fair that anyone with so much beauty should be given so much talent. This spoiled and shallow girl wouldn't do anything with her gift. It had been wasted on her.

In spite of his misgivings, he heard himself saying, "Stay after class for a minute, because I have a suggestion you might want to consider."

"All right, but I can't stay very long, as I have a luncheon engagement."

Judy thought of Ross Elderson and his sister, who would be waiting for her at the Palace Hotel. Ross was one of her most ardent beaus, and an eligible one, too. His father owned a shipping line and much property, as well as being a family friend.

At the end of the class, Judy put her art materials and smock away in her assigned locker and returned to the studio to see what Burke wanted.

When he was free of the other students, he turned to her. "You seem to have some talent with children. Your work today is the best you've done so far."

At last her eyes lit with interest.

"Do you like working with children?"

Judy shrugged. "I guess so."

He picked up his notebook and studied it. "Next session I'll be starting a new phase of this course, but I wondered if you would like to have some private lessons on painting children."

"Private lessons? Here?" She looked at him in surprise.

"No. It would have to be at my studio on Saturday mornings. You could use my niece as a model. She's a beautiful child. Five years old. But one leg is crippled so I don't bring her here; she tires quickly."

"I don't think I should come to your studio. My mother isn't well and can't accompany me." The nerve of this man!

"Don't worry. My mother will be there." He smiled at her. "You'll be properly chaperoned. I'd like to work with you. This is an area in which you'd do well."

"I'll talk it over with Mother and see if she'll permit me." She tossed her head. Actually, it might be quite exciting to have special lessons in painting children. Perhaps Burke would let her start oils or watercolors, instead of just using pastels. She picked up her purse. "I'll let you know next time."

"I don't see why I had to come along," Keith growled as they rode toward the address that Burke had given her. "I wanted to play ball with my friends."

"Mama said I couldn't go unless you came along."

"Surely I don't have to give up every Saturday morning."

"Of course not, silly. It's just this one time. Mama wanted to make sure that this Courtland Burke really did have a mother living with him."

When Judy saw the number on a cream-colored row house, she leaned forward and told Wilson to stop. "You can call for us in two hours."

Two bay windows protruded from the front of the house. Below them hung window boxes with red geraniums spilling over the edges. Judy and Keith climbed up steps leading to the front door. When the bell echoed through the house, a plump woman of about fifty answered it.

"Good morning. I'm Mrs. Burke, Court's mother. You must be Miss Hamilton. We've been expecting you." There was something reassuring about this pretty lady with gray-streaked dark hair. After Judy introduced her brother, the older woman went on, "Court and my granddaughter are back in the studio. Come with me."

As they walked down the hall, Judy asked, "Does Mr. Burke have many private pupils?"

"Only rarely. He likes to spend as much time at his own painting as he can." The large studio at the back faced north and overlooked a small back garden.

Courtland stood at an easel with a paintbrush in his hand. "Ah, here you are, Miss Hamilton." Once again her beauty hit him like a blow in the solar plexus. How he would like to paint her.

Judy introduced her brother. After they shook hands, Courtland pointed to a beautiful little girl who was curled up in an upholstered chair with a doll in her arms. "This is Rosemary, who has consented to be your model as a special favor to her old uncle.''

''Don't forget you promised to take me to the zoo this afternoon.'' Rosemary picked up a crutch leaning against the chair and with practiced skill got herself out of the seat and limped across the room to a platform. Courtland placed a straight chair on the riser and lifted his niece onto it.

Keith sat in an easy chair and assumed a bored, martyred air, but it wasn't long before he became interested in the way Courtland was setting up an easel and preparing a selection of pastels for his sister.

Disappointed, Judy said, ''I thought I was going to use oils for a change.''

''You will, eventually, but I want you to use these for the first portrait. Actually, you can get a stunning effect with pastels, as they're a perfect medium for children. Later, we'll have you try oils.'' He handed her a sketching pad and drawing pencil. ''First I want you to do a few sketches. Remember, you'll have to give Rosemary breaks, as she can't pose as long as a professional adult model.''

Rosemary spoke up resentfully. ''Uncle Court, I've posed for you loads of times. I know how to stay real still.''

''Of course you do, kitten. You're my most favorite model.'' He fluffed her curls lovingly and adjusted her head. He changed the position of the doll in her lap and straightened the skirt of her long, pink-checked gingham dress.

Soon Judy was sketching, hardly aware of her teacher's presence. Already the sketch was taking shape. When she put on the final touches, she looked up at him. ''What do you think?''

''It's all right for a start. Broaden her shoulders a bit. Her hands aren't very good.''

He's right, of course, Judy admitted to herself in annoyance.

He called out instructions to Rosemary to hold up one chubby hand and grasp her doll with the other. ''Take another piece of paper and just do hands,'' he told Judy.

Then Courtland walked over to his niece and said, ''We're going to change your position and see what Miss Hamilton can do with pastels.''

He returned to Judy's side. ''While you're working with pastels, I want you to think of the background and how you can make a more complex scene when you go on to oils. What can you do to give your viewer an emotional reaction?''

Puzzled, Judy glanced up at him. "You mean admiration? Or longing for a child as lovely?"

"Yes, perhaps. But dig deep down inside yourself. What do you feel as you look at her?"

Judy gazed at the ethereal child and the crutch by her side. She blinked back the tears that sprang to her eyes. An almost overwhelming pity struck her. How tragic that a little girl so beautiful should be handicapped.

"What are you feeling?" he whispered.

"Compassion." Her chin trembled. "That's what I feel."

"I hoped you'd say that." Perhaps this spoiled, self-centered girl had more depth of character than showed on the surface. "Rosemary looks something like you."

"Yes, she does. She could be my little sister."

"That's why I wanted you to come here. I thought you'd feel a rapport with her and could do something quite worthwhile with the child and her circumstances." He leaned toward her and said in a low voice, "Someday she'll be your age and just as beautiful. What if you—" He nodded toward the crutch.

Judy couldn't answer. Her throat tightened and tears flooded her eyes. What if she herself could never dance or run or walk without limping? She had always taken her fitness for granted. As if it were her right to be sound. To have the use of her legs and arms and to be able to see and hear. Why did she have those faculties when there were others who were handicapped? How could God have allowed this to happen to an innocent child? Finally, she asked in a soft voice that only Courtland could hear, "Was it an accident?"

He shook his head and mouthed, "Congenital."

Judy picked up her pastels and began. How easily the portrait took shape. Did she truly have a special gift for portraying children? she wondered. Never before had she been particularly interested in youngsters. In fact, at houses where she visited, they had always seemed rather pesty, and she was glad when their nursemaids came and took them away. But this was so different.

Fascinated, Courtland watched her work. Judy seemed to have a true instinct for composition, proportion, and color. The talent that came through, in spite of her being an amateur, excited him. If he could only help her make the most of her gift—inspire her to develop herself to her true potential.

At the end of half an hour, Rosemary began to droop. Burke spoke up, "We'll have to stop now."

Judy picked up one of her pencil sketches and walked over to the child. "You have been a marvelous model, dear. Here's a drawing I made of you. You can keep it."

"Thank you. I'll put it with some that Uncle Court has made for me."

"I'm afraid his are lots better than mine."

Courtland shook his head. "Don't believe that for a minute. You seem to have a special knack with children. Far more than I have."

Pleased with his rare praise, Judy began gathering her materials together.

Courtland walked over to his niece and lifted her off the platform. "We're going to stop now. Why don't you take Keith outside and show him your rabbits, while I work with Miss Hamilton."

When they were alone, he evaluated each of her drawings and the pastel and showed her how she could improve. "You can finish the pastel next time and we'll work on your preliminary sketches for an oil painting."

"That will be so exciting." Her violet eyes reflected her anticipation. She had never realized that art could be like this. Such a feeling of reaching out beyond her limited horizons. It was almost like having new worlds to conquer. A new challenge.

"I want you to think all week about what you are going to do with your painting. Try to transcend just a simple interpretation. Put yourself into this portrait. Paint what you feel about the tragedy of Rosemary's condition. It can never be changed. We have taken her to the finest doctors here and on the East Coast, and nothing can be done for her. We have to accept it. Of course, Rosemary has never known anything different, but the day will come when she will have to come to grips with it and make a good life for herself despite her handicap."

"Does she have your artistic talent?"

"Not that I know of." Courtland shrugged. "She seems to have some musical instincts. Perhaps she can develop them and build her life around music. The piano, cello, or some other instrument where she can sit. I hope so."

"Her mother is your sister?"

"Yes, but she's dead. She died of scarlet fever when Rosemary was only two. Just before she passed away, she had me promise to raise her baby, which I am doing, of course. But the main burden falls on my mother. Rosemary's father skipped out, so he's no help."

"Perhaps you'll marry someday. Then your wife can take over." Judy shrugged and thought to herself that the man *she* would marry would be handsome, rich, and without responsibilities like this. She glanced down at the exquisite gold watch that hung on a chain around her neck and saw that her two hours were up. "I must go. Our coachman will be waiting for us."

"We'll go outside and find Rosemary and Keith. They must still be looking at the rabbits," Courtland said.

"I don't like this one bit, Dorcas," Clyde Hamilton glowered at her, his eyes narrowed and his face flushed.

She felt a frightened, sinking sensation inside as she recognized the signs of his growing rage. How formidable her grandfather could be when he was aroused.

"Why didn't you telegraph me when you first suspected what was going on?" he demanded.

"I had no proof at all. Besides, I would have had to send a telegram from the general store and the whole town would've known about it. Someone would have been sure to tip off the men."

"But you fired them so out of hand. Never gave them a chance to explain."

"What was there to explain? I found the gold in their lunch boxes." Her mouth was so dry it was hard to talk. Her knees shook. "You would have done the same thing." She had to stand her ground and not let her grandfather intimidate her as he often did his employees.

"But you lost an experienced manager."

"He was a crook, Grandpa." She thrust out her chin. "He knew what the men were doing. Why didn't he stop them?"

"You have no proof that he knew about it. Just the word of thieves."

"He was right in the thick of it, all right. Probably took some gold himself. He thought they could all get by with the thefts because I am a woman. After this, I'll have the lunch pails lowered just before noon and have them hauled right back up again.''

"What are you going to do now?''

"Andy's lining up another manager for me.''

Clyde pounded his fist on the table. "Dammit, you're depending too much on that Andrew Woodard. He's just a henchman of the Richmonds. You can't trust any of them.''

"Oh, Grandpa, don't be like that. Andy's been a rock. I don't know what I'd do without him.''

"It seems to me you're getting in way over your head, young lady. I've had my doubts about this wild scheme of yours right from the beginning.''

"It's not a wild scheme to open a mine that we know can produce. Naturally, there are problems.''

"I warned you right at the start, didn't I?'' The old man drummed his fingers on the arm of his chair. "You're undercapitalized, and you're only taking Woodard's word that the mine will pay.''

"But I've read Papa's reports, and he was optimistic.''

"I don't like this plan of hiring such a big crew and putting up those buildings. Whose idea was that?''

"Well, Andy's. But I agree with him. I think he's absolutely right.''

"How do you know that he isn't leading you down the primrose path?''

"Why would he do that?'' Dorcas asked.

"To bleed you dry until you have to give up. Then the Richmond outfit will end up owning the Alpine.''

"Grandpa, I don't believe that for a minute.''

"I've lost all faith in you, Dorcas. You'd better quit before you throw away more money.''

"No! I'm not going to quit!'' Her chin trembled with hurt. "I've taken on this responsibility, and I'm going to see it through!''

Clyde Hamilton looked at the determined girl facing him and felt a flood of mixed emotions. Worry, annoyance, and pride. By God, she was amazing, all right. He'd never known a female like her.

Finally he shrugged, his anger gone. "I'll not say any more. You've got to learn the hard way, Dorcas. But I think you're just pouring money down a rat hole.''

Tears flooded her eyes. "But I sent in some gold. You got the check from the mint, didn't you?"

"Yes, I did. A small drop in the bucket."

"But that proves we can do it." She dropped down beside him and put her head against his arm. "Grandpa, don't lose faith in me. Just let me try."

He patted her hair. "I won't say anything more."

But Dorcas knew he had no real confidence in her.

Before she took on her mother, she went into the kitchen and made a cup of tea. The session with her grandfather had left her limp. Nibbling on a cookie, she planned her strategy. She had no choice but to borrow some money from her mother. Her funds were dangerously low. But her mother might not be willing to see her. Would she dare to borrow the money without Lenore's permission?

Finally she went upstairs and quietly tapped on the bedroom door. When her mother's maid came, Dorcas motioned for her to step outside.

"Rosalie, I want to talk to you. Can you leave Mrs. Hamilton for a few minutes?"

"Yes, she's napping."

"Then let's go to my bedroom."

They sat in the two slipper chairs by the window. Dorcas looked at the pretty young girl with her light brown hair tucked sedately behind her maid's cap. They were fortunate to have such a sweet girl who knew how to handle her mother.

"How is Mrs. Hamilton now?"

"She's much better, Miss Dorcas. She's still depressed, but at least she gets out of bed and sits in her chaise in her living room. For a while there she just lay in bed curled up in a ball all day. It was awful."

"When did she start to come out of it?"

"Right after your first letter came. She had me read it to her over and over. Every letter you've sent since, she can't hear often enough."

"That seems so strange. Why, I wonder."

"I don't know," Rosalie replied. "But she just devours them. It's a good thing you write so often, ma'am. I honestly believe that hearing from you has helped her on the road to recovery. It's as if she's carrying an awful burden inside and your letters reassure her."

Dorcas felt more puzzled than ever. Why would her mother find her letters reassuring? It wasn't as if they were from Judy or Keith.

"Do you think she's able to see me now?" Dorcas sighed worriedly. "I don't want to set her back."

"Why don't I go ask her, ma'am. She'll tell me if she doesn't feel up to seeing you."

"All right. I'll wait right here."

Lenore lay on the chaise in her sitting room, wearing a lounging robe with a light blanket pulled over her. She opened her eyes and smiled when her daughter came in.

How thin she is, Dorcas thought. Lenore's beautiful face looked sunken and deep; dark circles appeared under her eyes.

"Can we have a little visit?" Dorcas asked after she kissed her.

"I guess so," Lenore answered listlessly. "How are things going at the mine?"

"I'm making progress, but slowly." Dorcas told her about the thefts and having to assemble a new crew. "I'm afraid Grandpa's quite put out with me. He thinks I should have kept the manager."

Lenore shrugged. "Father Hamilton's always been so difficult. Sometimes I think I'll scream if he comes in here again and tells me that I ought to get out more and make an effort to pull myself out of the doldrums."

Dorcas kept herself from saying that she agreed wholeheartedly with her grandfather. Why was her mother so depressed? Was it because she dwelled upon her own feelings too much? Why didn't she get involved in church work or some women's club? It was ridiculous for her to lie around all day feeling sorry for herself. It was hard to be patient with her.

"I have a suggestion," Dorcas said aloud. "Judy was telling me that you both would like to get out from under Grandpa's thumb, so why don't you and Judy and Keith come up to Alpine Heights for a while this summer?"

"No!" The color drained from Lenore's face. "That's quite impossible."

"But it isn't. Keith and Judy could bring you up by train and I'll meet you in Redding." Dorcas tried to keep her voice low and calm. She told her mother about her plans to move into the manager's house. "That is, if you're willing to let me move to the mine some of our furniture that's in storage. I don't mean your choice pieces, but the less valuable ones."

"You must be planning to settle in."

"Yes, for a while. I thought Esther and I could live in the manager's house, which would save money. I'd like to be right there to keep an eye on things. Especially after this stealing episode."

"I can understand that," Lenore said, nodding.

"We'd have a comfortable place for you to get some fresh air and sunshine. You know how cold and foggy San Francisco can be in the summer."

"You can use what furniture you want, but I won't come."

"Keith wants to be with me up there as well."

"I can't permit that."

"But Mother, he's soon going to mining school. He should get some practical experience first. Papa did, before his training."

Lenore turned her head away and wiped her eyes. "Don't talk about your father. It's too painful."

"But you should talk about him and get your feelings out in the open. You're holding all your grief inside, and that isn't good for you."

"I don't want to discuss it," Lenore told her.

"Would you rather I left? I always seem to upset you so, although I don't mean to, dear."

"No, stay; I'm lonely. I'm glad to see you, Dorcas. Judy is at her art lesson and Keith is in school, so it's good to have you here."

"I'll tell you about the people I've run into at Alpine Heights," Dorcas began, although her mother closed her eyes and seemed to cringe. It was as if that subject was also taboo. "I saw Edna Trent in the general store. She sent her love to you and her sympathy about Papa."

Lenore sat up and cried out, "Tell me everything she said and how she acted."

Dorcas was startled by the desperation in her mother's voice, but at least she was paying attention. Then they discussed all her parents' former friends and neighbors who were still in the mining town.

Lenore asked question after question, as if she had an insatiable desire to know everyone her daughter had seen and talked to. It was not just an idle conversation but seemed to Dorcas more like being quizzed, which was strange. But her mother grew more cheerful as they talked.

"No one has asked why we left Alpine Heights?" Lenore demanded.

Dorcas herself wanted to know the answer to that question but didn't dare say so. "No, dear. They've sent their kindest regards and sympathy. You still have several friends in Alpine Heights. They'd love to see you again. That's why I urge you to come up for a while this summer. It would be a real change for you."

A strange expression, almost one of relief, came over Lenore's face. She was silent awhile and then said, "Perhaps we could all come. I think I'd get out and walk more. Judy could bring her paints and try some landscapes."

"Mother, I'm delighted. We'll have a wonderful summer together." Dorcas leaned forward and kissed Lenore on the cheek.

Did she dare ask her mother now if she could borrow some money? She'd pay it back, of course, as soon as they mined more gold.

"Mama, I'd like to talk to you about your insurance money. Could I use some of it? I'll repay it as soon as I can."

"Dorcas, I don't want to discuss money. It makes me upset knowing that it came from your dear father's accident." Tears gathered in Lenore's eyes. "If you want to borrow some, do so. Whatever you think is best, dear."

The next day Dorcas went to the warehouse and picked out the furniture she wanted shipped to the mine. She also cashed in some of her mother's bonds and deposited $25,000 into her own checking account. But as she did so, she felt half-sick with worry. Would she ever be able to pay it back?

CHAPTER 10

After Dorcas returned to Alpine Heights, the days seemed to be filled with countless problems to be solved and decisions to be made. It was a confusing, stressful time. The work on the bunkhouse and mess hall progressed slowly because of heavy rains. When the men couldn't work outside, they kept the mill running by processing the ore from the stockpile.

It was a long time between one cleanup and the next, so the amalgam balls accumulated slowly. But there was no point in hiring more miners until she had her new manager. Red Wallace was willing to leave his job in Nevada and would be able to start on the fifteenth of May. The October 1 deadline loomed more ominously than ever.

The papers were filled with news of Coxey's army, thousands of unemployed men marching to Washington to gain favorable attention from Congress to provide interest-free loans to communities to build roads and create jobs. The newspaper stories about the desperate men and their suffering families made her sick at heart. When "General" Coxey was arrested on May 1 for leading a demonstration, she was so upset she wrote to President Cleveland in protest. Not that she had much hope that he or any member of Congress would pay any attention to the letter of a mere female.

The only relief from her anxiety were the Sunday-morning rides with Philip. She looked forward to each time almost obsessively. How she needed that respite from her problems. They had to get the mine back into operation soon to produce another gold bar. The longer the delay, the more frustrated she became.

For the first time in her life, she felt unsure of herself. More than once she recalled her grandfather's words, "I've lost all faith in you. You'd better quit before you throw more money away." It was hard to keep up her self-confidence and optimism. She didn't feel it was wise to share her worries with Philip. He might not want to listen to her troubles, as he no doubt had plenty of his own.

The only one she could turn to was Andy. "This is strictly confidential. Just between the two of us. Don't say anything to Philip," she made him promise. She told him about her grandfather's financial affairs, the money she raised on her jewels and the amount she had borrowed from her mother. "You can see why I'm so desperate. Why I must make a success of this project. Our futures depend on it."

"You can do it, Dorcas. It will work out all right. Don't lose heart. Everything will fall in place."

"What a help you are, Andy. You bolster my self-esteem."

"I want to help you. Whatever you tell me in confidence will be a sacred trust." Secretly he was pleased that she confided in him.

By the fifteenth of May, the weather had cleared and the buildings were ready. Andy went into Redding for supplies and purchased more beds and mattresses for her. He also met Red Wallace and brought him back.

Dorcas liked her new manager immediately and felt he would work closely with her instead of opposing her at every turn. There was something quite wholesome and aboveboard about his freckled face and bright red hair. In his early thirties, he looked big, strong, and forceful enough to be a real boss.

"There's one thing I expect," she told him, "and that is for you to keep a close eye out for theft. I'm sure Andy has told you about our experience. I need every ounce of gold I can get."

Red grinned. "I may have faults—but I'm not dishonest. I don't rob banks or steal gold out of my employer's mine."

"Good. And something else—my former manager was surly and uncooperative. We didn't work well together at all."

"I'm sure you and I will do much better, ma'am. At least, I'll try my best."

Dorcas put out her hand. "I hope you don't object to the fact that I'm a woman."

Red smiled. "Andy told me that was one of the bonuses of this job."

Together they walked to the new bunkhouse and she showed

him his clean, private room. He put his suitcases down, and they looked over the big living area, furnished with the things from the manager's house.

"This looks mighty nice, Miss Hamilton. Far better than most quarters."

Within a few days, he had hired a new crew and the mine was in full operation. Red had a special way of handling the men so that they respected him and gave him their full effort. He and Andy explored every part of the mine and planned where they would excavate to the best advantage. They took Dorcas underground and explained everything to her.

"Looks fine to me," she said in approval. "Go right ahead."

Red kept one crew in the stope to exhaust that vein while he placed another at a lower level. It wasn't long before they shipped another gold bar and Dorcas's spirits began to rise.

When the furniture arrived, she and Esther moved into the little house. It was surprising what a change Lenore's possessions made. Although Dorcas had chosen the less valuable pieces, they looked luxurious here at the Alpine. Chinese hooked rugs covered the linoleum floor. The upholstered chairs in soft green brocade, the fruitwood tables, and the Tiffany lamps looked almost too formal with the stone fireplace. The largest bedroom barely held the French furniture that was such a favorite with Lenore. But it was all very beautiful and so delightful for Dorcas to have her own place.

On Saturday she ran into Philip as she walked along the wooden sidewalk in Alpine Heights. "Now that the weather is better," he said, "let's go fishing again tomorrow. And stay for breakfast, of course."

"I'd love to. My family will be coming the first of June, and I don't know if I'll be able to get away then."

"Then we'll make the most of our day. We'll try to bring back a big catch."

"We won't have to rush back for church, will we?"

"Not this time. We can fish as long as we like. And since I'll be picking you up at your mine, we won't have to bring Mrs. Austin along. No one will see us."

Dorcas made cookies and sandwiches for their lunch. When she told Esther she was going to be out with Philip for the day, she sensed the older woman's disapproval.

"Do you think that's wise?" Esther asked.

Dorcas told herself that it might not be wise, but she just had to have their day together. Perhaps if she and Philip had a wonderful time, he would declare himself.

Esther saw the dreamy look in Dorcas's eyes and was more convinced than ever that the girl was deeply in love with Philip Richmond. Oh, if it were only Andy. Now, *he* was a man who would put his wife first. She wanted to tell her employer that she was asking for trouble. That incredibly handsome Mr. Richmond, who could charm anyone out of their wits, was also very self-centered. He was only amusing himself with this horseback riding and fishing. Even if he was at least thirty, he didn't seem anxious to settle down with a family. Dorcas was deluding herself if she thought otherwise.

Dorcas was up at dawn. She looked out the window and rejoiced. The sky was clear and the air still. She washed and went into the kitchen for a small bowl of cereal and a piece of toast to sustain her until they cooked their breakfast. Almost bursting with happiness, she hummed a little tune. It was going to be her day with Philip. Her wonderful, wonderful day. Who knew what it might bring?

She returned to her bedroom and put on her own brown riding habit, which she had brought back from San Francisco. After she brushed her long thick hair, she tied it in back with an orange ribbon that matched the scarf around her neck.

It was delightful to have the privacy of her own house and not have to worry about the other boarders at Widow Hendricks's who might be watching out their windows to see Philip arriving with their horses. After she picked up her paper bag with the cookies and sandwiches, she walked outside. By the time she reached the road, she saw Philip approaching on Sultan, leading the mare. Just seeing him looking so splendid astride his horse sent the blood pounding through her veins.

"Good morning," she cried. "We're going to have a beautiful day. Not a cloud in the sky."

"I ordered this weather especially for us." Before he helped her into the saddle, he took her in his arms and kissed

135

her. Sultan whinnied. Philip smiled down at her. "He's telling us to stop the smooching and get going."

She stretched up and laid her cheek against his. She loved the feel of his skin, the fragrance of his shaving soap, just being near him. "Sultan can mind his own business," she said. But soon she broke away and walked over to the mare.

They rode to the Golden Star and took the back wagon road that wound through the forest to the falls. That way they didn't have to make the climb up the face of the cliff. Dorcas held on to her bag of sandwiches and cookies and hoped they wouldn't get crushed during the ride. Sometimes the two of them were able to ride side by side; more frequently, Philip led the way. But that didn't matter. Being with him was what was important.

She enjoyed looking at the back of his head and the way his hair came down to the top of his collar under his cap. Everything about him was so attractive. What could be more wonderful than riding through this glorious country with the ground lush with flowers and grass, the trees forming a cathedral arch above them, and the high white mountains just in front of them? Her worries about the mine and all its complications vanished.

When they finally arrived at the cabin, they took the saddles off the horses and let them graze in the meadow.

Dorcas loved the little domestic chores of getting fresh water, filling the coffee pot, and putting coffee in it while Philip brought in the wood and started the fire. She put her cookies and sandwiches in the cupboard. When they were married, they would come here often. She glanced at the bed again, and her cheeks flushed.

After they chose their rods and flies, they walked out to the stream. While they fished, she kept glancing toward Philip, still daydreaming about their life together. What would it be like living with him in the big Richmond house? She'd be the most important young matron in town. She smiled to herself. Alpine Heights was so small, that wasn't much of a privilege.

But she felt that being Philip's wife would be the greatest honor possible, whether they lived here in this mining town or in San Francisco. Inwardly she prayed, *Please propose to me. I want you so*. Perhaps later in the day he would. While they were talking after eating. Was there something she could say or do that would make him declare himself? If he did propose, they could have a quiet wedding after her family came. Philip would help her run the mine. Just think of all the advice he could give her.

Poor Andy was doing so much for just a small consultation fee. He gave her far more time than she deserved. It would be a relief to him to have Philip take over helping her.

They were both catching fish, so they soon had enough for breakfast.

"I'm starved, so let's eat. We can fish more later," Philip suggested.

Once again, she set the table while he cleaned the fish. He brought them in, rolled them in cornmeal, and dropped them into the big iron frying pan.

"I brought sandwiches so that we don't have to have fish again for lunch."

He picked up her hand and kissed it. "You're a girl after my own heart. What kind of sandwiches?"

"Ham."

"You're my true love."

She glowed with pleasure. Of course, he was making a little joke, but he meant it underneath. She was a girl after his heart. And his true love. They had so much in common. Their mining background. Their love of the outdoors. Their enjoyment of San Francisco and their friends there. What couple could be better suited?

Now she watched the careful way he split the trout, laid one half back, and loosened the bones in the other piece. Everything he did was so precise. She loved his perfectionism.

After breakfast they fished all morning, cleaned their catch, and wrapped the trout in wet leaves. Back in the cabin, they rolled up their sleeves and washed the odor of fish from their hands. Out of the corner of her eye, she saw the soap bubbles clinging to the dark hairs on his arms. Somehow it made her all too aware of his masculinity.

They ate their lunch and cleaned up the table. Surely this was the time Philip was going to talk to her. He would propose. She knew it.

He took her in his arms and kissed the hollow of her cheeks. "I've had a wonderful day, Dorcas." He smiled down at her.

"So have I." But there were no words for the ecstasy she

felt. Nothing could describe it. She put her arms around his neck and laid her cheek against his.

"I've never known a girl that I felt so at ease with, who was so willing to do the things I enjoy." His hand caressed her back, sending shivers of desire through her. "We belong together."

"Oh, Philip, I think so, too."

He pressed her closer and closer and kissed her eyelids, her sensitive, throbbing temple, and her lips. As his passion grew, she responded and felt she was caught in a current of longing, a force greater than she had ever known. It was impossible to resist. When he began unbuttoning her jacket, she couldn't protest. She wanted him as badly as he desired her.

They stayed all afternoon in the cabin making love, sending each other into heights she had never known before.

Over and over, she told him, "I love you, Philip. With all my heart." As they lay wrapped in each other's arms, she told him about falling in love with him when she was only fourteen. "I know some people would think that's impossible, but it's true. When I had to move to Colorado, I grieved for you."

"Oh, my darling, I didn't know."

"When I saw you at the grand-opening ball, it all came flooding back."

"I sensed something special about you." He caressed the planes of her face.

"Those years when I was away from you, I must have kept all my feelings for you in a special place, because they came rushing out when I saw you again." She pulled his face down to hers and kissed him. "I've never told anyone about this before."

"Then it's a secret just for us." He rose up on his elbow and looked out at the fading light. "It's getting late. We'd better go."

As he locked the cabin door and closed the iron shutters, he said, "I won't be able to come up here next Sunday. I'm entertaining a group of mining men from Nevada. They're interested in a special process we use here. There's no way I can get away."

"Then the following week, my family is coming." She threw her arms around his neck. "But we've had today. Our special, wonderful day."

"I know, my dearest girl, and I'll never forget it. We'll see each other soon."

It was only as they rode back to town that she realized he hadn't proposed to her. But hadn't he said, "We belong together"? Didn't that mean that he was making plans for their future? Of course it did.

But a guilty feeling came over her. She had been wanton. Given herself to a man before marriage. Something she'd sworn she would never do. But was it so terrible? They'd be married soon. Now they were one, mates in every sense of the word, so of course they should spend the rest of their lives together.

It was late afternoon when Dorcas entered her house.

"I'm so glad to see you, Miss Dorcas," Esther cried as she rose from her chair in front of the fire. "As it started to get dark, I was terribly worried about you."

"Well, we were fishing and fishing. We wandered way up the stream. I brought quite a few trout home. I'll put them in the cooler and take them to Sing Lee tomorrow. He can make chowder for the men."

"I hope you'll save a couple for us," Esther said, and smiled.

"Of course. I'll go and get out of these clothes."

Esther watched the glowing, excited expression on Dorcas's face and she knew that far more than fishing had gone on. She'd grown deeply fond of her employer and wanted only happiness for her. But somehow she doubted that Philip would bring it to her.

During the next few days, Dorcas and Esther prepared the house for the arrival of Lenore, Judy, and Keith. Dorcas moved out of the largest bedroom to prepare it for her mother. Esther could stay in the small bedroom, which left the sun porch for the two sisters.

"We'll have to put Keith out on the front porch. The weather will be warm while he's here, so I don't think he'll mind," Dorcas said.

"We can get some apple boxes for him to use as a cupboard," Esther suggested.

Almost every evening on his way home, Philip stopped by the office to see Dorcas. She waited all day for his visit; even if they had no chance to be alone, it was wonderful to know that he was thinking of her.

Her days were busy, but at night she lay in bed longing for Philip and trying not to feel guilty. How angry her grandfather would be if he knew she had given herself to a Richmond. What would he say when she told him that she would marry Philip this winter? She dreamed of her wedding and wished she were formally engaged.

Finally the time arrived when her family was to come by stagecoach from Redding. Esther stayed at the house to prepare dinner while Dorcas drove a wagon from the mine into Alpine Heights. While she waited for the stagecoach to arrive, she worried about how her mother had survived the journey. Perhaps the long train ride and the rough stagecoach trip, with the overnight stop in the crude station, would be too much for Lenore. She thought of how wan and frail her mother had looked lying on the chaise the last time she'd seen her. What condition would she be in by the time she got here?

Dorcas saw the coach coming slowly down the grade, leaving a plume of dust behind. Anxiety made a leaden ball in her stomach. But when the stage pulled to a stop, her mother waved from the window.

The driver climbed down from his perch, opened the door, and pulled down the step. He helped Lenore to the ground.

"Mama!" Dorcas rushed over to her parent and hugged her close. "I'm so glad to see you. I've worried terribly about you. How did you make it through the trip?"

In spite of Lenore's pale face with dark circles under her eyes, she seemed surprisingly sturdy. "I'm terribly tired, but I stood it better than I expected."

Dorcas still held her mother as she kissed Judy and Keith. The driver took their luggage down from the rack on top and tipped his hat before he climbed back up to his seat.

Soon they were all in the wagon and on their way.

"I just can't get over Mama," Judy exclaimed. "She took the journey like a real trouper. It was amazing."

From his perch on the luggage in the wagon bed, Keith added, "She didn't complain at all."

"My goodness, I've made this trip before," Lenore said. "I used to live here. I knew what to expect."

Judy put her arm around her mother to ease the motion of the wagon. "I'll help you right to bed when we get to the house."

On the way, Dorcas asked about her grandfather. "He's awfully down in the mouth," Judy answered.

"And crabby as an old bear. I'm glad to get away for the summer," her brother added.

"I haven't seen much of him, thank goodness. I have my dinner upstairs," Lenore said, sighing with weariness.

Only Dorcas had any sympathy for her grandfather. He was probably worried sick. Thank goodness she'd been able to ship another gold brick just the day before. That made three. He'd soon get the check from the mint and perhaps that would cheer him. He must be glad to have the mansion to himself for a while. The confusion of having all of them there must have been hard on him.

The last time she'd seen her grandfather, he had reminded her that he must make a payment of $125,000 on the first of October. That meant she would have to ship at least ten more bars before that time. Now that they were in full operation, of course they could do it. Things were going smoothly with Red in charge. Still, a nagging sense of foreboding bothered her. She tried not to think of her mother's money, which had to be repaid, as well as buying back her jewels.

When they arrived at the house, her family all seemed pleased with the living arrangements. Even Keith remarked, "Gosh, this is just like camping out. I'll be able to watch the stars at night."

While the others put their things away, Dorcas helped her mother undress and get into bed.

"I'm too tired to eat right now," Lenore said.

"Just rest, Mama. Before I go to bed, I'll bring you some chicken soup and a piece of toast."

"That will be fine."

"I'm proud of you, Mother. You did so well."

But her mother was already dozing off. Dorcas closed the door as she tiptoed out of the room.

When she, Judy, and Keith sat down at the table, Esther brought in a big platter of boiled beef, potatoes, and vegetables.

While they ate, Judy said, "I can't understand it. The minute we started out on the trip, Mama perked up. It was as if she hadn't been sick at all."

Esther put in, "I've heard of that before with people who suffer from depression. A real change will snap them out of it for a while."

Dorcas helped herself to some more beef. "Well, let's hope it lasts for the summer."

Judy added, "It's all so mysterious. Remember how upset she was when you first said you were coming up here? But as you kept writing about seeing her old friends, she began to get over it. It's so hard to figure out."

Within a few days, Lenore was rested from her trip and began to take short walks in the woods close to the mine grounds. Judy always went with her. Sometimes Judy would take her sketch pad and pencils and would draw while her mother watched. The fresh air and exercise brought color to the older woman's cheeks; she looked better than she had in years.

One evening Dorcas suggested, "Why don't you come to church with us on Sunday, Mother? So many of your old friends would like to see you."

But Lenore's face paled and her eyes looked haunted; she shook her head. "No. You mustn't ask me to do that."

Judy frowned. "Don't press her, Dorcas. Wait until she asks to go. I think all those people would remind her too much of Papa."

"That's right." Lenore twisted her fingers together. "Tell anyone who inquires that I am still in mourning."

But Dorcas suspected it was more than that. "Of course, Mother, whatever you want to do. I'm sorry I suggested it. What if someone asks to call?"

"If anyone drives clear out here, I'll receive them, of course."

Two of Lenore's friends soon came to call, but as soon as they'd left, she went to her room to lie down. She ate very little dinner that night. While they sat at the table, Dorcas watched her mother closely and decided that something very deep-seated bothered her. Something that might even have been the cause of her depressive spells all these years. But what could it be?

When they were in bed in the sun room that night, Dorcas said, "I have the feeling that Mother is holding some terrible secret deep inside her."

"Oh, Dori, you're letting your imagination run away with you," Judy said sleepily. "The doctor told me that Mama had a high-strung, nervous disposition and was having a particularly hard time going through her forties."

"But she wasn't in her forties way back when we first moved from here to Colorado. That's when it started."

Dorcas turned on her side and looked at her sister, barely discernible in the faint moonlight. A wave of affection came over her. "Judy, I want to tell you again that I think you've been wonderful with Mother. Lots of times I've thought you were a spoiled brat, but when it comes to helping Mama, you've been great."

"I do seem to be the only one who understands her."

"I admit I don't." How hard it was to be patient. Sometimes she wanted to grab her mother and give her a good shaking. There was no sense in Lenore's giving way to her moods like this. She ought to put aside whatever was bothering her. A little common sense would solve a lot of her problems.

"You've been a good sport about coming up here, too," Dorcas went on. "There isn't much entertainment here, especially after San Francisco."

"Well, the social season there is over, and everyone is going to his summer home. I didn't mind leaving. Besides, I hope to see something of Philip and Andy here. They're as attractive as anyone I ever met in the city. Do you think we could invite them over sometime?"

"What about Mother? Would that upset her?"

"I'll ask her tomorrow when we go for a walk. I was planning on taking her with me to do some sketching."

"At least you can get on with your art work up here."

"I'll do some. To be perfectly frank, I'm glad to get away from Courtland Burke. He's such a slave driver and can be so horrid. He started me on oils, painting his niece. Everything I did was wrong. 'Scrape it off and do it over.' That's all he could say. 'Scrape it off and try it again.' "

"Did you ever finish the painting?" Dorcas asked.

"Yes, after working on it for weeks and weeks. I've never tried to please anyone so hard in all my life. But when I got it done, he never gave me one bit of praise. I hate him."

"What do Mama and Keith think of it?"

"They never saw it. Courtland Burke kept it. He wanted to

get it evaluated, whatever that means. I think he's just awful.''

Dorcas laughed. ''He's probably the first person in your life who's ever made you get in and really work hard at something. You've always gotten by with minimum effort.''

Judy giggled. ''So, besides being a spoiled brat, I'm lazy, too.''

''That's right.'' Dorcas threw a pillow at her. ''Will you continue with your art lessons when you go home?''

''I suppose so. Courtland is a good teacher and practically never takes a private pupil. I don't know why he took me.''

''Probably for the same reason that men rush to help you out of a carriage or open a door for you.'' Dorcas slumped back in her bed. ''We'd better go to sleep. Good night, Sis. I'm so glad you're here.''

''So am I.''

But Judy couldn't fall asleep. She lay in her bed thinking about Courtland Burke and all the agony she'd gone through trying to get that darn painting done. There was something about the whole experience that haunted her. How her teacher had probed at her. ''What are you thinking? What are you feeling? Put yourself into this portrait.''

That was the trouble. She could see herself in that beautiful, crippled child. They really looked a lot alike. What if she were lame? She could never dance or run or even walk without a crutch. Just imagining herself in that condition was an agonizing experience.

Finally, she had begun to paint. She portrayed Rosemary curled up in her chair holding her doll. Her crutch leaned against the side of the chair. Then she painted a window. There was a cyclamen plant, white, as perfect in its beauty as the child, sitting on the sill. Outside on the street were five children. Two were turning a rope while a little girl just Rosemary's age was jumping. Two other girls waited their turn. It was all she could do to keep back the tears while she worked. There was always a great lump in her throat, and she could hardly swallow. More than once she had caught Courtland staring at her with a strange expression on his face. She was glad to be away from him. She didn't like feeling so exposed, with all the emotions deep inside her being brought to the surface.

*   *   *

It was with some misgiving that Dorcas invited Andy and Philip for dinner after her mother agreed to having them. She would have to be very careful around her lover. She didn't want her family to guess what had gone on that day in the cabin. Her cheeks burned with shame every time she thought about it. But why should she feel so guilty when they belonged together? When they were true mates? No doubt Philip intended to discuss his plans to marry her with her mother before he asked her. Wouldn't that be the thoughtful thing to do in light of all the trouble that had gone between the two families? But oh, how she longed for his proposal. She wanted to know that the rest of her life she would be with him.

The dinner party was scheduled for the following Saturday. That morning she washed and dried her hair and brushed it while sitting outside in the sun. Just the thought of seeing Philip again brought color to her face. Lenore had agreed to eat dinner with them, so Judy helped her mother bathe and dress. When Keith came in after a day underground with the miners, he had to take a shower and dress quickly to be ready in time.

Dorcas set the dining-room table for seven, grateful that she had brought some of her mother's good linen, as well as silverware and dishes. She placed a bouquet of wild azalea blossoms in the center, keeping it low enough so the diners could see over it. She hoped her simple voile dress, in a soft lavender with little sprigs of flowers over it, was becoming. Behind her pompadour, she had pinned a big lavender bow.

When she saw the two men walking across the path, she called to Judy, "Here they are."

Dorcas ran outside to meet them. Philip took her hand and squeezed it. "I've been looking forward to this all day." As he smiled at her, the blood raced through her veins.

Andy handed her a life-size carved bird. "It's a Townsend warbler."

"Oh, it's so lovely." She examined the exquisite carving with its head carefully painted in a bold black and yellow pattern. The wings and back were a shaded gray and the underbelly, yellow. "It looks so real." She caressed it gently. "Thank you so much."

"I've always been a bird watcher. Sort of a hobby of mine.

I study them and try to whittle and paint them as exactly as I can,'' Andy said.

''He's got quite a collection. And you ought to hear him imitate their calls,'' Philip spoke up.

''Later you'll have to entertain us.'' Dorcas took them each by the arm and led them into the house.

After they had all greeted one another, she said, ''Just sit down here in the living room while I help Esther finish dinner.''

Andy felt disgusted as he watched his boss. Philip sat on a love seat with Judy, unable to take his eyes off of her. Oh, the girl was a beauty, all right. A vision in a pink silk dress, with lace ruche framing her face. They were flirting with each other, which made Andy want to get up and give his friend a good punch in the nose. How could Philip behave like this when he must know that Dorcas was deeply in love with him? Anyone could tell that. It showed every time she looked at him. Her big brown eyes revealed her feelings all too well. Her voice softened when she spoke to him and her cheeks turned a lovely pink. She was besotted with the man, and he wasn't worthy of her.

A dull ache gathered around Andy's heart. Why did everyone have to care for the wrong person? If only Dorcas felt this way about him instead of Philip. Each day he worked with her he seemed to fall more deeply in love. But it was no use telling her so. He could never care for anyone else. In his estimation, Dorcas would always stand head and shoulders above any other girl.

Soon dinner was served and they all gathered around the table. After Lenore said grace, Esther carved the roast lamb and served it with new potatoes and parsley. There were tiny carrots, fresh peas, and coleslaw. For dessert, she had baked a big chocolate cake.

Later, when they sat in the living room, Dorcas asked Andy, ''Won't you give us some bird calls?'' She tried not to look at Philip, sitting on the sofa with Judy and obviously quite enchanted with her. Jealousy and heartache caused a tumult in her. She asked herself over and over, How could he do this to her? How could he, after their afternoon at the cabin?

She turned her attention to Andy, who was saying, "This is a grosbeak. Its warbling resembles the robin or western tanager but is more vigorous." When he finished that call, he turned his face up and whistled *"Wheee-ur-r-r.* That's a poor baby asking for food." He looked so funny they all had to laugh.

When he finished his recital they clapped, for he was amazingly skilled. What a darling he is, Dorcas told herself. She was especially grateful to him when they began to play cards later on. Andy made sure that he was the one sitting next to Judy, not Philip.

To forget her anger and hurt over Philip, Dorcas threw herself into her work at the mine. She didn't blame Judy, because flirting was as natural to her as breathing. Besides, her sister had no way of knowing about the fishing trips and the intimacy at the cabin.

But Philip did. She had confided in him, told him of her love for him. Her cheeks burned in mortification, not only for being wanton but for telling him her inner feelings, which she should have kept to herself. Surely the time would come when he would say he loved her as well. Oh, if they could only get off by themselves and go on their rides again, but she knew her mother wouldn't approve of any unchaperoned meetings. And it hurt that Philip had made no attempt to see her alone. It was as if she really didn't matter all that much to him.

By the end of the month, she was able to ship another gold brick, which now made four. She still had nine to go. The old stockpile was shrinking and the new one beginning to build up. All day long the stamp mill thudded and roared. But she was spending some of the free gold, rather than keeping it all for bars. It took a lot of money to pay her grocery bill at the general store. And there were always other supplies to buy.

But she must get nine more bars shipped off as soon as possible. Then her mother had to be repaid, plus her jewelry redeemed. It all loomed as an impossible task, but somehow she would have to do it.

At least her crew was working out well. Red was a conscientious manager who got the best from his men. He had also taken Keith under his wing. The two of them examined every tunnel in the mine. Now her brother was more determined than ever to make mining his lifetime career.

Everyone in Alpine Heights looked forward to the Fourth of July. The whole town planned to take part. But when Lenore heard about it, she demurred. "I don't feel up to it, Dorcas. Don't ask me to go. I'll stay home by myself."

Esther smiled and said, "You young people go. It sounds mighty strenuous to me, too. I'd rather be here with Mrs. Hamilton."

Dorcas suspected that Esther would really like to go, or at least attend the barbecue in the late afternoon and watch the fireworks, but when they spoke privately, her assistant said, "Miss Dorcas, you've been so good to me that I'm determined to help you as much as I can. I know you wouldn't leave your mother alone all day, so I'm going to stay with her. I don't want to hear another word about it."

Keith drove them into town and they found a place on the wooden sidewalk to watch the parade. Both Philip and Andy were to march in the volunteer fire squadron, but they planned to meet afterward. When the parade finally came by, it was surprisingly long for such a small town.

The band, various church groups, the Odd Fellows Lodge, schoolchildren carrying flags, and firemen marching alongside a splendid new engine were cheered as they passed.

As soon as the parade was over, the men joined Dorcas and Judy. When Philip took her elbow and led the way to the Methodist church where the ladies were serving lunch, Dorcas was ready to forgive him anything. It was enough to be near him, to match her stride to his, to feel the pressure of his hand. In his red fireman's shirt, he seemed more virile and masculine than ever.

Excitement pulsed through her. How attentive he was all afternoon. Then he insisted on treating them to the evening barbecue set up in a vacant lot. After dark they watched the fireworks and then went to the square dance held in Richmond Hall, which had been built some years ago by Philip's company.

Dorcas had a wonderful time, even more so than if she had been attending an elaborate ball in San Francisco. All the time they whirled together or locked elbows, she imagined what fun they would have here after they were married. Surely Philip would propose soon. He knew how deeply she loved him. Of course he cared for her as well.

Later, though, when she noticed that both Judy and Philip were missing, her suspicions were aroused. She tried to dismiss the feeling but couldn't.

Andy brought her a glass of cider and looked around. "Where are the others?"

"I suppose they went outside for a breath of fresh air."

"It's hot in here. Let's go out and find them," he suggested.

They walked outside and joined a group of dancers, but Judy and Philip weren't among them.

Slowly, Philip caressed Judy's back as he held her in his arms. They stood together in the dark shelter of a fir tree at the back of the hall. He kissed the hollows of her throat again and murmured, "You're so beautiful. So incredibly lovely."

As his lips crushed hers, excitement and desire for this exquisite creature throbbed through him. Judy was his kind of girl. Flirtatious, adorable, and frivolous. It was fun to be around her, for she expected no commitments, nor did she make him feel guilty. Not like Dorcas, who took him entirely too seriously, as if he had some duty toward her. After all, they weren't married or even engaged. He pushed any thoughts of Dorcas to the back of his mind as he kissed Judy again.

Soon the fiddlers started playing a lively piece and the caller cried, "Form a circle. Ladies on the inside, gents on the outside."

Andy took Dorcas's elbow and started to lead her back into the hall. "No, I want to find them." She twisted away from him.

"Better leave them alone." But Dorcas started around to the back of the hall, so Andy followed.

When Dorcas discovered Philip and her sister in their tight embrace, kissing each other feverishly, she gasped and cried, "How dare you!"

Judy whirled around. "Sis!" She ducked out of Philip's arms and ran back to the dance.

Philip grabbed Dorcas's wrist. "Look, I can explain!"

"Don't bother!" She yanked her arm away. "What a despicable man you are! I don't care if I never see you again." She turned to Andy. "Would you please take me home? Right now?"

"Of course, Dorcas." Andy put his arm across her shoulders and led her to his buggy. "I'm so sorry you saw that. I had a hunch we'd find them like that."

"I hate them both! How could they do this to me?"

Andy didn't answer but helped her into the buggy and drove toward the mine. When he came to a lane, he pulled off the main road and stopped.

"You don't want to go home just yet and have to make a lot of explanations to your mother and Esther," he said gently. He took her in his arms. "Go ahead and cry. Get him out of your system."

Dorcas leaned against him. Sobs shook through her. Finally, she said, "I can't get him out of my system. I've loved him for years."

"But how could you, when you were gone from here for so long?"

She told him how she had felt when she was only fourteen. "I've been in love with him all this time. I want to marry him. Oh, Andy, what am I going to do?"

"Just be patient, I guess." But Andy doubted that Philip would ever marry her.

"What hurts most is that I'm not as important to him as he is to me."

Andy caressed her and tried to comfort her. "Darling, some things just aren't to be, and we have to accept that fact." He kissed the top of her head. "I think I fell in love with you the first day we were together at the midwinter fair. I'd give anything on earth to marry you, but I won't ask you, because I know how you feel about Philip." If he could only wring that man's neck.

She started to cry again. "I'm so sorry, Andy. So terribly sorry. It breaks my heart to think you're suffering like I am. And that I'm the cause of it." She lay back against his shoulder, the sobs still shuddering through her. "Philip knows how I feel, and look what he's doing."

He held her closer. "You've got to understand Philip and take him as he is. He's always had women swooning around him. His kissing Judy doesn't mean anything."

"I can hardly believe that."

"Oh, Dorcas, she's just another pretty girl to amuse him for the moment. Just as he's a man for Judy to flirt with. Don't take it too seriously. They don't."

"I have to take it seriously," Dorcas protested. Hadn't she given herself to him? She started to cry again. "You don't understand."

But he did, only too well. His heart ached. Finally he asked, "Tell me the truth, Dorcas. I won't pass judgment. But has Philip made love to you?"

She didn't answer, but she burst into a fresh torrent of sobs, so he knew for certain it was true. He closed his fist as rage pulsed through him. He'd like to beat his boss to a pulp. Kill him!

"Are you in the family way, darling?" he asked softly.

"No. But I feel so guilty. I did wrong, and I want to marry him so I won't seem so wanton. Besides, I love him."

"I know you do. And anyone who cares for him as sincerely as you do could never be wanton." He kissed the top of her head again.

"Promise me you won't tell anyone. Ever."

"Of course I won't."

"It hurts me that Judy could be so disloyal." Dorcas's anger at her sister welled up in her. The spoiled little brat. All she was interested in was having a good time. Never mind how someone else suffered.

"Oh, Dorcas. She didn't consider whether she was being loyal to you or not. Making conquests is a game to her. Don't take this so to heart."

A long sigh passed through her. "Darling Andy, you're so understanding."

"I want to help you all I can."

"What a good friend you are. Telling you my troubles makes me feel better."

"I'll always be there when you need me, so turn to me, dearest girl. I don't think Philip is worth a hair on your head, but if he's what you want, I hope he does ask you to be his wife." Andy caressed her shoulders. "Just give him time. He's got sense enough to recognize a jewel when he sees one. He'll come around."

"I hope so." She sat up and wiped her eyes. Andy took out his watch and struck a match to see the time. "Look,

Dorcas, it's eleven-thirty. Surely the women are asleep by now, so I'll take you home. You can slip in through the back and get into bed without waking them. The dance will be over by midnight, and Keith will be bringing Judy home.''

"Yes, take me home. I don't want to talk to my sister tonight.''

All the way back to town, anger boiled in Andy. He'd kill Philip for seducing his beloved. He'd get revenge. Kill Philip dead! That's what that lowdown skunk deserved. Andy had his rifle with him in the compartment under the seat. Good thing he always carried it with him. A man never knew when he'd need it in this country.

Philip would be walking home from the dance. He'd be a perfect target when he passed under the gaslight at Center Street. When Andy neared the light he turned the buggy into a sidestreet and parked in a dark spot where he couldn't be seen but had a good view of the corner. He reached down, pulled the rifle out, and took off the safety catch.

Insane with rage, he waited until he heard footsteps. He raised the rifle and sighted the pool of light shining on the dirt. Philip walked across the street.

But what would this do to Dorcas? Wouldn't it compromise her honor when his motive came out? Mark her for life?

When Philip stepped into the light, Andy lowered the gun without pulling the trigger.

"Oh, my God!" Andy whispered aloud, shocked at what he had almost done. As cold sweat broke out on his brow, he slumped down limply against the seat.

CHAPTER 11

A few days later, Keith and Dorcas walked over to the mine. "Gee, Sis, this has been a great experience. I know I'll get a lot more out of college having had this chance to see how a mine really works. Papa seldom let me go underground with him."

"I don't like your going down so much, either. Actually there's far more to mining than that. You ought to spend more time in the stamp mill. Harry could teach you a lot about it. I think you ought to be under his wing for a while. I'll speak to Red about it."

"Not today, Sis. Red has something he wants to show me. Some special method we're not using anymore. It's in tunnel nineteen, near the Richmond property."

"But we're not working there."

"I know. But if we ever have a chance at the Andromeda Lode, it would be there."

She ruffled his hair and smiled. "If you find it, maybe Grandpa will split it with you."

"Okay, Sis." He grinned. "I promise I'll spend more time in the stamp mill beginning tomorrow."

"Remember to take your lunch pail down with you," Dorcas called after him.

She unlocked the office and began a long-overdue report to her grandfather. The morning flew by. Just before it was time for the lunch break, she heard the cables whirring and whining on the skip. Why were the men coming above ground so soon?

One of her foremen burst through the door. His face ashen, he cried, "Miss Hamilton, I hate to tell you, but we've had a cave-in."

"Oh, dear God, no! Where?"

"Not where the crews are working. It's in tunnel nineteen—"

Dorcas screamed. "Keith! He was going there!"

"I know, ma'am. That's why it's so awful."

"I'll blow the emergency whistle." She rushed out and pulled the cord three times and waited, then pulled again. It was a sound the whole crew dreaded.

Almost in a trance, she waited until the men came running out of the stamp mill. She told them what had happened. "Al Harris will show you where to go. Be sure to take shovels. Walt, you saddle the horse and go get help from the Golden Star. Tell Mr. Woodard to come right away."

As she ran toward the house, she whimpered aloud, "How can I tell Mother?" She prayed, Dear God, don't let anything happen to Keith and Red.

In the midst of her heart-wrenching terror, she couldn't grasp the enormity of what had happened. It seemed unreal. But it was all her fault. She should have forbidden Keith to go underground. Why had she ever taken that chance? Sobs tore through her by the time she reached the house.

Esther came running out. "What is it? I heard the whistle."

Dorcas told her. "Where are Mother and Judy?"

"They've gone for a walk." Esther wrung her hands. "I'll try to find them."

But they saw Judy and Lenore emerge from the woods and hurry toward them. Her sister called, "We heard the blast. Is something wrong?"

Dorcas ran toward them. "Oh, Mama, there's been a cave-in. Keith—"

The color drained slowly from Lenore's face. Before Dorcas could finish speaking, her mother slumped to the ground. Her daughters dropped down beside her. Judy gasped, "What about Keith?"

"We don't know. Only that there's been a cave-in. Apparently only Keith and Red were in tunnel nineteen." Tears streamed down Dorcas's face.

Esther ran to them. "You get back to the office, Miss Dorcas. I'll help with your mother."

Dorcas rose to her feet. "I'll let you know the moment I hear anything. But you're right. I must get back. I sent word to the Golden Star for help."

She could hardly see through her tears as she staggered back to the mine office. Keith, her adored brother. It was too terrible to bear the thought of him trapped behind a wall of earth.

When Andy came, he held her close while she sobbed. "Dorcas, keep up your courage. We'll find them. Chances are, they're safe. Philip is getting his crew together to help with the rescue." He kissed her cheek and wiped the tears from her eyes. "You'd better go to the house and tell Esther to start making sandwiches and coffee. This could take come time."

Numbly she watched Andy gather the available men and go underground. She shook with fear as she ran back to the house.

Esther met her at the door. "We've put Mrs. Hamilton to bed. Miss Judy's given her a sedative, but she's still hysterical. I wouldn't go in to see her just yet."

"I suppose she blames me."

"I'm afraid she does. Says she was opposed to reopening this mine right from the first."

Dorcas recalled her mother's words: *"It's an evil place. It will destroy us all."* She tried to pull herself together. "Andy says you'd better start making sandwiches and coffee. This could take a long time."

As she walked back to the office once more, all the anguish of their long vigil in Colorado came back. The men had dug out the cave-in for days, only to find that it was too late. Her father and three others trapped there were dead. She moaned aloud. That mustn't happen here.

Soon Philip drove up with a wagonload of men carrying shovels and holding wheelbarrows upright. Dorcas ran out to meet them. By this time she was beyond tears.

Philip climbed out of the driver's seat. "Dorcas, I'm terribly sorry. It doesn't seem possible that this tragedy could happen to you again."

She glared at him. "Please leave your men, but I don't want you here."

"Don't act like a damn fool. You need all the help you can get, and I'm here to take charge of the rescue operation." He pointed to the five men climbing out of the wagon. "I'm going to set up teams. These men and yours already underground will work until four and then they'll come up for a break. More of mine will arrive and take over until eight. Then we'll send the first group down again."

Reluctantly, she had to admit that he was right. Of course

it would take an experienced mining man to handle this emergency.

"Won't we need a lot more men?" she asked.

"There's only room for just so many. It's better to keep our teams small enough so they can work without getting in one another's way. Trust me. I've done this many times before." Philip led the way to the skip.

"I'll send down coffee and sandwiches."

"All right. Now, chin up. We'll find them."

"I pray it won't be too late." She turned and ran back to the house. Judy came out to meet her. "Mama's still in hysterics. I can't do anything with her. The sedative doesn't seem to have taken effect yet."

"I'm going to her room."

"No, Dorcas, don't! She blames you."

"I know. But if she lashes out at me, she might get rid of some of her terror and be able to relax."

Dorcas ran through the house, opened the door to her mother's room, and dropped down beside her bed. "Mama, it's Dorcas. I came to tell you that Philip is down in the mine with a crew. He's going to do everything possible—"

Lenore turned to her, her eyes wild, her face haggard. "It's your fault! Every bit of it!"

"I blame myself, too."

"You should never have come back here or reopened this mine. Didn't I tell you that it was an evil place?"

"Mama, try to calm yourself."

But Lenore pounded Dorcas's back with her fist and screamed, "It's your fault. Damn you! You should never have let him go underground."

"I know, Mama. I should have kept Keith in the stamp mill."

"It's too dangerous in those horrible tunnels. Rocks could fall on him. Another man could accidentally hit him with a sledgehammer."

Lenore's blows fell on Dorcas's shoulders. "You're right," she agreed. "You warned me right from the start. But try to get yourself under control. You'll just exhaust yourself, Mother."

But her mother shouted, "I'll never forgive you as long as I live. I'd like to kill myself and you, too. First my husband and then my son!"

"Mother, you mustn't give up hope so soon. The men have just started to clear the debris away. Philip was telling me—"

"He can't do anything."

"But he will. He's got the men organized. They're working as hard as they can." Dorcas thought of Philip taking charge. Gone was her heartache over seeing him with her sister in his arms. She'd forgive him anything if he brought out Keith and Red alive. Just the thought of her adored brother brought fresh tears to her eyes. Despair twisted her heart.

By now her mother's sleeve was torn from her flailing. "Mama, I insist that you get out of your clothes and into a nightgown. You'd better go right to bed for the rest of the day."

Lenore started to twist hysterically back and forth again. Dorcas grabbed her by the shoulders and shook her. "Mother, that's enough! I told you to calm down!"

Surprisingly, Lenore did get herself under control and climbed off the bed. Dorcas went to the closet and took a lace-trimmed rose gown off of the hook and helped her mother out of her clothes. She straightened the bed and folded down the covers. Soon she had the exhausted woman back in bed. "You're to rest, Mama. We have a long, hard day ahead."

When she went out into the kitchen, she found Esther and Judy making sandwiches.

Judy looked up. "How is she?"

"I think she'll doze off."

"I heard her carrying on."

"She pounded me on the back until I'll be black and blue. But I didn't stop her. I wanted her to give vent to her feelings. Otherwise she'll slump back into that withdrawn state that makes her so hard to deal with."

"I can understand how she feels," Esther said.

Dorcas nodded. "It brings back all the agony that we went through when Father was trapped. We can only pray that this turns out better."

"Your sandwiches are ready. I put the coffee in big thermos bottles," Esther told her.

They packed the sandwiches and thermos bottles in an apple box.

"I'll go to the cookhouse and get tin cups," Dorcas said.

"Do you want any help?" Judy asked, her eyes brimming with tears again.

"No, you'd better sit by Mama in case she's still awake. If

she wants to talk, let her. She must get her feelings out. If she cries, that's all right, too. But try not to let her get hysterical again.'' She gave Judy a quick hug. At least this terrible crisis had brought them back together again.

Sing Lee saw Dorcas coming and opened the screen door to the cookhouse. He bobbed his head up and down as he tried to tell her how sorry he felt. ''Keith a good boy.''

''The men are doing their best to rescue him and Red.'' It was hard to talk through her thickened throat. ''It's up to us to provide them with feed to keep them going.''

''Yes, missy.''

She told him about the arrangements Philip had made. ''You be ready with a good hot meal when they change shifts at four and at eight.''

He nodded. ''Will do.''

The next hour dragged by. Dorcas paced the office nervously. She couldn't settle down to finish the report. In fact, she couldn't do anything but move restlessly around the office or go outside to walk to the mine entrance and back. Just before four o'clock, twenty-five men came from the Golden Star, ready to take the place of those who had been working so hard.

One of the new men came to her with his cap in his hand. ''We want to tell you, ma'am, that we hope for the best. We're so sorry about this.''

''Thank you. I appreciate your sympathy and all your help. We'll have a hot meal ready for you at eight.''

It wasn't long before a weary, hungry crew came through the entrance and headed for the cookhouse. While Philip gave instructions to the new group, Andy walked over to Dorcas.

''I want to study the maps before I go to eat.''

''How's it going?'' she asked nervously.

''We're working as fast as we can. Philip has it very well organized. We're not trying to bring the debris to the surface, but instead we're piling it in the other tunnels. We're using the ore cars as well as wheel barrows.'' He entered the office and pulled down the map showing tunnel 19.

Dorcas saw Philip climbing up onto his wagon, so she ran outside to speak to him. ''Aren't you going to eat? You must be starved.''

''No, I had a couple of sandwiches, so I'm all right. Tell Andy I'm going into town now. I have a special tool at home

I want to bring back.'' He leaned over and took her hand and pressed it to his lips. ''Don't lose hope. We'll get through that mess sooner or later.''

Dorcas walked slowly back to the office.

Andy studied the map a long time and made some notes on a piece of paper. ''I'll eat now and then I'll walk back to the Golden Star. There's something I want to check,'' he said.

''Why don't you use my horse and buggy and save your strength?''

''Thanks, I will.'' He put his arms around her and held her to him. ''I'd give anything on earth if I could spare you this agony.''

She leaned against him and started to cry. ''I'm so terribly afraid. I keep thinking of Keith down there, crushed under all that earth.''

''Men can very often hear the timbers crack as they begin to break, so they get out of the way. If the timbers fall right, they act as a lean-to and create a space where the men can wait.''

''But they can run out of air, and then—''

''I know, dearest girl. We'll get to them before that.''

She moved away from him. ''I'll go hitch up the buggy while you eat, Andy. That'll give me something to do.''

Later, when she'd brought the horse and buggy back to the office, Andy came in with a plate full of beef stew and a big piece of bread. ''I was sure you hadn't eaten all day.''

''But I'm not a bit hungry.''

''Better have something while you can. You have a long vigil ahead.''

Back at the Golden Star, Andy pulled down map after map. Finally he stopped and studied one carefully. He took out his notes and read them over again. There was one tunnel that had been abandoned years ago, long before he had come to work for the Richmond Mining Company. It must go fairly close to tunnel 19, as the two properties were adjacent to each other. Couldn't they get another crew working from the Richmond side? At least they might be able to drill a hole through to the Alpine tunnel so they could get an airhose in to the captive men. He'd read of other cases where rescuers had dug down to the trapped men from a neighboring mine. But first he'd better go down and look the situation over. Perhaps the old Richmond tunnel, number 10, would be in such bad shape they wouldn't be able to get in there to work.

He found a lantern in the shaft house and went below. He walked through the dark cavern with the lantern light flickering eerily on the walls. Water dripped down steadily from the top of the tunnel. It smelled dank and dead. When he came to the end, he found that it had been completely sealed. Why? Was it unsafe beyond? He wanted to break the barrier down, but he had no tools. There was nothing to do but get back to the surface again.

When he returned to the Alpine, he found Dorcas and Judy talking with Philip. After the girls left to go over to the house to make lemonade for the men below, Andy turned to his boss. "Come on into the office. I want to show you something."

After he pulled down the map, he went on, "The men are trapped someplace between here and here." His finger traced along a line. "Our tunnel ten must end pretty close by. Of course, it's above. But we could dig a slanting shaft down to them, I should think."

"That tunnel's sealed off. My uncle closed it years ago."

"Dammit, I know it's closed off. But it can be opened!"

"I wouldn't want to do it without his permission."

Andy's temper flared. He grabbed Philip by the shirtfront. "This is a rescue operation! We don't have to get anyone's permission. Lives are at stake. Don't you understand that?"

"Of course I do, but—"

"I'm going to get a sledgehammer and go down there and bust through." Andy put his nose close to Philip's. "And neither you nor your uncle is going to stop me!"

Philip twisted himself away. He yanked his shirt down. "Keep your hands off me. I'm not going to have any part of it!"

"You yellow-livered coward."

"You can be the one to answer to Elliott Richmond. I'm not going to be."

"I'm not afraid to tell that son-of-a-bitch that it was more important to rescue two trapped men than it was to comply with his orders." Andy's face reddened in fury.

"If you're smart you'll leave tunnel ten alone. There must be some reason for its being sealed. It hasn't been worked for years. It was closed long before I came here."

"I'm not going to leave it alone!" Andy shouted.

Philip stepped closer. "As your boss—"

"To hell with you! I'm going to break through whether you like it or not."

Angrily, Philip whirled around. He slammed the door as he walked out of the office.

With a big sledgehammer, Andy banged away at the wooden barrier at the end of tunnel 10. He kept hitting against something unyielding behind the wood. When he broke away part of the obstruction, he could see padlocked steel doors.

"What in hell?" he cried aloud.

Why erect steel doors and then build a wooden wall in front of it? It didn't make sense at all. He hit the sledgehammer against the steel, but it didn't yield at all. There was nothing to do now but go to the nearest underground magazine and get dynamite and a fuse. He might have to go to the surface and get a drill. This job could take hours, but he was going to break through at all costs. For a moment he considered getting some men to help him, but that might not be wise. What if Mr. Richmond did get riled up? It might mean that others would lose their jobs, and he didn't want that to happen.

The endless hours dragged by. Dorcas and Esther helped Sing Lee set the table in the cookhouse for the shift that would be coming to the surface at eight o'clock. There were more sandwiches to be made for those who would be going below. Fortunately, both Esther and the Chinese cook had baked bread the day before.

When the men came to the surface, it would be for only a short respite. There was no way of knowing how long it might take to remove all the debris. How frustrating and frightening it was to wait and wait.

All they could do was pray. But the longer they had to wait, the less likely that the men would be alive when they were found.

Philip was Dorcas's source of strength. Whenever she saw him, he gave her a report. "We're trying to get a small opening in to them, first. As soon as we make contact, we'll force an air hose in. Then we'll dig a bigger aperture to bring them out.''

''What about Andy?''

''He's trying to reach Keith and Red from one of our tunnels at the Golden Star. I don't hold out much hope of his getting in that way, but he insisted on trying.''

''We're so fortunate to have you two to help us. I'll never forget this as long as I live. Thank God I had you.''

All the love she had ever felt for Philip came rushing back. No one could be more wonderful and caring than he had been. He'd worked all day directing the crews to make the most of their efforts.

She filled his coffee cup. ''Tell me exactly how the rescue operation works. It will give me something to tell my mother.''

As he sipped his coffee, he explained, ''One gang shovels the dirt into wheelbarrows and ore cars. Another pushes them into auxiliary tunnels and brings back empties. The third group unloads the filled containers. The trick is to get the debris far enough away so that you have room to work. It's going smoothly, without any bottlenecks. The men are working their hearts out.''

''I suppose they're thinking, There but for the grace of God—''

''That's right. They'd want someone else to do the same for them.''

Her chin quivered. ''I don't dare let myself think of what you'll find.''

He patted her arm reassuringly. ''We're going to find them alive.''

''I hope and pray so.''

''I'll be here all night. My manager has been told to send men here from every shift.''

''You work all three shifts, then.''

''Only in the summer.''

She leaned her head back into the hollow of his shoulder. ''What if I didn't have you and your men to fall back on? The rescue operation would have been too much for my small crew.''

He kissed her and gave her a final hug. ''I'm going underground again.''

When Dorcas returned to the house, she told Judy and Esther that she would sit with her mother awhile.

"Then we'll go to the office and wait for any word," Judy decided. "You'll come with me, won't you, Esther?"

"Of course. You don't want to be over there alone."

"And I don't like walking back and forth in the dark." Judy shuddered. "I'm a city girl at heart. I love living in San Francisco." Tears came to her eyes again. "If we can just get Keith out of the mine safely, I hope we'll be leaving. I don't ever want to get near a mine again."

"I don't blame you, dear," Esther murmured sympathetically. "You'd better put on a sweater. It's chilly this evening."

After they left, Dorcas went into her mother's room and sat in a chair beside the bed. A faint glow from the living room barely lit the area.

Lenore stirred and turned in bed. "Judy?"

"No, it's Dorcas. I thought I would stay with you for a while. The others have gone over to the office to wait for news."

Lenore put her hands to her face. "There'll only be bad news." She moaned and turned back and forth. "Tragic news."

"Mother, we mustn't give up hope yet."

"I have no hope at all."

"But the men are working so hard." Dorcas told her how Philip had organized the rescue effort. "There'll be a breakthrough. Probably tonight sometime."

"It's too late. Much too late." Lenore's red, puffy eyes and ash-colored skin added ten years to her ravaged face. The pink satin nightgown with its exquisite lace looked pathetically inappropriate. A sackcloth would have been much more in keeping with her grief.

"Mother, we must keep up our courage. We just can't give in. The search is not over yet. Don't say it's too late, because it isn't."

"Don't argue with me and get that impatient tone in your voice. I've had enough to bear today."

"I'm sorry, Mother. I know you've had a terrible time of it. Were you able to sleep at all?"

"Yes, I think so. I hope I can doze some tonight. God knows what lies ahead." A deep sigh shuddered through Lenore.

Dorcas gripped her mother's hand as pity for her brought

tears to her eyes. "Mama, I'm so sorry you had to go through all this. You were just beginning to feel so much better."

"Keith was such a precious boy. He was never rough and mean like some boys."

"He takes after Papa. And Judy, after you, Mama. I guess I'm the maverick. More like Grandpa." Dorcas studied her mother and thought what little rapport they had.

"Keith is all I have left of your father. I see the likeness growing stronger and stronger all the time. I've always been able to feel your father's presence when I'm around Keith." She turned away and moaned. "I can't bear losing my boy."

"But we haven't lost him yet, Mama."

Lenore gripped Dorcas's hand and stared at the ceiling with the most haunted look in her eyes. "I'm being punished, Dorcas. This is all my fault."

"Your fault?"

"Your father was killed as a punishment, and now my poor Keith is being taken from me as well."

"Mama! What on earth are you talking about?"

"I did wrong." Lenore began to sob again. She thrashed her head back and forth. "I'm being punished."

Horrified, Dorcas stared at her mother. Was she completely mad? "Darling, you're just imagining things."

"No, I'm not. I mean every word."

For a long time Dorcas had felt that her mother carried some terrible burden that was eating away at her very sanity. Some secret that was throwing her into these deep spells of depression. Dorcas knelt beside Lenore and took her hand. "Mama, we're in the house all alone. Tell me what's troubling you so."

"I can't! I can't! You'd never understand."

"But I would, Mother. No matter what you've done, I won't think less of you."

"You don't know how awful—" Lenore's voice died away.

"Please let me help you. Something is troubling you. Share it with me, darling."

"But you'd think I was a wicked, wanton person."

"Mama, no matter what it is, I wouldn't think you were wicked or wanton." Who am I to judge anyone else? Dorcas asked herself. Haven't I been wanton, too?

"You'd despise me."

"No. I'll always love you. Now I want to help you get rid of that worry you've carried for so long."

"I've wanted to tell someone for years. To confess my sins and ask for forgiveness, but it has all stayed bottled up inside of me."

Dorcas placed her mother's hand comfortingly against her own cheek and whispered, "Tell me about it, darling, so you don't have to go on bearing it all by yourself."

Haltingly, Lenore began, "It happened when we lived here in Alpine Heights. Early in the autumn. Right after you children went back to school. I'll always remember that day," her voice faded away as the memories came back.

"Go on, Mama."

"I went riding up the path to the falls. It was quite early in the morning. Your papa had just gone to the mine in the buggy we had at the time. You were getting Keith and Judy ready for school when I left. I knew I was doing wrong to go on that trail, because it entered Richmond land. You know how your father and grandfather felt about that family. There were always hard feelings over the Andromeda Lode. In fact, your father had expressly forbidden me to ever go up to the falls. But I was feeling rebellious that day."

Dorcas quietly caressed her mother's hand and whispered, "Tell me what happened."

"I wasn't the only one on the trail. I ran into Elliott Richmond. If you think Philip is handsome, you should have seen his uncle in those days."

"I remember him."

"He could have been an actor. He was so suave and charming. What a picture he made astride his horse! A big stallion with a coat that shined like copper."

"I can imagine how you felt," Dorcas whispered, thinking of her own feelings for Philip.

"I remember saying, 'Good morning, Mr. Richmond. I hope you don't mind my trespassing on your property.' " A long shudder went through Lenore.

"Go on, Mama."

"He said, 'You're welcome to ride here anytime you want. I'm delighted to see you. I think it's high time our two families buried the hatchet, don't you?' "

"I have to agree with that," Dorcas murmured, her thoughts still on Philip. "Then what happened?"

"We began riding along the path together. How deliciously wicked I felt. I was bored to death here in Alpine Heights. I wanted to live in a city where there were real balls and parties to go to. Shops where one could buy the latest imports from France. I could look ahead only to years of staying in this nothing town, missing out on all the fun and growing old without having lived at all."

"I know." Dorcas patted her arm.

"We didn't really need to live here. Father Hamilton begged your father to join him in the office, and I wanted to go. Then we would have lived in San Francisco." A sob shook Lenore. "Your papa was so displeased with me for nagging him to leave. He was so angry and horrid. Can you imagine how I felt?"

"Of course I can."

"I was ripe for an adventure. For something different. For some excitement." Her voice faltered. "I flirted outrageously with Elliott Richmond. I know Judy would understand. She's so like me, but of course I've never told her."

"That was for the best, Mama." Dorcas couldn't help remembering Judy with Philip at the Fourth of July dance.

"He told me to call him Elliott and said that he'd admired my beauty ever since we had come to take over the mine. Well, we rode to the foot of the falls, and he said he had to get back so he could go to the mine. But we made plans to meet the same time the next day.

"Yes, and every morning that week." Lenore continued after a moment. "Within a few days he had taken me in his arms and kissed me. If only I had stopped right then and told him I mustn't see him again, but I was bewitched by him. All I could think about was Elliott Richmond. I was completely besotted by him. As if I lived in an enchanted world with him. Can you understand how I felt?"

"Yes, Mama, I do," Dorcas said. Oh, how she did! Didn't she feel the same way about Philip?

"We met every day and rode up to the falls. Finally we were clambering up the rocks to the top. He had built a charming log cabin there."

Dorcas cringed inside. She knew so well what was coming. Her own feelings of guilt came surging back.

"The next thing I knew, we had gone inside the cabin and—this is the hard part to tell you—he took me in his arms again and kissed me and then began taking off my riding

166

habit. He caressed and kissed me until I caught on fire. Nothing mattered but that the two of us should make love. I hope you won't condemn me too much. Please understand."

"Mama, I do understand. You thought you were in love with him."

"I was completely obsessed by him. Your father and you children didn't exist. All I wanted was to be with Elliott, to have him hold me, make love to me." She started to sob. Dorcas held her hands, murmuring quiet reassuring words.

"The most terrible part is yet to come," Lenore went on. "We met every weekday morning and went to the cabin. This went on for days. I knew what I was doing was sinful. I was committing adultery. Breaking all of my marriage vows. But I couldn't stop. It was as if a power stronger than me urged me on."

"Then what happened?" Dorcas asked, her voice very low. She knew well that her father, who had been a very astute man, would soon have become suspicious.

"Your father burst into the cabin one morning and caught us in the act. Naked in bed, making love. You can't imagine the look of wrath and hatred on his face. He yanked Elliott off of me. Struck him a terrible blow on the jaw so that my lover was sprawled unconscious on the floor. Then your father turned to me and commanded me to get my clothes on and meet him down at the foot of the falls, where he would be waiting." Lenore started to cry.

Dorcas could imagine the terror that her mother must have felt. When her father was stirred to anger, he'd been as formidable as her grandfather.

"Oh, Mother, what did you do?" she cried out.

"I was beside myself. Almost in a trance I dressed, somehow got myself down the rocks, and faced my husband by the horses. He was in a cold rage. He looked me up and down in utter contempt. 'Lenore, I will never forgive this betrayal. Do you understand? Never! I no longer consider you my wife.' "

Dorcas stared at her mother in horror.

Lenore went on. "He said, 'I don't want any scandal for the children's sake, so we will go on living together.' It was so awful. 'We're going to leave as soon as possible,' he told me."

She put her hands to her face. A sob shook her. Finally she continued, her voice haunted. "He grabbed me by my shoulders and gave me a look that seared me to my very soul. 'You will be punished for this. Every day for the rest of your life you will suffer!' ''

"Oh, no!" Dorcas put her arms around her mother and rocked the sobbing woman back and forth. For the first time, she understood her mother's deep spells of depression. Her near madness. How utterly cruel and unforgiving her father had been. "Oh, I think that was terrible of Father."

"He never forgave me. We were never husband and wife again. We had separate bedrooms." A terrible shudder tore through her. "I was punished all right. As the years went by, I realized how deeply I loved your father and how I had ruined both our lives. He was desperately unhappy. But that wasn't enough punishment. Oh, no, that wasn't enough. He was killed, and it was all due to my terrible sin. I know that. And now Keith." She started to sob. "My dearest son. God is punishing me. I sinned, and now I am paying for it."

"Mama, that's not true at all. You had nothing to do with either cave-in. You were never in Papa's mine. You didn't go underground and set up the conditions to make that tragedy. Get that out of your mind! It wasn't your fault!"

"Do you think so? Can you really forgive me for what I did?"

"Of course I forgive you, Mother. And I'm sure the dear Lord has, too. I only hope He has forgiven my father for condemning you to a living hell all these years."

"Forgive your father?"

"Yes. What he did was far worse than your indiscretion. You've paid a thousand times for your sin. Over and over again. Wasted years of your life. No person has the right to cause that much suffering."

Lenore whispered. "It never occurred to me that your father did wrong, too."

"I only wish you'd told me all this while he was alive. I would have shown him how bitterly cruel he had been. It was terribly wrong of him." She held her mother close and rocked her back and forth. "Now you must put the past behind you. Make a new beginning. You have years ahead of you. You can still find happiness."

"But not if dear Keith—"

"Mother, regardless of what happens to Keith, you must never consider this your fault. You didn't cause it. So don't think you did. Nor did I bring it about, though I do blame myself for letting Keith go underground.''

Neither spoke for a long time, but they held each other tightly. They seemed to understand each other for the first time. Finally, Dorcas kissed her mother.

''Mama, it's nearly twelve o'clock, and the men will be coming to the surface to change shifts. I want to talk to them, so you must lie down and try to rest. Remember, you are not to blame for this cave-in or Papa's death. Put that completely out of your mind.''

''Dorcas, I'll never forget this night. A terrible burden has been lifted off my shoulders. I'm so glad I confessed everything to you. I didn't think you would take it so well.''

''Mother, I'm not one to sit in judgment over you.''

''Promise me you'll never tell anyone about this.''

''Of course I won't. It will always be just between us. Now all I ask is that you put it aside and start living.''

''Perhaps I can, if Keith is rescued,'' Lenore murmured. ''Perhaps I can.''

CHAPTER 12

Andy finally assembled all the tools he needed to break down the tunnel barrier. As he drilled the holes for the explosives, he recalled being told that this was the tunnel where the Andromeda Lode had originally been found. This fabulous lode had been a series of rich quartz veins that had yielded eight hundred to nine hundred dollars a ton. For years they had followed the lode as it petered out and reappeared at different levels. It would disappear and show up again like an illusive Lorelie that beckoned them on and on.

After they finally lost it, the company had hired specialists to find it again, but to no avail. ''It's been exhausted,'' one consultant told them. Now they were fortunate to get a hundred dollars per ton of ore. But even so, the Golden Star was profitable.

When the holes around the frame of the steel door were ready, Andy filled them with the least-powerful dynamite sticks in the magazine. He did not want to disturb the earth any more than necessary and possibly start more cave-ins. Also, he wanted to keep down the poisonous fumes the explosives would cause, as there was no time to let air in. He lit the fuse and ran down the tunnel to get away from the blast.

After the explosion, when the dust had settled, he went back to see if the door had been wrenched free. It still hung crookedly in its frame, but by twisting it at an angle, he was able to slide his pick and shovel to the other side and crawl through. His lantern cast a long beam of light down the black tunnel. Water dripped from above and ran in a rivulet down the center. Fortunately he had remembered to put on rubber boots. He hurried along, expecting to come to the end of the tunnel, but to his surprise it kept going. Surely they must be near the boundary line of the Richmond property.

But on and on he went, slipping in the mud, stumbling over fallen rocks. Fortunately there were no ore-car tracks to make the going even more hazardous. They must have pulled them up before they sealed off the tunnel.

The farther he went, the more puzzled he became. This has to be Hamilton property, he told himself. There's no way it can still be part of the Golden Star. No way at all.

He held his lantern high. It had been mined, all right. Had the Hamiltons and Richmonds had a joint venture at one time? If not, why was this tunnel here? Who had mined it? Was this done years ago before either of the present owners had come here? Slowly a suspicion formed in his head, a completely unthinkable thought. Had Elliott Richmond deliberately followed the rich vein of the Andromeda Lode across the boundary into the Alpine and stolen the gold? Would he take such a risk?

Andy leaned against the wall of the tunnel, trying to grasp the enormity of the implications. He shook his head in astonishment. If this were true, Elliott was a downright crook. No honorable mining man, especially a man of Richmond's stature, would knowingly cross a property line. He might go over a few feet by mistake, perhaps, but not all this distance. How had he gotten by with this chicanery? Perhaps the general manager of the Alpine had been in on the scheme and gotten a cut. It must have happened before Dorcas's father had taken over running the Alpine. Had he suspected something, and was that what had caused the rift between the two families? Andy couldn't prove anything unless he got access to the Richmond records.

"Good lord," Andy shouted. "Think what this could mean to Dorcas! If we can prove what happened, the Hamiltons could still go after their share of the lode."

As he hurried on, Andy determined that he would keep everything to himself until he could gather proof. He must be very careful. He didn't know enough yet to make any accusations. If he acted rashly, he'd get fired, and he must keep his job in order to have access to the old records. Ones that went back twelve to fifteen years, at least, and maybe longer. No, no one must know what he had discovered.

Soon he saw something that jolted him to the very core. He held his lantern high. In the distance, the floor of tunnel 10 had fallen down. Andy caught his breath in shock. That's what had caused the cave-in. The Richmond tunnel must be directly above the Alpine for part of the way. Even if there were several feet between them, any movement in the earth's crust could cause a disaster. The stress of tunnel 19 would be just too much of a load to bear.

When Andy reached the edge of the cave-in, he peered down into the sunken pit. Did he dare climb down there? Would it make it worse? What if Keith and Red were trapped directly below? He held his lantern up but couldn't see the end of the collapsed tunnel. That meant there were tons of earth and debris for the rescuers to remove from the Hamilton side. On the other hand, if the trapped men were at this end of the tunnel, just below him, they could be rescued comparatively easily.

Gingerly, he lowered himself into the pit, hoping that his weight wouldn't cause more shifting of the ground below him. He knew he was taking a terrible risk. He reached up and grabbed his shovel, then the pick, and at last, the lantern on the edge. He braced the light against the wall of the pit. Before he began to shovel, he had to decide where to begin. If he could break an opening through to tunnel 19, by shouting he might be able to get Red or Keith to answer. Just to locate them would be an enormous accomplishment. Even to get air to them might keep them alive until he could get help.

A shiver ran along Andy's spine. He was assuming that they *were* alive.

Finally, he chose the space near the edge of the cave-in that meant the least amount of dirt to be removed. He began to dig. It went slowly. At first it wasn't so bad, but as he got deeper, it became harder and harder to lift each shovelful to the top. He had to make the opening large enough to be able to manipulate the shovel. His arms ached, his back hurt, and the perspiration ran down his face. But he worked and worked.

The hours went by, one after another, until he was so tired he labored like an automaton. Push the shovel in, lift the dirt out. Over and over, until he was near collapse. It seemed endless, and it might all be in vain. He could smell the dank, soggy earth, hear the water dripping from above, and feel every muscle strain. Just as he felt at his lowest possible ebb, ready to give up, his shovel broke through into tunnel 19.

He made a little hole, squatted down the best he could, took a deep breath, and yelled, "Red! Keith! Can you hear me?" His heart almost stopped as he waited for an answer. He called again.

A faint answer came: "Yes."

"This is Andy. Are you both all right?"

"We're both hurt. But at least we're alive. Need air," Red gasped.

"I'll make this opening bigger so it'll let fresh air in." Andy frantically dug away at the dirt. "Do you feel a current of air now?"

"Yes, thank God. We couldn't have lasted much longer."

"I'll go get help. We'll get you out of there as soon as possible."

"Bring stretchers," Red called.

"All right. I'm going now." He braced his shovel and put his foot on it to give himself leverage to get out of the hole.

Andy hurried as fast as he could to get out of the long tunnel and up to the surface to find help. When he got to the office he looked at the clock and saw that it was just past three in the morning. He ran to the nearest bunkhouse and routed out some men. He looked around for the Golden Star's best teamster and shook him awake. "Svend, I found the trapped men. I need you to take them to the hospital in Redding. Bring the powder wagon. Get it hitched and ready."

As he rushed back to the office, he was thankful for the

special wagon that Philip had designed to transport nitroglycerin and other dangerous explosives. The wagon bed lay in a framework of leather straps and springs so it would receive the least amount of bumps and jars. The vehicle would make an excellent ambulance for an injured person when a mattress was placed in the bottom of the bed.

As soon as the rescue crew reported, Andy gave orders. "Mike, you take my horse and buggy and go over to the Alpine. Tell Miss Hamilton that her brother and manager are alive and we're taking them out through tunnel ten. They are injured, so they'll have to go into Redding to the hospital. We'll bring them by her office first, before going on to Redding."

Soon the men had assembled crowbars, ladders, shovels, picks, and powerful lights. Two men went to the first-aid room for the stretchers, bandages, disinfectant, and splints. At last they were on their way, underground, into tunnel 10. When they came to the battered barrier, Andy left three men to tear it away and enlarge the opening so the stretchers could get through. The others went on with him. The strong hardrock miners, used to shoveling, soon had the hole in the bottom of the tunnel large enough to lower a ladder to the trapped men. Andy, who had been trained in first aid, went down first.

Keith and Red were stretched out near the end of the tunnel. The timbers that had broken now formed props that held the remaining roof.

"Take care of the kid," Red said weakly. "He's hurt worse than I am, by far." He grasped Andy's hand and squeezed it. "Damn glad to see you guys. We were about ready to cash in our chips."

Keith was too weak to talk aloud. He whispered, "My leg and knee are hurt bad."

"It's okay. We'll get you out of here and to the hospital in Redding." Andy suppressed a gasp as he cut Keith's pant leg and saw the broken shinbone sticking through the skin. The surrounding area looked red and ugly. "Grit your teeth. This may hurt." He painted the area with disinfectant and wrapped it with a bandage before he attached the splint.

The stretchers, specially designed for use in mine accidents, had a harness arrangement to hold a patient in place. A metal shield folded across the body to protect it from falling rocks. When the men carefully and gently lifted Keith and put him on the stretcher, he moaned in pain. Andy gave him a drink of straight whiskey before he was strapped into the harness. Two strong men carried him up the ladder and started on the journey back.

Now Andy could turn his attention to Red.

"I've been spitting blood, so something's hurt inside." Red looked like he wanted to break down and bawl with relief at being rescued at last, long after he had given up hope, but instead he let out a string of cusswords to give vent to his feelings.

"I'm going to strap splints onto your sides, Red. You could have broken ribs or 'most anything, so we don't want to make it worse."

"I sure thank you for that. I'll be damn glad to see the last of this hole."

As she sat slumped at her office desk, Dorcas heard the horse and buggy coming through the still night. All the lights were on outside, so when she ran out she could see the buggy as it turned in the gate.

At first she thought the driver was Andy, but a man she didn't know stuck his head out and yelled, "Mr. Woodard found your brother and manager. They're alive."

Dorcas's heart jumped to her throat. "Thanks be to God. Are they hurt?"

"Yes, ma'am. Some. They're going to be taken to the hospital in Redding. They'll stop here on the way."

Tears of relief poured down her cheeks. "Thank you for coming. You couldn't have brought better news."

She rushed inside and blew one long blast without stopping, the signal giving the wonderful word that the men had been found. The whistle was wired to the tunnels below, so the men would soon be coming to the surface.

Dorcas grabbed a lantern and ran to the house. "They've been found! They're alive!" The women had been wakened by the blast and were getting into their bathrobes. She ran to her mother and held her close. "It's all over now, Mama. They've been saved." Sobbing in relief, Dorcas and her mother clung together. She told Lenore and Judy all she knew and added, "As soon as I can talk to Philip, I'll be back to pack so I can go with them to the hospital in Redding."

"I wish I could take Keith to San Francisco," her mother said.

"I think you should, Mama. But I doubt that Keith will be able to make the trip just yet. If he goes to the hospital, he'll get care and they'll nurse him through the worst of it, so he can go on."

"You're right, Dori," Judy said. "You go ahead with Keith. Mama and I will take the stagecoach tomorrow and meet you in Redding."

"Fine. Now I must go back to the office and tell the men the good news." Dorcas gave her mother a final hug and ran out the door.

Philip came up with the first load of men. When she saw his dirt-streaked face and bloodshot eyes, a wave of adoration rushed through her. No one could have tried harder to be helpful than her beloved.

"Good for Andy," Philip cried when she told the men the details. "He wanted to try that approach, but I didn't think he could get into your tunnel that way."

"Good thing he did," one middle-aged miner spoke up. "We had a long way to go before we could get through. It'd have been too late."

Dorcas explained that she was going to the hospital with Keith and Red. "Russ, I want you to be the acting manager while I'm gone. I know all of you will cooperate with him."

Philip spoke up. "If you have any problems, Mr. Woodard or I will help you."

Dorcas went on. "I want to thank all of you for working so hard. You were all great. Also, I want to tell my miners that you can take tomorrow off with pay. You more than deserve it."

Philip walked with her to the house. "I'm sure Andy will bring Red and Keith here in the powder wagon." He explained what it was. "We have a special teamster, Svend Olsen, who can handle that wagon like a baby's cradle. He's the one who takes all our accident cases to the hospital. He's got the endurance of an ox, and he'll drive right through."

Dorcas wiped her tears away with the back of her hand. "You and Andy have been so good. There's no way I can thank you enough."

"Out here in the woods we must all help one another. And

I especially want to do what I can for you. Now, if you're going to go with them, you'd better get ready." He took her in his arms and kissed her tenderly. Dorcas thought her heart would burst with love for him.

When she went back to the house, the women were dressed and helping Esther prepare a food basket. Dorcas changed her clothes and pulled her suitcase out from under the bed. It was hard to think what she would need while she was gone. All the time she folded clothes, tears of relief welled in her eyes and spilled over. As she brushed them away with the back of her hand, a half-shuddering sob went through her.

Everyone was on hand when Svend and Andy came with the powder wagon. The miners cheered and cheered and slapped one another on the back in their joy over the successful rescue.

Lenore rushed to the side of the wagon and looked at her son, who was stretched out on the mattress and covered with blankets. "Oh, my darling. I was so frantic."

"Don't worry, Ma. I'll be okay. My leg's hurt bad, but it'll heal."

Dorcas threw her arms around Andy and began to cry. "What would we have done without you? I can't tell you how grateful I am."

For a long moment Andy held her. "When you get back, dearest, I'll tell you all about the rescue. I know you're anxious to get off now."

"Shouldn't they have something to eat and drink before we go?"

"No, we cleaned them up and fed them a little before we loaded them into the wagon. Svend is anxious to get off. The sun is about ready to come up."

"I'll take care of them along the way."

"Fine. Say good-bye to your mother and Judy, and I'll help you climb aboard."

After she said her farewells, Andy boosted her up onto the seat. "As soon as I get back to my office, I'll telegraph the hospital so they'll be expecting you," he promised.

She leaned out and kissed him on the cheek. "You're so thoughtful. I love you for it."

*　　*　　*

Svend was not much of a talker. Dorcas was too exhausted after the crisis to carry on a conversation anyway. Every few minutes she looked back to see how the men were doing, but they both seemed to be sleeping as they lay huddled under the blankets. It wasn't long before she began to doze and was soon sound asleep herself.

Hours later, when they reached the summit, Dorcas jolted awake as Svend pulled the wagon into a turnout place in the road so the horses could rest. Her face flushed as she realized she had been leaning against his shoulder.

"I'm sorry, Mr. Olson." She sat up straight and pulled down her coat.

"No harm done, ma'am." His own face reddened. "You must be mighty tired after all you went through."

She smiled at him. "But very, very happy." She looked back at the two patients. "I'll see if they can drink some cider."

She climbed out of the seat and went to the back of the wagon. She found a thermos of cold cider in the food basket there. Both men were able to drink, and although very weak and in considerable pain, they were holding up.

There were other stops along the way to change horses or to eat and stretch. The hours seemed endless as they plodded along. The sun had gone down by the time they dropped down into the valley, but the simmering heat still lingered.

When they finally reached the town of Redding on the banks of the placid Sacramento River, Svend found the small hospital next door to the doctor's big Victorian house.

After Svend had helped the doctor and nurse take the injured men into the hospital, Dorcas sent him to the hotel to engage rooms for the night.

She waited wearily while they examined Keith's leg. Finally the doctor came out. "It's a bad break, and I think the knee is involved as well. But I want to get the swelling down before I attempt to set it. Therefore, I've ordered ice packs put on tonight. I won't do anything more until tomorrow."

She told him about her mother's plan to take him to San Francisco.

"Yes, that's wise. Your own physician can take over then. He'll probably call in a doctor experienced in cases like this. I'll do the minimum and put the leg in a temporary cast so that it will be immobilized."

"I think we should have a nurse to take care of him on the train, don't you?"

He nodded. "I'll find someone." He smiled. "Almost any nurse would be glad to have a free trip to San Francisco."

"What about Mr. Wallace?" Dorcas asked, concerned about her mine manager.

"He has internal injuries; if necessary, I will operate. But I'm hoping he'll respond to complete bed rest. I won't make a decision about him just yet." He looked at her face, gray with fatigue, and her glazed eyes. "Young lady, you need to rest. If we don't watch out we'll have to put you in the hospital as well." He patted her shoulder. "Now, you go to the hotel and get to bed. We'll take good care of your brother and Mr. Wallace."

When Dorcas went outside, she found Svend waiting patiently for her. By the time she entered her hotel room, she was too tired to unpack her suitcase. It was all she could do to take off her clothes and climb into bed.

The next morning she walked to the telephone and telegraph office to get in touch with her grandfather. The operator had her enter a special booth for the call.

From his voice, Dorcas knew her grandfather was in an irritable mood. "I suppose something's wrong," he said gruffly. "I'm ready to leave for the office."

"I'm afraid so, Grandpa." She told him about the cave-in.

"From the beginning I knew this was a foolhardy scheme of yours. I told you so. Oh, no, you wouldn't listen to me. I've been in mining all of my life, but you knew better, didn't you?"

"Grandpa, now don't be cross." Her heart constricted as his voice lashed out at her.

"No one should reopen a mine after eight years without doing a lot more preliminary work than you did. You took that Woodard's word that everything was in order. You're lucky your brother wasn't killed." How angry he sounded.

"I am grateful for that, Grandpa. That's why I'm calling." She told him about the plan to take Keith to San Francisco. "I want you to order an ambulance to meet him, Mother, and Judy. I'll telephone or wire the exact time they are arriving. Better get in touch with our doctor, too."

"Yes, I'll do that, but don't hang up, yet young lady. I'm not through with you." His voice shook with fury.

Dorcas's dry throat made it hard to speak. "Grandpa, don't be—"

"Listen, girl, you aren't up to such a big undertaking. You don't know what you're doing. I want you to close the mine and get yourself down here as fast as you can before all your men get killed!"

"I'm not going to close the mine. I won't do it!"

"But it's not safe to keep it open."

"My manager was showing Keith something in tunnel nineteen. It's an old part of the mine. We're not working it anymore. That's where the cave-in took place. Not where we're mining now. Besides, Andy—"

"You shouldn't listen to anyone connected with the Richmonds. They're all a bunch of crooks," Clyde snapped.

"You mustn't say that! Philip and Andy worked like dogs trying to rescue Keith and Red. No one could have done more, so it isn't right to call them crooks. In fact, it was Andy who found Keith. I don't know just how, but I'll write you when I've had a chance to talk to Andy."

"Don't bother writing. Close the mine and get yourself back here to San Francisco. You can't solve my problems, and you're throwing more money away. Risking everyone's neck, besides."

"Haven't I sent you four bricks? That's worth over thirty-six thousand dollars, isn't it?"

"Listen, young lady, when I need as much as I do, four bricks aren't going to help much. Besides, you're not deducting your investment, so you're not really ahead. I think your bookkeeping is as scatterbrained as your mining methods. You're totally incompetent and making matters worse. Don't go on with it."

"Well, Grandpa, I *am* going on, in spite of what you say. I'm too much like you to give up yet."

"Well, mark my words. You're going to get into more trouble! Just you wait and see."

The telephone was abruptly disconnected. Her grandfather was in a rage, all right. Her hand shook as she hung up the receiver. But she wasn't going to give up. In spite of what he'd said, she was going on. She'd show him what she could do.

She wiped her eyes and tired to compose herself before she faced the operator to pay her bill. All the way to the hospital she tried to put away her feeling of despair. Perhaps Grandpa was right. She might be foolish to go on. What more was in store for her?

After Clyde slammed the receiver down he picked up his cane and stomped out the front door. All down the steps, he thumped his gold-headed cane and snarled to himself, "Drat that girl! She's defying me. Drat her!" She was the only person who dared oppose him. He gave orders and they were obeyed without question. But Dorcas stood her ground. Drat her!

As he rode in his carriage, he tried to get over his anger, but his granddaughter had gotten him all riled up. Drat her! He shook his head as his jaw clamped shut.

So she'd had a cave-in. He didn't dare think about what might have happened to Keith. It was too awful to contemplate. Nothing must happen to his grandson. He was the only one left to carry on. How could Dorcas take such a risk as to permit her brother to go underground in such a dangerous mine? She'd listened too much to that Richmond outfit.

Besides, it was ridiculous to think that a girl like her could reopen the mine and get it in operation. He should never have agreed to it. Anyone with a grain of sense would give up on such a harebrained idea. It wasn't going to work.

He recalled her words—"I'm too much like you to give up yet." So she thinks she takes after me, does she? Perhaps she does.

Actually, he had always had more rapport with her than anyone else. Even his son. But she was a stubborn, foolish girl to insist on staying up there. Now he was all upset. It was all her fault. He thumped his cane again. Drat her!

Clyde's first appointment was with his legal advisor. As the lawyer took some papers out of his briefcase, he said, "Mr. Hamilton, I went around to various bankers and tried again to borrow money on your mining holdings, but I was turned down."

The old man shook his head. "Same old story. No one wants to take a risk on closed mines."

"Money is still very tight. And of course it would mean a considerable investment just to get the mines back in condition again."

"I know. I know. My granddaughter just telephoned me

that she'd had a cave-in at the Alpine. Fortunately there were no fatalities.''

"Mr. Hamilton, under the circumstances I would advise you to deed your mines over to your grandson right now, while they are unencumbered. At the present time they aren't producing, but the day may come when he'll be able to get something from them. It would simplify your estate to get rid of them now.''

Clyde made a steeple of his fingertips and thought about the lawyer's suggestion. It would be one less worry, he supposed. He had always owned mines. It would be strange not to have any. "I'm sure you're right.''

"I'll take care of it at once, Mr. Hamilton. What about the Alpine? Do you want it to go to Keith? Or to your granddaughter Dorcas? After all, she is up there trying—''

Reluctantly, in spite of his annoyance with her, Clyde muttered, "Well, deed the Alpine to Dorcas. But I don't want you to tell my grandchildren. They don't need to know about it just yet.'' If Dorcas knew the mine was hers, she'd be more determined than ever to keep it open. Besides, he'd lose what control he had over her. She was too headstrong to be given full rein.

"I'm sorry, Mr. Hamilton, but they'll have to be told. There are papers they will have to sign.''

"Well, all right, if it can't be helped.''

By the time Lenore and Judy arrived in Redding on the stagecoach, all the arrangements to go on to San Francisco had been made. Keith and the nurse would ride in the baggage car on the way to Sacramento. When they transferred to the transcontinental train from the East Coast, there would be a lower berth available.

The night before they were to leave, Dorcas had a chance to talk with her mother alone. She kissed Lenore on the cheek. "You must make some plans for yourself. I want you to make a fresh start on your life. A wonderful new beginning.''

"I really will, Dorcas, Since Keith has been spared, I feel anything is possible.''

Dorcas looked at her mother with an outpouring of love and compassion. For the first time in her life she felt she really understood Lenore. Dorcas's heart ached as she thought of the suffering the poor woman had endured. How terribly guilty she must have felt, until it drove her to the brink of madness. And to blame herself for Papa's death. What a waste, and how sad.

Tears flooded Dorcas's eyes. "It hurts me so to think of what you went through with no one to turn to."

Lenore looked down at her hands. "I felt so utterly alone. It all just ate away at my very soul."

"I know I didn't help you much. I'm so ashamed of myself. Thank goodness Judy was some comfort to you."

"But I couldn't unburden myself to her. I couldn't bear to have her disillusioned about me. I'd rather she thought I was frail and inclined to nervousness. So you must never tell her."

"No, Mama. I won't." Dorcas took her mother's hand. "I love you so much. More than I ever have in all my life."

"And you've forgiven me?"

"Of course, Mother. But I don't feel worthy enough to pass judgment on you. Let's just say I understand you now and admire you more than ever." She caressed her mother's hand. "In a way, I've been as cruel to you as Papa was. I should ask *your* forgiveness."

Lenore seemed too moved to speak. Finally she whispered, "This is a new beginning. Now that I've unburdened myself, I can start living again."

"Mama, make the most of it. Make up for all those lost years."

"I will."

The nurse the doctor had hired was a reassuring, plump, middle-aged woman. She seemed delighted to make the trip to San Francisco and have the chance to visit relatives there. When it was time to board the train, she soon had Keith settled on a cot in the baggage car. Except for the fact that it was hot, he looked as if he could stand the trip.

Dorcas kissed him good-bye. "I hope this won't discourage you from being a mining engineer."

"Of course it won't, Sis. Would a jockey quit just because he'd gotten thrown off a horse? If I get well in time, I'll be back before you close for the winter."

Dorcas laughed. "Don't say that to Mother."

She said farewell to Lenore and Judy and watched them climb aboard their car. When the train had pulled away in a cloud of steam, Dorcas walked back to the hotel and settled her bill. Then there were the doctor and hospital to pay for the two patients, as well as the nurse's fees. Leadenly, she added up all the bills.

Her bank account was shrinking again. Of course, she should offer to pay wages to the men from the Golden Star as well. Her shoulders slumped in discouragement as she rode the stagecoach back to Alpine Heights. Was her grandfather right? Had all this been a waste of time? Throwing good money after bad? It was tempting to just give up and rationalize that Clyde wouldn't let her go on. But she gritted her teeth and determined to keep trying, in spite of his orders.

If all went well, she could get enough to him to make his payment by the first of October. But would the remaining months go smoothly?

CHAPTER 13

The fog blotted out the view of San Francisco Bay as Lenore and Judy sat in the hospital waiting room on the fourth floor. There were other people there, their faces sagging in resignation as they too waited for news about their loved ones.

For the tenth time, Judy opened the case of the small gold watch hanging on a chain around her neck. "It's eleven o'clock. They've been in that examination room for an hour."

"I suppose Dr. Reese is discussing Keith's condition with that bone doctor he wanted to consult. I'm glad he called in someone. He's a good doctor, but as he said, he wanted an opinion from a colleague who spends most of his time working with fractures."

"At least we have Keith here, in the hospital. Thank goodness that ghastly train trip is over." Lenore shuddered as she recalled the long hours they'd spent trying to keep him cool and comforting him as he groaned in pain.

"Here they come now," Judy said.

Lenore looked down the hall and saw the elderly Dr. Reese approaching with a tall, distinguished-looking man who towered over him.

"Mrs. Hamilton, may I present Dr. Prescott Fuller? He has particular expertise in these difficult cases. He studied in France under Dr. Ambrose Peret, the leading orthopedic surgeon."

Lenore held out her hand and was impressed with his air of confidence—as if he could handle any case.

"I can understand how worried you must have been," Dr. Fuller said, smiling. His blue-gray eyes showed genuine concern. His brown hair showed some gray around the temples. He must be in his late forties, Lenore estimated. How thankful she felt that someone like this was taking charge.

Dr. Reese said, "Dr. Fuller will report the results of our examination to you, so if you'll excuse me, I have patients to see." He walked away half-stooped, as if all the responsibilities of the hospital were on his aged shoulders.

Dr. Fuller waved his hand toward a settee. "Why don't you sit down? I'll pull up a chair." When they were settled, he took a pad and pencil and drew Keith's leg-bone. He took time to explain the complications of the fracture.

"It will be necessary to operate, and it should be done as soon as possible. I need your permission, of course," he said.

"Whatever you think necessary. I give my full permission," Lenore assured him. What a relief to know that something was going to be done at last. "When will you operate?"

"This evening at eight o'clock. That's the earliest time a surgery room is available." He rose and put out his hand to take her arm. "If you'll come along with me, I'll take you to the office so you can fill out the necessary forms."

On the way home, Lenore leaned back and sighed. "I think the worst is over, Judy. Somehow I have so much confidence in Dr. Fuller."

"I don't think Dr. Reese would have recommended him if he weren't good. Isn't he attractive? Not handsome, exactly, but so tall and manly." Judy glanced at her mother and noticed a slight flush on her face. She reached over and took Lenore's hand. "I know everything is going to be all right now. When we get home I want you to get into your negligee and lie on your chaise. Rosalie can bring you some lunch."

Dr. Fuller came out to the waiting room about nine that evening. "Keith came through the operation fine. He's asleep now. I was able to position the bones so that he should recover fully."

Lenore asked anxiously, "Then he won't be lame?"

"No, he shouldn't be. We'll keep him here in the hospital in traction for a while. After he goes home he'll have to do special exercises to strengthen his leg muscles. The therapy was developed during the Civil War."

"We'll do anything to help him—" Lenore said.

Judy interrupted. "Mother, I think I should telephone for Wilson to come and get us."

"My coachman is outside waiting for me. Please allow me to escort you home." Dr. Fuller took Lenore's arm and they walked to the elevator used only by the staff.

"Now that the operation is over, I'm starved," he said when they reached the street. "I'm afraid I didn't eat much dinner. Could we stop at a cafe and have some supper on the way home?" The doctor smiled at them. "I doubt that you ladies were able to eat dinner, either."

Lenore felt a pleasant flush come over her at his invitation.

Soon they were sitting at a window table with all the lights of the city spread out below them. Dr. Fuller began talking about the art exhibits and concerts he had attended.

"My daughter took art lessons before we left for Trinity County. Tell Dr. Fuller about them, Judy," Lenore said.

"My instructor was Courtland Burke. He's connected with the new art museum. Have you heard of him?"

"Of course. Courtland Burke is considered to be one of the finest artists in the West. How fortunate you were to have lessons with him. In fact, I just today received this invitation to a private showing and reception for Burke." Dr. Fuller pulled an envelope out of his pocket. "You probably know that this one-man show opens to the public on Sunday."

Lenore glanced at him. Was he going to ask her to go with him? She hoped so.

"I'm unable to go, but I thought you and Judy might want to attend," he continued, handing the invitation to Lenore.

She looked at the small envelope, trying to contain her disappointment. Then she gave him a smile. He was probably just shy; there was plenty of time. "Thank you so much, Dr. Fuller," she said.

When the doctor left them at the front door of the mansion, Judy spoke up. "I'll go with you to Courtland Burke's exhibit, Mama. We could have lunch at some nice restaurant first."

"Perhaps you can arrange to start your lessons with him again," Lenore said. "Of course, we didn't expect to be here this summer, but you might as well take advantage of it."

"I'll see." Actually, Judy had no intention of taking more lessons. Especially from Burke. He was too demanding. Got her all upset. Besides, painting was too much work. She wanted to have fun with her friends instead. That was exactly what she intended to do.

For the rest of the week, she mulled over her mixed feelings about going to the exhibit. On one hand, she wanted to forget Courtland and all his demands. On the other, it would be interesting to see what he had painted. He was always so critical of her work. What did Mr. High and Mighty himself do that was so wonderful?

Then it was Sunday and time to go to the gallery.

"What a surprise. I thought you were gone for the summer." Courtland shook Judy's hand as she and her mother entered the exhibit.

Judy shrugged. "I did expect to be away, but my brother was injured in a mine accident, so we returned early."

"I hope he's recovering."

"Thank you, he is."

Others were waiting to greet Courtland, so, relieved, she stepped away and started walking around the room, looking at his work.

How powerful and disturbing the paintings were. You couldn't just glance at them. They had to be studied. Savored. She wanted to reject all the feelings they inspired in her—the deep-seated longing to be as great. To achieve. She wished she hadn't come. She glanced toward her mother but saw that Lenore was talking with old friends. Judy shrugged and walked into the next room.

For a long time she stood in front of a painting of an old man sitting on a park bench. His gnarled bony fingers gripped a cane that reminded her of her grandfather's. The old man's shabby blue serge suit hung on his thin frame. Where had he gotten the suit? It was too big for him. Had someone given it to him? Perhaps he'd bought it in a secondhand clothing store. A small boy of about eight stood in front of the aged man, showing him a kite he had made. How young and fresh the boy's face looked. His whole life was ahead of him, in contrast to the ancient one with his sunken eyes so full of despair. Tears came to her own eyes. A big lump formed in her throat.

"What is the old man thinking, Judy? How does he feel?"

Startled, she whirled around and faced Courtland. She couldn't speak. Two tears rolled down her cheeks. Angrily, she brushed them away and rummaged through her handbag for her handkerchief. As her face flushed, she wiped her cheeks and patted her eyes. Damn this Courtland Burke. He had no right to sneak up on her. She felt so exposed. He seemed able to peer right into her very soul.

"Your work is very nice, Mr. Burke," she said at last, hating the tremor in her voice.

"Nice?" His lips parted in a sardonic smile. "Don't insult me. That's the last thing I intended."

"Well, moving, then," she admitted as tears flooded her eyes again.

He placed his hand on her arm. "When are you going to resume your lessons?"

She looked away. "I told you that my brother was injured. Very badly. He's still in the hospital, so I must devote—"

"Must you? Couldn't you spare a little time for your lessons?"

"I couldn't possibly give up three mornings a week. I have too much to do."

"I wasn't thinking of three mornings a week. I'm willing to go on with private lessons at my house. Every Saturday."

"No, that's not possible at the present time," she said.

*   *   *

He stared at her with a contemptuous expression in his dark, piercing eyes. So much talent wasted on this shallow girl. What a tragedy. How could it happen? There were others so eager to achieve. So willing to work. But they had none of the potential that this stunningly beautiful girl had.

It was like a blow to see her again in her pink street dress with a matching parasol. He was so aware of her tiny waist, high, rounded breasts, and flawless complexion. He'd almost forgotten the impact she had on him. He wanted to take her by the shoulders and shake her until her teeth rattled. Damn her, anyway.

Judy saw his disdain. How she resented it. "I want my painting back, Mr. Burke. When may I call for it?"

"I'll be working in my studio Tuesday morning. Come then."

"I'll be there." Tossing her head, she walked away. She glanced back to see him joined by a group of admirers. All the rest of the afternoon, she walked around and looked at the paintings, not even admitting to herself how shaken she felt. Drat Courtland Burke. She wished she'd never come to this exhibit. Why did he always have such an effect on her? How she hated him for stirring up this undefinable need, for making her discontent with her life.

She'd been perfectly happy going to parties and flirting with her admirers until she'd started studying with this horrible man. He pulled at her so. She put her chin in the air. She wouldn't let him. She'd get her painting back and never see him again.

When she joined her mother and her friends, one of the men was saying, "We should all buy Burke's paintings now, before they get too expensive."

Another put in, "Burke's still young. Give him another ten years and he'll be known throughout the country. One of the great ones."

Judy didn't want to hear any more. "I'm ready whenever you are, Mama," she said.

When they arrived back at the mansion and walked into the entrance hall, Judy saw the mail on a tray. She picked up an envelope addressed to her and read the letter. "Barbara Allinton has invited me to a house party next weekend. She's with her parents at their summer home down the coast."

"You must go, darling," Lenore urged. "I was there with your father once. It's a magnificent place looking out over the ocean."

"I intend to accept. It'll be fun."

Judy thought of all the eligible young bachelors who would be there. That's what she wanted, to have a good time at parties. There'd be lots of house parties, now that her friends knew that she was back in town. At Lake Tahoe, Monterey Bay, and all the exciting places. She intended to accept any invitations that might come her way. She'd have a wonderful time. Why should she drudge away at painting when she didn't have to? Why do all that hard work? She flipped her head in the air and ran up the stairs.

Judy's painting stood on an easel in the living room at Courtland Burke's house. Something seemed to grab at the pit of her stomach as she stared at it. She'd forgotten how moving it was. Rosemary, her crutches, the children skipping rope. A sob shuddered through her. She had painted this. She, Judith Hamilton, who had never achieved very much in her life, had performed this miracle. Of course, Courtland had taught and guided her, but it was her hand that had held the brush. Her very own. She looked down at it in amazement, as if it couldn't possibly belong to her.

Swallowing hard, she looked at the portrait again. She thought of Courtland's painting of the little boy showing his kite to the old man. She stared back at her own work. A long gasp escaped her. This one was just as moving. She blinked away tears. Of course, hers was not as skillfully executed. But her teacher was a professional. A rising star in his field, while she was only a beginner.

Leadenly, she walked down the hall toward Burke's studio. He stood at an easel, putting finishing touches on a scene of the park in front of a bandstand. She avoided looking at the expressions on the faces in the painting.

She cleared her throat. "Good morning."

Burke whirled around. "I didn't know you were here. The bell didn't ring."

"I met your mother coming out of the door. She's on her way to the market."

He put his brush into a turpentine jar. "Sit down."

"I just came for my painting."

"I want to talk to you."

There was nothing to do but slump down into chair. She couldn't refuse; it was as if he had some power over her.

He drew another chair close and took her hand. "Judy, you have real talent. Can you understand that? A true gift from God. I've never told that to any of my students."

She shrank back, afraid of his intensity.

"You owe it to yourself to continue with your lessons and to paint," he persisted.

"I don't want to."

"But Judy, you mustn't waste your gift. Begin again. Right away."

She shook her head. Her mouth was dry. "I don't want to," she repeated.

His face reddened. He grabbed her shoulder angrily and gave her a little shake. "If you don't want to study with me, that's all right. There are lots of good teachers here in San Francisco. It's one of the great art centers of the country. You have a marvelous opportunity here."

She twisted away from him and started to rise. "I have no desire to study with anyone."

His jaw tightened, his eyes narrowed. "Why not, you foolish girl?"

She rose to her feet and he stood up as well, towering over her.

"I have too much to do this summer," she said weakly.

"Doing what? Going to parties? Kissing boys? Playing croquet?"

"I don't have to tell you."

"Why were you given such a gift? You're a spoiled-rotten heiress who'll just throw it away. It isn't fair. It's tragic!"

She felt condemned. Scorned.

He grabbed her shoulders again and shook her with all his might. "My God," he shouted. "Do you have any idea what you're doing? You damn fool!"

Truly frightened now, she began to cry. "Leave me alone, you horrible man. It's none of your business if I paint or not."

His fingers bit into her flesh. He put his face near hers, his dark, pointed beard nearly touching her cheek. He shook her again. "Damn it! It is my business. It's just as if I were seeing someone ready to smash a piece of priceless porcelain.

You're destroying your gift by not using it. You owe it to yourself and to the world to share the talent you have inside of you!''

"Let go of me!" She yanked herself away from him and ran to the door.

"Go, you little fool! If you ever come to your senses, I'll still be here."

Judy ran through the house not even glancing at her portrait. She didn't want to be reminded of what it represented. Down the stairs she flew, crying, "No! No!"

Outside in the carriage, Wilson stared at her. "Miss Judy, are you all right?"

She nodded. "Please drive me to the conservatory at Golden Gate Park."

When they arrived at their destination, Wilson helped her out. "You can go home now and take my mother to the hospital to see Keith," she told him. "Tell her I'll meet her there later. I want to take a walk."

"I'll return for you after I deliver Mrs. Hamilton." Wilson drove off.

Judy walked through the hothouses, glorying in the beauty of the orchids and tropical plants. It soothed her to stare at their exquisite beauty. She tried not to think of Courtland and the bitter words he had flung at her. No, she wouldn't be forced into something she didn't want to do. Instead, she'd go to her house parties and have fun. She'd buy pretty clothes and enjoy herself. Let someone else be torn apart as they painted. Why should she?

Her mother must never know that Courtland thought she had real talent. Lenore would urge her to go on with her lessons. Then, of course, Dorcas would find out as well. Her sister, who had such drive, wouldn't understand her position at all. Even Keith would have a lot to say. Judy shook her head. She'd keep it all to herself so no one could force her into anything.

The rest of the week flew by for Judy. There were clothes to pack for the house party. It took two large suitcases to carry all the dresses she would need; the girls would change several times during the day. Some outfits were appropriate only for morning. Then there were sport clothes for horseback riding, tennis, or croquet. Of course, everyone changed for lunch. Finally, one's loveliest gowns were put on for dinner and dancing afterwards.

She took the train down the coast. Others in the party were aboard and she had a delightful time. Who needed to drudge when it wasn't necessary? She was a Hamilton and intended to take her part in society.

There were sixteen guests at the house party. Eight young gentlemen and the same number of girls. Some of the parents had also been invited, so the guests would be carefully chaperoned. Just as her mother had told her, the home was huge, with plenty of room for all and an adequate staff to take care of every need. Separate servants' quarters housed all the help and an orchestra hired for the occasion.

Try as hard as she could, Judy couldn't forget her confrontation with Courtland. His words kept mocking her. He had upset her so, and she hated him for it. Of course she wasn't a shallow fool. She had painted the portrait, hadn't she? That had taken a lot of self-discipline, hadn't it? A lot of it. Darn that horrid man.

By throwing herself wholeheartedly into the house party, she was able to blot out Courtland from her mind. She was the most vivacious and popular girl in the group. One young man in particular, Jeffrey Lathrop, a senior at an eastern university, interested her. Not only was he in college, but he had made the grand tour of Europe. His family owned a vast shipping line and had homes in both San Francisco and Hawaii. He was by far the richest and best-looking man at the party. What a catch he would be as a husband.

On Saturday night, Judy found that he was placed next to her at the dinner table. As he helped her with her chair, he whispered in her ear, "I begged Barbara to let me be your partner tonight."

She smiled up at him. "I'm glad." She looked at the other girls and caught their envious glances. What fun to be the most sought-after girl at the house party. Excitement ran through her. Here was a conquest worthy of her skill. "What courses are you taking in college, Jeff?" she asked.

"The easiest ones I can find. I only study enough to get by."

"Aren't you training for a profession? Doctor? Lawyer? Pharmacist?"

"Why should I take all those hard courses? Especially all those sciences?"

"Then you must be planning to go into the family business."

"I suppose so. Dad will find me a spot somewhere. But frankly, I see no reason to work hard. My grandmother left me a trust fund. I'll let my older brothers be the tycoons." He grinned at her.

"What do you like to do?"

"Lie on the beach in Hawaii and enjoy myself with the Polynesian girls. The Hawaiians taught me how to ride a surfboard on the waves. Nothing like it. I sail. I like to do anything but work."

She laughed gaily, but in the back of her mind she could almost hear Courtland chuckling to himself. She was thankful he hadn't overheard this conversation. His opinion of her and her friends would be lower than ever. Drat that man, anyway.

Jeff chatted on about the sailing races he had won and the tennis matches he had played. They ate dinner and danced most of the evening together. "You're a girl after my own heart," he murmured as they walked outside to see the moon. "Why haven't we seen each other before?"

"You've been away at college, and I lived in Colorado until this past year."

"We must make up for lost time. Let's go to the Slipper Club next week. It's a cabaret. Has an excellent show."

Judy had heard of the Slipper Club. Although it was located near the docks in a less desirable part of the city, many of her friends had gone there. "Sounds like fun. Let's find some others to go with us, though. I know my mother wouldn't want me to go with you alone."

"I'll round up some of the gang here to go along. We'd better make it Wednesday night, since we're all going to Pat's house party on Friday."

The new show at the Slipper Club attracted a full house, so it was just as well that, as it turned out, only one other couple came with Jeff and Judy. Jeff slipped the head waiter a big tip so they had a table right next to the tiny dance floor. As soon as they were seated, Jeff ordered a magnum of champagne. Every time Judy emptied her glass, he filled it again. When the bottle was empty, he ordered another one. It wasn't long before she felt dizzy. When she got up to dance, she staggered a little. The whole room whirled around them. She hoped that none of her mother's friends were here to see her hanging on Jeff's neck so she could stand up. She knew her mother wouldn't approve at all.

A long, crowded bar took up one wall beside the tables. As they went around and around the small floor, she felt more unsteady than ever. Perhaps she should ask Jeff to take her home. When her eyes focused on the men at the bar, one figure seemed familiar. She tried to remember where she had seen him before. A tall, slender man with a dark, pointed beard.

Appalled, Courtland Burke watched Judy on the floor. She'd been drinking champagne ever since she had arrived. Now she could hardly stand up. This was no place for a kid like her. What was her escort thinking of, bringing her here? The show was too risqué for a properly brought-up girl of her class, anyway. Should he get her and take her home? But her escort looked like the type who would cause a scene, which would be even worse, as it might make the papers.

Before Courtland could decide what to do, the music ended and the master of ceremonies stepped out on the stage to announce the show. At least Judy was seated now and the room darkened. Perhaps she'd drink some coffee and clear her head.

Judy did sip some coffee, but all through the show she was aware only of a hazy blur of half-naked dancing girls, singers, and a comedian who caused wave after wave of laughter to reverberate throughout the room. She didn't understand many of his jokes.

As soon as the show was over, the other couple left. Jeff wanted to finish his champagne, so they stayed on at the table. Finally they made their way to the door.

"We don't want to go home yet," Jeff declared, his tongue so thick she could barely understand him. "The night's young. There's another place around here I went to once." When they climbed into a waiting cab, he instructed the driver to take them to the Starlight.

* * *

Courtland waved down another cabby and followed. They were going in the opposite direction from the one he'd expected. Why didn't they head straight for the Hamilton mansion? The closer they got to the wharves, the seamier the cabarets became. This was certainly no place to take Judy. Even a man wasn't safe here.

As they entered the crowded place, Judy glanced around at the rough-looking sailors, stevedores, pimps, and thieves, who turned to stare at her.

Her heart pounded in fear. "Jeff, I don't think we should come in here." Her head cleared as she pulled her light cape around her. "Let's leave."

"I came here once before." He shouldered their way between the men. "They have a great show."

"But this is no place for us." Smoke hung in the air. The smell of sweaty bodies, stale beer, and cooking odors from the kitchen made her ill. "Come on. Please let's get out."

Jeff's voice turned ugly. "I'll leave after the show."

He staggered over to a table that a man had just vacated and shoved a whiskey glass that sat there onto the floor. "Sit down." Jeff pushed her into an empty chair.

A burly man with tattoos on his huge arms came back with another whiskey glass in his hand. He put it down on the table and grabbed Jeff by the shoulder. "This is my place. Didn't you see the glass I left here?"

"We're using it now." Jeff brushed his assailant's hand away.

A massive fist flew out, caught Jeff on his chest, and knocked him to the floor. Jeff slowly raised himself and reached for Judy. "Let's go."

But the man was leering down at Judy. He braced his muscled arm across her. "She stays. You git before I beat you to a pulp."

Judy tried to scream, but no sound came. She shrank back in horror, paralyzed with fear. She looked for Jeff, but he had vanished in the crowd.

"You're quite a filly." The big man grabbed a chair and sat down as close to her as he could get. "What's your name?"

"Nora." She said the name of one of their maids. Watching, the other men crowded around the table, eyeing her jewels and the purse she clutched in her hand.

"Well, Nora, why should we wait for the show?" He leaned toward her and leered, showing his blackened teeth, some of which were missing. His foul breath hit her. "You're more of a beaut than anything they've got on the stage here." He glanced up at the onlookers. "Ain't that so?"

Terrified, Judy looked to the other men for help, but they only nodded in amused agreement. "Yeah," one said. "Can we join the fun?"

Courtland paid the cabby and started for the door. Just then the young man Judy had been with came running out alone and jumped into the cab.

"Go! Hurry!"

Courtland ran toward the vehicle, crying, "Wait! Where's Judy?"

But the horses were galloping down the street. Where the hell *was* Judy? Burke almost panicked as he pushed his way in the dive. That rat must have left her here! He ran into the main room and saw all the men gathered around a table. He caught a glimpse of her golden curls as one drunk held her hair aloft.

He couldn't rescue her alone. Not from that crowd of drunken toughs. They'd soon have him pinned to the floor. He rushed to the bar and asked one of the bartenders, "Who owns this joint?"

The man jerked a thumb toward a huge man behind the end of the bar. "Spike."

Courtland pushed his way through the crowd at the bar until he stood in front of the giant. "Spike, I came to get a young lady, and I need your help. She came in with a friend who left her here."

"I'm busy. I don't pay no attention to what goes on out on the floor."

Courtland grabbed him by the shirt. "Look, Bud, she's the granddaughter of one of the most powerful men in this city. If you don't help me get her out of here right now, I'll call the police. And you'll be damn sorry."

"What the hell is she doing in here, where she don't belong?"

"I don't know. But I'm going to take her home. You come right behind me so those thugs know they'd better let her go."

"I ain't responsible for what they might do to you."

"I'll worry about that. Come on!" Courtland shoved himself toward the table. "Out of the way! Out of the way!" he ordered authoritatively as if he were a plainclothesman. His bluff worked. The men fell back, leaving a path open.

When he reached the table, he pulled Judy's captor's arm away from her. "Come on. We're going home," he said.

"Courtland!" she screamed, and jumped up. He put his own arm across her shoulders and held her to him.

The massive owner of the bar stood next to them. Courtland looked over Judy's head. "Thank you, Spike." He turned to the others. "Good evening, gentlemen."

The surprised onlookers fell back as he led her out of the place. Spike followed along with his hamlike fists on his hips to see that they got outside safely.

Courtland waved down a cab, helped Judy in, and gave the driver the address of the mansion as he climbed aboard himself. "Get out of here as fast as you can!" As the horses sped away, he looked over his shoulder at the dive. Only then was he able to settle back in relief, with the sobbing Judy in his arms.

"I came to thank you." Judy stood in the doorway of Courtland's studio.

He glanced at her, his eyes narrowing. He continued with his painting. "Sit down. I'll be with you in a minute."

She dropped into the big easy chair, put her head back, and closed her eyes. She still felt wretched but decided she should come in person to thank Courtland for rescuing her. She had spent the previous day in bed, telling her mother and the servants she had an upset stomach from food she'd eaten the night before. She thought of her friends who were no doubt eating lunch at Pat's country home. How relieved she'd been to be able to call and say she was too ill to join them. The last person she ever wanted to see again was Jeff. Her lip curled in disgust.

Finally, Courtland put his brushes in turpentine and pulled up a chair close to her. "You look as if you're still recovering from the hangover of all time. I'm surprised they let a kid like you drink at the Slipper Club.''

''Well, it wasn't whiskey or anything like that. It was champagne.''

''Is that so? The way you were pouring it down, I thought it must be water.''

Her face flushed. She put out her hand and grasped his. Tears flooded her eyes. ''Courtland, how can I possibly thank you? If you hadn't come, I don't know what might have happened to me.'' Her voice trembled.

''Shall I tell you? It might do you good, young lady.'' He pushed a lock of hair out of her eyes.

She nodded.

''You would have been pulled into a back room, stripped, your jewels and money taken.''

The color drained from her face. ''How awful!''

''That's not the worst of it. You might easily have been raped by every tough who was hanging around you.''

Her eyes widened in horror. ''Oh, no!'' She grasped his arm. ''Then I owe you my life. I would have killed myself if that had happened to me.''

''Well, it didn't. Fortunately I saw you at the Slipper Club and followed you just to make sure you were all right.''

''Oh, Courtland. I'll be grateful the rest of my life.''

''Put it out of your mind now.'' He made a fist. ''Have you heard from that no-good you were with?''

''Not directly. One of the maids told me that someone telephoned yesterday morning and asked if I was home. When she said she would call me, he said 'never mind,' and hung up. I suppose it was Jeff.''

''That damn coward. I could wring his neck. Why didn't he go right to the police station and get help? Why did he leave you in that dive to fend for yourself?''

Judy put her hands to her face and started to cry. ''I expected him to come to see me yesterday and make sure I was all right. And apologize. Or at least send flowers and a note. But he didn't do anything. I hope I never see him again.''

Courtland took out a clean handkerchief and wiped her face. ''You still look under the weather. You'd better go home and go back to bed.'' He pulled her to her feet.

She stood next to him, looking up into his face. ''I've

decided I want to take lessons again. I'm going on with my painting."

"Fine. I know some excellent teachers. I'll write you a list."

"But I thought you—"

"The offer's withdrawn." He walked to his desk and found a piece of paper. He dipped a pen in an inkwell and wrote down three names and addresses.

"But Courtland, you're the one I want to teach me. Just you."

"You should have said that when I made the offer. You turned it down instead, so I'm no longer interested. I know damn well you'd start, work a little while, and then want to quit."

Judy ran to him and grabbed his sleeve. "No, I won't. Please, Courtland."

He yanked her hand away. "Here are some good teachers. They need the money and I don't. Enough of my paintings were sold at my show to support me for years. My time is too valuable to waste on you."

"Please, I beg you. I'm serious now. I'll work hard. I promise."

"No!"

How stern and uncompromising he looked. She felt ill with disappointment. Now she wanted to study with him more than anything in the world.

"I'll try my best. Please believe me."

"Judy, if you're serious about your work, ready to put your very heart and soul into your painting, any good teacher will show you the way. You don't need me."

"But I do. Oh, Courtland, it's you I want. I need you. Not just any good teacher. You!"

"I think you'd better leave."

She stamped her foot. "No!"

He shook his head.

It was one of the few times in her life that she had been denied anything. She stared at him in shock. He was not going to have her as a student. He meant every word he said. A stab of disappointment shot through her. She picked up her handbag, then walked down the hall and out the front door. Courtland followed her and stood in the doorway.

As she turned and looked at him, tears flooded her eyes.

"Oh, Courtland, I won't see you again." She could hardly bear the thought. How important he had become to her. "Anyway, thank you for everything." She grabbed the rail and hurried down the stairs. From now on she would throw herself into her social affairs and forget all about art.

Courtland fought his despair. It was like tearing out a very part of him to see her go. But she had to grow up. Find herself. Perhaps underneath all her beauty and shallow immaturity were the makings of a true artist. But first she would have to develop a true, gut-wrenching drive to achieve. A sob tore through him. Oh, God, would she?

CHAPTER 14

Two months. That was all the time left. Just two months. With a sinking heart, Dorcas stared at the entrance to tunnel 19, which was still filled with debris. At long last, the men had cleared the other tunnels, which had been shoveled full of rocks and dirt while they were trying to rescue Keith and Red.

Now the miners were able to blast and work the veins again. Could they mine enough to make the nine bars still needed before the October 1 deadline?

So many interruptions. So much time had been wasted because of the cave-in. Now that Keith was well on his way to recovery and Red was back on the job, she could concentrate on the immediate problem: how to recover enough gold to make the payment.

A faint glow flickered from the end of the tunnel as Andy walked toward her. She braced herself with her hand against the tunnel wall. The rough surface bit into her palm. She could smell the damp, musty air and the faint odor of powder from the blasting the night before. The mud squished as she shifted her feet. She could feel the cold wetness through her rubber boots.

"I've inspected all the timbering, and it looks solid," Andy said as he drew near. "I have one crew extending the tunnel in order to follow a vein."

"Is it a rich one?" Dorcas asked, hoping against hope for an encouraging answer.

"I'm afraid not. But it might get better as we move along. From the color of the quartz, I have reason to believe it will."

"Oh, Andy, I sometimes get awfully discouraged. Time is running out on us. There are only two months left."

"Of course, the cave-in set us back." He put his arm across her shoulders. "We're not giving up yet. The ore is rich enough to mine, and we'll put it through the stamp mill. You might be surprised how much we can get out of it."

"The stockpile is getting lower, though. That old ore that we're now processing from the pile is not as rich as it was at first," she pointed out.

"Keep on using it up to recover what you can. I'd suggest that you now send all your concentrate to the smelter so we can add that to the rest."

They walked slowly toward the skip. Dorcas asked, "Exactly where are the crews?"

Andy reviewed just where he had placed the men and outlined the work they were to do. "I had to take into consideration the state of the timbering to make sure the men were safe. I don't want to take them away from mining to put in new timbers, so we haven't worked some of the old tunnels. In tunnel 8, which goes deeper into the mountain, I'm having some side stopes dug to see if the vein branches inward. That's where I expect the best results."

"If something good shows up, you'll concentrate on that, won't you? We want to recover as much as we can as fast as possible."

"Of course." He took her arm and helped her into the skip. "By the way, Philip has house guests. A distant cousin and her mother. He wants us to come to dinner Saturday night. Then riding on Sunday morning."

"That sounds delightful." The hurt that had been building inside of her eased a little. She had only seen Philip once since the night of the rescue. "Have they been here long?"

"Yes. That is, here in California. They are making a tour of the West and have been staying with the Richmonds in

Sacramento. Philip went down there to see them and brought them back with him.''

She breathed a little sigh of relief. That explained why she hadn't seen him. But it was strange that he hadn't come to say good-bye before he left for Sacramento.

Back in her office, Dorcas opened the ledger and studied her finances. She was going to need more money. There was no way she could meet her expenses without borrowing more from her mother. With a sinking feeling, she wrote to their broker in San Francisco and asked that more bonds be sold and an additional twenty-five thousand be deposited in her bank account. Now she would owe her mother fifty thousand dollars. How could she ever pay it back? Of course, she would just have to keep the mine open as long as possible this fall and try to make up the sum. And that would be after she sent the required nine bricks to the mint for her grandfather. She drummed her fingers on her desk and sucked in her breath, trying to control the panic she felt. What if they didn't recover the expected amount of gold? They would all be wiped out. Her mother as well as her grandfather. How naive she had been to think that all they needed to do was open the mine. Her grandfather had been right. She didn't know what she was doing and had taken on an impossible task. Her throat thickened and tears stung her eyes.

On Saturday afternoon, Dorcas shampooed her hair and sat in the sun. When it was dry, she brushed it out carefully. She bathed, dusted powder over herself, and put on her clothes. She chose a white dimity with pale yellow sprigs of flowers scattered on it. She combed her hair into a pompadour with soft waves across the top and pinned a yellow bow at the back of the bun.

Andy was calling for her, so she pulled a white shawl around her shoulders, picked up her purse, and walked along the path to the office. Excitement bubbled up at the thought of seeing Philip again. How she had longed for him every day and dreamed about him at night. Her large dark eyes glowed and her cheeks flushed faintly. Long before the buggy turned into the courtyard, she could hear the horse's hooves beat a steady clip-clop on the road.

"You look very beautiful this evening," Andy said while helping her into the buggy. It was all he could do to keep from gathering her into his arms.

As he climbed into the driver's seat, he wanted to warn Dorcas that Philip was quite taken with his distant cousin. That damn woman chaser; he ran after every skirt he could. Loyalty wasn't one of Richmond's strong points. Andy glanced at the lovely girl by his side. Anger flared in him again as he thought of how she had been seduced by his boss. And she was going to be hurt again; of that he was certain.

When they pulled up in front of the Richmond home, Dorcas's blood raced in anticipation of seeing Philip again. Andy tied the reins to the hitching post and came to help her out of the buggy.

"You'll like Heather. She's lively and full of fun."

"Where did they come from?" Dorcas asked.

"St. Louis."

Philip opened the door and walked out to greet them as they shut the wrought-iron gate. "Hello, there." He took her arm. "How lovely you look this evening, Dorcas." He smiled, and she felt as if she were melting inside.

"I hear you've been in Sacramento." Dorcas smiled as she spoke. He must never know how neglected she felt over his not even saying good-bye before he left.

"I made up my mind in a hurry and grabbed the next stagecoach," he explained, as if he sensed her hurt. "I was gone just a few days. I had something to discuss with my uncle, and I wanted to meet my relatives. Fortunately, I persuaded them to come back with me."

When they entered the parlor, a small, attractive girl of about twenty jumped to her feet and came toward them. Philip put his hand on her shoulder. "Heather, I want to present Dorcas Hamilton."

Heather gave Dorcas a charming smile as she took her hand. "I've heard so much about you, Dorcas. Philip assured me that we'd become friends. Now you must meet my mother, Mrs. La Pointe.''

As they settled down in the parlor chairs while Philip served sherry, Dorcas studied Heather. It wasn't just the thick, wavy brown hair that framed her piquant heart-shaped face or her lively gray eyes that made her so enchanting, but her vivacious personality.

It was Andy who escorted Dorcas in to dinner and held her chair. Philip sat at the head of the table, with Heather on his right and Dorcas on his left. Andy sat next to Dorcas, with Mrs. La Pointe at the foot. It was all too obvious that Philip had paired her and Andy, Dorcas thought miserably, while he considered the witty Heather his partner.

After dinner they returned to the parlor, where Philip served brandy. ''Heather brought some of the latest sheet music from St. Louis. I've asked her to play the piano and sing for us.''

''I'll play, but you must all gather around. We'll sing together,'' Heather insisted.

So they did. Heather played with great skill and had an excellent voice. It was fun, Dorcas had to admit, but she tried not to notice how Philip kept his hand on Heather's shoulder as they sang. Mrs. La Pointe excused herself early and the four young people spent a lively evening singing and talking.

''Let's go riding in the morning. I promised Heather I'd show her the falls,'' Philip said as it grew late.

Heather looked up at him. ''You also promised me breakfast when we got there.'' Her eyes danced.

He patted her arm. ''Of course. I'll make us the best hotcakes you ever tasted. We could all go fishing first and catch some trout. Dorcas and I have gone several times and had good luck.''

Dorcas felt her cheeks flush. She didn't want to be reminded of the last time they were there.

As she and Andy prepared to leave, Philip laid her shawl across her shoulders. He held her back as if he wanted to speak privately. She looked up at his handsome face eagerly. ''I just wanted to ask. How is Keith?''

She answered, trying to hide her disappointment that he'd spoken no tender words of love. She thanked him for the dinner and walked out of the house with Andy.

Shivering with cold, she climbed into the buggy. Andy put his arm around her. ''Sit close to me. I'll keep you warm.''

"I should have worn a coat." But she snuggled against him as much for comfort as for warmth. Tears began to run down her cheeks, so she rummaged in her bag for a handkerchief. She leaned her head against Andy's shoulder. "Philip only thinks of me as a friend; that's all. He's not in love with me."

"I know he admires you very much," Andy tried to reassure her.

Dorcas began to cry harder. "But I don't want just admiration. I want him to care for me the way I do for him. I want him to ask me to marry him so we can be husband and wife."

"Perhaps he isn't ready to get married yet."

"But he's thirty years old. He's not some young boy. Of course he's ready. He just doesn't think I'm the girl for him. Oh, Andy, I feel so frustrated. He was far more interested in Heather than in me tonight."

"I have to agree to that. If you should ever marry Philip, you'll have to be willing to share his attention. He's simply not a one-woman man. He likes to play the field."

"In other words, he's a woman chaser." Her sobs smothered her voice.

"I guess you could say that," Andy admitted.

"Do you mean he might be untrue to me? I couldn't bear that."

"I'm not the one to predict that he might commit adultery. He could be very faithful once he settles down. All I can say is that he likes the attention of lots of ladies."

"And he gets it, too." There was a bitter note in her voice. "I wish I could forget him—drive him right out of my mind—but somehow I can't. I truly love him."

"I know you do," Andy answered sadly. "And he doesn't deserve such devotion."

"I don't deserve yours, Andy darling. But it means so much to me." She snuggled against him. He was truly one of the nicest men she had ever known. If she could only care for him instead of for Philip.

He held her close to him. "I'm afraid we both love the wrong people. We're just asking for heartbreak."

"Don't say that. I keep hoping and hoping."

"And so do I.'

* * *

The next morning Heather wore the riding habit that had been too small for Dorcas. It fit her perfectly, and she bubbled with excitement as she rode next to Philip. Dorcas and Andy rode side by side until the trail became too narrow and they had to form a single line.

While they rode, Dorcas relived the times she had come with Philip and been almost beside herself with happiness. But today the flowers did not look as bright, nor the snow-covered mountains as glistening. Instead of joy, she felt a dull ache in her heart.

She also thought of her mother riding here day after day with Elliott Richmond. Her beautiful mother, so bored with life in Alpine Heights and ready to find some excitement. She could visualize her father following them and catching them at their rendezvous. What a price the poor woman had paid for her unfaithfulness. Dorcas's eyes stung with tears.

When they came to the veillike falls, Dorcas, Andy, and Philip carried the breakfast things as they scrambled up the rocks, leaving Heather free to use both hands to hold on.

At the cabin, Dorcas rushed to the picnic table on the outside. "Let's eat out here in the lovely fresh air." She wanted to be inside the cabin as little as possible. Every time she thought of the double bed in there, she cringed. If she had only restrained herself, and also not confided so much in Philip. She felt not only wanton but deeply humiliated. There was nothing left of her pride now.

While Philip started the fire inside and put the coffeepot on, Heather and Dorcas set the table outside and put the benches in place. Soon they were all down at the stream, fishing for trout.

A jealous ache surged through her as out of the corner of her eye, Dorcas watched Philip showing Heather how to cast. She hated herself for being so vulnerable, so open to hurt.

When Andy came up to her, she turned to him with relief. His constant admiration bolstered her sagging self-esteem.

"I'm going to tramp around the woods this afternoon looking for birds to draw. Do you want to come with me?" he asked.

"Yes, unless Philip has plans for us all."

"I don't think he does. He told me he was going to work in his office later. His uncle wants some special report sent to Sacramento."

"Then I'd love to go. It'll help take my mind off my troubles." Andy must know that she wasn't referring to the mine.

It was delightful sitting in the sun, eating their breakfast. Heather looked around at the glorious setting. "Wait until I tell my friends in St. Louis about this. They won't be able to imagine how beautiful these mountains are. No wonder they're called the Trinity Alps."

Dorcas couldn't resent Heather, as she was utterly beguiling. No wonder Philip seemed taken with her. Who could blame him? This charming girl from St. Louis was all gaiety and fun, while she herself must seem like a drone with all her problems.

Later the two girls washed and wiped the dishes while the men carried everything into the cabin and put it away. Soon they were climbing down the rocks again. It was a relief for Dorcas to get away. Too many memories haunted her here.

That afternoon Dorcas and Andy rode as far as they could in the horse and buggy and then walked back into the deep woods. She carried his sketching materials and a book to read, while he brought their lunch and a blanket.

As he spread the blanket beside a stream in the middle of a clearing, he said, "It's easier to see the birds here away from the trees. I'm hoping to spy a golden-crowned sparrow. I don't have one in my collection."

"I envy you and Judy in your ability to sketch," Dorcas commented.

"Don't mention me in the same breath with Judy. She really has talent. All I can do is get a crude sketch down just to help me with my carving." He put a finger to his lips and whispered, "There's a sparrow now." He nodded toward a bird about six inches long.

Dorcas watched him sketch the dainty bird with colored pencils, putting in a brownish-yellow crown and a heavy black band over the eye. The sparrow pecked at some seeds on the ground, tiptoed to the water's edge, and drank. Suddenly it burst into a plaintive, flutelike song of three notes that suggested "Three Blind Mice." Andy whistled the same notes and the bird answered before it flew away.

"You're amazing, Andy. You must have a true ear."

"Guess I do." His face came alive with his beautiful smile. It caught at her heart.

*   *   *

Andy glanced at her, saw her expression, and put his arm around her shoulders. He lowered her on to the blanket and moved his fingers over the planes of her face.

"I love you, dearest. I want you to be my wife. If you ever change your mind about Philip, I'll be waiting for you." His lips pressed down on hers with desperate longing and passion.

CHAPTER 15

"Aren't you feeling well, dear?" Lenore asked her maid one morning as she noticed the dark circles under the girl's eyes.

Lenore had been so engrossed in her own affairs, especially going to the hospital to see Keith, that she hadn't noticed until now how wan Rosalie looked. She was extremely fond of her personal maid, who had been so helpful to her during the dark months of her depression.

"Yes, ma'am, I'm all right," Rosalie replied. Then she glanced away as if she had something to hide.

"You don't seem as lively as you did before I went to Trinity County. Have you had the grippe?"

"Not really, ma'am." But the maid avoided her mistress's eyes as she helped her dress.

Lenore joined some friends for lunch at the Hamilton Regency before she went on to the hospital. All the time she was there visiting Keith, concern for her maid nagged at her. Something was wrong. She was positive of that. When she came home she sought out Mrs. Williams, who was in her own living room, mending table linen.

"May I speak to you? I'm worried about something," Lenore said.

"Of course. Just sit down in that rocker and I'll bring us a cup of tea."

When the housekeeper returned with a tray of tea and

cookies, Lenore asked, "Is there something wrong with Rosalie? She doesn't act like herself at all."

"While you were gone, Mrs. Hamilton, Rosalie got to chasing around with a sailor boy. A nice-enough young man named Henry Brown. His freighter was here in dry dock being repaired, so he was in the area for at least three weeks. I was lenient with her, probably more than I should have been. But since you were gone, I gave her extra time off. She promised to make it up."

"I see," Lenore said thoughtfully. "That might explain a lot."

"I hope I didn't do anything wrong."

"Of course you didn't, Mrs. Williams. Rosalie put in a lot of extra hours when I was ill. She deserved some free time."

"I'm afraid our Rosalie got quite smitten with Henry. She's been grieving for him ever since he left," the housekeeper said.

Lenore finished the last of her tea and put her cup on the tray. "In other words, she's suffering from lovesickness and not the grippe."

When she went upstairs to her room, she found Rosalie putting freshly laundered petticoats away. As the maid helped her out of her street clothes, Lenore said teasingly, "I understand you have a sweetheart."

Rosalie's face flamed. "Who's been talking about me?"

"No one, dear. I've been worried about you, so I spoke with Mrs. Williams. She told me about your Henry Brown. She spoke very well of him. There's nothing wrong with having a sweetheart, Rosalie. That's only natural for a young, pretty girl like you."

"As soon as he returns to port, we're going to get married."

"I hope that won't be too soon. I'd miss you terribly. When do you expect him back?"

Tears flooded Rosalie's eyes. Her chin trembled. "I don't know, ma'am. I haven't heard from him."

As Lenore slipped on her lounging robe, she studied the stricken expression on the girl's face. She settled herself on the chaise and patted a spot next to her. "Sit here by me, Rosalie, and tell me all about it."

Soon the distraught girl was sobbing beside Lenore with her face in her hands. "Oh, Mrs. Hamilton, it's so awful. I

don't know what to do. You'll never forgive me." The words
came out in gasps.

Lenore caressed the girl's soft dark curls. "You're afraid
you're in the family way, aren't you?"

"Yes, but Henry's going to come back. I just know he is."

"I wouldn't count on it, dear. Henry wouldn't be the first
sailor who betrayed a sweetheart here in San Francisco."
Lenore's heart ached with compassion.

"But he promised to come back. He said we'd get married."

"Rosalie, don't plan on that. He probably meant every
word at the time. But now that he's gone away, he may have
forgotten all his promises."

"But what am I going to do?" A fresh torrent of sobs
shook the maid's shoulders.

"You won't have to do anything for a while. Stay right
here with us until you begin to show too much."

"But then—"

"Don't you have a family you can go to? I know your
mother is dead, but what about your father?

"I can't go to him. He'd kill me."

"I doubt that, dear. He'd probably want you to turn to him
if you were in trouble," Lenore said gently.

"No, you don't know him. He's a mean drunk. I haven't
heard from him for ages. He wrote and asked me for money
and I wouldn't send it to him. He'd just drink it up."

"Now, calm yourself. I'll keep you right here with me as
long as I can. Of course, it's Mr. Hamilton's home, and he's
the one—"

"Don't tell him. Please, I beg you. He'd throw me out in
the street."

"Hush, Rosalie. He wouldn't do that. But we don't have to
tell anyone. However, I'm going to see what we *can* do."
Lenore tried to think of someone who could advise her.

"Don't tell Miss Dorcas or Miss Judy. I don't want them
to know. Promise me."

"Now hush, child. I promise. I won't even discuss this
with Mrs. Williams. We'll keep this our secret for as long as
we can."

"Oh, Mrs. Hamilton, I'm so glad I could talk to you." A
sigh shuddered through the girl. "I thought you'd be angry
and insist I leave at once. I don't know where I could go."

"I'm too fond of you to do that." Lenore gave Rosalie a

quick hug. "You're to stay right here as long as possible. In the meantime, I'll see what we can do."

For the next few days Lenore wondered whom she could turn to for advice. Surely there must be homes for unmarried mothers-to-be. How could she find out about them? Would Dr. Fuller know? He seemed to confine his practice to fractures and bone surgery. But he was so friendly every time she saw him, perhaps he could help her.

When she visited the hospital the next morning, Dr. Fuller announced that Keith could go home the following day. "I suggest that you have a nurse come in during the day," he told her. "I know of one who is skilled in exercises and therapy. I'll have the nurse at the desk call her if you agree."

"Of course." She followed him out into the hallway. "I have another problem I'd like to discuss with you, if I may."

"Certainly." He turned to look into her eyes. "Perhaps you'll dine with me tonight and we can talk it over leisurely."

"Thank you. I'd like that."

"Then I'll call for you at seven, Mrs. Hamilton."

Her face flushed with pleasure as she watched his white-coated figure disappear down the hall.

Lenore looked around the luxurious setting of the new French restaurant. "You didn't have to bring me here. Any place would do."

"Hardly. One doesn't take a Hamilton to just any place." He smiled at her. "Actually I'm delighted to have an excuse to ask you out."

"You didn't need an excuse, Dr. Fuller." Her eyes shone as she looked at him. How nice he looked in his dark blue suit. So distinguished.

"Do you want to tell me your problem, or would you rather wait until we're finished eating?"

"Let's enjoy our meal first."

After they finished their dinner and were sipping black coffee, she told him about her maid. "I dearly love the girl and I feel so sorry for her. Do you know of any homes for unwed mothers we could investigate for later?"

"There's a desperate need for such places, Mrs. Hamilton.

Some of the churches have facilities, but we need far more of them. In fact, a woman I know, a former nurse, came to me for help not long ago. She wants to start just such a home. She already cares for two or three girls at a time in her apartment, but she'd like to buy a big house and take in several girls."

"I wish she had her place now. I worry about Rosalie."

Dr. Fuller reached across and took Lenore's hand. "It would be a marvelous project for a society woman like you to help raise the money. Perhaps you could get some support from your friends. This nurse has the will and ability, but not the money."

"I wouldn't know how to go about it. To raise a lot of money, I mean." Just the idea of it frightened her. She didn't even handle her own money, let alone try to raise a lot for charity.

"Would you talk to this woman, at least?" The doctor pressed her hand. "It could be a real challenge for you."

"Yes, I'll talk to her. If only to see if she'll care for Rosalie when the time comes."

Dr. Fuller took a card out of his pocket and wrote the woman's name and address on the back. "I'll telephone to tell her you're coming. And I want a report from you afterward, so we must have dinner together again. A week from this evening?"

Lenore laughed. "You're forcing my hand. Making me take some action."

"I read in the paper all the time about this charity tea or that fashion show to raise money for some cause. Why couldn't this be a worthy project?"

"Well, it could be, of course. It's just that I don't feel adequate to take it on. I've never done anything like it before."

"But you could, Mrs. Hamilton. I think you're capable of doing anything you want."

She smiled, but there was a sad expression in her eyes. "You don't know me very well, Dr. Fuller. I've suffered from depression for several years and have just recovered from a severe spell."

"But getting deeply involved in a project like this would be the best possible treatment. I guarantee you'll like Mrs. McDonald. By the time you see what she's trying to do and how enthusiastic she is, I'm sure you'll want to help her."

Mrs. McDonald greeted Lenore at the door. The nurse was a tall, middle-aged woman with her hair drawn back in a bun. Her eyes twinkled with friendliness, and she had the sweetest smile Lenore had ever seen.

"Do come in, Mrs. Hamilton. One of my girls is going to serve us tea in the living room." She led the way to a settee in front of a bay window.

Lenoe looked around the immaculately clean, cheerful room with house plants in the windows and a big yellow cat sunning itself in a chair. Soon a young girl in a maternity smock brought in a tray with a silver teapot and plate of cucumber sandwiches and raisin cookies.

Mrs. McDonald put her arm around the girl. "This is Mary Jo. She made these all by herself." The girl smiled shyly.

When Mary Jo left the room, the older woman went on in a whisper, "She's only thirteen. A neighbor raped her."

"Thirteen!" Lenore gasped in shock. "Where is her family?"

"They don't want to have anything to do with her now. They think she enticed the man. Anyway, their minister brought her to me. Her father sent some money to pay her way and says she can come back home after the baby is put up for adoption."

Indignantly, Lenore cried, "I can't understand treating your own child like that." She looked around the cozy room. "What a haven this place must be for a girl in trouble."

"I try to help them. I'm a widow with my family grown and on their own, but I still want to be useful. A doctor got me started with my first little mother-to-be five years ago, and I've been taking care of them ever since."

"I came to ask you to care for my personal maid, who is in the family way. She can stay with us until she begins to show too much. I'd pay her way, naturally."

"Of course I will, Mrs. Hamilton." She refilled their tea cups. "Dr. Fuller told me you might also help me raise funds for a larger place. I can only keep four girls at a time here. It breaks my heart to turn a girl away."

"I just told him I would think about it." Lenore just couldn't turn the eager woman down flat. "What do you have in mind?"

"I'd like to care for about twelve girls at a time."

"But that would take a huge place."

"If I could find a rooming house with plenty of bedrooms and some space to turn into a nursery and a delivery room, that would be fine. I could hire a woman to help me."

"And you could manage with just one helper?" Lenore thought of the large staff that kept the Hamilton mansion going under Mrs. Williams's supervision.

"Well, the girls help, of course. Each one has her chores to do. They all pitch in to help with the babies when they come. That way they learn to care for their own child if they keep it."

"You haven't found a suitable place yet?"

"No. I've looked some, but I'm really too busy to leave here very often. Besides, one of my girls is due any day now." The good-hearted woman told Lenore some of her experiences with her girls.

"I don't know what I can do to help you, Mrs. McDonald, but at least I could try to find some places for you to consider. I'm not as tied down as you are."

All the way home, Lenore thought about the need for a larger home for Mrs. McDonald's girls. She wanted to push all the sad stories out of her mind, but she couldn't. Besides, it wouldn't hurt to look at some places. At least she'd have that to report to Dr. Fuller when he took her out to dinner next week. But she shrank from taking on too much responsibility. How could she help raise money even if she did find a place?

With Keith home, Lenore's days were full. She waited on him when the nurse took her breaks, and of course she walked with him while he tried to get around the house on his crutches. However, she spent one afternoon going out with a real estate agent to look at rooming houses and small hotels that were for sale.

"They all seem so dreary and dirty," she reported to Dr. Fuller when they had dinner. "I can't imagine Mrs. McDonald being interested in any of them."

"You can do wonders with a little paint. I have an idea. Why don't the two of us look this Saturday?"

"I'd like that. I've really had so little experience in dealing with real estate. My husband always provided me with a home. So I'm not one to judge what would be suitable, Dr. Fuller.''

"I wish you would call me Prescott." He held her hands in his.

"I will if you'll call me Lenore."

"I'll look forward to Saturday, Lenore."

"So will I."

On Saturday he called for her at ten o'clock. They met a real estate salesman who took them from one property to another until they were exhausted but had still found nothing that seemed suitable. They stopped for lunch and then went driving around on their own.

"Let's go farther out where we might find something less expensive," Prescott suggested. "There's no reason that the building should be located downtown like a rooming house."

Toward the end of the afternoon, they found a large, older house on a sizable lot. The sign announcing that it was for sale also said, "Open for Inspection." A real estate agent opened the door as they approached. "I was just ready to lock up."

"Do you have time to show us through?"

"Of course. Just come with me. Now, this place is a real buy. The widow who owned it died about six months ago and left it to a nephew back east. He's anxious to sell and get it off his hands."

He led the way through a large front parlor and a back parlor as well as a dining room and sunroom. There were two extra bedrooms downstairs and quarters for a housekeeper, including a small living room and bedroom. The upstairs contained five bedrooms in addition to a big master bedroom.

"What about the furniture?" Prescott asked. "Does that go with the house?"

Lenore had been noticing the pieces, some of which looked as if they had been expensive in their time. Most of them were still in fair condition.

"Well, the furniture's supposed to be extra, but I imagine I could arrange the whole package if anyone were interested," the salesman said.

"When was this house built?" Lenore asked.

"In 1858, by a ship captain. He brought his whole family out here from Connecticut."

"There's someone I want to bring to see this place." Prescott said. "If you'll give me your card, I'll arrange a time."

The salesman handed him a card and added, "I'll be here all day tomorrow. It's a real buy. Five thousand dollars will get you the whole place."

"And the furniture?" Lenore asked.

The salesman smiled. "We'll have to see about that."

Later, as they ate dinner, Lenore said, "Now that house looks like a real home to me. I'm sure Mrs. McDonald would agree. I can just see that back parlor as a nursery."

"And one of those downstairs bedrooms as a delivery room. It would take some repair work and cleaning and painting, but it's an excellent place for the purpose. And a lot of house for the money. I think the reason they have to sell it cheap is because the rest of the neighborhood is made up of small houses or row houses. It looks out of place.

"I suppose the captain was the first one to build there and no one else built one as big. But the house seems to suit our purpose beautifully."

Prescott ordered dessert and turned to her with a smile. "I'm glad to hear you say 'our.' I want you involved in this."

Lenore shrank back. "I don't think I can do anything more."

"Of course you can. Now this is how I think we should proceed. If Mrs. McDonald is as enthusiastic as we are, we should see a lawyer and get ourselves organized as a legitimate charitable association. We should have a board of directors and hire Mrs. McDonald as the salaried manager."

"That's a good idea. She should be paid."

He pointed his finger at Lenore. "You should be president of the board."

"Oh, Prescott, I couldn't take that responsibility. I couldn't possibly. I've never done anything like that."

"Then that's a good reason for you to try. You underestimate yourself, Lenore. I'll serve on the board and get another doctor as well. A nurse or two. And a couple of your friends, if possible. Those who work in charitable organizations. But you should chair the board."

"But why me? I'm not even one of the leaders of society."

"But you do have a famous name. You will attract others

to the cause. And you could be a leader of society if you so chose. Most socialites also tend to have a favorite charity. Some of them work very hard to support them. This could be your charity.''

"Really, Prescott, it's absolutely out of the question. I can't even consider it. I'm afraid I've never been much of a leader, social or otherwise. I was in poor health—''

"Lenore, you're not in poor health now. I've never seen a more beautiful, radiant lady. Put your past problems behind you and make a fresh start. You can do all kinds of interesting things. Look ahead.''

She smiled at him. "You sound just like my daughter.''

"You mean Judy?''

"No. My other daughter, Dorcas. Someday you'll have to meet her. She's such a spirited girl with real initiative. She's the one who has reopened the Alpine, our mine in Trinity County.''

"Sounds like a girl after my own heart. I admire a woman who gets things done. And you can, too, Lenore. I think of you as a sheltered lady, but one who has loads of latent ability. You should take on this project and not be afraid to try. You'll surprise yourself.''

"Oh, Prescott, how could I ever raise five thousand dollars? I doubt that I could even bring in five hundred dollars. Just the thought of it scares me.''

"No one is asking you to raise the whole amount. I'll donate some money, and I'm sure several of my doctor friends will be glad to help out. In fact, if Mrs. McDonald approves of the house we found, I'll put up enough to hold it until we can form a legitimate charitable organization.''

The more Prescott talked, the more Lenore became enthusiastic about taking part. But that night, as she tossed and turned, unable to sleep, all of her self-doubt came rushing back. She couldn't possibly take on the responsibility. She was quite incapable of heading a fund drive or presiding over the board of directors. The whole project was beyond her. She'd tell the doctor the next time she saw him. She wouldn't have anything to do with it. Of course, she would make a donation, but that was all.

She dreaded telling Prescott of her decision. She wanted him to admire her. And she would miss her meetings with him. It had been a long time since she'd been so attracted to a man.

On Monday Lenore lunched with a friend she had known all her married life. Before she realized it, she was telling Virginia Reston about Mrs. McDonald and the need for a new home for unwed mothers.

"Can you imagine poor young girls being in such a tragic predicament, with nowhere to turn? The doctor who is taking care of Keith wants me to take this on as a project and raise funds—"

"You should do it, Lenore. You'd enjoy it once you got started."

"Oh, Virginia, it's out of the question. I haven't the slightest idea how to go about it."

"The thing to do is to put on a big charity ball. That's where you'd make the money. Perhaps a costume ball. Everyone would come as a famous character in a book or something like that. I've worked on fashion shows, luncheons, musicals, and almost every kind of party you can imagine. Nothing brings in the money like a well-planned ball."

"It sounds impossible. I wish the doctor had approached you," Lenore said with a sigh.

"I'll help you. We could be cochairmen of the ball."

"Would you serve on the board of directors as well? Dr. Fuller is going to get it all set up."

Virginia picked up her gloves and began putting them on. "It looks like I'll have to get you started. Wait until my husband hears this. He thinks I run half the charities in town already."

"Of course, I might decide not to go on with the project myself."

"Lenore Hamilton! I don't want to hear another word about your backing out. You need to get started again instead of staying home grieving for your husband. You can't be in mourning for the rest of your life. We'll do it together."

As Lenore returned home, she kept wondering how she could ever go ahead with all this. One part of her was intensely interested and the other still afraid to try.

That evening Prescott stopped by on his way home to check on Keith. When the doctor finished his examination, Lenore asked him into the parlor to have a drink of brandy.

"I also came to tell you that I took Mrs. McDonald to see the house, and she is most enthusiastic. I've made an offer; if it's accepted, we'll go right ahead," he told her.

He studied her as he sipped his drink. "We'll need your help, Lenore. Not only to serve on the board and to raise money, but to counsel the girls as well." He leaned toward her. "You have so much to give, if you would only let yourself."

"Well, I'm thinking about it." It would be wonderful to have something to work for in common with this charming man.

"You'll find that as you help these girls with their problems, you'll solve many of your own. As the Bible says, 'As you give, so shall you receive.' By reaching out away beyond yourself, you'll be too busy and involved with others to be depressed. A person who turns inward too much destroys himself. You'll be helping yourself as well."

She smiled at him. "Of course you're right. The more downhearted and depressed I became, the less I thought of anyone else. Even my children ceased to be important to me. I hope I'll never be like that again." She told him about her luncheon meeting with her friend. "Perhaps you've met Virginia Reston."

"Yes, I have. She's a charming lady. Very active in the community."

"She's willing to serve on the board and help in any way she can. In fact, she has offered to be cochairman of a charity ball to raise money."

"That's marvelous news. Exactly the kind of support we need." He finished his drink and rose to go. When Lenore stood up, too, he took her hands in his and raised them to his lips. "What about you, Lenore? What is your decision?"

She looked into his eyes. "In spite of all my misgivings and feelings of inadequacy, I guess my answer is yes."

"You'll never regret it, my dear. And it will give us an opportunity to get to know each other better. I'm looking forward to that."

"So am I." Her heart sang happily as she escorted him to the door.

CHAPTER 16

The weeks raced by until it was the first of September. Andy's heart ached for Dorcas as he watched her becoming more worried each day. She shipped another gold bar, but she was still a long way from reaching the goal.

One morning Andy went over to her after he had been underground. "I've been examining some new core samples at the end of tunnel fourteen." He pulled down the map and showed her where it was located. "It runs parallel to the face of the cliff at the six-hundred-foot depth."

"I remember reading in my father's records that he picked up a vein in there, but it petered out on him."

"But according to my core samples, it might show up again. Anyway, I've placed a crew there. As soon as we extend the tunnel, we'll see what we have."

When Andy reported to work at the Golden Star, he found Philip packing some material into a briefcase.

"I got a wire from my uncle. He's called a meeting in Sacramento of all his mine managers. I don't know what's in the works." Philip told Andy what he wanted him to do while he was gone. "You'll be in charge, of course. All together, I'll be gone about a week."

When Philip left to go home and pack before he caught the stagecoach to Redding, Andy sat at his desk and let out a long sigh of relief. This was the perfect chance to get the evidence he wanted about the Richmond skulduggery against the Hamiltons.

At the end of the day, when his work was done, Andy prepared for his investigation. He took a high-powered camera out of its special cupboard, along with film, a tripod, flash powder, and a custom-made rack to hold the powder. Somehow he managed to get to the skip and down into tunnel 10 without being noticed. Fortunately the office workers had already left for home and it was between shifts. Even if someone had seen him, it would not be unusual for the chief engineer to be using the camera.

His burden became heavy and awkward as he trudged along the tunnel, trying to keep his light in front of him without dropping any of the equipment. At last, when he came to the barrier they'd had to break through, he put his lantern down, erected the tripod, and screwed the camera to it to hold it steady. The iron door hung loosely on its hinges. A few boards had been placed across the opening with the sign DANGER! KEEP OUT! in full view. He shook a small amount of the flash powder in to the rack, got the camera focused, and snapped it as soon as the opening became illuminated.

"This will be the 'after' picture," he told himself. As soon as he finished his photographing he would have the barrier put back the way it was before they'd broken through it, and take a picture of that. What he wanted was real evidence of how the tunnel, with its illegal workings, had been sealed off.

He picked up his equipment and walked on down the tunnel until he came to the cave-in. Here he took more pictures. He made sure he got photos of the opening the rescue team had made to put the ladder down into the Alpine tunnel just below. In fact, by aiming his camera carefully, he even got a shot of the end of tunnel 19, where Keith and Red had been trapped.

When he returned to the office he searched through all the old maps until he found one that showed the extension of tunnel 10 across the property line. Of course, it didn't say so on the map, but there were small dots indicating its length. He hung the map on the wall and took pictures of it.

By the time he was through, it was quite dark. He knew his landlady would be keeping his supper warm, so he put the camera equipment away and determined to go on with his investigation the next morning. He had to make the most of every hour of Philip's absence.

The following day Andy hunted up one of the Golden Star's oldest carpenters. "Bernie, do you know who put the iron door and the barrier at the end of tunnel ten? It must have been done about twelve years ago."

Bernie scratched his head. "I think I did. I had a helper then, and Mr. Richmond, the older one, ordered us to seal it off. He said it was too dangerous to leave open."

"It's even more dangerous now since we rescued the Alpine men through there. I don't want anyone hurt. Will you fix it just the way you did before?"

"Yes, sir."

"Tell me as soon as it's finished. I want it taken care of before Mr. Richmond returns," Andy said.

"I understand. He's quite a stickler for safety."

"Take someone to help you, Bernie."

That night Andy warned his landlady that he would be late the next evening. "But please don't worry about me. It's just that with Mr. Richmond gone, I have more work to do. His as well as my own."

The elderly lady smiled. "Don't fret about your supper, dear. I'll fix something that you can heat up easily. Probably stew."

The next day, as soon as Andy had completed his necessary work, he took his photographic plates into the darkroom and developed them. He had quite a few clear pictures. The last step was to look up the old records. The pictures alone wouldn't be enough to get the result he wanted. If he only had the exact dates, it would help. When he found the evidence, he hoped he'd be able to capture it on film, but he knew he was in for hours of work trying to search it out. It wasn't going to be easy. Elliot Richmond was no fool. Whatever he had done would be safely buried in the files. Perhaps there was nothing at all recorded. All Andy could do was try.

As the days passed, Dorcas's hopes faded. None of the veins they were following had paid off well so far. She saw little of Andy, as he was especially busy with Philip gone.

Each morning as Dorcas climbed out of bed, she had to convince herself that something would happen soon to help them. She worried about her grandfather. What was he thinking? Had he given up all hope and resigned himself to bankruptcy?

Clyde Hamilton sat in his office, holding the calendar and staring at the date. It was September 7. He had just three weeks and two days. He took a red pencil out of the desk and drew a scarlet circle around Monday, October 1. Doomsday.

He reached in the back of the top drawer and picked up the

small revolver. It felt good in his hand. He had brought it from home with the ammunition. The bullets still lay in their box at the back of the drawer. In spite of his promise to Dorcas, he made his plans. September 30? October 1? He would have to decide between the two dates. In any case, he would come here early in the morning and end his life.

Let one of the clerks find him. It was better than shocking the folks at home. Especially if it were Keith who discovered him. That poor boy had had troubles enough this summer. Clyde gripped the barrel, then let his fingers trail over the trigger and the roughness of the handle. This was the only friend he had left.

One thing he couldn't face was the gloating of all his creditors. They were just waiting for the end. There was no way that Dorcas could send enough gold bars from the mine to save him. It was too late now. After he was gone, the gold would be hers to use as she pleased. Perhaps she could recover enough to redeem her jewelry. One gold brick would almost take care of that. What about Lenore? What did she have left? He had a hunch that Dorcas had been using some of her mother's money. But pretty soon he wouldn't have to worry about anything anymore. He caressed his gun and put it away. For the next three weeks he would just be marking time. It was practically all over.

Lenore looked at Rosalie one morning when the maid came in with the breakfast tray. "We may have a lovely place ready for you by the time you need to leave us."

"That would be very nice, ma'am, but I'm sure Henry will be coming for me soon.

The girl's air of complete confidence made her so vulnerable that Lenore hated to say anything. But she had to face facts.

"Don't get your hopes up too much, dear. I'm afraid you'll never see him again. If he were interested in you, wouldn't he have written? You haven't heard a word."

"I know, ma'am, but likely he's no hand to write. He doesn't know about the baby coming. He just said he'd look me up again as soon as he got into port, and I know he will."

"I certainly hope so."

Rosalie put the tray on a table, and while Lenore ate, she

made the bed and straightened the room. "What clothes shall I put out for you, Mrs. Hamilton?"

"My green linen suit. You know how warm San Francisco can be in early fall. So I'll need something cool."

It was delightful to look forward to having lunch with Virginia Reston. Their plans for the charity ball were making great strides. Today they would decide on the theme so they could order the invitations to be printed up.

Virginia Reston sat at an outdoor table in the courtyard of a charming French restaurant. As usual, she was beautifully turned out, in a pale blue dress and a straw hat covered with matching flowers. She waved as she saw Lenore coming.

"Have you any ideas about a theme?" Virginia asked after she greeted her friend. "I want you as involved as possible in this project."

Lenore studied the menu, deciding on crab louie and iced tea. "Well, I like the idea of a costume ball. You say there hasn't been one for some time. I've been considering using a book as the theme, but on the way down I wondered how the sea would work. We're right here on the Pacific Ocean, so it should be appropriate, of course."

"Marvelous. We could call it the King Neptune Ball."

"We could even have someone dress up as King Neptune, and he could preside over the event." Lenore suggested.

"Of course. We could have a throne for him on a stage and some pretty girls to be his handmaidens. Your daughter, for example."

Lenore's face showed her enthusiasm. "Speaking of my daughter—I've told you what an artist she is. Why not have her design us a cover for the invitations?"

"And we could repeat it on the dance programs. Let's hire some entertainers to put on a show dancing to the hornpipe and singing nautical songs."

"By the way, Dr. Fuller has called a board meeting on Saturday to get organized. Luncheon at twelve-thirty and meeting right afterward. He's going to call you. You can come, can't you, Virginia?"

"Of course. Vince likes to play tennis on Saturday, so he is delighted when I have my own plans."

For the rest of the week, Lenore looked forward to going to Prescott's home for the luncheon meeting. She dressed with special care in a flowered voile afternoon dress in the latest style—bell-shaped and ending in a short train. The background of the material was a soft pink that brought out the coloring in her skin.

Before she left the house, Judy brought her some drawings of King Neptune on a throne shaped like a shell and holding his forked spear.

"Judy, they're excellent. I'll be so proud to show them to the board." She took her daughter's hand. "You have so much talent. It's a shame you aren't continuing your lessons with Mr. Burke. Why aren't you, dear?"

"Because I don't want to anymore." A flush rose in Judy's cheeks, and her jaw set stubbornly. "Someday I might, but not now. I'm going to enjoy myself and go to all the parties I can."

"Don't forget your art entirely. So few have the gift you have for it."

After Wilson helped Lenore into the carriage, she handed him a map. "We need to go to 937 Victoria Way. It's in Pacific Heights. I've marked it on the map."

She settled herself back in the seat. This outing was particularly meaningful. What if Prescott proposed to her someday? He might not, of course. But if he did, and if she accepted, would he want to live in his home in Pacific Heights? Just the thought of marrying again stirred her. Prescott was a most eligible widower in a respected profession. With her social background, they could take their places in San Francisco society and have a delightful life.

But she'd better not make too many plans. Prescott might not have the slightest intention of every marrying again. She knew he still missed his wife. Apparently, they had been very devoted. Yet he had been most attentive and seemed to be attracted to her. At least, the project of the home for unwed mothers had given them many opportunities to be together.

As the carriage entered the fine district of Pacific Heights, she looked at each home. Would Prescott's be as nice? They turned down Victoria Way. She hardly breathed as they drew closer to 937. Would it be a gingerbready Victorian, appropriate to the name of the street? Actually, she wasn't enthusiastic about some of the examples of the era, especially since they were approaching the twentieth century. Besides, the queen was seventy-five now.

She suddenly saw the house and let out a gasp. It was a

handsome mansion of Georgian architecture, her favorite. It looked out over San Francisco Bay and the hills of Marin County to the north. The wrought-iron gates stood open, so Wilson turned the carriage into the circular driveway at the front entrance.

The other members of the board turned out to be interesting, busy people. Another doctor, a banker, and a lawyer. Besides Virginia and Lenore, there were a social worker and a nurse, so the board was evenly divided between men and women.

After lunch in a splendid dining room with a breathtaking view, they went into the living room and Prescott called the meeting to order. "The main order of business today is to get organized as an official body with an election of officers. I would like to nominate Mrs. Hamilton as president."

Before Lenore could protest, Virginia seconded the motion and she was elected. Soon Prescott was named vice-president; Virginia, secretary; and the banker, treasurer. "I'll now turn the meeting over to Mrs. Hamilton," Prescott announced, and settled back in his chair.

Lenore's natural poise took over, and soon she was proposing that they hold a charity ball to raise money. She skillfully brought Virginia into the discussion and showed the pictures that Judy had prepared. The project was unanimously approved. It was decided that the ball would be held the first Saturday night in November.

As Lenore alighted from the carriage back at the Hamilton mansion and started up the stairs, she heard someone running toward her. She turned and saw a young man with a peaked cap on the back of his head and a duffel bag slung over one shoulder. "Mrs. Hamilton," he called, his face red with exertion.

Puzzled, she waited for him. Who could he be? She had never seen him before. He came to the bottom of the stairs and looked up at her, panting for breath. "You're Mrs. Hamilton, aren't you, ma'am?"

"Well, yes. But who are you?"

"I'm a friend of Rosalie's. Could I possibly see her for just a minute, ma'am? I know it ain't her day off, but—"

"Are you Henry?"

"Yes, ma'am. Henry Brown. I've been out to sea and I just got into port."

She looked at his clean denims and freshly cut hair and smiled. "You're a welcome sight, Henry Brown. Do come right in with me."

When he reached her side, Lenore put out her hand. "I've been telling Rosalie that she would never hear from you. Thank goodness I was wrong."

"I expected to return all along."

They shook hands and she thought, I like this young man. As she unlocked the door, she said, "I hope your intentions are serious toward Rosalie."

"Yes, ma'am. I want us to get married. I'm not going to sea anymore. I want to find a job right here in San Francisco."

"Good. You've come back none too soon. Rosalie is expecting your child."

His face flamed. "Gosh, she is?"

"Yes, and I want you to do right by her." They walked across the entrance hall and up the stairs.

"Oh, I will. That's why I came back."

"I imagine Rosalie is working in my room. You wait out here in the hall until I tell you to come in."

Lenore found her maid cleaning her bathroom. "There's someone to see you, dear. Go into my sitting room."

Rosalie got off her knees, washed her hands, and straightened her cap while Lenore hurried through her bedroom into her sitting room. She opened the door to the hall and motioned for Henry to come in.

When Rosalie came into the sitting room, she cried, "Henry!" and burst into tears. Lenore stepped into the bedroom and closed the door to leave them alone. Well, this day would be a happy one for her sweet little maid. She took off her afternoon gown and hung it in the closet. After she put on a simple dress, she opened the door to her sitting room and found the two of them in an embrace.

"Rosalie, you can take the rest of the day off, dear. I think you and Henry have some plans to make."

"Oh, Mrs. Hamilton, you're the nicest lady in the world."

* * *

The next morning, Rosalie brought in the breakfast tray. Her eyes shone with happiness. "I'm afraid I'll be leaving you, ma'am. We've found a little flat, and Henry wants me to stay home and take care of it and get ready for the baby."

"When are you planning to be married?" Lenore asked.

"This coming Saturday. Henry has to look for a job during the week. We have to get a license and then find a preacher who will marry us."

"Would you like to be married here in the back parlor?"

Rosalie's face beamed with joy. "I'd like it, Mrs. Hamilton. The staff could all see me. You folks are the only family I've got."

"I'll ask Mrs. Williams to bake you a cake and fix punch. Tomorrow we must go find you a pretty dress to wear. I'll pay for it."

"You're so good to me, Mrs. Hamilton."

"I want you to have a nice wedding, dear."

Before they left to go shopping the next morning, Prescott telephoned and she told him the news about Rosalie. He said, "I hope you'll still continue to work on the board."

"Of course. Not all the girls are as fortunate as Rosalie. Too many of them are left with no one to help them."

"Is there anything I can do?" Prescott asked softly. "Does the young man have a job?"

"I doubt it. If you hear of anything, please let us know."

"I'll ask around the hospital. There's usually need for an extra orderly or two. Or perhaps a driver." Prescott laughed. "I feel very much obliged to Henry. He's the one who was responsible for getting us together."

"You forget that you were Keith's doctor," Lenore said.

"But that was a physician-patient relationship. I needed more than that to approach the beautiful Mrs. Hamilton."

"Then I'm grateful to Henry, too. By the way, I thoroughly enjoyed your luncheon yesterday, Prescott."

"I'm glad. Would you have dinner with me and go to a play next Saturday evening?"

"I'd be delighted. I'm sure the wedding will be over in plenty of time."

"In the meantime I'll find out what I can about a job for Henry. At least something to get them started."

* * *

The following Saturday afternoon, Lenore's eyes misted as she watched the wedding ceremony. She doubted that there was ever a happier couple who exchanged vows. Rosalie looked so pretty in a new fall outfit with a ruffled white blouse. The jacket hid the slight rounding of her figure. Henry stood tall and proud in a dark brown suit with a boutonniere in his lapel. The gardener had filled the back parlor with flowers and made a bouquet for the bride. The whole staff, along with Judy, who skipped one of her innumerable parties, Keith and herself, witnessed the ceremony and enjoyed the reception afterward. When it was all over, they loaded the gifts and Rosalie's clothes into the carriage, and Wilson took the newlyweds to their flat.

Before Rosalie left, Lenore put her arms around her maid and kissed her. "I'm going to miss you so. Be sure to come and see me, dear. Especially after the baby comes."

"I will, Mrs. Hamilton. I've been so happy here with all of you." She added in a whisper, "I hope you'll marry Dr. Fuller."

Lenore whispered back, "So do I."

Sleep eluded Dorcas. She lay in her bed, staring into the darkness and wondering how long she could hang on. There was so little money left to run the mine. A shroud of worry wrapped around her as she thought of the October 1 deadline drawing closer and closer.

As soon as she saw the first rays of sunlight in the east, she climbed out of bed and put on her clothes. She'd walk over to the office and work awhile before breakfast. She knew that if she didn't keep busy, she'd soon be a bundle of nerves.

When she stepped out into the fresh, chilly air, her breath made a white cloud in front of her. She shivered, not just from the cold but from a feeling of apprehension that suddenly came over her. She walked briskly along the path, hearing the squeak of her footsteps in the frost. Something urged her to hurry. Was someone prowling around the office area? Should she go on or turn toward the bunkhouse and rouse some of the men? But she broke into a run and headed in the direction of the mine buildings.

Soon she entered the inner court and ran toward the office.

She tried the door and it was still locked. She glanced through the window and nothing seemed disturbed. Frantically, she glanced all around. Should she check the stamp mill? As she started in that direction she saw a slight movement near the mine entrance. Was it an animal or a man? It was bigger than a dog, but it could be a stray deer. Whatever it was had slipped behind the hoist house and was no longer in view.

"What do you want?" she called as she ran that way. Her heart thrashed in fear.

Soon she heard the pounding of hoofs, and she ran around the hoist house just in time to get a glimpse of a man on horseback before he disappeared among the trees. His back had been toward her, but there was something familiar about the shape of his shoulders, his brown plaid lumberman's jacket, and his build. But who was it?

"Wes Ferguson!" she cried aloud. What was he doing here? Her heart constricted in dread as she remembered the threat he had made the day she had fired him: "I'll get even with you!" What had he done?

But when she entered the hoist house and looked around at the big cable and the spool it was wound on, she couldn't see anything amiss. She shrugged and walked toward her office. Later, when she saw Red and the others in the crew preparing to start their shift, she came out and told them about the unexpected visitor. "I guess he heard me coming and left before he could do anything."

"We'll look things over carefully, Miss Hamilton," Red assured her. "No use taking any chances."

"I'll be in my office. Let me know if you find anything."

Soon she heard the machinery turned on and then the men shouting. Dorcas rose from her chair and hurried out the door. When she reached the hoist house the miners were all talking excitedly.

Red looked up at her, his face flushed in anger. "The man you saw cut the cable. My God, we could all have been killed!" He showed her the partially severed cable, with its dozens of small wires splayed apart instead of being wound into a strong whole. "This is malicious vandalism of the worst kind."

"It was cut from the inside so no one would notice it at first glance," one of the miners said, his face white with shock. "It'd never have held up with the weight of all of us on the skip."

A wave of horror washed over Dorcas as she looked at her crew and realized what might have happened if they'd tried to go underground. "It was Wes Ferguson. I'm positive of that. But why would he put your lives in danger? I'm the one he wanted to get even with."

Red pushed his cap back and scratched his head. "I suppose he assumed we'd discover it before we started down. I can't believe that he'd want to kill us all. That doesn't make sense."

"Maybe he intended to cut it clear through but he heard me coming, so he beat it," Dorcas suggested. She looked at the men, one after another. "But why?"

"The delay, ma'am. It'll take us some time to fix the cable," one of the men answered.

Dorcas hardly listened as Red explained what they would have to do. She was too angry to put her mind to the problem. "I'm going into town to find Ferguson. I'll call the sheriff when I do."

"Be darned careful, Miss Hamilton. Ferguson might be pretty desperate if he knows you saw him."

When Dorcas returned to the house, Esther was ready with her breakfast.

"I don't want anything. I have to go into town at once," Dorcas told her.

After Esther heard about the cut cable, she said, "Wes Ferguson already has a good start if he's heading out of town. Now, you sit down and eat some of this hot oatmeal while I change my clothes. I'm going into town with you. If you do meet up with that scoundrel, you certainly don't want to be all alone."

Dorcas sat impatiently at the table. She was anxious to get away, but she knew that Esther was right. Her former mine manager was too dangerous to confront alone.

Although they searched for Wes Ferguson all day, there was no sign of him in town. None of the people they questioned had seen him. By midafternoon they finally gave up and returned to the Alpine. Completely discouraged, Dorcas put the horse in the small barn and unhitched the buggy. "I suppose he's ten or fifteen miles away by this time."

"Perhaps. But he may just be hiding out in the woods until after dark," Esther warned her as she filled the feed bin with oats. "I have a hunch he'll hang around to hear what happened out here."

"In other words he might go into a saloon in town tonight to get something to drink and pick up any news."

"That's right."

"Then let's us go back after dark and see if we can find him."

"Oh, Miss Dorcas, let's ask Mr. Woodard—"

"No. I'm going to handle this myself. After all, I'm not even sure that the man I saw was Ferguson."

But Dorcas didn't feel so brave when she and Esther sat in the buggy outside of the Alpine Saloon. They watched several hard-rock miners push against the swinging doors as they entered the noisy establishment. The tinny sound of an old piano cut into the quiet night.

When a tall, broad-shouldered miner stopped by her buggy, he tipped his cap and said, "Good evening, Miss Hamilton. I'm Jake Adams from the Golden Star."

"Of course. I recognize you. You worked so hard the night of the cave-in. I'll always be grateful for your help."

"Could I give you a hand tonight, ma'am? Are you looking for someone?"

"As a matter of fact, I'd like to have a few words with Wes Ferguson. I haven't seen him go inside. But when you go in, would you look around for him? If he's in there, please ask him to come outside. Just say that someone wants to see him."

"Be glad to, ma'am."

Her heart pounded against her chest as she climbed out of the buggy and stood in a circle of light in front of the wooden sidewalk outside the saloon. Soon Wes Ferguson stepped out of the swinging door, followed by six big miners who lined up in a row behind him. She didn't recognize any of them, so she guessed they must be from the Golden Star. How huge and menacing they looked. Probably all Ferguson's buddies. Her blood seemed to turn to ice as she faced them.

She swallowed hard and stared right at her former manager. "Ferguson, when I fired you, you said you'd get even. Well, you have, haven't you? At daybreak this morning you sneaked into my hoist house and cut my cable."

"I don't know what you're talking about," Ferguson answered gruffly.

One of the other miners spoke up. "Why do you think it was Wes?"

"Because I saw him riding away on a horse just before he vanished into the woods."

"Did you see his face?"

"No, but I recognized him."

Wes sneered. "She don't know what she's talking about."

"It was you, all right. You had on your brown plaid jacket."

Ferguson looked around at the other men. He pointed to his dark blue jacket. "Does this look like brown plaid to you guys? She must have seen someone else. I don't know nothing about a cut cable."

"Well, I say it was you, Ferguson. I'm positive of it. Will one of you get the sheriff for me?" Dorcas asked.

A huge man stepped forward. A dark beard covered most of his face. "I'm Mike Tuttle, ma'am. I've been sworn in as a deputy sheriff. What makes you think that Ferguson is the man who cut your cable?"

Her heart sank leadenly. She was sure these men were all Wes Ferguson's cronies. Likely he'd spent most evenings hanging around this saloon when he worked at the Alpine.

Esther leaned out of the buggy. "Miss Dorcas, I think we'd better leave now." Her voice rose with fright.

Dorcas squared her shoulders. "No! I'm not leaving. Not until Ferguson's arrested for malicious vandalism. All my men could have been killed."

Mike Tuttle took another step toward her. "Tell me again exactly what you saw."

Dorcas tried to keep her voice steady as she explained again about the man on horseback.

"Can you describe the horse?"

Dorcas looked at the horses tied to the rail. She pointed to one. "I think it was that one."

Tuttle turned to Ferguson. "Is that yours?"

The former mine manager shrugged. "What if it is? There are lots of brown horses in this town."

The deputy sheriff turned to Dorcas again. "Actually, it sounds like you only caught a glimpse of your intruder this morning. You didn't see his face at all. You just think it was Ferguson."

"Of course I think it was Ferguson. He threatened me

233

when I fired him. Then as soon as he comes back to town, something terrible happens at the Alpine." She stuck her chin out determinedly and blinked back tears of anger. "Arrest him!"

"I can't do that, ma'am. There's not enough evidence."

Ferguson laughed. "Come on, guys. Line up at the bar and I'll treat you to a drink." He turned to go back into the saloon.

But Tuttle grabbed his arm and swung him around. "Not so fast, Ferguson. We don't want your kind around here. Now get yourself onto your horse and get out of town. And don't come back!"

Wes Ferguson stared at the deputy sheriff in shock. "What the hell do you mean?"

Tuttle tightened his huge fist and held it before Ferguson's nose. "All of us miners at the Golden Star have an understanding among ourselves. Nothing is to happen to Miss Hamilton! She's earned the respect of every one of us. And by God, neither you nor anyone else is to harm her! Now get out right now!"

Two of the biggest miners stepped forward and grabbed Ferguson's arms. They marched him down the sidewalk to the hitching post and lifted him up into his saddle. One of the men untied the horse and handed him the reins. As soon as Ferguson had the animal turned around, one miner gave it a smart clap on its flank.

As the sounds of the horse's hooves faded away in the darkness, the deputy sheriff stepped off the sidewalk and came up to Dorcas. "Here, let me help you back into your buggy."

"Thank you, Mr. Tuttle. I'm ever so much obliged to you and the others." She climbed in and then turned to wave to the men still on the sidewalk.

"Remember, Miss Hamilton, if you need help, just call on us," Tuttle said.

Dorcas put out her hand. Her voice trembled as she murmured, "At least I found out that I have some friends."

CHAPTER 17

As Philip took his place at the conference table, he felt a sense of dread, almost foreboding. Why had his uncle called together all the mine managers at the company headquarters here in Sacramento? This was the busiest time of year for all of them. They always tried to make the most of the good weather before the winter season began. Soon the rains would start, making the roads almost impassable. So why take them away from the mines now?

Two of the managers were Elliott Richmond's sons, Sidney and Matthew, both in their twenties and graduates of the Mackay School of Mines in Reno. Now they each managed a large silver mine in Nevada. The three other men were from the Richmond gold mines in the Sierra, about fifty miles east of Sacramento. And, of course, he himself was from the north.

A big overhead fan whipped the air around to keep them reasonably cool. When Philip had walked over from his hotel, the valley heat, so necessary to ripen the fruit and grains for which this great region was noted, had struck him in full force until he felt as if he were in a furnace. He hung his coat jacket over the back of his chair, grateful to be indoors at last.

Copies of their financial reports were placed in front of them. A feeling of shock came over Philip as he studied the balance sheets and realized that of the six mines, the Golden Star was the least productive.

During the morning each manager gave a report and Elliott Richmond summed up their discussion. "We must make some long-term plans and see what properties are getting depleted and should eventually be phased out."

Philip seemed to freeze inside. He couldn't look at his uncle.

But Elliott went on. "Unless something unusual comes up, it looks as if the Golden Star is reaching that point."

"But it's been our major mine," Philip protested. "The

one we've been noted for. The Golden Star and the Andromeda Lode."

Elliott's lip curled. "But we don't have the Lode anymore. You know that. You were right there when we had the consultants come. It's mined out." He let out a long sigh. "Those were the glory days when we were working the Lode. Eight to nine hundred dollars per ton of ore. But that time is over. It's played out."

"But Golden Star's still making a profit."

"Marginal, Philip. It won't be long before we'll have to replace the obsolete equipment. In light of that, it's not so profitable."

"How can you close it down and throw all those men out of work? Alpine Heights will be a ghost town." A frantic note crept into Philip's voice.

Matt spoke up. "You're an experienced engineer. You should realize that all mines have a certain life span. When they're mined out, you close up shop."

"But the miners—" Philip persisted.

Elliott frowned in irritation. "We're not running a charity. Your men will just have to go somewhere else." His lip curled again. "And so will you."

Philip stared at him, too shocked to speak. He had assumed that he would always have a job with the company.

Elliott went on. "It won't happen for a while. I'm just making some long-term projections. Well, it's time to take a break for lunch. I've made reservations at the River Hotel."

As they left the room, Elliott put his hand on Philip's arm and held him back. "Let the others go ahead of us. I want to discuss something with you." While they walked down the stairs, Elliott continued in a low voice. "If the Alpine falls into our hands, we'll combine the operations and keep both mines with you in charge."

"Have you ever considered making Hamilton an offer for the Alpine?" Philip asked.

"Why? All my reports indicate that the old bugger hasn't a ghost of a chance to make his October payment. Then the axe will fall and the mine will be ours."

"Don't underestimate him. He's a wily old fox. And his granddaughter is—"

Elliott turned and scowled at his nephew. "Speaking of his granddaughter brings up a point I want to discuss with you.

I've been told that you're very friendly with her. Taking her horseback riding. Giving her a lot of help with the Alpine. Mooning around her. I don't like that a bit, Philip, and I want it stopped at once!''

Philip's face flushed in anger. ''I didn't realize that you had spies watching me and reporting to you.''

''That's enough, young man. I don't need any of your smart talk. I thought I made it perfectly clear that you were to make things as difficult as possible for Dorcas Hamilton.''

They were outside on the crowded, hot sidewalk. ''I've carried out your orders to the letter, Elliott, I'm ashamed to say,'' Philip muttered.

''We want her to give up and go home. Old Hamilton must be in his dotage to have sent her there in the first place.''

Philip tightened his fists in annoyance. ''One can't help but admire her. She's made a valiant effort to make the Alpine pay.''

Elliott snorted in disgust. ''It's up to you to force her out of there as soon as possible. That's an order.'' When Philip didn't answer, he went on. ''Now, if you want to court someone, why don't you go after Heather La Pointe? Her mother hinted to me that Heather is quite sweet on you. She's a real catch—pretty, talented. There's plenty of money in that family, I can assure you.''

''Look, Elliott, the fact that I work for you doesn't give you the right to run my private life. For your information, I'm not interested in courting anyone, so let's drop the subject.''

''Well, you could do a lot worse than Heather La Pointe, don't forget.''

Privately, Philip had to agree with him.

For the first time in weeks, Dorcas felt some hope. Red had asked her to come underground to see the mine face in the new workings. As she followed him though tunnel 14, the light from their lamps caught the walls, making them look like demon caves. At times she splashed through puddles of water.

''I think two rich veins are coming together. I wanted you to see it for yourself, Miss Hamilton.'' Red's voice showed his growing excitement.

When they reached the spot where the men were working,

Red picked up a bucket filled with water that had dripped from the tunnel ceiling. "You can see the veins better when they're wet." He tossed the water against the face of the workings and for a minute she could see the two veins coming together to form a thick V. Before the water ran off, she could see tiny sparkles and pockets of gold in the wall.

"This is the best we've seen yet." His voice rose again. "I think we're really onto something."

"Put as many men as you can here. We can let the other places go for now," Dorcas said.

"I will in the morning. We're going to drill as much as we can and blast just before we go off shift. I'm anxious for Mr. Woodard to see this."

"He's been very busy since Mr. Richmond went away." She felt a little hurt that Andy was so engrossed in the affairs of the Golden Star now that she was coming down to the wire. He'd given them very minimal time each morning.

"Well, I know that we are going to concentrate on this face, so it doesn't matter if he can give us much time or not right now. This is the best color we've seen."

After Red gave orders to the foreman, he walked back to the skip with her. "One thing we could do is divide the men into two shifts and have them work day and night for a while to get as much ore out as possible."

"That's a good idea. If it really is as rich as it seems, we might reach our goal yet."

"It's possible, all right. I've heard of mines that brought in as much as ten thousand dollars a day when they struck a rich vein. It might not last long, but it pays big for a while."

Back in her office, Dorcas was almost tempted to walk over to the Golden Star and tell Andy her news. But then she decided not to. Perhaps he would stop in on his way back to town at the end of the day.

But Andy worked until midnight. He knew he had to make the most of every day that Philip was gone. At long last, in a record book he'd found tucked away at the back of a storage closet, he'd discovered the records he wanted. It had been easy to break the code name used for the illegal workings, Pinemill, a combination of Alpine and Hamilton. Now it was a matter of taking photos of the entries.

He stood the open record book on a low shelf with the pages he wanted exposed. By bracing the ledger open with heavy inkwells, he could take the pictures he needed. Now all he had to do was write a report summarizing his findings. At last he had all the facts and figures he wanted.

When his report was finished, he put the old record book back where he had found it and stored the camera, tripod, and flash equipment in their proper places. He even cleaned the developing trays and put them away so that nothing looked disturbed. He gathered all the pictures and report sheets together, placed them in a large heavy envelope, and secured the fasteners on the outside.

As soon as he got home, Andy put the envelope in his briefcase and hid it on the top shelf of his closet. Now he had to wait for Philip to get home.

The next morning, when Andy stopped at the Alpine mine, Dorcas ran out to greet him. She brought him up to date on the developments in tunnel 14.

"Red thinks it's going to pay off big. We're going to concentrate all our efforts on those workings." She told him about the plan to have day and night shifts.

"It might pay you to hire another crew and work twenty-four hours a day," he suggested.

"Well, let's try this for a few days and see what happens." If they came close to their goal, she'd take the gold bars to the mint herself and use the rest of the money she'd borrowed from her mother to make up the difference.

Now it was the middle of September. They only had fifteen precious days left. At best, they would have to work very fast to get the money to her grandfather in time.

That day went very well. Ore car after ore car came to the surface. It was rich, all right. Her stamp-mill foreman told her it was running seven hunded dollars a ton, an astounding figure. Lately the ore had been one hundred dollars a ton, which was the usual amount but not nearly enough to produce gold bars as fast as she needed them.

The next day, Dorcas went underground with Andy as soon as he came. She had to see for herself how successfully it was going. The men were working at top speed. Everything augured well. If they could keep this up and the ore stayed as rich, they would be able to reach their goal.

As they came back up to the surface, she said, "We're having pot roast for dinner. Will you come and eat with us, Andy? Esther was saying last night that she hadn't seen you for some time."

"I'd love to come. I've been terribly busy on a project that I wanted to complete before Philip returned. But I have it all finished now, so I can relax a bit."

"*I* won't relax until I have all the gold bars I need. I'm considering taking them to San Francisco myself. I can hardly wait to present them to Grandpa."

That night they ate dinner and then the three of them sat out on the porch watching a full moon rise and the stars come out. Dorcas could see in the distance the very tips of the mountains, glistening in the silvery light. Her heart sang with happiness. They had two rich veins to mine. Philip was expected home any day. Her dear friend Andy was right here by her side, giving her every support. As soon as she had the gold bars ready, she would wire her grandfather that she was on her way.

At ten o'clock, Andy said he had to get home. "I haven't had much sleep the last few nights, because of this special project. Don't say a word to Philip. I don't want him to think I've discussed it with you."

"Of course I won't," she promised.

Andy thanked Esther, and Dorcas walked with him to where his horse and buggy were waiting.

The moonlight cast a silver glow over the mine buildings, the head frame, the tramway, and surrounding trees, turning it all into a magic fairyland.

Before he climbed up into the buggy, he took Dorcas in his arms. "I love you, my dearest, with all my heart. I want you to always remember that, no matter what happens."

Tears glistened in her eyes. "I know you do, Andy. And I'll always cherish your love. It's given me so much courage."

He kissed her tenderly, then whispered, "Promise me that you'll tell me if you ever feel the same toward me. I'll always be there, waiting and hoping that you'll be my wife."

* * *

He held her close and dreamed of living with her always. How he longed for a home and a family, a little girl to come running to him with her arms outstretched, some little boys to go exploring with him in the woods. He would teach them what he knew about birds, carve toys for them, and dress up like Santa Claus. He kissed her eyelids and then her lips again. "Good night, my love. Sleep well."

Dorcas walked back to the house feeling his love and protection surrounding her but nevertheless longing to see Philip again. Surely he would come and visit her as soon as he returned. She had such good news to tell him.

The next morning, Dorcas went underground with Andy. He stayed just a short time and then said he had to get over to the Golden Star, but she remained below with Red and the men. Excitement coursed through her as she walked from one ore car to the next and saw that they had all been filled by the night shift. Soon they would be sent to the surface. She ran her fingers over the shining white quartz, exalting in its beauty and grateful for the riches that each piece contained. In just a few days the ordeal would be over. As soon as she took care of her grandfather's payment, she would concentrate on paying back her mother.

Of course, her first priority was her grandfather. Lenore had written to tell her how despondent Clyde was. "He's given up and is just waiting for the end." Well, he ought to see all this rich ore, Dorcas thought.

She picked up one piece of quartz, rich in free gold, and walked over to Red. "Isn't this beautiful?"

"It's all looking mighty good, Miss Hamilton."

The words were hardly out of his mouth when they heard a terrible roar from deep in the earth. They looked at each other in alarm. Suddenly the ground began to tremble.

"An earthquake!" Red shouted. "Get down on the ground."

Scarcely breathing, Dorcas sat down on the wet ground as the earth rumbled and shook. She suppressed a scream. She wasn't going to act like a scared female in front of all these men.

"Put your heads between your knees and cover the back of your necks," Red ordered.

They all huddled together while the earth pitched and rolled. It felt like a great ocean wave surging below them.

Rocks fell from the walls of the tunnel and thudded onto the ground. Would there be a cave-in? She pressed her fist to her mouth to keep from screaming. Ore cars pitched over on their sides. The newly mined quartz splashed in the water.

Frozen with fear, they waited out the tremor. They rocked from side to side, trying to keep their balance. Would a piece of the wall crash down on them? Wave after wave of motion hit them. Then, at long last, it was over.

One of the men laughed in relief. "That was a bad one, all right. I remember being underground at Nevada City when—"

Another roar came from the center of the earth's crust as the great plates shifted and moved to relieve the pressure that had been building up from below. The earth began to pitch and roll again as they swayed helplessly back and forth. Dorcas felt trapped. There was no place to hide. The very walls seemed to close down on them. She grabbed Red's arm and screamed in terror. Would it ever stop?

At last the rumbling died down. They started to rise. Again a violent quake hit as if a giant hand had tilted the ground below them.

Just as it seemed to end, another jolt cracked the end of the tunnel. Hot steam and boiling water gushed out.

"Run for your lives!" Red yelled.

They scrambled to their feet and stumbled along the tunnel, trying to get to safety. They could feel the terrible heat from the water even as they tried to pick their way through the spilled ore and scattered rocks.

"It's a hot spring that's broken through!" one man shouted as he fell over an ore car. "Dammit, we'll be cooked alive." He got to his feet again and lunged onward.

Red grabbed Dorcas's arm and pulled her after him. Steam filled the tunnel, making it hard to see and breathe. Perspiration poured down her face. There was no time to grasp the enormity of this catastrophe. All she could think about was keeping ahead of the onrushing boiling water. She gasped for breath, afraid she was going to faint.

At last they reached the safety ladder to the next level.

"Let the men go up first. They can climb faster than I can," Dorcas gasped.

Red directed the men as they ascended the ladder. "Leave room between you so you don't step on anyone's fingers."

When the last of the crew had reached the top, Red turned to her. "Now it's your turn. I'll be right behind you."

Steam billowed around her as Dorcas climbed onto the first step and reached up as far as she could for the rungs above.

Her arms shook as she strained to hoist herself from one rung to the next. She felt dizzy and faint in the cloud of steam. Her hands grew slippery. How easily she might slip off! Red pushed her from below. "Keep going, Miss Hamilton. You'll make it all right."

She glanced upward. The ladder seemed endless.

A big miner with shoulders twice as wide as her own climbed back down the ladder to her. Holding on to a rung with one hand, he reached down and grabbed her upper arm. "Easy does it, ma'am. You can't fall off with me holding you. Come on. We've got to work together. Let's all step up another rung."

"My skirt is getting in the way," she gasped.

"Lift your feet and I'll pull it out," Red ordered and gathered her full skirt into the hand he was using to push her upward.

Somehow the two men kept her on the ladder in spite of the fact that perspiration was running down her forehead and blinding her. Gradually, taking one rung at a time in unison, they managed to get to the five-hundred-foot level. At last they were in the waiting skip, which took them to the surface.

Once at the top, the men shouted with relief. One of them lifted Dorcas out of the skip. She tried to walk but slowly slumped to the ground, gulping the fresh air. "I'll be all right as soon as I catch my breath."

She was vaguely aware of Esther's concerned voice. "I'll get her a glass of water." From far away she heard Red explaining about the hot spring that had broken through.

When Esther took her in her arms and brought the glass of water to her lips, Dorcas drank and began to recover.

"I think we're jinxed," she said at last. Her mind cleared slowly and she was able to think. "Will it fill the whole mine?" she asked in despair.

"Oh, no. But I'm afraid it will ruin tunnel fourteen until we can figure out a way to drain the hot water out," Red said. "No man could work in that cauldron."

Tears filled her eyes. "But all our ore cars are now under water. We can't process the ore."

Red answered, "We have ore cars in the other tunnels. We'll just have to go back to our other workings. Maybe Mr. Woodard can figure out a way to solve this problem."

Red explained that the whole area around Alpine Heights was water-saturated and it wasn't unusual to tap underground springs and artesian wells as tunnels were dug. Some of the water had seeped down deep fissures in the earth's crust and was heated to the boiling point by the hot inner core of gases and metals. The water then gushed back up to the surface in the form of hot springs. "It was there all along. The earthquake cracked the crust just enough to let it escape into the tunnel."

Esther spoke up, "Miss Dorcas, you're soaking wet and covered with mud. Come on home and we'll get you cleaned up."

Red helped Dorcas to her feet. "If it's all right with you, Miss Hamilton, I'll tell the men to go back to the bunkhouse and take showers and clean up."

"Yes, and tell Sing Lee to fix them a good meal, as they've lost their lunch boxes. This afternoon we'll talk things over and see what we can do."

Esther put her arm around Dorcas's waist and helped her along the path to the house. "What you need is a good bath and shampoo."

As Dorcas sat in the sun later, letting her hair dry, her mind was numb with disappointment and despair. It was hard to think. This final disaster was more than she could grasp.

Then she saw Andy come around the house. He ran to her and dropped down on the grass beside her. "Darling, I heard about your close call." His face was pale with fright. "You could have been boiled alive!"

"We were so lucky to get out at all." She leaned against him and started to cry. "What are we going to do? We were so close to those rich veins—but now there's no way to mine them. What am I going to do about Grandfather?"

"Perhaps he can get an extension on his loan payment. Let's not worry about him for the moment. Tell me exactly what happened."

She went over the whole terrifying experience again. More than once she had to stop to get her voice under control so that she could go on. "The earthquake was dangerous enough. I was afraid a rock would dislodge and hit us or that the tunnel would cave in. I never dreamed that a hot spring would break through."

"It's not too surprising, though. Think how close we are to the inactive volcanoes, such as Mount Lassen and Mount Shasta." He caressed her arm. "My dearest, it frightens me to think how close I came to losing you. I assumed, of course, that you were perfectly safe in your office when I felt the earthquake. I was underground and had to check out all the Golden Star men to make sure none of them had been injured by falling rocks or cave-ins."

"Were they all right?"

"Yes, fortunately. We have some cleaning up to do, but that's all. You folks are the ones who took the damage."

Dorcas wiped the tears away from her eyes. "Do you think we're hexed? You know that old belief that a woman in a mine spooks it."

"No, of course not. All mines have their ups and downs."

"Maybe I've brought the Alpine bad luck." But then she squared her shoulders and said, "I'm not giving up. Not as long as we have even a day left."

Andy cupped her face in his hands. "Darling, I've never loved you as much as I do right now. You're the bravest, most wonderful girl I've ever known." He kissed her. "I wish I could spare you all this trouble."

"Oh, Andy, you're the sweetest, nicest person I've ever known." She kissed him tenderly in return. "I know you must get back to the Golden Star, but please walk over to the office with me first." She pinned her hair back with two combs and let the rest hang loose.

Before they went into the office she led him to a spot at the edge of the road that overlooked the canyon below. She stared at the face of the cliff, trying desperately to think of a solution to their problem. "Isn't there some way of draining the hot water away?"

Andy looked at her pale face, her lovely dark eyes so full of despair and felt so sorry for her. If he could only help. "You could pump it out, I suppose," he said hesitantly.

"But wouldn't it just keep bubbling out through the crack into the tunnel?"

"I'm afraid so."

"Then we'll have to divert it somehow, make that hot water flow somewhere else."

"It's not that simple, darling. I don't want to discourage you, but—"

Her chin trembling, she turned to him. "I'm already discouraged. I could easily throw over this whole deal here and give up." Tears spilled out of her eyes and ran down her cheeks. "But I can't, Andy."

He took her in his arms and gently caressed her hair as she sobbed against his shoulder. Diverting the hot spring could be a major undertaking. The steam and extreme temperature complicated the problem. As an engineer, he couldn't see any way they could accomplish it in such a short time. He kissed the top of her head and felt the softness of her thick hair.

"I'm so sorry this has happened to you." What would be best? Should he be honest and tell her right out that there was no chance at all of getting the gold out of that tunnel in time to help her grandfather?

Finally she stopped crying and wiped her eyes and blew her nose. "Look, I still have almost two weeks. I'm not giving up yet!"

"Good for you." He took his own handkerchief and wiped her wet cheeks.

"We're so close to those rich veins. We must find a way to get to them."

"I think you should forget them for now. Concentrate on the rest of the mine. You might—"

"No! That's too slow. It would take months to pay off my debts. I know that gold is there. If we could just get it out . . ." She pulled away from him and looked down the face of the cliff again. "Couldn't we drill a tunnel from below and find the spring?" Her voice rose in excitement. "Wouldn't that divert the hot spring so it would run out this way instead of bubbling up into the mine?"

"I suppose so. There might be a slim chance."

"Then let's get started—"

"No, I have to think about it first; study the maps."

"It needn't be too big a tunnel. Just enough to let the water flow through."

"But it would have to be large enough so that the men could work in it and bring out the dirt," he said gently. He hated to point out the realities of their problem.

"I didn't think of that."

"We'd want to keep it to a minimum in circumference, however. Otherwise, we'd have to timber, and that's slow and costly. Remember, we'd be going through earth close to the face of this cliff. There's no support on this side. So we'd have to be aware of slippage or landslides. We'd want to disturb the face as little as possible."

Her face fell. "I suppose so."

"First we must calculate as best we can where the spring is. Then we should start below and slant upward toward it."

"But why? That would take longer. Couldn't we tunnel straight in?"

"No. We'd want to let the water drain by gravity."

"Of course you're right." She sighed.

"I must go back to the Golden Star now. But I'll return as soon as possible," he promised.

She put her hand on his arm. "Come and have dinner with us tonight and we'll talk it over." She clenched her fist. "There has to be a solution."

Andy felt doubtful, but he patted her on the shoulder. "Perhaps we can find it. I'll come as soon as I can."

After dinner they returned to the mine office and Andy studied the geological reports, maps, and surveys.

Finally he said, "It's just possible to run a tunnel in from the face of the cliff, but I must warn you that it will be a lucky break if you find the source of the hot water."

"Why do you say that?" She peered over his shoulder, trying to make some sense out of all the curved lines on the paper. It certainly took training to understand them.

Andy drew a line with his pencil. "The source of the spring might be in one place, like here, for example, and the water flowing out might have found a fissure in the rock and been diverted, so tunnel fourteen might not be near the spring's source at all."

Dorcas felt a wave of discouragement. Everything was so complicated. There were always so many variables. It could be this or it could be that. "But the water gushed out with such force. Wouldn't that indicate that we were near the source?"

"Perhaps. It depends on the pressure below."

"Look how tunnel fourteen runs parallel to the face of cliff. Deep inside, of course. If we can come anywhere near the tunnel, we're apt to run into hot water, and we could drain it off. Isn't that true?" she asked.

"Theoretically, yes. But I can't promise you anything. I don't know how it will work out when we actually get in there. You know how capricious a rich vein can be. It shows up, disappears, and then is found again. A hot spring is just as difficult to pinpoint. It could drain down toward the center of the earth in one place and be subject to forces there that might send it upward in another spot. I must warn you that it's no small undertaking to try to drain a hot spring."

"Oh, Andy, don't be so discouraging."

He took her arm, his eyes sincere and pleading. "You'd be much better off concentrating on the parts of the mine that haven't been flooded. You might run into something good there."

"If we had lots more time, I would agree with you. I know you're making sense. But we're coming right down to the wire. We must get the gold mined now, not months from now. Those rich veins in tunnel fourteen will pay off right away if we can just get to them."

"Yes, that's true." Andy stared at the material spread out before him. "It's a damn shame that the earthquake had to occur at such a critical time and in the one place we wanted to mine. Before that happened, you stood a real chance of recovering the gold you needed."

"That's why we must return as soon as possible!"

Andy let out a long breath. "Dorcas, even if by a wild chance you do hit the right place and drain the tunnel, it's unrealistic to think you can recover enough gold to make the payment in time. You might as well face facts. I know it's heartbreaking, but I can't let you go on deceiving yourself."

"But if I can get to the veins and prove to a bank how rich they are, I might be able to get a temporary loan to take care of Grandpa's payment. The bank would have its money back very soon."

He studied the determination in her face. How he hated to discourage her. "But you told me that your grandfather had tried to use the mines as collateral and the banks refused."

"At that time, all of Grandfather's mines were closed. But if the Alpine is running and I could convince them of its potential, I'm sure I could work out something. As soon as we drain the tunnel, I'll leave for Sacramento. I'll talk to the bankers myself. Maybe Philip would write a letter of introduction for me.''

"Of course, the Richmond name would open doors for you.''

"And you could include a report.''

He took her hand. "I'd do anything on earth for you.''

She kissed him on the cheek. "I know you would, dear Andy.''

"Then at this point I guess there's nothing to do but tunnel in and try to hit the spring. I'll come early in the morning and do some measuring.''

"Let me help you.''

"All right. You can hold the tape. We'll pick out a spot that seems most promising. But I want it thoroughly understood that this could be a bitter disappointment. If you hit the spring, it will be a lucky fluke.''

Tears swam in her eyes. "I have to take that chance. It's the only one I've got.''

They got up and walked out to his buggy.

"Say an extra prayer tonight, dearest girl,'' he said.

"I will, Andy. You're a brick to help me so much in spite of the fact that you don't think I have a chance. And with my luck lately, maybe I don't.''

"Perhaps your luck will change.'' He took her in his arms. As he kissed her good night, he laid his cheek against her soft one and whispered, "I love you, my darling. I'd give anything on earth if I could spare you all this worry.''

At six o'clock in the morning, dressed in her oldest clothes and stoutest boots, Dorcas walked rapidly toward the cliff. She looked down and saw Andy already there. He pointed to his left to indicate that there was an easier trail to climb down.

In spite of all her worries, it felt good to be alive on such a beautiful morning. The rising sun cast long shadows across the dry creek she was following as she made her way downward toward the river bottom. She listened to the water tumble over great boulders, smelled the fresh, pine-scented air, and looked at the wild rhododendron with its long, graceful branches.

When she joined Andy, he greeted her warmly. "I'm glad you're here. It's almost impossible to use this tape in this underbrush without help."

They worked for an hour scrambling around the trees, pushing the tape under bushes, and holding it taut in the clear spaces. Finally Andy drove a stake into the side of the canyon wall and tied a piece of red cotton to it.

"This is the best I can do. If you insist on going ahead, I recommend that you begin here."

She smiled at him. "I insist. We'd better go find Red and explain what we have in mind."

They reeled in the tapes and made their way up the riverbank to the dry creek. It was far harder climbing up than coming down, and by the time they reached the top, she left the perspiration running down her face. But she wiped it away with the sleeve of her dress, straightened her hair as well as she could, and brushed the dust off her clothes.

They found Red coming out of the stamp mill. When Dorcas explained what she had in mind, he stared at her in disbelief. Finally he shook his head. "I think you're making a mistake, Miss Hamilton."

Her cheeks burned. "You could be right, Red, but I'm going ahead with it."

Andy explained where he had driven in the stake and what percentage of slope was needed for the tunnel. "We only want enough angle to allow the water to run out by the force of gravity."

"If we find the spring at all," Red answered glumly. "I'm not in favor of this scheme. I think it's a cockeyed idea." He scowled.

Dorcas wanted to snap at him that no one had asked his opinion. It was his job to carry out her orders and not question them. But how could she be short with such a loyal employee as Red? He'd kept them going all these months.

She controlled her voice and answered pleasantly. "You could be right, Red. But I'm going ahead with it. Divide your men into three shifts so the tunneling can go on around the clock.

His mouth hung open in shock. "Surely you don't mean that!"

"Yes, I do. As soon as possible, pull the men away from wherever you've assigned them and get them started on the tunnel."

Andy shook his head. "Don't you think it's better to keep some of the men where they are and put a limited crew to work on the tunnel?"

"No." Dorcas straightened her shoulders. "I want that tunnel dug as soon as possible. Every day and night counts. We have no time to spare."

"Miss Hamilton, I've spent my whole life mining. I don't mean to be disrespectful, but you don't have a chance in hell of draining tunnel fourteen. I speak from experience. In a mine near Nevada City, we once tried to divert a heavy spring, and it didn't work. Had to give it up as a bad deal. It'll be the same thing here." Red took out a bandanna and wiped his face. "Besides, in this situation you're dealing with boiling water. That's a lot worse."

"That's what I've been trying to tell her," Andy put in.

Dorcas looked at the two men who had done so much for her. They both had experience, training, and judgment. Was her scheme as foolish as they seemed to think? Should she abandon the whole idea? Was she just throwing more borrowed money away on an impossible project?

Yanking at her skirt, which had been caught on a buckthorn branch, she thought awhile. Finally, she looked at them and said firmly, "I know neither of you men agrees with me, and I don't blame you a bit. However, I'm not going to take your advice. I want to go ahead with the drainage tunnel. An all-out effort will be made."

Her manager's face turned an angry scarlet. He didn't meet her eyes. "I'm to get three shifts organized?"

"That's right."

"It's not going to work."

"If it's a flop, I'll take all the blame."

"You'd better, because I don't want it on my neck."

"I won't let that happen, Red. But I do want your cooperation."

"Haven't you always had that?"

She put her hand on his arm. "Yes, Red. You've gone far beyond the call of duty to help me, and I appreciate it. Just bear with me now."

"It's going to take the morning to get things organized. I'll start a swing shift on the tunnel.'' But she still felt his angry disapproval. He turned away and walked toward his office in the stamp mill. She could imagine how he was swearing at himself for getting tied up with a female boss. Nothing but trouble.

''I have to get back to the Golden Star,'' Andy muttered.

As she watched them both leave, tears of discouragement flooded her eyes. ''We must find the hot spring,'' she whispered. ''We must.''

CHAPTER 18

A tremor of excitement ran through Lenore as she dressed for a luncheon meeting of the board of directors for the home for unwed mothers. She was still a little surprised to find herself in the role of president, but she was gaining confidence each time she presided. Most of all, she loved looking at Prescott and seeing the approval and admiration in his eyes.

She missed having Rosalie around as her personal maid. But the upstairs maid had pressed the outfit Lenore was to wear today. Now it hung on the door.

She took the beige linen suit off the hanger. How pretty it was, with its brown braid trim and silk blouse. It seemed strange to be wearing only one petticoat, but it was the style now to emphasize the hourglass figure. At least it was lined, snug-fitting to the knees, and then flared below. It was made of her favorite taffeta, which she loved because of the rustling sound.

First she slipped on the gored skirt, which was lined with silk cambric and stiffening. She glanced in the mirror at herself and noted that although the train was short, it still fanned out gracefully on the floor. Next, of course, was her long gold chain with a diamond-enrusted watch hanging like a pendant.

Before she put on her leg-of-mutton-sleeved jacket, she covered her shoulders with a dressing cape so that she could comb her hair. She loved to brush her thick, wavy hair and pin it in a chignon with tortoiseshell combs at the back of her head. She thought again of Rosalie, who had always been so skillful at arranging her hair. But the dear girl was happily awaiting her baby and feeling secure and protected by her new husband. At least that crisis had ended well.

Finally Lenore put on her jacket and a brown toque trimmed with beige feathers. Her whole outfit was fashionable for fall, but not too warm on this September day. She wished Judy could see her, but her daughter was having lunch with one of her beaus.

When she stepped outside to wait for Wilson to bring the carriage around, she looked out at the clear sky and the sparkling water of the bay. Autumn was her favorite time in San Francisco, with September and October the most delightful months of all. It was not like summer, when the city was often shrouded by fog, pulled in by the valley heat, or was chilled by winds whipping around the buildings. No, this was perfect weather, with the warmth tempered by a gentle ocean breeze.

When Wilson came and helped her into the carriage, she settled back and thought how luxurious it was to be delivered to the restaurant without having to board a streetcar.

Glancing back at the mansion, she was thankful for once that her father-in-law had given them a home this past year. Just as Dorcas had told them, it was wonderful to have this setting.

As they drove through the streets, Lenore hummed a happy tune. She arrived at the meeting place just as Prescott alighted from a cab. A surge of pleasure came over her as she saw him. How attractive and manly he was. So distinguished in his dark gray suit. Her cheeks flushed and her eyes sparkled as she waved to him.

He came over to the carriage and helped her down. As he greeted her, she felt he held her hand longer than necessary. "How lovely you look," he said. "All you need are fresh violets to complete your beautiful outfit. And we can correct that right now." He led her to a flower stand on the corner and chose a shoulder corsage. As she pinned on the flowers and thanked him, her heart thudded wildly.

At the door to the restaurant, he murmured, "I read of a wonderful concert being performed Saturday night." He name the artists. "Will you accompany me?"

"I'd love to."

"Then I'll get tickets. We'll have supper afterward."

If only he'll propose then, Lenore thought longingly.

The meeting and luncheon went well. All the other board members had sizable checks to present toward the project.

"I'll go right to the bank from here," Lenore explained. "My daughter has been taking care of all my financial affairs, but she's out of town right now." She turned to the treasurer. "I'll mail you a check for one thousand dollars."

Prescott had to leave the meeting before it was over to return to his office. The others also had engagements, so Lenore was alone for the rest of the afternoon. Perhaps that was just as well. It was high time she visited the bank and found out exactly where she stood financially. Now that she was feeling so much better, she could take over her own affairs. She would relieve Dorcas of that burden. The poor girl was so busy with the mine. It had been some time since she'd last written, but of course Clyde must be receiving the gold to pay off his debts. It would be good to have Dorcas back with them again.

Lenore stepped into her carriage and directed Wilson to take her to her bank. She looked out happily at the busy streets as they drove along. Suddenly life seemed so full of interest for her. Keith had just started school again, with only a slight limp to show for his accident. Prescott had assured her that even that would go away. Judy was busy with her social affairs. She must be the most popular girl in San Francisco. Hardly a day passed that she didn't go out in both the afternoon and evening. Now she herself had this project of the home for unwed mothers. And there was Prescott, of course. She mustn't get her hopes up too high, but every instinct told her that he was interested.

Lenore faced the bank vice-president, Mr. Stanley. "I'm thinking of making a donation to a charity, so I came to see exactly where I stand."

"One moment, Mrs. Hamilton." He signaled to a teller and soon the records were on his desk. The banker cleared his throat as he picked up the report. "You have exactly $534.27 in your checking account and $19,792.00 in your investments."

Lenore stared at him in shock. She couldn't believe her

ears. The color drained from her face. "That can't be right! I turned my insurance check for $75,000 over to you."

"You remember, of course, that you gave your daughter Dorcas the power of attorney to handle your financial affairs."

Lenore's heart thudded dully in her chest. She fought down a wave of nausea. "I know that, of course, but—" Surely Dorcas hadn't used so much of her money. Five or six thousand dollars, perhaps, but not fifty thousand dollars! It just couldn't be. Lenore's throat felt so dry she swallowed hard. A sickening lump formed in her stomach—fifty thousand dollars?

The banker handed over two letters. "We received orders to sell your bonds and put the money into your daughter's account, which she uses for the mine, I understand. Here are her letters. Altogether we've disposed of fifty thousand dollars." He stopped, but after a long moment went on. "I've never favored giving anyone the power of attorney. Keep control of your own affairs, I always advise. It's too easy to watch your money slip away; just as it has in this instance."

Lenore tried to speak, but the words wouldn't come. She only made a little gasping sound. The vice-president rose and got a glass of water from his own cooler. "Here, drink this. I'm sure my news has been a blow to you, Mrs. Hamilton."

"It's nearly all the money I have." Tears came to her eyes while she fought for control.

"Perhaps I should have notified you before this. I assumed, of course, that you'd been informed. I'm so sorry, Mrs. Hamilton."

"It's not your fault. Not at all. Dorcas didn't use the money for herself. She opened our family mine and needed capital. I realize that, and I don't blame her for an instant. She asked my permission to use my money, and I gave it to her."

"That's understandable. I'm sure she's worthy of your trust."

"Oh, she is. But I had no idea that she would need so much. The mine is producing gold, and I know she'll pay me back." Lenore tried to compose herself.

"I'm sure she will, Mrs. Hamilton. She seems like a most remarkable young woman. There aren't many young ladies with the initiative and courage to open a mine. And you do have some money left. Nearly twenty thousand dollars. Try to conserve that balance as long as possible. I suggest that you postpone any large donations or expenses until later."

"Oh, I will, of course." She felt as if her mouth were full of cotton. She tried to swallow again and had to take another drink of water.

"Perhaps Mr. Clyde Hamilton will replace the fifty thousand dollars, since the money was used for his mine."

"I'm sure he will," Lenore murmured. Didn't this banker know that the great Hamilton dynasty was ready to collapse like a house of cards?

As soon as she could, Lenore rose, said her farewell and somehow got out of the bank building. Her heart pounded a steady rhythm—fifty thousand dollars—fifty thousand dollars. She couldn't believe that her fortune was so depleted. Now she was worth only twenty thousand dollars, instead of a comfortable sum nearly four times as great. And she had foolishly assumed that the income from her money was paying all the expenses of her family, but instead she had used up five thousand dollars from her capital.

Her knees shook, her hands trembled, and it was hard to breathe. A policeman stepped up to her and asked, "May I help you, madam? You look as if you were ready to collapse on the sidewalk."

"Yes, please signal my carriage. I don't feel well. I must get home."

He waved his arm toward Wilson, who was waiting just down the street, and she was soon on her way. It was hard to grasp the fact that so much of her money was gone. As she leaned back and closed her eyes, fear gripped her. For the first time in her life, she had to worry about money. Always before it had been there to satisfy her every wish.

When she arrived at home, she rang the bell instead of unlocking the door herself. When the maid answered, she said, "Please help me upstairs and to bed. I feel faint."

Lying on her chaise with a damp cloth on her forehead, wearing a loose dressing gown, she murmured to the girl, "Tell Miss Judy to come to me as soon as she comes home."

At the end of the day, Judy entered the darkened room. "Mama, is something wrong?" she asked.

"Yes. Sit down, dear, and I'll tell you about it."

Judy's eyes widened in shock as her mother told her about

their financial affairs. "I can't believe it. But surely Dorcas will pay you back."

"She will if she can."

"Oh, Mama, don't be discouraged. It may take a little time, but you know how conscientious Dorcas is. She'll find a way."

"I'm afraid she's out of her depth this time." Lenore took Judy's arm. "I've written Dorcas a letter. Find Wilson and have him take you straight to the post office. I want you to mail it as soon as possible."

Within forty minutes Judy was back. "It's on its way. Now I'll have to change my clothes and get ready for dinner."

"Make my excuses to your grandfather. I couldn't possibly eat anything. I can't receive any calls, either."

"Yes, Mother." Judy leaned over and kissed Lenore on her pale cheek. "I'll run along and let you rest now."

Judy sat at her place at the dining room table, wishing that dinner were over so she could escape. She glanced at her grandfather and thought he looked like some great bird of prey with his long beaked nose and his thin face. His sunken eyes stared at her without really seeing her. His skinny, long fingers looked like claws. She had always been a little afraid of him, and now he terrified her.

Only Keith ate his dinner with any appetite. Fortunately, he had played in a baseball game after school and was eager to tell them about it. Otherwise, there would have been complete silence.

When they had eaten the last of the lemon pudding, Clyde Hamilton spoke. "I want you to come to the library. I have something to tell all of you. Judy, go up and get your mother."

"But Grandfather, she isn't feeling well. She's not dressed."

He glowered at her. "Lenore can come down in her dressing gown. What I have to say concerns her as much as it does you two. Perhaps more. Go get her now."

"Yes, Grandpa. I'll bring her right away." Oh, how difficult he is, Judy thought as she ran for the stairs. She would be so glad if they could just move away from here.

When she told her mother, Lenore shook her head. "I'm not able to go downstairs."

"Mama, you'll have to. I know Grandpa'll fly into a rage if you don't. He said for you to come down in your dressing gown. It's terribly important and concerns you most of all."

Lenore swung her feet over the edge of the chaise and put on her bedroom slippers. Judy took her arm and led her down the stairs.

"I'm sorry to disturb you, Lenore. But this is important. I'm calling the servants together in the morning, but I wanted to tell the family first."

As fear permeated her whole body like poison, Lenore watched her father-in-law. He was in a terrible mood. She could tell that. When he was in this state, like a volcano ready to explode, she avoided him as much as possible. If only Dorcas were here. She was the only one who knew how to handle him.

Scowling, Clyde glanced at his grandson. "Keith, don't just stand there." His voice rose in irritation. "Get a chair for your sister and one for yourself. I don't know how long this will take." As the old man waited for them to get settled, he drummed his long, thin fingers on the arm of his chair.

When they were all seated, he began. "As you know, I've suffered severe financial reverses this year. I'm not going to make any excuses for myself. But the fact of the matter is that I am deeply in debt and about to go into bankruptcy. On October first, a payment is due on my numerous debts, which I can't pay."

Keith spoke up. "But I thought Dorcas was sending gold to the mint and they were paying you."

Clyde turned to him. "Your sister has made a valiant effort. If you turn out to be half the person she is, you'll be a fortunate young man. So far, however, I have received less than fifty thousand dollars from the mine. Far short of the hundred twenty-five I need."

"But there are still several days left, Grandfather," Keith pointed out. "It's not October yet."

Clyde's face twisted in scorn. "Since it took Dorcas six months to come up with this much, I don't expect the rest in a few days."

Keith shrank back.

"As painful as it is, we must face facts," Clyde went on. "We'll have to get out of this house. All the servants will have to be dismissed. My creditors will take over everything."

Feeling unreal, as if she were in some horrible nightmare, Lenore stared at him. So he really was going into bankruptcy. It was too enormous a disaster to grasp. Finally she asked, "What shall we do?"

Clyde turned to her. His voice shook in disdain. "For once in your life, Lenore, you might act like a grown woman instead of a spoiled girl. I have just said that we must leave this house. I suggest that you start looking for a place of your own. A comfortable flat, perhaps."

Lenore felt as if he had struck her. She tried to answer, but the words wouldn't come.

Judy spoke up. "We'll start looking tomorrow. I'm sure we'll find something." Then she ventured, "I'm so sorry about your bankruptcy. I know how hard this has been."

Clyde turned his hawkish face toward her, his thin upper lip curling in a sneer. "How could you know how hard this has been on me? You're just like your mother. Spoiled. You have no idea what hardship is. All you do is run around to parties. You've never known what it is to lose everything you've struggled for. This past year has put me through hell."

All the color drained from Judy's face as she slumped back.

No one said anything until Keith put in, "Well, anyway, I'm sorry, too, sir."

"Thank you, Keith." Clyde tried to keep his voice controlled. Of course they're sorry, he told himself. They won't have any inheritance now.

"What are you going to do, sir?" Keith asked. "I mean, where will you live after the first of the month?"

Clyde thought of the pistol and the bullets all ready in his desk. "I've made some arrangements."

"Will you be with friends?"

Clyde nodded. He wanted to believe that he would be joining his lovely wife. At least she'd been spared this downfall. How good it would be to have it all over with and not have to worry anymore.

Lenore sat up. "Judy, Keith, and I will start looking right away for a place to rent."

Clyde turned to her. "Thank God you have some money of your own, Lenore."

"Not very much. I just learned today that I only have about twenty thousand dollars left."

Clyde half rose from his chair. "Dammit, woman. You

had an insurance settlement of seventy-five thousand dollars a year ago. How could you have squandered it all away?" He pounded his fist on the arm of the chair. "I told my son more than once that he made the mistake of his life when he married you!"

"Grandfather!" Judy shouted. "How dare you say that to Mama? You know how easily she gets upset. She hasn't been well for years."

"If she's been upset and depressed for years, it's her own damn fault. That's right, isn't it, Lenore?"

Lenore rose to her feet. "I'm not going to stay here and listen to this. Besides, I didn't squander my money away."

"Then just what did you do with it, besides buying clothes and furbelows?"

"Dorcas used it in that damn Alpine mine of yours. That's where it went." She started to cry and headed for the door. "I don't suppose I'll ever get it back!"

Judy jumped up and put her arm around her mother's shoulders. "Come on, Mama. You should go to bed."

Keith rose from his chair as well. "I'll take her other arm," he offered.

After they were gone, Clyde slumped down in his chair, slowly clenching and unclenching his fist. He shouldn't have spoken to his daughter-in-law like that. Of course Dorcas would have had to use Lenore's insurance money. The ten thousand dollars from the jewels wouldn't have lasted long. He shut his eyes in despair. This was the final straw. The bitter end.

Hour after hour, Lenore lay in bed, unable to sleep, staring into the darkness while an aching depression descended over her in a smothering blanket. She curled up in a ball, her knees to her chin, wishing she could die.

The next morning, Judy brought her breakfast. Lenore glanced down at the dishes of stewed prunes and charred toast. The coffee pot had spilled over, leaving a brown spot on the tray cloth.

"I'm sorry, Mama. I fixed this myself. All the servants are meeting with Grandpa in the back parlor."

Lenore murmured wanly, "Never mind. I don't want to eat anyway."

"Try to get something down. At least drink your coffee. Then I'll help you dress. We've got to go hunt for a place to live."

"Oh, no, I couldn't go anyplace today. I want to stay here in bed."

"Then I'll go," Judy said.

Lenore groaned. "You can't go into strange buildings by yourself. Perhaps Wilson will hunt with you."

"I'll ask him when the meeting is over. In the meantime, I'll look in the paper to see what places are listed."

Late that afternoon, Judy came back into her room. "I found a place, Mama, that I'm sure you'll like. It's so sunny and nice. A lovely six-room flat. There's living room, dining room, kitchen, three bedrooms, and a bath. The only thing is, it's not in the most fashionable neighborhood."

"That won't matter anymore. Once the news of your grandfather's bankruptcy gets out, we'll be dropped from all the social lists. The important thing is—is it reasonable?"

Judy named the rent and Lenore nodded. "I guess we can afford that."

"I explained that you weren't feeling well right now, so the landlady is going to hold it a few days until you're able to see it."

Tears flooded Lenore's eyes. "I'll try to go soon."

"Oh, Mrs. Williams gave me a message for you. Dr. Fuller called and he'll phone again this evening."

"I don't want to talk to him. He plans to take me to a concert Saturday evening. You tell him that I'm unable to go."

"Oh, Mama, try to pull yourself out of this slump. Go with Dr. Fuller in spite of everything. You owe it to yourself."

But Lenore shook her head and settled herself under the covers again. She wanted to hide from the whole world. Before her daughter left the room, she murmured, "Go ahead and rent the flat tomorrow. We'll move in as soon as we can. I can't wait to get away from your grandfather."

"Neither can I. I never heard him be so mean to you. I thought he was terrible. He scared me to death."

"I've always been afraid of him," Lenore admitted.

"I don't blame you."

"And the nerve of him accusing me of squandering my money. Who is he to talk? He wouldn't be going bankrupt if he'd kept hold of his fortune instead of pouring it into that hotel."

The next day Lenore didn't try to dress. She didn't even comb her hair. It hung in a disheveled mess around her face. She put on her oldest dressing gown and set about packing her clothes.

After she found her suitcases, she pulled her gowns out of the wardrobe and piled them on the chairs. Soon her whole room was in chaos. There was no Rosalie to straighten out the confusion, and she was determined not to call another maid. She assumed they'd be busy packing her father-in-law's possessions.

But there was so much to do. So many things to pack. She'd have to get everything out of storage. All of a sudden it overwhelmed her. She couldn't face it. She crawled back into bed and gave way to a paralyzing sadness. If she could only die. Get away from everything.

Suddenly Prescott Fuller shoved open the door to her room and burst in. For a moment he stared around at the upheaval and then strode to the bed.

"Lenore, what's wrong?"

She sat up and stared at him through her disheveled hair, her eyes nearly closed, her red face puffy. "What are you doing here?" She cringed in embarrassment.

"I came to help you."

Her chin trembled. "No one can help me. Go away. Just go away." How awful to have him find her like this.

He pointed to her clothes piled in heaps. "What are you doing?"

"I'm going to move. As soon as I can."

"Move? Out of this magnificent place?"

She nodded. "Just go, Prescott. I'm moving, and I can't tell you why."

"But what about the concert tomorrow night?"

She shook her head. "I can't go. Didn't Judy tell you?"

"Yes. But it was all very mysterious. I wanted to see for myself."

"Well, you've seen me now. I'm not very pretty, am I?"

"Darling, have you called a doctor?"

Instead of answering, she started to cry. She wanted to die of humiliation.

He put his hand on her shoulder, but she jerked away. "Please leave me now."

"I'm not going until you tell me what's wrong with you!"

"No. You shouldn't have come in here!"

"If you need help tell me. I'm a doctor. Perhaps I can take care of it."

"No one can. No one at all."

"What do you mean, no one can? That's ridiculous. There's any kind of medical help here in this city."

"I don't need medical help." She turned away from him.

"Then explain yourself."

"I told you I had spells of depression, terrible depression. I'm in one right now. So please go and leave me alone."

"My dear, we all get depressed sometimes. That's not so terrible. Tell me how I can help you."

"You can help me the most if you will leave. Right now!" she cried out.

For a long moment he looked at her, then he took her by the shoulders and pulled her toward him. She pushed him away. "I don't want you here. Go!"

Without another word he got to his feet and left the room.

She dropped back onto her pillow and started to sob. She had lost him. And her money. And her friends, because she was sure they wouldn't be bothered with her anymore once Clyde went bankrupt. Her world had come to an end.

She would live in an ordinary flat in a grubby part of town, unable to entertain or go to expensive luncheons. The whole future looked bleak. There was nothing to live for now.

Finally she stopped crying and got out of bed. When she looked at herself in the mirror she gasped. She didn't recognize that hag. That red, swollen face with puffy eyes wasn't hers. That hair hanging down like a crone's. She looked around her room. The disorder revolted her. Her dressing gown hung on her like a mussed, wrinkled rag. She, who had always prided herself on her appearance, couldn't have looked worse. No man would want a woman like her.

To make matters even bleaker, she had refused Prescott's help and told him to leave. There was no question in her mind now. She had lost him.

CHAPTER 19

The old shirt and man's overalls were too big for Dorcas, but she rolled up the sleeves and tucked the pant legs into her boots. On her way out of the house she picked up a battered felt hat and pulled it on over her hair. She expected Andy to come by on his way home from work; they were going to crawl into the drainage tunnel that was moving along so slowly.

By the time she arrived at the office, he was there. Just seeing his sweet smile gave her lagging spirits a lift.

"Hello, Andy. How do you like my outfit?"

He kissed her cheek. "No matter what you wear, you look beautiful to me."

"What a good friend you are. You always pay me a compliment however I look. And now I'm dragging you into the tunnel to get your advice."

"You're not happy with the progress on the drainage tunnel?"

"No. The men think I've lost my mind. They're not in favor of digging this tunnel, and I think it's affecting their work. It's going so slowly. I thought by now we would surely be close to the hot spring."

"Perhaps you're underestimating the size of the project. Come on. Let's get some lights and see."

"The swing shift will be working there. I didn't warn them that we'd be coming. I want to see if they're working."

Andy and Dorcas walked out of the office and went to the storeroom for their lanterns. Andy shook his head in mock disgust. "You women! Lord save me from a female boss!"

"I'm sure that's the way Red feels about now—maybe all twenty-five miners, for all I know. Anyway, it's slow, slow, slow! Perhaps you can make them more enthusiastic."

"As you know, I'm not all that enthusiastic about it myself. I'm afraid it's a wild goose chase."

As they climbed down the creek bed to the bottom of the canyon, loose rocks tumbled ahead of them to land with a clatter.

"If you think you're going to surprise them, you'd better forget it. These rocks will announce us. And remember, the men can look out of the tunnel and see us coming in," Andy said.

"I suppose they'll really throw the dirt around when they realize I'm on hand."

"Of course." He put his arm around her waist to keep her from slipping. "What did you expect?"

She was glad to have his help down the treacherous path. Feeling his arm around her gave her such a sense of protection. Dealing with all these disgruntled men over the past few days had been very trying. More than once she'd wanted to throw up her hands in despair.

Perspiration broke out on her forehead and ran down the side of her face. By the time they were at the entrance to the tunnel, she had to take out a bandanna and wipe her neck and face.

Andy handed her a pair of heavy leather gloves and knee pads and put some on himself. Soon they were down on their hands and knees crawling into the narrow tunnel.

From deep inside, Dorcas heard one of the men call, "Hello, there. Who's coming?"

"Just Miss Hamilton and Andy Woodard."

"Okay. Mind that you don't whack your head."

It was rough going. Dorcas felt the jagged rocks on the bottom cut into her legs. The uneven places in the roof caught at the straps of her overalls. In spite of the miner's warning, she hit her head more than once on the roof.

"The men seem to be judging the grade okay," Andy whispered. "Just enough to let the water run down when we reach it, but not too much of a slope."

"If we can just reach the spring soon. I feel more panicky every day."

"You don't have many days left."

When they reached the men, Dorcas said, "I thought I would see for myself how you're coming along."

The foreman sat down before he answered. "I'm glad you came, Miss Hamilton. You know now what a tough job this is. It's a killer working in this position for a whole shift."

Andy squeezed a damp clod of earth in his hand. "I can see that. At least in a regular tunnel you have more room."

"I hope it won't be much longer," Dorcas put in. "I thought surely by now you'd hit the spring."

"Naw. Nowhere near it. Feel the wall. If we were closing in on hot springs, that earth would be warm. It's not, is it?" the foreman asked.

She put her hand on the side. It was damp and cold. A leaden feeling of disappointment hit her.

One of the miners spoke up. "We all think this is a bust. We ain't going to hit hot water at all. You don't hear any steam hissing or feel any heat. Don't mean no disrespect, but this ain't going to work."

The foreman added, "He's right, ma'am."

For a long minute there was complete silence in the tunnel. No one shoveled dirt or pushed a makeshift cart to carry the debris away. They were all waiting for her reply.

Should she give up? Was she foolish to continue spending all this money on a scheme that wasn't going to work? Everyone else was against it—Andy, Red, and all the men who had to carry out her orders. She had only herself to blame. She'd taken a chance, and so far it hadn't paid off. Why not write it off and go back to mining the other tunnels with some hope of return? What would be gained by just digging further into the cliff if she could never reach her goal?

"Dorcas, perhaps you'd better call it quits. It was a fine idea in theory, but it's not working out," Andy said in a low voice.

It was up to her to make the decision. What should she say?

Finally she shook her head. "I'm not ready to give up yet. Continue digging the tunnel." She turned around and started out. She sensed the men's disgust and disapproval. Even Andy's.

The morning sunlight tipped the top of the trees in gold as Dorcas walked to the office. It was only six-thirty, but she had awakened early after a restless night. Hearing a horse clopping along the road just outside the wall, she stepped through the gate and waved at Andy.

"You're an early bird, too," he called to her, and pulled on the reins.

"I couldn't sleep. I worried all night about my decision to keep the men working on the tunnel."

Andy climbed down from the buggy and put his hands on her shoulders. "Darling, I don't agree with you, and neither do any of your men. As far as we're concerned, you're throwing your money down a barrel. But it's your decision to make."

"But it's not just my money I'm throwing away. It's my mother's. I only hope and pray she doesn't find out how much of her estate I've spent." Worry twisted in her. Everything was going wrong.

"Well, I do have a bit of news. I found a wire when I got home last night. Philip is coming back today. He'll be on the afternoon stage. I knew that would please you."

"Oh, it does, of course." It would be wonderful to see Philip again. But even that news failed to lift her spirits.

"Dorcas, there's something I want to tell you. I have a personal matter I must take care of, so I'm going to be gone for a week."

Appalled, Dorcas looked at him. "Andy, how can you leave me right now?"

"I'm sorry, dearest girl, but this can't wait any longer. It's some urgent business I must take care of."

"When are you going?"

"Tomorrow, I hope." He patted her arm. "When Philip was gone I had to manage the mine, but now I can go."

"But what will I do without you?" She touched his hand. "What if we do hit the spring? What happens then?"

"Red will know what to do. He's very experienced. If he needs help with the engineering, you can always turn to Philip."

She threw her arms around his neck. "Oh, Andy, please don't leave me right now."

"You know I wouldn't go away if I could help it." He held her close. "I love you more than anyone on this earth, and I wish I could stay right here with you. But I can't this time. Trust me, dear one. I'll be back as soon as possible."

"But *why* do you have to go?" Tears gathered in her eyes. She couldn't imagine how she could go on without his help. He'd been such a support through all this time.

"I'm not free to tell you yet. I hope to be able to when I return."

She wiped her eyes with the back of her hand. "I'm being selfish. Besides, I'm acting like a child. Forgive me, Andy. I'll manage somehow."

"You can always ask Philip for his help. In fact, he might come up with some fresh ideas about the tunnel."

"He'll probably be as opposed to it as you and the miners are."

Her chin trembled as Andy tilted it and looked into her eyes. "Whether I agree with your ideas or not, remember, I'll always love and admire you for trying." He spread his hand over her cheek and wiped away a tear. "I wish I could take you away from all this trouble and cherish and protect you for the rest of my life."

"What a wonderful friend you are."

He kissed her lightly on her lips. "If only I could be more than a friend. I'd give my soul if you'd become my wife."

She slipped out of his arms. "You'd better go to work. I'm keeping you."

She watched him drive away, wishing that she could feel for him what she knew she still felt for Philip.

Judy came into her mother's room. "I paid the deposit, but the landlady says we can't move in before September thirtieth. She's having some painting done and laying new linoleum in the kitchen. She hopes you'll feel better tomorrow so you can come by. She wants to know what colors she's to use."

"Oh, dear. I suppose she'll paint it all in horrid dark colors. Remember how light and cheerful that place Dorcas fixed up at the Alpine mine looked? That's what I want."

"Then go tell her, Mama. It'll do you good to get out."

For the rest of the day they sorted through the clothes in Lenore's closet. They would have to last for years, so she had to take care of them. In the attic, Judy found boxes and tissue paper, which they used to pack the garments for moving.

As they worked, Judy brought up the subject of their future.

Lenore sighed. "I doubt that Dorcas will ever be able to pay me back."

"Poor Dori. She's tried so hard to solve all our problems."

"I'm afraid she's just made matters worse."

"Mama, what will you do when we move out of this house? Do you think your friends will—"

"No. I'll be dropped when they hear of the bankruptcy. No one will call at the flat."

"What about Dr. Fuller?" Judy asked.

"That's over as well. What man would want to be burdened with a woman who has spells of depression? Besides, when he saw me last, I'd never looked so terrible. Like an ugly witch, a slovenly fishwife." She shuddered as she recalled her humiliation.

"But what about your work with the unwed mothers?"

"I've been thinking that over very carefully. I know those girls need me. I'd like to devote my life to helping them. They won't care whether I have money or not. Nor will they care where I live. Even a has-been socialite like me could have a place helping them."

Judy threw her arms around her mother's neck. "Mama, I'm so proud of you! Of course they need you. Why don't you talk to Mrs. McDonald?"

"I'll do that. You know I promised a thousand-dollar donation, and I'm going to make it, in spite of not having much left. How can I face the others on the board if I don't?"

"You can't, Mama, so draw a check and send it to them right away."

"And I'll go visit Mrs. McDonald tomorrow."

Wilson drove Lenore to the new apartment, and she looked it over carefully. It was everything Judy had said it was. Lenore and the landlady soon came to an agreement on what colors should be used. It would certainly be a comedown from the mansion, but she made up her mind to make a comfortable home for her children here and do the best she could without servants.

Her next stop was the bank, where she withdrew enough from her savings to write a check for the girls' home to send to the treasurer of the board. Later I might regret losing that thousand dollars, she told herself, but we'll have to manage without it.

Mrs. McDonald greeted her enthusiastically. "I telephoned

you the other day, but a maid said you weren't feeling well. I'm so glad you came. We must get started on deciding what we're going to do with the new house. There's so much to take care of. It's in escrow, you know. It's almost ours."

"Could we go over there right now and look at it? My carriage and driver are outside."

"Yes, I think I can leave the girls for an hour or so. Just give me a few minutes to change my clothes." Mrs. McDonald turned to a pretty girl, about twenty, who was dusting the living room. "Elizabeth, you entertain Mrs. Hamilton while I put on another dress."

Elizabeth smiled at Lenore shyly. Her slender face flushed as she finished the dusting. Finally she said, "You're the lady who is helping us get a new home, aren't you? Mrs. McDonald said it's going to be lovely."

"It will be just as cozy and homelike as we can make it. That's where we're going now, to see what has to be done. And once we have it all ready, I want to get to know all of you girls better," Lenore went on. "Perhaps there are things I can do to help you."

"Oh, you can. Writing letters, for one. Some of us don't know how to write good or read very well. We never went to school much."

A thrill ran through Lenore. Of course some of them would be less than literate. Perhaps she could give reading and writing lessons.

"Most of all, we'd like someone to talk to. An older lady who could give us advice." Elizabeth's tone grew sad. "We girls could sure use friends at a time like this." She glanced down at her swollen stomach.

Lenore stepped over to the girl and put her arm across her shoulders. "I'd like to be your friend, Elizabeth. I know Mrs. McDonald is already, but she must be very busy. I'll be happy to spend time with you girls."

Soon Mrs. McDonald returned to the room. "I brought a notebook and paper so we can write down some of the things we need to do." She took a key out of her purse. "The realtor lent me this key."

On the way, Lenore said, "I was telling Elizabeth that I would like to devote as much time as I can to helping the girls. She suggested that several of them needed instruction in reading and writing so we ought to set aside some place where I could give lessons.''

''That would be marvelous, Mrs. Hamilton. And there is another way you could help them tremendously.'' Mrs. Mc-Donald's kindly face broke out in a smile. ''I have often thought how someone like you could train these girls to be housemaids. That way they could earn a living when they're through with their confinement. There's always need for a trained maid.''

Lenore's face lit up in interest. ''Well, I'm an expert in that field. I've certainly trained a lot of household help myself.''

''When we get back to the house, could you stay for lunch? I'd like to have you get acquainted with more of the girls. It will be the first time most of them have ever been in contact with a real aristocrat like you. You could be a marvelous influence on them.''

''Of course I'll stay.'' A surge of excitement came over Lenore. For the first time in years she had a real niche for herself. She wouldn't allow her depression to control her life. Whenever she began to feel discouraged and blue, she'd reach out to the girls who needed her so badly.

Late in the afternoon Philip and Andy stopped by the office of the Alpine. Dorcas ran out to greet them. How handsome Philip looked as he climbed out of the carriage. The breeze ruffled his dark wavy hair. In spite of his journey from Sacramento, he looked perfectly groomed.

''It's good to see you again,'' Dorcas cried after Philip kissed her lightly on the cheek. And it certainly was. No one else could imagine how exciting it was to be near him.

''Andy tells me you've been having your problems.''

Dorcas looked at Philip and shrugged. ''That's all I've been having. I would have given up a long time ago if it hadn't been for Andy.'' She turned to her friend. ''And now you're leaving tomorrow.''

''I know. But Philip's here,'' Andy said graciously.

''I'll be glad to help you,'' Philip agreed as he leaned against the buggy. ''Why don't we take a ride early tomorrow morning and you can tell me all about it? I'll bring the horses here about six.''

After Andy said his good-byes and the men left, Dorcas

271

locked her office door and walked toward the house. Just the thought of seeing Philip again in the morning sustained her and lifted her spirits. Perhaps he could come up with a solution to the filled tunnel.

There was a chill in the early-morning air, a hint of the autumn to come. As they rode along, Dorcas told Philip about the earthquake and the hot spring gushing into tunnel 14. "There are two rich veins but they're impossible to mine. Even the ore cars are covered with water. That's why I'm having a drainage tunnel dug—to tap the spring so it will flow out instead of into the mine."

"Andy doubts that it will work," Philip commented.

"Not only Andy but Red and all the men. They think I'm wasting my money."

"I'm afraid you are if there aren't any signs that you're near the spring. I'll think about your problem, though, and see if I can come up with some ideas. Actually, Andy is more ingenious than I am," he admitted.

They rode along in silence until Dorcas asked, "Isn't this a new way? I don't remember coming here before."

He looked back at her. "No, we never have. But in a little while we'll see a magnificent view of the lake and the mountains."

A few minutes later he said, "We'll tie the horses here and then walk about half a mile through the trees."

When they stood at last on the edge of the cliff and looked out at a shimmering lake and glaciated mountains towering on the other side, Dorcas felt a soaring ecstasy at its grandeur. A heron as blue-gray as the water stood in the marshy edge. Its long slender legs made up half of its four or more feet in height. Suddenly it uncurled its slender neck and stuck its sharp-pointed bill into the water, causing a series of circles to form on the surface. Other than that, nothing disturbed the perfection of the early morning.

Philip put his arm across her shoulders. "I wanted you to see this." His voice barely rose above a whisper as if he too was deeply moved by the sight.

Her every nerve responded to his touch. Her whole body came alive. She turned to him and he drew her into his arms.

"I missed you, lovely Dorcas." He kissed her and trailed

his lips along the planes of her face, then pressed his cheek against hers. "You're an amazing woman. I've never known anyone like you."

Her heart pounded wildly. Was he going to propose? How she longed for that. Why didn't he ask her? He knew how she felt about him. She had certainly bared her inner soul to him. Why didn't he ever say that he loved her? What was holding him back? But he said nothing, so she slipped out of his arms, almost sick with disappointment. She looked out at the view but only half saw it through the tears that flooded her eyes. She fought for control. He mustn't see her cry.

Finally he gave her a quick kiss. "We'd better go. We both have work to do."

All day, thoughts of Philip haunted Dorcas. He was an enigma. What was behind that handsome exterior? How did he really feel about her? If she could only talk it over with Andy. But she couldn't discuss anything with her good friend, as he was on his way to Sacramento. She wouldn't see him for a whole week. Already she missed him and felt a longing for his caring support.

Later, as she sat at her desk and worked on her books, she became frighteningly aware of how little money she had left. And there wasn't any more she could draw on. She couldn't take every cent her mother had. At the most, she could keep the mine open for only two or three weeks. Was she foolish to try to dig the tunnel and use up all her capital? Perhaps she should give that up after all and put her men back to work in the rest of the mine. That meant she couldn't save her grandfather, but she might recover enough gold in time to keep the mine open and at least pay her mother back. Poor, poor Grandpa. He must be deeply disappointed in her.

The day dragged by and finally, at the end of the afternoon, she walked back to the house, thinking how badly she had managed everything. At every turn, she had made mistakes. And trying to dig this drainage tunnel was the worst one of all.

As the evening went on, she felt oddly disquieted, but she couldn't quite put her finger on what was bothering her. Of course there was the looming deadline, as well as the bitter disappointment that Philip hadn't proposed to her, but this was somehting else. Almost a foreboding.

After she went to bed, she felt too restless to sleep. Then, along toward morning she heard someone pounding on her door, calling, "Miss Hamilton! Miss Hamilton!"

Dorcas jumped up, grabbed her night-shift robe, and ran to the door. Red stood there with the night-shift foreman. "Sorry to wake you up, ma'am," her mine manager began. "But Chuck here tells me they've run into real trouble."

"Come in and tell me." Her heart plummeted. The two men stepped inside. She dreaded the bad news, whatever it was.

After they sat down, she asked, "What is it, Chuck?"

"Well, ma'am, it looks like we've run smack into granite. A big wall it is."

"And nothing will touch it," Red added.

"We couldn't imagine what was wrong, ma'am," Chuck went on. "All of a sudden we kept hitting this hard barrier. The picks didn't do much but nick it. Well, we scraped all the dirt off the wall and threw water on it. We scrubbed it, and saw it was granite, just as sure as I'm sitting here. You can come and see for yourself if you don't believe me, Miss Hamilton."

Her voice cracked in her dry throat. "Of course I believe you." She was too numb to fully grasp this latest development.

Red rubbed his leg nervously as if all these problems were too much for him to deal with. "Chuck told the men to get out of the tunnel."

"Nothing more we could do. I asked the men to wait at the mine buildings while I went and woke up Red."

"That was right, Chuck," Dorcas said.

Red turned to her. "If it's all right with you, I'll have the men finish the shift in the main part of the mine. We might as well get back to normal again."

"Yes, you might as well." She felt as if she were pronouncing her doom. It was all over. Any hope she had of saving her grandfather from bankruptcy was gone.

The men got up to go. At the door, Red turned to her. "I'm so sorry it didn't work out for you. We all tried hard."

"It's not your fault. I appreciate all the hard work you and the men have done. Please tell them so."

"I will, ma'am.

"Thank you for coming. At least I know now where I stand."

After the men left, Dorcas saw Esther waiting at her bedroom door. "More trouble?"

"Yes. They've run into granite. Red is putting all the men back in the mine on a regular schedule again." Dorcas walked heavily back to her room and climbed into bed. But she lay there until daybreak unable to sleep. Oh, if only Andy were here to advise her.

When the sun finally came up, she rose and put on her overalls and old shirt. "I'm going to crawl into the tunnel and see for myself," she told Esther.

"Aren't you going to take someone with you?"

"No. If I don't come out by the end of the morning, send someone in to get me."

"I hope the tunnel doesn't cave in on you."

"Oh, if it only would. That's how I feel. Like burying myself someplace," Dorcas said bitterly.

It was hard going, crawling back into the dank-smelling black tunnel. How could she justify this whole fiasco to her grandfather? She heard the water drip, drip down the walls.

When she came to the end, she lifted her head so the miner's lantern would shine on the wall. She put her hand on the cold, repelling surface. It was granite all right. A terrible barrier keeping her from her goal. A surge of despair stabbed through her. It was as cold as a tomb. No wonder they hadn't been able to feel the warmth of the hot spring.

Where could she turn? What could she do now? Her control snapped. Over and over she banged her fist against the rock. "Damn! Damn! Damn!" she screamed. Her cries echoed back at her. Finally she put her head down and sobbed. Oh, if only Andy were here to comfort her.

CHAPTER 20

As Andy walked from the railroad station, carrying his leather suitcase, perspiration broke out on his forehead. He stopped in the shade of a storefront, put down his suitcase, and took off his hat to wipe his face. It was late afternoon, the warmest time of day in Sacramento.

While he slipped off his jacket and hung it over his arm, he considered stopping in at the Richmond company headquarters and making an appointment with Elliott Richmond for the next morning. He could see the building ahead and was half inclined to go there. But wouldn't that give his boss the advantage? Wasn't it better to catch him by surprise? Andy decided he'd have to take a chance that the head of the company would be in first thing the next morning.

Right now it was important to get to the hotel and out of the heat. He'd have a good wash and go to the restaurant next door, which was noted for its excellent steaks. He could hardly wait for one, as he was starved. Then, after dinner, he'd practice what he was going to say. He had to sound convincing and really give Elliott a jolt. However, his boss was a formidable opponent, and this was going to be a real clash of wills.

"Well, Andy, this is a surprise," Elliott exclaimed when his engineer was shown into his paneled office. "Sit down." He waved his hand toward the heavy oak chair across from his desk. "What brings you to Sacramento? You're not having trouble up there at the Golden Star, are you? Philip didn't mention it when he was here."

"No, sir. Everything is about the same." Andy put his briefcase on top of the desk and opened it.

"Well, then, why have you come?" Elliott's affable expression changed. He frowned. "Who gave you permission to leave? We're paying you a good salary, so why the hell aren't you up there earning it?''

Andy looked him straight in the eye. "I came to hand in my resignation, for one thing." He took a letter out of the briefcase and watched while Elliott opened it, scowling.

"Andy, you're our best engineer. You can't quit the company!" Elliott slapped the letter with his hand. "And what does this mean—'effective immediately'? You know we expect at least two weeks' notice.''

"I think you'll be willing to let me go when you hear what else I have to say.''

"Does Philip know anything about this? He didn't say a word to me." Elliott banged his fist on the desk.

"No. I haven't told him. I just said I had to take care of a personal matter.''

"Well, dammit, explain yourself. Stop talking in riddles. What kind of a personal matter would make you want to resign?" His face reddened. "I suspect some woman is mixed up in this. That Hamilton female?''

"You can leave her out of this discussion, Mr. Richmond." Andy resented this man calling his adored Dorcas 'that Hamilton female.' ''

Elliott settled himself back in his chair but still seemed tense, on guard, as if he was wondering what was coming next. "I'm listening, Woodard, and you'd better have a damn good explanation for resigning, or I'll make it impossible for you to get another job. The idea of your barging in here with this news and no warning. I don't like it a bit.''

"You'll like what I have to say next even less.''

"Well, begin. Don't pussyfoot around.''

"I'm sure you heard about the cave-in at the Alpine in July.''

"Of course I heard about it. Philip wrote about it in his report, but I didn't pay much attention to it. What goes on in the Alpine is of little concern to me.''

"But surely you're aware that young Hamilton and the mine manager, Red Wallace, barely escaped with their lives?'' Andy asked.

"I didn't give it much thought." Elliott reached into the humidor on his desk and selected a long cigar. He spent some time trimming the end with a special snipper, then lighting it as if to show his complete disinterest. His attitude was that of a man with supreme self-confidence, aware of his handsome appearance, wealth, and power.

Elliott blew a cloud of smoke. "That's part of the mining game. Besides, what the hell does that have to do with me?"

"Because, Richmond, you're indirectly responsible. It's your fault."

Elliott stared at Andy in shock. He sat up straight, his cigar halted halfway to his mouth. "My fault! Have you lost your mind? It had nothing whatever to do with me!"

"Oh, yes it did."

Elliott put his hand on the table, still clutching the cigar. "Dammit to hell, explain yourself!"

Andy pulled out a drawing he had made. "You will see that tunnel ten from the Golden Star extends directly over tunnel nineteen from the Alpine mine. That's what caved in and trapped the men."

The color drained from Elliott's face. Perspiration broke out on his forehead. His expression changed from shock to fear. But he blustered, "And you expect me to believe this? You think you can show me some drawing you've made and thus prove your point? You're bonkers, Woodard."

"But there's more, Mr. Richmond. A lot more."

Angrily, Elliott shoved his chair back. He stood up and leaned over his desk. "All right, Woodard. I've had enough of you and your innuendos. I accept your resignation. Now, get the hell out of here."

But Andy settled back in his chair and crossed his legs. "I'm not ready to leave yet. I have more to say."

"Whatever it is, I'm not interested. Now, get out!"

Andy shrugged. "If you're not interested, I'm sure a lot of government agencies would be." He nodded toward the state capitol building, with its golden dome rising above the trees. "And federal ones as well." He reached for his briefcase and half rose from his chair.

"Sit down!" Elliott Richmond roared, his face red with rage. "I demand a few explanations. You can't come in here with all these accusations and then just walk back out. Whatever you have to say, say it now."

"I've said that you and your mining practices are responsible for that cave-in at the Alpine in July."

"I heard you the first time. Why should I accept some crackpot theory like that? It's ridiculous."

"Is it, Richmond? I can assure you that it's more than a crackpot theory. In fact, the Alpine men were rescued through your tunnel ten. All we had to do was dig through the debris and put down a ladder."

Richmond's face turned ashen. "How did you get into tunnel ten? It's permanently sealed off."

"I broke down the barrier."

"You had no right to do that! Why didn't you telegraph me for permission?"

"Young Hamilton and Wallace would have been dead if I'd waited any longer. Surely you wouldn't want to be responsible for that, as well as the cave-in."

"I'm not responsible for a damn thing, and you have no right to say so."

"I don't think the government agencies would agree with that statement. There are strict laws against crossing boundary lines and mining another company's claim. And that's just what you did, wasn't it? You followed the Andromeda Lode right into the Alpine, didn't you?"

Elliott's mouth moved, but the words didn't come. He spluttered and stammered.

Andy went on. "You didn't notify the Hamiltons, did you? You didn't go to them and say, 'Look, the Lode's on your side of the line. Mine it and get your share.' Instead you just extended tunnel ten and took it all. Then you sealed off the tunnel and even packed dirt against the barrier so it would look like the end, in case an inspector came."

"What a bunch of hogwash," Richmond snarled at last.

Andy leaned forward. "I realized what you'd done at the time of the cave-in. I kept going on and on through tunnel ten. There was no way it could still be on Golden Star property."

For a long time, Richmond sat in his chair and stared at Andy. "What are you getting out of all this, Woodard? You've given up your job and are running the risk of being blacklisted at every mine in the country. To what purpose?"

"I'm representing the Hamilton interests on behalf of the Alpine mine. I want to see justice done."

"Who authorized you to speak for them?" Elliott looked at Andy through narrowed eyes.

"Dorcas Hamilton. The mine is in her name now." To say that she had authorized him was stretching the truth, Andy realized, but he knew she would approve. He thought back to the time she'd shown him the papers from the lawyer deeding her the Alpine.

He studied Elliott and noted a hint of fear in his eyes. The news that Dorcas owned the mine was a surprise to him, Andy was sure.

"Exactly what do you want?" Elliott asked at last.

"I'll tell you what I want. A fair settlement for the Hamiltons. As a first payment you can give me a check for a hundred thousand dollars, made out to the Hamilton Company. I'll personally deliver it to Clyde Hamilton in San Francisco."

"You must be out of your mind!"

"But I'm not. I've never been more lucid." Andy sat back in his chair and crossed his legs. "By the way, the check must be a certified one or a cashier's check. I want it negotiable at once."

"This is extortion."

"Is it? Not when I'm representing a legitimate client. Not when I'm asking in the name of the person entitled to it. I estimate that you realized at least three to four hundred thousand dollars from the Hamilton share of the Lode. The cave-in was caused by your illegal mining, which weakened the roof of their tunnel nineteen. That caused extensive damage and expense besides putting at risk the lives of two innocent people. If you come out of this with a settlement for a few hundred thousand, you're lucky. They could cause you trouble from which you'd never recover, Richmond."

The older man's lip curled. "You come in here with all this big talk and no proof at all. A judge would throw such a case out of court." But the bluster had gone out of his voice.

Down in his gut he's afraid, Andy told himself. Now is the time to pull the big surprise.

"I think a judge or a state mining official would rule very much in favor of the Hamiltons. It so happens that I do have proof. I went to considerable trouble to get it."

He opened the briefcase again and took out the pictures and laid them face down on the table. "You're not to touch them, Richmond. I don't want them out of my hands." One by one, he held them up for his former boss to see. "First, here's the picture of the way the tunnel was sealed and hidden. I took this after I had the opening repaired, but you'll have to admit that this is the way it looked."

Andy went on. "Now here's a picture of the way I broke through to look for a way to lead the rescue party. Here we are, right at the cave-in. Here's a picture of how narrow the ledge was between the two." Andy looked Richmond in the eye. "Now can you say that this case wouldn't hold up in court?"

Richmond sneered. "We'll see about that."

Andy picked up another picture. His hand covered one corner. "The government agencies will find this photo the most interesting of all. It shows how the vein has been mined on the Hamilton side."

"That picture could have been taken anyplace in the Golden Star. It doesn't prove a damn thing."

"Doesn't it?" He took his hand away from the corner. "Look it at now. Here you can see the beginning of the cave-in."

At first Elliott looked as if he'd lost all his composure. Nervously he picked up a stack of papers from his desk and rearranged them. Then he scraped his chair back and paced the room. Finally he stopped and turned to Andy. "You may think you've got a case, but a smart lawyer could shoot it full of holes."

With an air of confidence, Andy gathered the pictures up one at a time, looked at them carefully, and slowly put them into a paper folder. He wanted to drag out the procedure as long as possible, as he knew it was upsetting Elliott. Finally he slid them into his briefcase and leaned back in his chair. "How could a smart lawyer shoot the case full of holes?"

Elliott apparently thought he had the upper hand. He raised the cigar to his lips, took a long draw, and slowly expelled the smoke. It hung in a delicate cloud over the desk. "How can you prove that I personally had anything to do with this? It happened a long time ago, remember. Some employee could have gone in there and set it up without my knowledge. After all, I was gone a lot of the time."

"I'm so glad you brought this up, Mr. Richmond. I almost forgot to show you the rest of the evidence."

Elliott stopped his pacing and stared at Andy. "What do you mean?"

"After careful searching, I discovered some secret reports. They were very well hidden, but I found them. I photographed them as well. Of course, they were written in obscure language. Nothing is said outright about working the Alpine side. Just the measurements of how tunnel ten was extended. But this chart I made shows the Golden Star boundary, and the broken dots represent how far the tunnel extends into the Alpine. I used the figures straight out of the report you signed. Here is your signature, right near the date.'' Andy carefully pointed to the name on the bottom of the photo. ''And I have even more evidence that you were directing the whole operation.'' He reached in his briefcase.

Richmond stepped over to him and grabbed his arm. ''You are a sneaky, underhanded son-of-a-bitch. You did all this while in the employment of my mining company. Where was your loyalty? Your sense of honor?'' He stuck his red, furious face close to Andy's.

A tremor of fear ran through Andy, but he grabbed the older man's arm and yanked it away. Looking squarely at Elliott, he said, ''How can you speak of honor? You don't know the meaning of the word.''

Richmond clamped his jaw shut. Only his lips moved. ''I'll get you for this. I'll contact every mining company in the country. I'll have you blacklisted—''

''If you do, I'll sue you for slander. I'll see that every newspaper in the state gets a full report of this chicanery.'' Andy stood to his full height. ''Of course, all the government agencies involved in mining will know about it as well. I have complete proof of every accusation I have made. Rest assured that it will stand up in court.''

''Then you'll have to take it to court. I'll see my lawyers today. You're not going to get by with these threats.''

Andy tucked the briefcase under his arm. ''I suggest that you think this over very carefully. That we settle this whole affair between us.''

''Do you think I'm that big a fool?'' Richmond's lips curled into a sneer.

But Andy ignored that and went on calmly, ''As a gesture of your sincerity, you can make a preliminary payment of a hundred thousand dollars. Remember, it's to be a cashier's check payable to the Richmond Company. I'll pick it up tomorrow at twelve o'clock sharp.''

Elliott's fist slammed down on the desk. ''I'll see you in hell first. Now, get out before I throw you out.''

Andy acted as if Elliott's words meant nothing at all.

"I'll be here at noon tomorrow. I want to catch the two o'clock train to San Francisco." Andy threw his shoulders back as he walked to the door. He opened it and strolled through the outer office. The clerks looked up at him curiously. Had they overheard the commotion?

He tipped his hat. "Good day." But his knees shook as he walked down the stairs and out onto the street. He entered a saloon on the corner and ordered a double whiskey. He needed something to calm his nerves. What would Elliott Richmond do now? Would he find some way to squirm out of the trap that had been set for him?

That same afternoon, Lenore, wearing one of her most expensive gowns, presided at a tea party in Mrs. McDonald's living room. She sat behind a table covered with a lace cloth. A silver tea service, which she had brought from home, and a plate of cookies were placed in front of her.

"How many of you would like to learn how to be housemaids?" she asked the four girls seated near her. Across the room, Mrs. McDonald was watching their reaction with interest.

All four girls raised their hands. "It's better than some jobs," one of them said. "At least you'd have something to eat and a roof over your head."

"That's right," Mrs. McDonald put in. "There are lots of advantages to working in a wealthy home. Mrs. Hamilton has always had help and knows what is expected of them. I suggested that she come and train you. I think it's very kind of her to agree."

Lenore smiled at the eager girls. "It's lots easier to get a desirable job if you know what you are doing. Besides, you'll be saved a lot of embarrassment after you go to work."

"I'd be scared to death to be a maid in some la-di-da house like yours," a fifteen-year-old put in. "I wouldn't know what to do."

"That's why I want to show you some things while you're here." Lenore smiled at them to put them at their ease. "This training will also help if you work in a first-class hotel or resort. And, no doubt, you can use some of it when you entertain in your own homes."

"I'll likely marry some guy who'll want me to serve beer to our guests instead of tea," one of the girls said, giggling.

"Pay attention," Mrs. McDonald admonished. "We're pretending that we're maids."

"Well, to begin. I wore one of my best afternoon gowns, because it's a compliment to your guests to look as nice as possible." Lenore glanced down at her blue chiffon dress trimmed in matching lace. "Notice my pearl necklace and earrings. They are more suitable for daytime than something glittery."

Elizabeth let out a long, admiring sigh. "You're so beautiful, Mrs. Hamilton. Just like a fairy godmother."

The girls all laughed. Lenore said, "I just wish I had a magic wand and could make all your dreams come true. Anyway, we're going to begin with our first party. I want each of you girls to take turns being the maid. Elizabeth, you be the first. But all of you watch how I put the cup on this saucer along with a spoon, and pour the tea. I won't fill it too full, because it might spill." She went on about the proper way a maid should handle the dishes. "Now, whom should Elizabeth serve first?"

"Mrs. McDonald," they all cried.

"That's right. She's the most important person here, so she should be served first."

Lenore gave more instructions, and each girl had a turn at being the maid. The delightful party was nearly over when the doorbell rang. Mrs. McDonald put her teacup down and went to answer it.

Lenore looked up and saw Prescott Fuller in the hallway. To her chagrin, she heard Mrs. McDonald invite him to the tea party. Her cheeks reddened but she told herself that she would have to face him sometime. Wasn't it better to get it over with now than at a board meeting? Although she avoided his eyes, she murmured a greeting.

Mrs. McDonald introduced him to the girls and pointed to a chair. "Sit down, Dr. Fuller, right here by me." She explained what was going on.

"An excellent idea," Prescott said as he settled himself. "In these hard times you need training to get a job. There are too many people out of work."

Lenore turned to the girl whose turn it was to serve. "Martha, you take this pot into the kitchen and refill it. And put more cookies on the plate."

Although she felt self-conscious, Lenore went on with her

lesson with all the poise and dignity she could muster. Soon she heard the clock strike four, which meant that Wilson would be waiting for her. When the doctor had finished his tea, she could leave and get this ordeal over with. What was he thinking? About that horrible afternoon he had caught her in such a dreadful state? No doubt he had come to discuss some business about the home with Mrs. McDonald. Was he as flustered as she over this unexpected meeting? Being face to face again?

As soon as she gracefully could, Lenore said, "I'm afraid I must go now. We'll have more lessons soon."

"Please wear another beautiful gown and your jewels for us," Martha begged. "We've never known a society lady like you before."

"You've given me an idea," Lenore smiled. "When we have our next lesson I'll bring some of my jewels. I'll teach you how to take care of fine jewelry and when is the suitable time to wear each of the various pieces. It's in just as poor taste to be overdressed as it is to be too plain. You might have to help your mistress in this way." She rose and picked up her silver set to take back out to the kitchen and pack into the box she had brought.

When she was finished and walked into the hall with the box she found Prescott there with his hat in his hand, ready to leave as well.

"Here, allow me to carry that for you," he said.

"Thank you." She was grateful for his help so that she could pick up her train, which was dragging on the porch. It was longer than usual, since this was one of her most elegant gowns. Surprised, she looked for her carriage, but only the doctor's was out in the street. "Wilson was supposed to be here. I can't imagine—"

The doctor walked to his carriage and handed the box to his driver. "I called your house and left a message that I was picking you up. We need to talk, Lenore, so I'm taking you back to my house."

"About the home, I suppose." She accepted his help getting into the carriage. It was true that there was a lot to discuss. Perhaps there were complications over the sale. Also, they needed to decide just how much they could spend on redecorating. And he might be wondering if she was going to continue on the board. But why take her to his home? Did he have papers there he wanted her to see?

Her thoughts were in a tumult. Every time she recalled that day he'd surprised her, when she was so depressed, she wanted to shrink down into the seat. All the embarrassment she had felt came rushing back. Perhaps he had discussed her situation with the others on the board and they'd decided that she should be replaced. How humiliating! If only she had resigned instead.

The horses clip-clopped along the street, heading toward Pacific Heights. The driver slapped their flanks with the reins. Lenore stared out at the other carriages and the people on the sidewalks, trying to think of something to say to relieve the silence between them.

Finally she asked, "How did you know that I would be at Mrs. McDonald's this afternoon?"

"I telephoned her this morning and she mentioned it. That gave me the idea of coming to pick you up. She told me about your lessons and I wanted to see one for myself. I think they're an excellent idea."

"Of course, two of the girls are still too young to go into domestic service, but at least it's a start."

"When we have the big house ready and take in more girls, it would be a good idea to have many kinds of training programs. They won't all want to be maids."

"Oh, no, of course not. Some might want to work in department stores, for example. Or be waitresses."

Prescott's voice softened. "You looked so beautiful presiding at the tea table, Lenore. Think what it must mean to those girls to have you around."

She laughed. "One told me I looked like a fairy godmother. Now if I only could work a miracle and get them out of the predicament they're in." She thought of the sweet girls with their swollen figures, facing so many problems ahead.

"No one can accomplish that. We can only offer help."

"Sometimes I wake up during the night and worry about them. Will they keep their babies? Will they put them out for adoption? Will they return to their families afterward? No matter what they do, they will carry the scar of this experience."

"That's true, but I don't think any of them have had an easy life. I imagine they come from pretty poor backgrounds. Abusive parents. Drunkenness. Their fathers and brothers out of work. This is just one more problem in their lives," Prescott pointed out.

"Yet, in spite of that, those girls are as sweet as can be. I just hope the future holds something better for them."

Prescott glanced at her. "We all have problems, don't we?"

She nodded and looked away from him. Was he preparing her for the discussion about her staying on the board? At least he was taking her home to talk about the situation in private. He was sparing her the humiliation of bringing it up before the board.

They pulled up in front of his house. Prescott instructed the driver to bring the box with the silver set inside, while he helped Lenore out of the carriage. After they were in the house, he ushered her into the parlor. "We've already had tea, but perhaps you'll drink sherry with me."

"Yes, thank you, that would be nice." She sat down on the sofa.

"Take off your hat and be comfortable."

As she pulled out the pins, removed the hat, and laid it on the table beside her, she watched him pour out sherry from the cut-glass carafe at the sideboard.

When they were settled, he began. "I want to apologize for barging in on you that day. The maid told me that you weren't receiving company, but I came in anyway."

Her cheeks flushed. "And you saw me at my worst. Perhaps it's just as well. At least you know the truth about me."

"That's what I want to discuss—"

Tears gathered in her eyes as she looked at him. "You want me to resign from the board, don't you? That's why you brought me here, isn't it?" As the words tumbled out, she realized how much the project meant to her. "I'll make it easier for you and resign right now, but I hope I can continue helping the girls. Surely . . ." Her hand began to tremble so, she put her wine on the table.

Prescott set his glass down, got out of his chair, and joined her on the sofa. "No, that's not at all why I brought you here. I think you're the most important member of the board, and you must stay on."

She let out a long sigh of relief. At least she would have that much of her life left.

"When I saw you sitting there this afternoon, so gracious and stunning, I thought what a rare opportunity you are giving those girls. You're showing them a whole new world. I studied the expressions on their faces, so full of wonder and

admiration. Oh, my dear, think what you're doing for them."
He took her hands in his.

"Then why did you bring me here?"

"I want to discuss us." He raised her hands to his lips and
kissed them. "I'm in love with you, Lenore. I want you to
marry me."

The color drained from her face. This was the last thing she
had expected. "But I—"

"Oh, I know I'm not from the same background. I'm a
professional man, of course, but hardly on the same plane as
a Hamilton. I suppose I'm not worthy—"

"Oh, my God." She turned away from him. "It is I who
fall short, not you, Prescott."

He slid his hand from the back of the sofa to around her
shoulders and held her close. "What do you mean?"

"You saw me. I told you I had depressive spells. Do you
want to be saddled with that?" Her voice rose in despair.

"Darling, I'm fifty-one years old. I've been a doctor for
half my life. I've seen it all. Every human frailty. I neither
expect nor want perfection in my wife."

He caressed her hair. "Dearest, I want a human being like
you, with all your strengths and weaknesses. God knows I
have more than my share, too."

"But there are my children—"

He smiled. "I'm quite aware that you have children. In
fact, that's one of your attractions. Your lovely family."

"But they'd have to live with us, Prescott," she protested.

"Of course. I didn't expect you to leave them with your
father-in-law in the mansion."

"Prescott, that's something else you should know. Clyde
Hamilton is going into bankruptcy, and there'll be no mansion. No fortune. Nothing. Even my money—" She told him
about Dorcas's using her insurance money for the mine.

"Then we'll live on mine, dearest Lenore. I do earn a
living from my practice."

"Oh, Prescott. How kind you are." It seemed unbelievable
that he wanted her in spite of what he had just heard.

"I want you to marry me and be my companion and share
all the years we have left to us. It's you I want. Not your
money or material things," he said.

"I don't know what to say."

He kissed her on the lips. "Say yes and make me the happiest man in California."

Her eyes shone as she looked up at him. "Then it's yes."

He kissed her for a long time. Finally she put her hand on his cheek. "Oh, my darling, before you found me that horrible day, I dreamed of being your wife. I hoped against hope you would propose. Then afterward I lost all hope; I didn't think you would want me at all."

"You're all I've ever wanted since I met you." He caressed her high cheekbones. "I've been so terribly lonely since my wife died. Let's get married as soon as possible."

"But I want Dorcas to be here for the wedding. I don't know when she can come."

"Just so it's not too long. I want a wife and family around me. Someday your children will marry and have children and we can gather them all around us for the holidays. That's what I want—a real home again. Children, pets, grandchildren."

"And friends." Lenore's face had never been more radiant. "Think what fun we'll have entertaining our friends."

"I don't know that I'll be able to keep up with your social life."

"But I'm going to be very selective about what I do. I won't have many free days, either, as I still want to devote a lot of time to my poor expectant mothers. I suppose we'll always have plenty of those."

"I'm so proud of you. You're just great." He kissed her again. "I know that being so interested in those girls will help you with your own problems. And from now on, you won't be trying to cope with your spells of depression alone. You'll have me for support."

She blinked away sudden tears of happiness. For so many years she had felt so completely alone. "I'm going to love having you for a mate." She kissed him and snuggled in his arms. "And I'm going to be very busy in other ways as well." She looked around the room. "This is a beautiful home, but there's lots of work to be done on it. But we'll tackle that later. Right now I have to move." She told him about the apartment.

"It's a shame you have to leave the mansion now, when you'll soon be coming here."

"I wish I didn't have to make two moves. I'd even put up with my father-in-law for a while longer if I could."

"You could move right in with me before we're married." He grinned at her. "I wouldn't object at all."

She looked up at him and laughed. "Think of all the scandal we'd cause. It'll be bad enough when poor old Clyde goes into bankruptcy. I can see the headlines now."

"Then we'll have to wait until you're my wife to cohabitate." He took his arms away and stood up. "I put some champagne in the icebox to chill before I came for you. I was hoping I'd have something to celebrate. I'll go get it and some glasses."

They proposed their toasts and sipped their champagne in a daze of happiness.

"We've got a lot to decide," Lenore said at last. "Where should we hold the wedding? Whom should we invite? Where will we have the reception?"

"I'll go get a paper and pencil so we can make a list." When he returned he said, "Your family. Mine. Mrs. Mc-Donald. I don't want the wedding too big."

"Well, neither do I, but I think we should have a few close friends. I have four or five couples I'd like to invite, and surely you have some."

"Yes, a few. But I only want intimate ones. And I'd like to have my housekeeper and coachman, the nurse who helps me in my office, and there's another couple I'd like to ask."

"Who is that?"

"Rosalie and Henry. After all, they started this romance of ours."

She reached up and kissed him on the cheek. "I'd love to have them. It all just goes to prove that the most unexpected things can change our whole lives."

CHAPTER 21

To pass the morning, Andy wandered around the state capitol grounds, which were filled with specimens of trees and shrubs brought to Sacramento from all over the world. Blooming flower beds, velvety lawns, and spreading trees made it one of the most beautiful parks he had ever seen.

When he wandered through the state capitol itself, he found the agency that handled mining matters and recognized the name of the director with whom they had corresponded from the Golden Star.

After some deliberation, he walked into the office and asked the male clerk, "Would it be possible to see Mr. Wellington early this afternoon?"

"You can see him right now, if you want. He had an appointment, but it was canceled."

"I'm not sure it will be necessary to see him. I won't know until noon."

Just then the door to the inner office opened. A florid-faced man with mutton-chop whiskers stepped out with a letter in his hand. He glanced up and saw Andy.

The clerk spoke up. "This gentleman might want to see you early this afternoon. You'll be back from lunch by one, won't you?"

"Of course. What's your name, young man? I could see you now." Wellington put out his hand.

The men shook hands and Andy almost winced from his strong grip.

"I'm Andrew Woodard. From the Golden Star in Trinity County."

"That's right. The Richmond Company. And you're the chief engineer. I've read your reports. Come on in and let's get acquainted."

Andy liked the big, hearty man. There seemed to be an aboveboard, honest air about him. No wonder he had such an excellent reputation in the mining industry. "You can't buy off old Wellington," someone had once told him at a conference.

"How's the situation up your way? I understand that Hamilton's granddaughter has opened up the Alpine again. Never heard of a female running a mine before."

"She's doing an excellent job, but she's had some serious problems." Andy told him about the cave-in and the earthquake.

"That'd be enough to discourage anyone, let alone a young lady like that. You seem to know a lot about it. Have you been helping out some?" Wellington asked shrewdly.

"Yes. And when I return, I expect to work for her full-time. She has a serious problem with that hot spring."

"You can expect anything when you get down into the bowels of the earth. I suppose it's against nature to disturb them the way we miners do." Wellington's chair squeaked as he leaned back. "You say you're going to work for the Alpine full-time. That must mean that you're no longer with Richmond."

"Yes, sir. I resigned yesterday. That's why I'm here. We're trying to come to a settlement on a matter. I see him at noon. That's why I asked for a tentative appointment with you afterward. If we don't agree on a matter between us, I'm going to turn it over to you."

Wellington crossed his arms over his head and looked at Andy through half-closed eyes. "Let me give you a tip, Woodard. Don't let Richmond bamboozle you. Stick to your guns. Whatever you're trying to settle, don't give up. Let him bluster around, but don't quit."

"I wish I could tell you about it now, Mr. Wellington, but I'm not free to do so."

"Of course not. It's none of my business unless you refer it to me. But I will say this. Richmond is very much inclined to skate on thin ice with the law. In fact, we're looking into some deals of his right now. Nothing to do with the Golden Star, however."

"In other words, he wouldn't like my turning over my case to you."

Wellington grinned. "Indeed he wouldn't! Here, let me give you my card." He reached into his vest pocket and pulled out his card case. "I'll just write down our appointment. We wouldn't want you to forget it, now, would we?" He winked at Andy before he scrawled 1:00 P.M. and his initials.

Andy stood up. "Thank you, Mr. Wellington. You've been a big help. More than you know." He put the card into his side pocket. It would be handy just in case.

Mr. Wellington pulled his bulk to his feet and put out his hand. "Good luck, son."

"If I'm not here waiting for you when you come back from lunch, you'll know everything is settled."

The temporary exhilaration that Andy felt after his talk with Wellington evaporated as he strolled around the capitol grounds again. Had Elliott consulted with his lawyer? Had they found some legal angle that he'd overlooked? His former boss was slippery; it would be dangerous to underestimate him.

By the time Andy returned to Richmond's office, his heart thumped so hard and his throat was so dry that he was afraid his voice would be affected. He wanted to appear assured, cool, confident of being successful. But would the tremor in his voice give away the doubts he was feeling? Of course, he had proof in his briefcase, but had Elliott Richmond found a way to discount it?

"I have an appointment," Andy said as he walked right past the clerk's desk and opened the door to Elliott's office. He caught the man by surprise.

"I don't appreciate your coming in unannounced," Elliott said with suppressed anger.

Andy ignored the remark, pulled a chair up in front of the desk and sat down. "I'm ready to do business."

Elliott stood up, leaned on his desk, and said, "I have no intention of doing business with you. We have nothing to settle. I won't even acknowledge that I have any kind of a problem with the Hamiltons."

"Is that right?" Andy hooked his arm over the back of the chair and nonchalantly placed his briefcase on his lap. He said nothing more.

Richmond waited. Andy looked out the window and pretended to be very interested in the street scene below him.

The big wall clock ticked loudly. A fly buzzed around the room. Elliott was the first to break the silence. "You might as well leave. I have to go to lunch now."

Andy looked at him square in the eye but kept his poise.

The two men glared at each other until Elliott snapped, "Get the hell out of here. My attorney told me that you have no case at all. The statute of limitations makes it totally invalid. Clyde Hamilton should have brought it to court years ago. The time limit has expired now."

"Expired? When the cave-in happened slightly over two months ago? On July tenth to be exact."

"That has nothing to do with the question."

"Oh, yes it does. Your illegal mining caused the cave-in. You're responsible for enormous damage to the Alpine. You'd better get yourself another lawyer." Andy held his breath as he waited for an answer. This wasn't going to be an easy victory.

"You're not going to get any settlement out of me." Richmond's lip curled into a sneer. "You must be crazy if you think I'm going to write a check for a hundred thousand dollars."

"Oh, no. You're not going to write a check. I don't trust you, Richmond. You'd stop it as soon as I walked out of the office. It must be a cashier's or certified check."

"You know, Woodard, you're going to be in deep trouble with the state agencies. You had no permission to do the things you did up there at the Golden Star. My attorney advised me to report you. And that's what I'm going to do. I'm telling Wellington—"

"Good. Let's go together." Andy reached into his pocket and pulled out Wellington's card. He slapped it down and shoved it across the desk. "As you can see, I have an appointment for one o'clock." He took out his pocket watch. "It's twelve-fifteen. Plenty of time to get your papers together." He patted his briefcase. "I'm all ready."

Richmond looked down at the card, picked it up, and flipped the edge against his fingernail. There was no question but that he recognized the initials. He bided his time as if he was considering what to do next.

Andy slapped his fist down on the desktop. "Richmond, I want that check, and I want it now!"

Elliott flushed. He opened a folder and closed it again. "All right, dammit, here it is." He opened the folder once more and drew out a cashier's check. "But, by God, you have to sign this statement before you get it."

"Let me read it first."

Angrily, Richmond pulled out a paper and shoved in across the desk.

Andy picked it up and read: "This check for $100,000 is full settlement for any claims the Hamilton Mining Company has against the Richmond Mining Company." There was a line for him to sign. He read it through again. It was amateurish. Elliott hadn't gone to a lawyer. This was something he had written himself. Should he sign it even if he didn't like the wording? Would Clyde Hamilton be so grateful for this settlement that he wouldn't care about possible future claims?

Andy remembered Wellington's warning: "Don't let him bamboozle you."

"I'm not going to sign this. I don't know what the Hamilton Company might want to do in the future. You can write another statement, Richmond. But it must read, 'This check for one hundred thousand dollars is settlement for claims made by Andrew Woodard on September twenty-seventh, 1894, on behalf of the Hamilton Mining Company against the Richmond Mining Company.'"

"But the Hamiltons could go on blackmailing me the rest of my life." Elliott's face turned livid with rage.

"Then it's up to you to work things out with them. Meet with Hamilton and his lawyers and come to a permanent agreement."

"I'll be damned if I'll write out another statement."

Andy leaned forward and picked up Wellington's card. He studied it carefully and then pointedly put it back in his coat pocket. He put his arm over the back of the chair again as if he was prepared to wait. For a long while he sat. Finally he took out his watch again. "It's twelve-forty-five, Richmond."

His former boss reached into his drawer and took out another piece of paper. Hastily he scrawled the statement Andy wanted. "Write another copy so I can keep it," Andy put in.

When Elliott shoved the two papers across the desk, Andy read them carefully. "All right. These I can sign." He dipped a pen into the inkwell and wrote his name. "Now hand me the check."

Hardly believing his good fortune, Andy walked back to his hotel to pick up his suitcase. He relived the scene. He'd outwitted Elliott Richmond, as slick a character as you could find anyplace. More than once he put his hand inside his coat pocket to feel the check and make sure it was really there.

Before he boarded the train, he went to a saloon, ordered a beer and helped himself to the free lunch on a side table. At one-fifty-five he climbed on board the train with a newspaper under his arm. But when he tried to read, the words swam in front of his face. He was too tickled with himself to settle down. In Oakland he had to board the ferry to complete the journey to San Francisco. The late-afternoon sun highlighted the tips of the waves in the bay. Sea gulls swooped and squawked. When a passenger threw a piece of bread overboard, they dived down and fought over it.

Excitement ran through him as he thought of the wonderful days ahead. Presenting the check to Clyde Hamilton first thing tomorrow morning. That would be Friday. Then he could spend the whole weekend seeing old friends. Going to the theater. He couldn't stay too long, though, because Dorcas needed him. He walked around the deck. Imagine how happy she would be when she heard the good news.

"Mr. Hamilton is not seeing anyone," the office clerk said.

"Tell him that someone is here from the Alpine mine with a message from his granddaughter. It is very important. I must see him this morning. As soon as possible," Andy insisted.

"But my orders are—"

"Never mind your orders. This is too important to wait. Now, go in and tell him or I'll barge in unannounced."

Clyde Hamilton looked up when Andy was ushered in. He frowned at the intrusion, but he stood up and put out his hand. "Good morning, Mr. Woodard. This had better be important, as I am seeing no one today."

"That's what I understand, sir."

"You have a message from my granddaughter?"

"Not exactly. I just used her name to get in to see you. As a matter of fact, she doesn't even know I'm here."

Clyde flushed in anger. "Young man, you—"

Andy pulled out the check and put it on the desk. He shoved it across. "Before you have me thrown out, I want to give you this."

Clyde Hamilton's face turned gray. He looked down at the check and gasped. "A hundred thousand dollars! What is this? Some kind of cruel joke?"

"No, sir. I can explain. But it's quite a story." Andy put his briefcase on the desk top and took out his papers. He talked for nearly an hour. "As you can see, Elliott Richmond deliberately cheated you out of your share of the Andromeda Lode that was in tunnel ten."

Clyde thumped his fist on the desktop and leaned toward Andy. "I knew it! I knew that crook was pulling something. I was ready to stake my life on it! But there was little I could do."

"Richmond would have been sure to cover his tracks."

"Oh, he did. That snake in the grass could hide anything."
He tightened his fist. "At the time, I tried to nail him myself,
but I had no proof, and there was no way I could get into the
Golden Star." His old eyes glowed in triumph. "If my son
were only alive to hear about this."

"As I told you, the only way I could gather the evidence
was when Philip Richmond was gone and I was in charge.
None of the others on the staff knew what I was doing. Then,
as soon as Philip returned, I went down to Sacramento and
confronted Elliott Richmond. I finally forced this partial settlement out of him on your behalf."

Clyde picked up the check and felt it with his fingers as if
to convince himself that it really existed. "Dorcas must have
told you about the deadline."

"Yes. She nearly killed herself trying to raise the money in
time, Mr. Hamilton. We both did everything possible to get
the money out of the mine, but we ran into so many unexpected problems."

"I know. She wrote me." Tears flooded Clyde's eyes.
"She's a girl in a million."

"I'm aware of that, sir." Andy nodded at the check. "This
whole incident should be kept strictly confidential."

"Of course. I'll just say that I received an unexpected
payment on an old debt."

Andy put the papers and pictures back into his briefcase.
"I'll turn all this over to Dorcas. You two can decide if you
want to file more claims."

"It'll be up to her. She owns the mine now." Clyde looked
at him. "Are you going to continue at the Golden Star? Or
did old Richmond give you the boot?"

"I resigned before he had a chance." Andy grinned. "Of
course, he threatened to blacklist me with the other mining
companies, but I told him I'd sue him for slander if he did,
and expose him to all the newspapers."

"You won't hear any more about that. But what are you
going to do now?"

"Go back and help Dorcas. I have some money saved, so I
won't expect a salary, but I want to find some way to drain
the hot spring that flooded a promising area of the mine and
free the vein they found there." Andy told him about the

drainage tunnel that the crew had been digging. "I'm afraid that's not going to work, but she insisted on trying."

The two men discussed the geological formation of the land at the Alpine until Andy finally said, "I have people to see, so I'll go."

Clyde Hamilton also got up and put out his trembling hand. His voice broke as he said, "How can you thank someone for saving you from bankruptcy? As soon as I can, I'll see that you are rewarded."

"No, I don't want a reward. I wouldn't accept it if it were offered. I just wanted to see justice done. That and to help Dorcas."

Clyde gripped him in a bear hug. "Thank you. That's all I can say."

"I'm happy, too, Mr. Hamilton. I'm glad it all worked out."

"I only hope that Dorcas finds a fine young man like you to marry."

"I hope that she finds someone who cares for her the way I do." Andy smiled wistfully. "But she's not in love with me, so—"

"More's the pity."

Andy shrugged. "You'll send her a wire and tell her that you can make the payment? Then I'll explain it all to her when I go back."

After Andy left, Clyde slumped down in his chair and picked up the check again. He felt numb, almost disoriented. That was the trouble with growing old. You couldn't feel as keenly anymore. Instead, there was this sense of unreality, as if it hadn't actually happened. And this was just a reprieve. In six more months, when another payment was due, there would be another terrible crisis.

How much of this worry and suspense could he take? He had so primed himself that it would all be over soon that he felt almost disappointed; as though he had been cheated out of his release. Wearily, he held his head in his hands. Of course he was grateful for the check. Young Woodard had gone to great trouble to get this. He'd lost his job as well.

Finally, Clyde reminded himself that he wasn't the only one affected by this unexpected windfall. His office staff could go on working here. He could stay in the mansion for at least another six months. The servants would have employment. He rang for his accountant, who was also the company's treasurer.

When Abel Long came into the office, his shoulders were hunched in discouragement. Clyde smiled at him. "Cheer up. For once I have good news. A surprise. I can hardly believe it myself. We can make the payment after all."

Abel's mouth fell open in astonishment. "Make the payment? How on earth—"

"I just had a caller. He brought me a settlement for a claim we've had outstanding for years. I'm not free to go into details just yet, but you can figure out some way to post it in your books." Clyde handed him the check. "It's for one hundred thousand dollars."

"What a coincidence." Abel sat down and ran his fingers through his silver hair. "Just the amount we need at the zero hour."

"It's not a coincidence, Abel. It was a friend of my granddaughter's. He knew about the deadline."

The treasurer let out a long sigh of relief. "You'll be able to keep the office open now."

"Yes. At least until the next payment is due. We'll worry about that later."

"I can't tell you what this will mean to Bertha and me. We were terribly worried. We really didn't know how we could manage without my salary."

"I know everyone in the office has been upset. I'll call a staff meeting and tell them the good news."

"But I have some questions first. I assume I'm to take this straight to the bank. Shall I write out checks to your various creditors? As soon as they're signed, I could deliver them personally so we'd be sure they get there in time."

"Yes, do that. But first send a wire to my granddaughter." He took out a pad and pencil and wrote, *Payment made. Letter follows. Clyde Hamilton.* "She'll be relieved." He wrote the address.

While his accountant was writing up the checks, Clyde decided how to make his announcement. Then he signed the checks, and Abel left with them.

Clyde called his clerk and told him to bring the whole staff to his office. When he made the announcement, they all cheered. "We'll have to celebrate, so I'm inviting all of you to lunch at the Hamilton Regency," Clyde said.

It was a happy group of men who sat around the table in the hotel's main dining room, drinking champagne. Clyde surveyed the room and was pleased that it was full. At least the hotel was breaking even, but it would be a long time before he'd see any real profits. Would he be alive then? But at least he had a reprieve, and there were six months ahead of him before the vultures could descend. He saw some of his associates at a table near the window and noted their curious looks. What were they thinking? They'd be surprised when they found out that the payment was made. With a glow of satisfaction, he sipped his champagne. As soon as this luncheon was over, he'd go home and tell his servants.

By the time he arrived at the mansion, both Judy and Keith were home and were eating a snack in the breakfast room. Lenore walked in the front door, back from a shopping trip.

"Come into the library," Clyde said. "I have some good news for a change."

After he told them the payment had been made, he watched their expressions of relief and delight. Judy jumped up and hugged her grandfather. "I'm so happy for you." The girl has changed, he told himself. For once she was actually thinking of someone else.

"I want you to understand that I'm not out of the woods yet. This is only a payment on my debts."

"But at least you're not going into bankruptcy," Keith put in.

"Not this time. Perhaps things will get better and I'll be able to unload some of my holdings at a profit to get myself in a more stable condition."

"I've tried to talk to you, Father Hamilton," Lenore spoke up, "but there hasn't been a good opportunity. I'm going to get married this fall to Dr. Prescott Fuller."

"Congratulations, Lenore. When?"

"It depends on when Dorcas can be here. I haven't written her yet. It all happened so fast. But I want her here, of course, and I don't know when she can come. Oh, I do wish they had a telephone line into Alpine Heights."

Judy clapped her hands together in glee. "It's going to be so much fun to have a wedding. And now, Grandpa, you've brought your wonderful news." She rushed over to her mother and kissed her cheek. "I hope I can be your maid of honor."

Lenore smiled at her daughter. "We're not ready to make those decisions yet. But there is something I want to ask you, Father Hamilton. When we thought we'd have to leave, we rented a flat and are ready to move into it. But I wondered if we couldn't just stay here until the wedding."

"Of course. It would be foolish to make two moves." I'll actually miss them, Clyde realized. Perhaps he could persuade Dorcas to stay with him during the winter.

"Thank you, Father Hamilton. I'll call the landlady and tell her we won't need the flat after all," Lenore said.

"She'll probably want to keep the deposit," Judy told her.

"Of course, that's only fair."

Clyde looked at his daughter-in-law. "Is this Dr. Fuller aware of your emotional problems, Lenore?"

Her face flamed in anger, but she quickly seemed to get herself under control. "Yes, quite aware. We have it all worked out."

"Good. It doesn't pay to spring an unpleasant surprise on a man." He got up wearily. "I'll call the servants together and tell them that we're going on just as usual—for the next six months, anyway."

When we left the room, Judy looked after him and scowled. "Grandpa didn't have to make a remark like that. I'll be so glad when we can leave here and live at Dr. Fuller's house."

"So will I!" Lenore added, still feeling resentful of her father-in-law. "Prescott and I will fix it up nicely so it'll be a real home for us." She couldn't understand how Dorcas got along with Clyde so well.

"I'll be darn glad to get out of here, too," Keith put in. "I don't dare ask my friends over or anything. This place is like a museum."

But the servants were more than glad to stay. Mrs. Williams burst into tears when Lenore told her the news. "This has been my home for so long. It would break my heart to leave."

When Clyde was alone in the library, he looked around. He belonged here. He hoped he could stay until he died. Here were all his memories. Everything that was near and dear to him. The only person in the family who really appreciated this place was Dorcas. He was glad he'd left it to her in his will. But would she ever have money enough to keep it up?

CHAPTER 22

When Dorcas woke up Thursday morning she looked out her window and saw the rising sun highlighting the tops of the trees. The birds sang their greeting. Off in the distance, the aspen trees showed the first color of autumn. It should have been a day to rejoice being alive, but for her it was one of dread.

Facing the fact that she had been a bitter disappointment to her grandfather, her mother, and most of all herself was the hardest thing she ever had to do. Nothing could save the Hamilton empire from crashing now.

But at least she could still try to salvage something from the workable part of the mine as long as her money held out. She hoped the Richmond Company would not claim the mine too soon in payment for the equipment installed by their supply company in San Francisco. Such moves took time, and perhaps she could replace part of her mother's money before she had to leave. The drainage tunnel had been a costly mistake. It was so hard to admit that she had been wrong and the men right.

After breakfast she walked over to the office and shivered a little in the chill air. The men were back on their regular daytime shift and already below ground. How she missed Andy's regular visits, his sweet smile and supportive attitude. He always boosted her morale and gave her courage to face the day.

She spent the morning preparing the pay envelopes. When she heard the mailman come up the road and stop at the big box outside she ran out to see what he'd brought. She found a letter from her mother that was postmarked a week ago. With a feeling of dread, she opened it and read her mother's careful handwriting.

Dear Dorcas:

It pains me to write this letter. First let me assure you that my deep love for you hasn't diminished at all. I have nothing but admiration for the way you tried to solve your grandfather's problems.

However, I went to the bank today and received one of the worst shocks I've ever had in my life. I couldn't believe the bank officer when he told me that there was less than $20,000 left in my estate. As you know, that's all the money I have in the world. When you asked permission to use some of my money, I thought it would be three or four thousand, not fifty thousand! I'm utterly appalled that my money is so badly depleted. Oh, I know your intentions were the best, but I am the loser, not you.

And as far as I can tell, you are not going to get anything out of the mine. Your grandfather has entirely given up hope. Likely we'll all have to leave here. If so, we will rent a flat or a house and I will take some of my furniture out of storage and do the best I can. Wherever we live, there will always be a place for you.

All I will have to live on for the rest of my life is my small estate. Somehow we'll have to manage on the income from it, which means I can have no servants, no social life, no carriage, or any of the amenities I am used to. When it is time for Keith to go to college, I'll have to dip into the capital.

Please, I beg you, do everything you possibly can to pay me back at least some of the money. I need it desperately. In spite of the worried tone of this letter, I send my love.

> *Mother*

Tears gathered in Dorcas's eyes as she read through it again. Finally, she crushed the letter in her hand. Why had she ever touched her mother's money? She had had no right to do so. She had taken every bit of security away from Lenore. Was Mama depressed again? If she could only telephone home and talk to her. Communicating by wire or letter wasn't the same.

In despair, Dorcas pounded her fist on her desk. This very day they were probably moving out of the mansion. She had to do something. She pushed back her chair and began pacing around the room. Wasn't there something, anything, she could do?

When she saw Red crossing the yard to the storeroom, she ran outside and called out. He turned and came toward her.

"I know you're going to object, but please, just carry out my orders, Red."

"What do you want me to do?" She saw him brace himself unconsciously, waiting to hear her latest harebrained scheme.

"I'm going to make one last desperate effort. I want you to send a crew into the drainage tunnel to drill and blast that granite. We might be able to find the hot spring after all."

He cringed. "Miss Hamilton, it's a damn waste of time. We've already set ourselves way back."

"Perhaps it is. But just do it! As soon as it's safe, I want you to crawl in there with me and see what it looks like."

He shrugged his shoulders in resignation. "I'll carry out your orders, but I'm not at all optimistic."

"If we're lucky, the hot water will come gushing out and we won't have to crawl in there. But if we do have to take a look, when will it be safe?"

"Not until morning. Remember, that tunnel is small. It'll take a longer time to clear out the gases. The men will have to work the rest of the day to drill into that granite and do the blasting," he added in a put-upon tone.

How disappointing. She had hoped to get in there today. How could she wait all night?

Red went on, his expression one of disapproval. "They'll have to use long fuses, and that's always tricky because sometimes they fizzle out and have to be relit."

"Then please take care of it."

"Yes, Miss Hamilton."

He didn't have to tell her how disgusted he was. It showed in the rigid way he held his body as he walked toward the mine entrance to go underground and round up the crew.

The endless day dragged by. If only Andy were here to comfort her. Of course, he'd probably try to talk her out of this latest effort. She wished that Philip would come by, but of course he was terribly busy taking care of his own mine. He, too, must miss Andy's help.

Finally she heard the blasts and counted as they went off. One. Two. And up to ten. The earth shook and rumbled from the explosives, reminding her of the time of the earthquake underground. Now, if the hot spring were only diverted, they could get back to the tunnel with the rich veins and ore cars full of quartz ready to stamp!

It wasn't long before all the men were aboveground again at the end of their shift and waiting for their pay envelopes.

"You saw no sign of water after you blasted?" she asked one of the men.

"No, ma'am. But of course that's a dangerous place to blast, so we didn't stick around."

"You ain't got any spare room in that tunnel," another miner said. "All we was interested in was getting out as fast as possible."

She arranged a time to meet Red the next morning and went home to talk over her mother's letter with Esther.

When Dorcas arrived with Red at the drainage tunnel entrance the next morning, there was no gushing stream of boiling water to greet them. A sickening stab of disappointment twisted through her. All night she had hoped and prayed that the blasts would tap the hot spring.

Red kicked the dry dirt. "Well, it's just as I thought."

"Perhaps the water hasn't reached here yet."

"Oh, Miss Hamilton, you know better than that. It wouldn't take too long to run out. The force of that spring was tremendous."

She nodded in disgust. Certainly it hadn't taken too long for tunnel 14 to fill with boiling water and steam after the earthquake. And this drainage tunnel was on a slope. The water would have run down here even faster. "Well, let's crawl in and see what we've got."

Red cried angrily, "It's a damn waste of time. I've got better things to do."

"But we waited until you had the men started this morning. Surely your foreman can carry on without you for a little while longer." How cross and out of sorts he was. She'd have to handle him with care and not push him too far. She didn't want him to quit. She must hold on to him as long as she could.

"Well, I have a hell of a lot to do on the surface as well," Red muttered.

"But I want to see what's at the end of this tunnel."

"I can tell you right now. There's a big dent in the granite."

"Well, we're going in anyway." She set her chin stubbornly. "Light the candles."

The acrid odor of blasting powder still hung in the air as they crawled into the narrow tunnel. Dorcas fought back her panic at being confined in a small dark place. She tried not to think of the spiders or snakes that might be in there with them.

As they neared the end, they found the floor of the tunnel filled with chunks of granite, dust, and layers of sharp gravel that cut through her gloves.

"Are you satisfied now? No sense in going closer. You might get hurt," Red said impatiently as the light from his miner's candle glowed eerily on the debris.

"I want to see what happened to the granite wall." She was going to get close enough to feel it; she was determined. If she detected any heat, they could blast again.

Dorcas carefully manuevered her way between the chunks of granite, wincing as she felt the sharp edges jab into her.

When she finally got within five feet of the face, she held her head up so the candlelight from her miner's lantern would shine into the ruptured granite.

Something glittered! Excitedly, she moved her head back and forth. A sparkle came from another spot. Was it gold? She hardly breathed as she bobbed her head up and down. The whole face came alive.

"Red! Come here!" she half stuttered in excitement. "Did you bring extra candles? Come as fast as you can!"

Had she discovered a vein? It had to be. Even from this distance, she thought she could see quartz.

As she crawled around granite chunks, she told herself, don't get your hopes up. It could be a false alarm. But the closer she drew, the more she could see something glittering in the wall.

Red half fell on her as he came up behind her. "My God!" he shouted as his miner's lantern, along with hers, illuminated the rock face. "It's gold, all right!" He reached into his pocket and pulled out four large candles. With shaking fingers, he lighted them and handed two to Dorcas.

They searched carefully the whole exposed surface. The

stronger light revealed chunks of gold embedded in the quartz. In awe he whispered, "I've never seen anything like this! Never!"

Her pounding heart raced the blood wildly through her veins. "It's real gold, isn't it! Not pyrite?"

"Yes, it's gold." He held his candles near the chunks of granite piled on the ground next to them. "Good lord, look at this!" Shimmering threads of gold wound like lace through the quartz imbedded in the granite pieces. He gasped for breath at the awesome sight.

Too stunned to feel anything at first, Dorcas tried to grasp the enormity of this discovery. She reached out and traced her finger along the spiderweb of pure gold. Finally a flame of excitement leaped through her. Gold! Gold! Gold! The flame consumed her. She wanted to shout with joy. She grabbed Red's arm. "We've made a strike, haven't we?"

"Yes. The like of which I've never seen."

"I wish Andy were here. I want him to share this with us," Dorcas cried.

"He could tell us just what this means."

Andy! How they needed him!

"Just look at this, Miss Hamilton." Red held his candle toward the top of the blasted cavity. Everywhere the light hit they could see the rich quartz, some with flecks of gold, and in other places larger streaks and even bigger concentrations of the pure yellow metal glittered back at them. Red let out a long whistle of admiration. It was too much to believe.

"I take back every objection I ever made to digging this tunnel and blasting yesterday. To think I didn't even want to come in here this morning. This is too much. How easily we could have missed this." He shook his head in wonder.

"I know. That's what scares me." Thanks be to God that Mama sent that letter, Dorcas thought.

"It's happened so many times. Some guy will give up too soon and the next one makes the strike." Red turned his head and smiled at her. "But that didn't happen to you, did it? It looks like your jinx is over."

"I hope so. We've had enough rough times." She shifted her position to get more comfortable. "Now what do we do?"

"We need some expert advice as to just how to proceed."

"I know we'd have to make this tunnel bigger, for one thing. Maybe we should keep this a secret."

Red shook his head. "That's what John Sutter said in 1848 when Marshall discovered gold in the mill he was building at Coloma. Look what happened! The Gold Rush! There's no way we can keep this a secret. It's just too big."

"It is a major strike, don't you think? Not something that'll play out in a hurry."

"As far as I can tell, it's major, but of course I'm not a mining engineer. Andy could tell us."

"Or Mr. Richmond. I could get him. He's back now."

"Yes, he'd know." Red touched the largest concentration of gold. "You could dig this out with a penknife. I think I'd better post some armed guards. Anyone could crawl in here from the river and steal some of this and we might never know the difference."

"Yes, do that. Come on, we'd better get out of here. We both have things to do." She maneuvered herself around so that she was headed out.

"I suppose you'll send a wire to Mr. Hamilton. He'll be tickled."

Grandfather! Her heart almost stopped. Perhaps there was still time to save him from going into bankruptcy! The payment wasn't due until tomorrow. She could send him a wire at once. "Yes, I'll telegraph him right away. I'll go into town."

Surely, if the lenders knew about this big strike, they'd give her grandfather more time. Or a bank would finance him. That was the first thing to do—get some wires sent. She could save him after all. She hardly paid any attention to the discomfort of crawling out. Her heart sang with each foot. She'd wire her mother, too.

As soon as she got near the house, Dorcas called, "Esther! Where are you? Something wonderful has happened!"

Esther appeared in the doorway, and when she heard the news, she grabbed Dorcas and hugged her. Soon they were both crying with happiness. "Oh, Miss Dorcas, somethng good has happened for a change."

"I have to go into town to send a telegram to my grandfather and mother. Come with me so I can tell you all about it on the way."

"All right. I'll hitch up the horse and buggy while you change."

It didn't take Dorcas long to shed her dusty overalls and old shirt. She gave herself a quick wash and put on a dark print dress with a white ruffled collar. As she brushed her hair, she had to assure herself over and over that she'd really made a strike. Every time she thought about the gold, ecstasy flamed in her again. It seemed too good to be true.

All the way into town, Dorcas and Esther discussed this sudden turn of events. "Red said he'd never seen anything like it. That granite wall looks like a jewel case."

"I hope you make a fortune, Miss Dorcas."

"Well, I don't expect to get much out of it for myself. But if I can keep Grandfather from going under and pay back my mother, that will be wonderful. And get my jewels back, of course."

"When I think of all you've put into that mine, you deserve something from it, too."

"I'm not going to say anything to anyone or expect too much until Philip looks it over," Dorcas told her firmly.

How proud she would be to send the wire. Never again could anyone say that she had used poor judgment. Or made foolish mistakes.

When they rode down the main street in Alpine Heights, Dorcas turned her head from side to side and greeted each person on the sidewalk. How surprised they'd be when they heard the great news. Some of the grizzled old miners sitting in front of the saloons would have to change their minds about the female at the Alpine.

The moment they walked into the general store, the grocer, who also acted as telegraph operator, motioned to her. "I just got a wire for you this morning. I was trying to find someone going out your way."

After he handed her the yellow envelope, she tore it open and read: PAYMENT MADE. LETTER FOLLOWS. CLYDE HAMILTON. Her mouth fell open in astonishment. She gave it to Esther and they exchanged a long look.

"Where could he get the money at the last minute?" Dorcas asked.

"Perhaps he sold a piece of property."

"But it was all mortgaged. No, he probably got another loan somewhere." Dorcas slumped down on top of a cracker barrel. What an astonishing piece of news! So Grandfather hadn't gone into bankruptcy after all. She breathed a long sigh of relief. What a day this had been.

Now they would be able to get him solvent again. How she

wanted to have him spend the last years of his life in peace and contentment with the fortune saved and Keith's future assured.

She scratched out the telegram she had prepared and wrote another. GLAD ABOUT PAYMENT. MAJOR DEVELOPMENTS HERE. GOOD NEWS FOLLOWS IN LETTER. At least he'd have something to be cheerful about, but still she wasn't giving too much away nor making promises she couldn't keep. To her mother she wired, RECEIVED LETTER. NO NEED TO WORRY. ALL IS WELL.

Philip bent over his desk, working on his quarterly report. His shoulders drooped in discouragement. He didn't like the figures he had to put down. The amount of gold he had shipped out of the Golden Star had declined again for the fifth quarter in a row. Just as his uncle had threatened at the meeting of managers, the Golden Star would have to be phased out in a year or so. This latest report confirmed that the mine was rapidly reaching the point at which it simply wouldn't pay to keep it open. Not only was the gold getting depleted, but much of the equipment would have to replaced. It was hardly worth making such a major capital investment.

He tapped a pencil against his teeth. Just what was his future with the Richmond Mining Company? Not rosy. The best jobs would go to Elliott's sons. That had been made clear from the start. When Elliott retired, Matt would take over. Philip and his cousin had never gotten along well. Where would he be when Matt was in charge? Out on his ear, that's where.

Philip longed for the days when the Golden Star was the major mine in the company. The legendary words *Andromeda Lode* evoked magic. All the Richmonds had grown prominent in the mining world because of it. Wealth; good luck; power.

But the Lode was gone now. Like a will-o'-the-wisp it had appeared and disappeared throughout the Golden Star, governed by the movements of the earth in ages past. There was no logic in where gold was discovered. It depended on geological conditions at the time the earth was being formed. This area had been blessed by the Lode. Why? Who knows? His grandfather had discovered it and made the most of his opportunities.

But now that largesse was gone. Instead of being the flagship, the Golden Star mine was now the least important in the company. A has-been. Of course, he could always get a position somewhere else. Perhaps in a copper mine or a tungsten mine someplace. In a silver mine in Nevada or another gold mine in the Mother Lode.

But it wouldn't be the same. He'd be just another employee, albeit an important one, as no major mine could be operated without engineers. But it would take forever to work up to being the general manager again, if he ever could. There was no chance to make a fortune on his own. Philip's spirits sank even lower as he contemplated his dismal prospects. His only hope lay in Elliott's acquiring the Alpine and possibly combining the two mines.

He heard someone come running lightly up the steps and into the outer office. He saw Dorcas through the glass partition and motioned for her to come in. He had never seen her looking so radiant and lovely. Her eyes sparkled and her face glowed with excitement.

"Philip! Guess what!" She slipped into the chair opposite him.

"Something wonderful has happened."

"Yes. But how can you tell?"

"You look ready to ascend like a balloon. What is it?"

She leaned forward and spoke very low. "I think I've made a strike. A big one!" Breathlessly, she told him her astonishing news. "I can't believe it! It's like a dream and I'm afraid I'm going to wake up."

"Well, don't get your hopes too sky-high. You could be disappointed." Inwardly he doubted that she had found anything very important.

"I know. That's why I came. I need your help to tell me just what I have." She put her hand on his arm. "Philip, please, could you possibly come with me now? I need expert advice so I'll know where I stand."

"Yes, I guess I could." He tapped his report. "I can do this some other time." Actually, he was grateful for an excuse to leave it until later.

"We have to crawl into that narrow tunnel, so why don't you get some old clothes," she suggested.

As they walked back to the Alpine, she told him in further detail about the discovery. Her big brown eyes sparkled and she hugged his arm. Her dark print dress emphasized her slim waist. How stunning she is, Philip thought. Always before he'd felt that Judy was the more beautiful of the sisters, but she'd be hard put to outshine Dorcas today.

He laid his hand over hers and squeezed her fingers. "If you're really onto something, I'm happy for you. You've tried so hard against terrible odds. Maybe fortune is shining on you at last." He honestly hoped so, for her sake.

"It's about time for a change," Dorcas agreed.

In high spirits, she laughed gaily, her feet hardly touching the ground. What could be more wonderful than walking with Philip and sharing such good news? "Come up to the house while I put on my overalls and old shirt. But I'll be embarrassed to have you see me like that," she added with a smile.

He lifted his bundle of old clothes. "Wait'll you see me decked out."

As they slipped down the dry creek bed a few minutes later on their way to the tunnel, he held her close so she wouldn't fall. How she loved the pressure of his arm around her. Once again he'd cast an enchanted spell over her and made her feel desirable in spite of her ridiculous getup. In fact, it didn't matter how they looked. Philip, at least, was handsome in anything. Everything about him was perfection. His strong, masculine face. The way his hair waved back from his forehead. His broad shoulders and well-shaped hands. He was virile, dynamic, and exciting. There was no one like him.

Soon they were crawling back into the tunnel. Their heavy leather gloves and knee pads helped them over the jagged rocks.

When they finally reached the end and saw the rock face glistening in the semidarkness, Dorcas cried, "Look, there it is. Hold up your lantern."

When Philip beamed his light around, he cried out in astonishment, "Dorcas, do you know what you have here?"

"A rich vein, I hope."

"Rich vein? It's a lode! The Andromeda Lode! It's shown up again."

She gasped in disbelief. "But how could it? This far from the Golden Star?"

"It's not so far. When we walked out of your mine grounds we came toward the Golden Star. It's all part of the same formation, but this time the lode has appeared on the Hamilton side, not the Richmond." He laid his head against hers and started to laugh. "How ironic! I can see my uncle's face when he hears about this. He'll be livid."

She began to laugh as well. "I can just see my grandfather's face when he hears about it, too."

"Think how our families fought over it years ago." He reached out and touched the gold. "Isn't it beautiful?"

"Right now it's the most glorious sight in the world. I still have this weird feeling that I'm dreaming."

Philip caressed the rock face. "The reason there's so much pure gold here is that it was locked in this granite, which acted as a protective shield. It couldn't wash away and eventually work its way out to the streams and riverbeds like placer gold."

"Do you think the lode is substantial? It isn't just here in this one spot is it?"

"Until you follow a lode, there is no way of knowing exactly where it will appear and then vanish. Of course, you can tell a great deal by core samples. But my guess is that you came across the beginnings of it in those rich veins you found in tunnel fourteen."

"But they were nothing like this."

"Perhaps not, but they could be the beginning. If so, the lode could very well run the whole distance to here and even beyond." He let out a long, low whistle. "Your grandfather'll be out of the woods now. He'll certainly be glad he still owns the Alpine."

"Actually, he signed it over to me."

"To you?" Philip gripped her shoulder. "To you?"

"Yes. But I think it's just a technicality. I guess he did it because he thought I was trying so hard to make it pay. No matter who owns it legally, all the profits will go to Grandfather, of course."

"But it's legally yours? You have full control over it?"

In the semidarkness, Dorcas saw a strange expression come into Philip's eyes. She answered, "That's right. And I'm glad, because I can make decisions without consulting him first. When I came here at the beginning, I had to wire him about every move I made."

"Clyde Hamilton's not the easiest man in the world to deal with, either," Philip commented.

"I should say not. He can be very difficult." She turned back to the glittering rock face. "Now I have to make some decisions. The first one is how to get this ore out of here. I need some more working capital right away. But Andy warned me right from the beginning not to make this tunnel too big.''

''I agree. Between Andy and me we might be able to figure out some way to get some of this ore out on a temporary basis to give you money enough to go ahead on a permanent one. Of course, you can always borrow money from a bank.''

''Oh, no. I have too many debts now. I'd rather take a little longer and use some of this gold.'' She gazed at it again in disbelief. ''Red said he's going to post a guard.''

''You'll need one, once the word gets out.''

''I've kept you away from your own work too long. We'd better go back.''

He squeezed her shoulders. ''But this big discovery calls for a celebration. I'm afraid I can't take the rest of the day off, but I'll pick you up on my way home. We can have dinner and break out a bottle of champagne.''

''That would be wonderful.''

''Shall I invite some of our friends to drop by afterward?''

''No, I don't want to do that. Not without Andy. Besides, I'd just as soon be as quiet about this as possible. Just the two of us can celebrate. Come on, let's go. I must write to my grandfather and my mother. Andy didn't say where he'd be, so I can't write to him.''

''He certainly was mysterious,'' Philip agreed.

Dorcas felt a twinge of hurt again. It wasn't like Andy to shut her out this way. But it would be wonderful to tell him all about the strike as soon as he returned. Dear Andy. As exciting as all this had been, she felt an underlying lack that he wasn't here to share her triumph.

Back at his office, Philip tackled his report again. There was nothing to do but include the news about the Andromeda Lode reappearing in the Alpine. He could imagine how furious his uncle would be. The report itself was bad enough. Hearing that Clyde Hamilton would enjoy the rewards of the lode instead of himself would only add more fuel to Elliott's anger. Even worse, though, would be to leave the information out and have his uncle learn it from someone else.

There was no way at all that the Alpine would fall into the Richmonds' hands now. Of course, all talk about Hamilton's bankruptcy would be forgotten. Philip threw his head back and laughed at this twist of fate. How ironic! And it served his uncle right. But his laughter died away as he realized that his own future was also affected. Elliott wouldn't keep the Golden Star open now that the Alpine was out of his reach. What, then, was in store?

When the report was finished, Philip sealed it and put it in the outer office to be given to the mailman. He turned to other work at hand, but it was hard to concentrate, because he kept thinking about Dorcas and how radiant and beautiful she had looked when she rushed into his office. How slender her waist was in that print dress. How her face had glowed as they walked together down to the tunnel. How adoringly she'd looked at him.

Thoughtfully he rolled a pencil back and forth on his desktop. Never before had he been interested in marriage, but what a prize she would be as a wife. A well-bred, attractive heiress to the Hamilton fortune. She would be at home anywhere, here in Alpine Heights or in San Francisco. They had the same interest in mining. And to think she owned the Alpine! That was almost too astonishing to comprehend.

Old Clyde had signed the mine over to her for some reason. Why had he done that? Was he getting senile, or did he want to reward Dorcas for her efforts in opening the mine? At the time, of course, Hamilton had had no idea that the lode would appear again.

Perhaps I should propose to Dorcas, he told himself. She would accept him, of course, since she had been in love with him for years. He felt a twinge of regret over Heather La Pointe, who was so enchanting, but she didn't own the Andromeda Lode, and Dorcas did.

His blood raced as he realized what it would mean to have Dorcas for a wife. It wouldn't take much persuasion to get her to turn the Alpine over to him. He was the one who could operate it most efficiently. Her experiences this summer would convince her of that. A shiver of excitement ran through him. If only he could get his hands on the lode. It beckoned and enticed him like a Lorelei. He visualized its glittering beauty. Untold riches were buried in the quartz through the granite.

Once he married Dorcas and controlled the Alpine, he'd

bide his time. When Elliott was about to close the Golden Star, he'd make a token offer at some ridiculously low price. He was sure his uncle would sell it to him. Who else would want it? Philip let out a long, excited breath. With the capital from the lode he could completely update both properties.

He'd get rid of all the obsolete equipment and install only the best so that they would have no breakdowns and wasted miners' hours. They could connect all the tunnels between the two mines and sink subsidiary shafts from one level to the other. Run the two mines as one. What an operation that would be!

Think of the power and wealth he would have! How heads would turn when he attended meetings of mining men. Think of the respect he would get from his peers. Even if he were married, the ladies would still fawn all over him.

Best of all, he would no longer have to kowtow to Elliott or be humiliated by his cousins, who never let him forget that he was illegitimate. With what delight he would invite them all to the wedding at which he, the bastard, was marrying one of California's great heiresses. A Hamilton.

His thoughts were interrupted when a clerk came in with mail. He took it and ordered, "Fred, run into town and tell my housekeeper that I'm bringing a guest home for dinner tonight."

As he glanced through the envelopes, his stomach tightened into a hard knot. There was one from his uncle. He always dreaded opening letters from Elliott, as they were usually full of criticism. With a feeling of panic, Philip noted that his uncle had written it himself. That meant trouble. Something of utmost privacy.

> *Dear Philip:*
>
> *I trust you arrived home safely.*
>
> *On Tuesday last, Andrew Woodard came to see me and made the most astonishing accusations. He told me about the cave-in at the Alpine in July and had the temerity to say that I was responsible for that accident.*
>
> *In the first place, where were you when he was breaking down the barrier to tunnel 10, which I had installed for safety reasons? Why did you just sit back*

and let him do that? He had no permission from me to enter that tunnel. Did you give it to him?

He also had pictures that he had taken in the tunnel and at the cave-in. In addition, he had photographed confidential reports that I had filed in a special place. I had never told anyone about them, not even you. No one else was supposed to see them. How did Woodard get access to them? Have you been so careless that they were available to him?

He blackmailed me with those photos and demanded money, saying he was representing the Hamiltons. I made a small settlement with him to get rid of this nuisance claim. Of course I fired him. If he should return to Alpine Heights, he is not to be allowed back on my property. Remember, under no circumstances is this scoundrel to set foot on the Golden Star grounds again. I have never had dealings with such an under-handed, disloyal employee in all my years in the mining game. He should be blacklisted at every mining company in the country.

Philip, I am very displeased with you. In the first place, you recommended Woodard as an engineer. You asked that he be assigned to the Golden Star. As General Manager, you should have prevented this occurrence. It is your responsibility to guard the private records.

You must have been most lax to let this happen. Since I plan to close that mine next year, anyway, I do not intend to replace Woodard. You can do his work. I suggest that you start inquiring about another position within the next few months, because once the Golden Star is closed, I don't want you on my staff. It's only out of my sense of responsibility to your late mother that I don't fire you outright along with your friend.

Yours truly,
Elliott Richmond

Philip let out a long gasp. He read the letter again. All hell had broken loose. So that was what Andy had been doing in Sacramento. What had he discovered here?

As Philip put the letter down, his hand shook. Anger boiled in him. What right did his uncle have to blame him? He didn't know about any secret records. Where were they?

Andy sure must have had the goods on Elliott or he never would have dared such a confrontation. Philip glanced at the letter again and noted that the terms ''should be blacklisted'' had been used. If his uncle were innocent, he would have said that he had reported and blacklisted Woodard already.

Well, that did it! Philip decided he'd propose to Dorcas that very evening.

CHAPTER 23

This was the last afternoon Andy would spend in San Francisco. Tonight he would take the riverboat to Sacramento and catch the morning train for the north. He loved this city by the bay. He wished he could spend a lot more time here, but Dorcas needed him. Since he had no job, he would give all his time to her and help her solve her multitude of problems.

How anxious he was to return to her and tell her all about his confrontation with Elliott Richmond. He could visualize her lovely face, her expressive brown eyes, and the approval she would show him. He smiled at himself. He was the knight in shining armor who went out to slay the dragon and came home to his princess in the tower.

Well, old Elliott certainly was a dragon—a crooked one at that. He'd probably written his version of the big brouhaha to Philip already. The threats of blacklisting were hollow. There was no way that his former boss was going to take any chances on being exposed.

Andy checked his suitcase and took a street car to the industrial district. He wanted to see his friend Fred Langley, who owned and operated a small but very successful company that manufactured custom-made equipment to be used in mines with special problems. Drainage, steep slopes, and land slippage were just a few of the situations that the Langley Company had dealt with. None was more puzzling than the hot spring in the Alpine, Andy was sure.

As he walked through the huge, barnlike building, he stopped more than once, fascinated by the work going on. He watched the skilled machinists study blueprints, then make adjustments on and take measurements of the pieces of steel in front of them. How carefully they worked with their calipers and slide rules.

Some of the pieces of equipment being built were large and others were very small, but all were necessary to machinery used in mining. He had ideas he would like to try out, if he had the chance.

Andy found his friend in his office. The big Welshman stood up, grinned, and put out his hand. After they had greeted each other, Fred took a set of blueprints off a chair. "Sit down if you can find an empty spot in this madhouse." He was from a long line of Welsh miners and had come to California to work in the gold mines in Placer County. "I hope you're looking for a job. I have more work than I can handle."

"Don't make a statement like that, unless you mean it. You might have me on your payroll one of these days. I resigned from the Golden Star."

"Really?" Fred cried eagerly. "You could go to work today."

"Well, hardly." Andy explained the need for him at the Alpine. "But I couldn't leave San Francisco without stopping by to see you." They talked about mining problems, including the Alpine's hot spring, for an hour.

When Andy finally rose to go, Fred stopped him. "I'm serious, Andy. You always have a job here if you want it. And it doesn't have to be full-time. You can come during the winter months, for example, when the Alpine is closed."

"I may take you up on that. I've always wanted to design mine machinery."

"Then this is just the place for you."

*   *   *

Dorcas left the office early to bathe and dress for her celebration with Philip. If only Andy were here to join them. Somehow it didn't seem complete without him. Hadn't he been in on all the catastrophes? Now that they had a big strike, he should be here for their triumph. And what could be more triumphant than discovering the Andromeda Lode again? It still seemed so unreal.

She rummaged through her closet to find a light wool dress in a pale gold. Dark brown braid trimmed the neck, which stood up to frame her face. It was one of her better outfits; she had brought it up from the city early in the spring. For the first time this fall, the weather was cool enough to wear it.

"Miss Dorcas, it's much too cold outside for you to go out to the shower room," Esther said. "I've brought the big wash tub into the kitchen, and there's plenty of hot water. You take a good soak right here."

It felt good to sink into the hot water, even if her knees were up to her chin. Dorcas soaked all the tension out of her muscles and scrubbed herself with her favorite lavender soap. When she finally got out of the tub, she wiped herself dry with a soft towel and dusted bath powder all over her glowing body.

After she dressed, she hung a gold chain with a large nugget on it around her neck. Her father had given it to her for her twenty-first birthday. The gold had come from the mine in Colorado. She rubbed the nugget between her fingers as memories of her father flooded back. Somehow she felt his presence as if he were rejoicing with her on this glorious day.

Little tendrils escaped from the pompadour she'd piled on top of her head. She tied a loose scarf over her hair and draped a brown wool cape across her shoulders, just as Philip rapped at the door.

"How stunning you look," he said as he walked with her out to his carriage.

"I thought you'd be on horseback." She laughed happily. "I was all prepared to ride behind you."

"Indeed not. We keep this carriage at the mine for special occasions. I had to escort my golden princess in regal style." He put his arm around her waist and helped her into the seat. When he climbed in beside her, he leaned over and kissed her.

"Someone might see us." Her cheeks flushed prettily. How attentive Philip was this evening. He had never been quite so gallant.

"Who? There's no one around. Your men haven't come to the surface yet." He kissed her again and laid his cheek against her own.

"Please go. Someone from the stamp mill might see us."

However, it pleased her very much that he made her feel so desirable.

He tucked her hand in his as they rode toward Alpine Heights.

"I've never been so happy," she murmured. "I guess I appreciate my good fortune now that I've had a lot of hard knocks. I used to take everything so for granted."

"Now you know that even a Hamilton can have bad luck."

"Yes, and even worse than bad luck—some out-and-out disasters. But I guess they weren't all bad. If it weren't for the earthquake and hot spring, I never would have had the tunnel dug."

"Against everyone's better judgment. Because of your stubborn insistence in going on with the tunnel, we're having a celebration tonight."

"I wish Andy could be with us. He deserves to be in on it, too; he's been so helpful. I keep wondering where he is," she added.

"I heard from my uncle today. Apparently Andy and he had a terrible row. Well, the upshot is that my chief engineer is no longer with the Golden Star."

Dorcas looked at Philip in astonishment. Had Andy been fired, or had he resigned? How puzzling it all was. "Well, I hope he comes back here, anyway. I need him more than ever."

"I'm sure he'll be back. He'll be able to work for you instead of me."

"But I can't afford—well, of course, I can pay him full wages now. I guess I can't believe that the lode is really mine." Happiness flowed through her again. "For the first time since I came, I won't have to worry about meeting a payroll."

"I know, my darling female Croesus, and I'm so happy for you," he said.

"Before we go to your house, I'd like to mail some letters. I want them to go out as soon as possible." She thought of her jubilant letter to her mother.

Mama, now that we've discovered the Andromeda Lode, I will be able to pay back every cent I borrowed from you, plus interest. I know I used far more from your estate than you expected, but it was necessary and certainly has paid off. Above all, I want you to have a sense of security for the rest of your life. Of course, you must send Keith to college, because he will need all the training he can get to take over the Hamilton Company. . . .

She'd not only written a long report to her grandfather but added:

I had Philip examine the discovery—now, don't be cross—as he is the best-trained person around here. He says it's part of the Andromeda Lode, just like in the glory days when it ran $1,000 a ton. It's incredibly rich. I will have as much mined from it through this drainage tunnel as I can and then next spring we can sink the proper shafts and go about the project to get the highest return.

Grandpa, I can't tell you how happy I am. I'm so glad that somehow you made your payment so you will be able to get the benefit from this big strike. I plan to pay back my mother as soon as possible and redeem grandmother's jewels from Angliers'. From then on, I want all profits devoted to paying off your debts so you won't have to worry anymore.

I'm also including a press release in which you make the announcement about the big strike. Send a copy to all the nearby newspapers and the ones in Sacramento as well. Let everyone know about your new state of affairs. There have been so many rumors about your impending bankruptcy, and you should put them to rest once and for all. Then you can go back to being my beloved Robber Baron, issuing orders right and left and scaring everyone to pieces.

As they drove up in front of the Richmond house, Philip wondered if he could buy the dwelling along with the Golden

Star. Of course he could. He would insist on its being part of the deal. Why would Elliott want the house if he didn't own the mine? Besides, it would only be appropriate for Dorcas and himself to live in the biggest, most luxurious house in town. He could visualize children playing in the yard.

This was the first time he had ever desired children.

But if Dorcas were busy raising a family, she would be less interested in the Alpine, wouldn't she? How could she climb into the skip if she were in the family way? Or take babies underground? Or toddlers to the office? How easy it would be to insist that he take care of everything. He could convince her that she would be better off in their beautiful home raising a family.

He could imagine their spending the worst of the winter in San Francisco, enjoying all the advantages of city life. There was the magnificent Hamilton mansion overlooking the Bay. Old Clyde wouldn't live forever. Who would inherit that place? Dorcas, probably. Hadn't she already received the mine? It was obvious that she was the apple of his eye.

They dined on roast chicken and mashed potatoes with gravy. There were glazed carrots and apple salad, and a light lemon cake for dessert. And, of course, they drank chilled champagne.

Afterward they sat in front of the fire and watched the flames leap and devour the wood. For a long time they talked about her unexpected discovery and how easily she could have missed the lode. He had brought another bottle of champagne into the parlor and refilled their glasses over and over while they toasted her good fortune.

When he heard his housekeeper tread wearily up the stairs and shut the door to her room, Philip took Dorcas in his arms.

"You have such beautiful hair. Like burnished mahogany. It's not just dark brown; it has highlights of copper. You should see the firelight shimmering on it." His fingers trailed around her neck and under her chin. Finally he tilted her face and his lips pressed down on hers.

At first Philip was ever so languorous, exquisitely tender, barely touching her lips in sweet torment. Dorcas felt herself floating, floating in a haze of passion and champagne. All the adoration she had ever felt for him came rushing back.

Her hand caressed his cheek and found its way to the back of his head, into the softness of his hair. She heard nothing but the crackling of the fire, his short hollow breaths, his soft moans.

"I love you, my darling," he whispered at last.

Her breath caught in her throat. This was the first time he had ever declared himself.

"I love you, too, Philip. Just as I always have ever since I first saw you. You've held such a special place in my heart."

"I realized how lovely you were at that first ball back in San Francisco. It seems so long ago now." He raised her hand to his lips and kissed the palm.

She felt the furious thumping of her heart. Something told her that this night was special—a culmination of all her hopes and dreams.

He pressed her hand against his cheek. His voice grew urgent and tense. "Darling, we belong together. You and I. Will you marry me?"

At first she was startled, stunned, simply too astounded to answer. She had half expected a breakthrough on this magic night, but now that it had come, she was overwhelmed. This was a dream come true. Dorcas closed her eyes and savored the moment. Every since she had first met Philip, she had visualized being his wife. Wanted it with her whole heart. Finally she gazed up at his face. "Yes, I want to marry you, Philip."

He pulled her closer and kissed the hollows of her neck. She could feel his warm breath on her skin. "Let's marry as soon as we can," he murmured. "I want you with me always."

"And I want to be with you." Hadn't that been her dream all these years? She leaned back against his shoulders. What a day! Almost more happiness than she could fathom. A great wave of joy engulfed her. First the lode and now this proposal from Philip. She felt a little numb, as if her very senses were trying to absorb more than they could handle.

"We'll have such a wonderful life together, my lovely Dorcas."

"I suppose we could live right here."

"Of course."

"I'll want my family to be at the wedding. I think it should be in San Francisco, don't you? It would be hard for all of them to come up here."

"Whatever you say, darling."

"Of course, you'll want the Richmonds to come from Sacramento." She was happily absorbed in her plans.

He kissed the top of her head. "I certainly want them to receive an invitation." He could hardly wait for that. How he would gloat! No longer could they look down their noses at him. Elliott Richmond had always been jealous of the prestige and power of the Hamiltons. Soon Philip would be one of them.

Dorcas let out a long, ecstatic sigh. "Now we have to decide just when."

"No doubt you'll be closing the Alpine down entirely by December first at the latest. The rains could be heavy by then and all the roads a quagmire. You'd be going to San Francisco anyway. We could get married then."

"A Christmas wedding! Wouldn't that be wonderful?" She kissed him.

"That will give you plenty of time to mine out the part of the lode that's been exposed. You wouldn't want anyone to get in there and take it while you're gone."

"No, of course not. You and Andy can help me decide how best to mine it on a temporary basis."

"Yes. It's wise now to wait until spring to sink your permanent shafts. That will take a lot of preliminary work. And you don't want to be interrupted by rain."

"Besides, I don't have the capital to finance such a big project yet. I can hardly wait for Andy to return so we can begin the planning, though. Surely he would have wired me if he weren't coming back at all."

Philip caressed her arm. "Let's not talk about mining. Let's discuss us. Besides, after we're married you'll be busy making a home for me and raising a family."

She snuggled closer. "But you'll have to admit that it'll be nice to have a wife who'll understand your mining problems too."

Dorcas twisted her fingers in his. How handsome his hands were. Long, slender fingers. More like those of an artist than a hard-rock miner. He had no calluses. Obviously he worked with his mind and engineering instruments, not physically.

Finally she asked, "Tell me about yourself. Where were you born? What branch of the family are you from?"

For a long time he was silent. Should he tell her that he was illegitimate? Should he spoil this triumphant day?

"You don't have to tell me if you don't want to," she murmured at last. "I've always been aware that there was something mysterious about you. I don't care what it is. I love you, my dearest. That's what matters most."

What should he tell her? He didn't dare ignore her request. It was far better that she find out from him about his background than from someone else. He could play on her sympathy. Pretend that his mother thought that she had married his father.

"Of course I'll tell you. But let me fill our glasses again and add a log to the fire. It's a long story." He got off the sofa, walked to the hearth, and tossed on a thick chunk of oak, watching the sparks fly while he collected his thoughts and planned what to say. He poured the champagne and then sat down beside her again.

"My mother was a saint, but she lived a tragic life. Of course, she was raised in luxury in San Francisco, but she fell in love with my father and ran off and married him against my grandparents' wishes." His voice died away as if it were too painful to go on.

"The poor girl. How she must have suffered."

"She did suffer." Philip murmured at last. "You can't imagine how miserable her life was. After she was expecting me, she found out that my father was already married. He deserted her, of course, and my grandparents would have nothing more to do with her."

"Oh, Philip, how dreadful. What did she do?"

"She went out of the state. At first to Idaho Falls and then to Salt Lake. Some friends took her in." He told her a little about what he could remember from his childhood. "She used her maiden name, but everyone called her Mrs. Richmond. Do you realize what that makes me? Technically, I'm illegitimate."

Dorcas gave a shocked gasp. "But your mother thought she had married. What happened wasn't her fault."

"That's true."

"Besides, it's no one's business but ours. I'll be so proud to be Mrs. Philip Richmond." She gave his hand a reassuring squeeze. "And she died when you were only sixteen. It's all so very sad."

He held her closer. "Anyway, the two of us will be a real family. The first I have ever had."

"I'll try my hardest to make up to you for everything you've gone through. I want you to have all the happiness you've missed all those years."

Philip reached up and turned off the lamp. Only the dancing flames faintly lit the room. He took her in his arms and gently placed her on the soft rug in front of the fire. All of her senses were lulled by the champagne, delight over her engagement and the incredible discovery of the lode. She savored her joy, felt surrounded by it just as she was by the fire's warmth.

"My darling," Philip whispered as he kissed her temples and the sensitive spot in front of each ear.

His arms crushed her to him until all she knew was the blood-racing, tantalizing nearness of him. He kissed her throbbing throat, awakening every longing in her, sending liquid fire through her veins until she made no objection when he fumbled with the buttons on her dress.

As the stagecoach approached Alpine Heights, Andy wanted to get out and urge the horses up the grades. It was so hard to be patient as the animals plodded slowly along. All he could think about was being with Dorcas again and telling her all the details of his confrontation with Elliott Richmond.

He imagined how she would throw her arms around his neck. "Oh, Andy, you saved my grandfather! So that is why he didn't have to go into bankruptcy. I wondered how he was rescued the very last minute. I can never thank you enough. Never!" In his mind he could smell the fragrance of her hair. Feel her heart throbbing against his own.

He closed his eyes to savor in the closeness of her lovely body, the softness of her skin, the adoration in her brown, velvety eyes. Had a man ever loved a woman the way he loved Dorcas? She was part of his very heart.

What did it matter that he had lost his job over her? She was worth every sacrifice on his part. All he wanted to do was cherish and protect her. He would devote himself to her mine so she could pay back her debts. It didn't matter that she couldn't pay him. He'd live on his savings.

His dream went even further as he imagined her saying, "I love you, Andy. I want to be your wife." He thought of their future together. The house they'd build on the mine grounds once he got it producing again. He dreamed of the children they would have. That's what he wanted. A home and a family. And above all, Dorcas.

The stagecoach swayed as it dropped into the ruts. He grabbed the strap to keep from sliding back and forth and bumping the other passengers. When they finally reached the town, the driver called out, "Alpine Heights!"

Andy leaned out and asked, "Would you mind dropping me off at the Alpine mine?"

In spite of being numb and tired from the long journey, he felt a great surge of energy at the prospect of seeing Dorcas. How excited she would be at the news he had to tell her. He could see the expression in her eyes and hear her say, "Andy, did you really talk to Elliott Richmond like that? How did you dare?"

When he came through the gate, Dorcas ran out of the office, crying, "Andy! Andy! You're back!"

He gathered her in his arms. "Oh, Dorcas, my dearest love." He held her close and put his head against her hair.

"I was so afraid you wouldn't come back, Andy. Where were you?"

"It's a long story."

"Come back into the office. I have so much to tell you." She ran ahead to unlock the door.

When they were inside, she went on. "Now, sit down, because you'll never believe this. Not in a thousand years!"

He took the chair across the desk from her, waiting until she was ready to hear the really big news about his triumph over Elliott Richmond. He put the briefcase with the damning evidence on his lap. He could hardly wait to spread the photos and charts out for her to see and to tell her about the check he'd taken to her grandfather.

Dorcas leaned toward him, her large eyes flashing in excitement. "Andy, we discovered the Andromeda Lode again! Can you imagine that? The real lode. Philip said it was just like the lode they mined at the Golden Star in its glory days. You've never seen anything like this. It's beyond imagination. Incredible!"

He stared at her. His jaw dropped.

"I knew you'd be thunderstruck. It took me a long time to believe it." Her voice rose while her face radiated with happiness. "I'll tell you all about it!"

While he listened, Andy's fingers absently traced the outline of the briefcase in his lap. He felt like a balloon with the air slowly going out.

Dorcas went on, her dark eyes snapping and her cheeks flushed in excitement. "While I was in that drainage tunnel looking at all those riches, I realized I had the means to save Grandpa after all. I crawled out and went into town as fast as I could, but just as I was ready to telegraph him about the lode, old Henderson gave me a wire. It was from Grandpa saying that the payment had been made somehow, so I just wired that I had good news for him. Just think, now I can pay off my mother and get my jewels back. Then I'm going to pay off all of Grandpa's debts so he won't have to worry anymore."

Finally Andy said, "I'm happy for you, Dorcas. I'm still stunned. I can hardly believe it."

"I know. That's just the way I felt. It was all so unreal. But I have something else to tell you. That wasn't the end of my fairy-tale day. Philip took me to his house for dinner that night to celebrate. We had champagne and talked. He proposed to me at last! And I accepted him. We're going to be married at Christmastime."

Andy winced. He fought for control. He steeled himself against the sobs that threatened to shake him. Finally he stood up, his face ashen. He had to get out of there.

"Congratulations. I hope you'll be happy." He picked up his briefcase and grip, then headed for the door.

"Andy!" Dorcas pushed back her chair. "Andy, wait!"

He hit his shoulder against the partially closed door but somehow managed to stumble outside. He hurried through the gate and out onto the road. He couldn't talk to Dorcas any longer. He'd only sob his heart out and make a damn fool of himself. He had to get away. Clear away. Back to San Francisco.

As he heard her calling him from the office doorway, a farmer drove by with a wagonful of hay. "Going into town?" Andy asked.

"Sure thing." The farmer pulled on his reins, and the horses came to a halt.

By the time Andy had climbed into the seat beside the bearded man, he had a grip on himself.

"I suppose you heard about the big strike here at the Alpine?" the farmer asked.

"Yes. Just now. I've been out of town. Got back today and Miss Hamilton told me about it."

"Funny thing, that slip of a girl coming up here and discovering that vein. Never did understand why she came here at all, when her grandfather owns half of Frisco. But all the same, she made that strike. Them who has, gits, I always say." The farmer droned on about his own poor luck. Andy hardly listened. He had his own troubles to think about.

CHAPTER 24

The farmer drove to the Alpine Heights stable to deliver his load of hay. After thanking him for the ride, Andy looked over all the vehicles in the large building.

When he found a light wagon that looked sturdy, he approached the owner. "Could I rent this wagon?" he asked.

"It's not very big. Now I got heavier wagons that'd really haul a load, Mr. Woodard."

"But I don't want anything bigger. Just large enough to haul my things to Redding."

"Surely you ain't leaving us."

"I'm afraid so. I was offered a job I couldn't refuse. In San Francisco."

The heavyset stableman put out his hand. "I sure hate to see you go. We all think so well of you here." He flushed in embarrassment and went on. "Come with me and I'll write up a rental contract."

After hitching up the horse and wagon, Andy drove home. He tried not to think of Dorcas. He had to keep in control.

"I've accepted a job in San Francisco," he explained to his landlady. "I'll pack my stuff tonight and leave early tomorrow morning."

"Oh, Andy, I'll be so sad to have you leave." Tears sprang to the elderly woman's eyes. She loved this fine young engineer with his sweet smile. She had hoped he would find some nice young lady here and get married. "I made some soup this morning. Just let me warm it up for your supper. I didn't know when you were coming back."

"I'll eat later. There's something I have to do first."

It wasn't long before Andy had changed his clothes and headed for Philip's house. This was prayer-meeting night, so he felt sure the housekeeper would be gone.

When Philip himself answered the bell he put out his hand. "Well, hello, Andy. So you're back. Come on in. I'm just eating my supper. I'm alone, so we have a chance to talk."

Andy took Philip's hand but hardly shook it. "Go ahead and finish your meal. I'll wait in your den."

"I'm all done except for eating some apple pudding. I can have that later." Philip led the way into the den. "Sit down in front of the fire. How about a drink of whiskey?"

"No. I'm not staying long." Andy sat on the edge of his chair while anger seethed through him.

"Andy, for gosh sake. I know my uncle fired you, but we can still be friends."

"Elliott Richmond did not fire me. I quit before he had the chance."

"That's not what he wrote me."

"Well, he's a damn liar."

"I'll grant you that." Philip laughed a little hollowly. "By the way, I'm not supposed to let you put a foot on his property. I mean out at the mine."

It was all Andy could do to control himself. He felt like a volcano ready to explode. "I have no intention of coming back to the Golden Star." Andy stuck his chin out. "You needn't worry about that."

"I'll miss you like hell. What happened between you and

Elliott? He wrote that you tried to blackmail him. Showed him some pictures you had taken—''

''I gathered proof that he deliberately crossed over into Alpine property years ago. Followed the Andromeda Lode and mined it all out. The fact that it rightfully belonged to the Hamiltons didn't stop him. I also accused him of being responsible for the cave-in.''

Philip stared at Andy in amazement. He let out a long whistle. ''He must have been livid.''

''He was.''

''What did he do?''

''He gave me a check for one hundred thousand dollars, made out to the Hamilton Company, in partial settlement for the claim I presented. He was guilty and he knew it.''

Philip gasped. ''Do you mean he wrote a check, just like that?''

''No, he didn't write a check. I insisted on a cashier's check, since I didn't trust him for five minutes and told him so.''

''I'm surprised he didn't throw you out.''

''He knew I'd go right to Wellington. It seems that your esteemed uncle was already in deep trouble over some other shenanigan. Up in the Mother Lode.''

''I still can't get over how you got him to buckle under. He's so slick.''

''It took some convincing,'' Andy admitted.

''Good lord, you've got courage,'' Philip said.

''Much more than that. I have proof that Wellington and the other government agents would like to see, I'm sure.''

''Well, after you got the check, what happened?''

''I took it to San Francisco and gave it to Clyde Hamilton so that he could make a payment on his debts.''

''Andy, please, have a drink and stick around. I want to hear all about it. Where did you get your proof?''

''No, I'm going home to pack my gear. I'm leaving in the morning.''

''Leaving? But Dorcas needs you. Have you talked with her?''

''Yes, I've talked to her,'' Andy said tersely.

''Then you know about the lode?''

''Yes.''

''She wants you to work for her full-time. At the same wages you got at the Golden Star.''

"We didn't discuss that. But I have no intention of working for her or you." Andy got to his feet.

"Look, Andy, we both want to be your friends. We can all go on as usual, even if—"

Andy watched as Philip rose from his chair as well. "Even if you and Dorcas are married. That's what you were going to say, wasn't it?"

"Well, yes."

Hurt and anguish welled up inside Andy. "She said that you were going to get married at Christmastime."

"I don't know why you're so resentful. You know that she's loved me for a long time."

Andy took a step toward Philip. "I resent the fact that you don't love her. I find it interesting that you never proposed to her in all these months, until now. You didn't even do the honorable thing after that episode at the cabin."

Philip paled.

"No, you never considered proposing to her and easing the guilt and shame she felt." Andy reached out and grabbed Philip's sweater at the shoulder and gave him a hard shake. "You son-of-a-bitch! You never considered marrying Dorcas until the day she found that lode."

"Let go! That's not true at all!"

"Did she tell you that she owns the mine now? That old Clyde Hamilton signed it all over to her some time ago?"

"I don't have to answer that."

"No, you don't have to, you skunk! You're no better than your uncle. You're just as big a crook as he is." Andy drew back his fist and struck him on the jaw.

Philip yanked Andy around and they fell to the floor. "You can't call me a crook!" He struck out his fist and caught Andy in the stomach.

Soon the two men were grappling on the floor. They tossed and turned. One minute Andy would be on top; the next minute it was Philip. Blow after blow rained down on their bodies. They gasped for breath, rolling back and forth, hitting against the leather davenport, the big chair, the table. A lamp crashed to the floor. An ashtray hit Andy on the forehead.

He grunted and gasped. Philip was bigger and stronger than he. But what Andy lacked in size he more than made up for in fury. He wanted to beat his rival to a pulp and let out his hurt and frustration once and for all. How dare a man as insincere as this one marry his beloved. With superhuman strength he pinned Philip to the floor and straddled his torso.

With his face down close to Philip's, he snarled, "You scheming louse. You didn't even wait, did you? The very day you saw the lode in that drainage tunnel you proposed to her. But, of course, not until after you found out that she owned the mine."

"Let me up!"

"That wonderful girl who is so superior to you. How she'll be demeaning herself to marry a rat like you! Sure, you're handsome. Sure, you sweep the ladies off their feet. But there's not a sincere bone in your body."

"Damn you, I said let me up."

Philip twisted and turned, but Andy kept him pinned down firmly.

"You don't love anybody but yourself. You're going to marry her at Christmastime and then see to it that she's pregnant as soon as possible. What a good excuse you'll have for getting the Alpine under your own control."

Philip yanked himself away. He shoved Andy off him and scrambled to his feet. "Get out of my house!"

Andy slowly pulled himself to his feet. He straightened his coat. "Congratulations, Richmond. You've pulled a real coup, but you're not worthy to kiss the hem of her skirt."

"You're just sore because you want her yourself."

"That's right. I do. But at least I would help her and not try to cheat her." He shoved his hand against Philip's chest and knocked him down onto the sofa. Then Andy turned and strode out the door, hardly hearing Philip muttering threats and curses behind him.

Andy ran back to his boarding house, hoping his landlady wouldn't notice his swelling eye and lip. But she did.

"Oh, my goodness. You must have gotten into a fight," she cried when she saw him. "Here, let me fix you an icepack. You can hold it against your face while I warm up your supper. Who could have done such a thing? Some scoundrel out in the street who'd been drinking?"

"That's right."

"We have too many saloons in this town. A body isn't safe here at all."

While he held the icepack against his face, he ached all over from the fight. As he thought about Dorcas, he felt a greater hurt. How could he live without her? He needed to be near her. And she needed him. Perhaps more now than ever. But how could he stay here and work for her, when it would be such torture? No, it was better to cut it off right now. Philip could do the engineering in her mine. Since he was going to reap all the benefits, let him do the work. In spite of all his shortcomings, his former friend was an excellent engineer. He had run the Golden Star as well as anyone could.

Andy wanted to be left alone in his misery, but Mrs. O'Brien fussed over him. "Where are you going to work in San Francisco? I didn't know they had mines there."

"They don't, Mrs. O'Brien. I am going to design special machinery in a place that builds custom mining equipment."

Tears flooded her eyes. She put her arm around his shoulders. "I'll miss you, Andy. I hope you'll be happy in that big city."

"Thank you. I'll miss you, too." He wondered if he would ever be happy again. He couldn't imagine living without Dorcas close by.

Dorcas lay in her bed, staring into the darkness. The look on Andy's face when she'd told him about her engagement still haunted her. He loved her so deeply, and she knew she had hurt him to the very core. Would they still be able to work together? Somehow she doubted it.

When he didn't come to the mine the next morning, she had a hunch that he had left town. When Philip stopped by on his way to work, she asked about Andy.

"Yes, he's gone. He said he wouldn't work for either of us. I'll talk to Red right now; he can get some men started on the lode." When he bent to kiss her, she noticed his bruised face, especially the puffiness over one cheekbone and around his eye.

"What happened to you?" She reached up and lightly touched his face.

"I exchanged a few blows with a guy who shot off his mouth. Nothing to worry about. I'll hunt up Red now."

When Dorcas drove Esther into town that morning to buy their groceries, she left her housekeeper in the general store and went on to Mrs. O'Brien's. She found the older woman on the back porch doing her washing.

"I understand that Mr. Woodard has left town."

"Yes, he has a job in San Francisco. I don't quite understand what he's going to do, but it's something about making special equipment for mines. I sure am going to miss that lad."

"And so am I."

"I hated to see him go off. He was plum wore out. Besides, he'd been in a fight. Some drunk had attacked him."

Dorcas gave a little gasp, thinking, he and Philip were probably fighting over me. She felt sick at heart.

Mrs. O'Brien scrubbed a bath towel up and down on the washboard. "I tried my best to get Andy to take it easy today and start out tomorrow, but he wouldn't hear of it. No sir, he worked most of the night packing his things into a little wagon he had rented, and left at daybreak."

As Dorcas drove the buggy back to the store, she thought about her conversation with Mrs. O'Brien. All the brightness went out of the day as she realized that she had lost Andy even as a friend. How bleak the future looked without him. Even the anticipation of being married to Philip didn't seem to make up for her loss. Her throat thickened and she blinked back tears. "Oh, Andy," she murmured aloud, "How can I live without you?"

Later in the day the mailman brought a letter from Lenore, about her plans to marry Prescott Fuller. Dorcas felt cheered. At least her mother would be happy.

Prescott wants me to continue with my work at the new home. I am teaching the girls how to conduct themselves if they find work as housemaids. Also, we have lessons in reading and writing. You'd be surprised how illiterate some of them are. They have had so little schooling.

Now back to the wedding. We want to get married the day after Thanksgiving. It will be a small wedding— just family and a few intimate friends. We have reserved the chapel at the Episcopal church close to town and will have a wedding breakfast at the Hamilton Regency. Of course, all these plans are tentative. I couldn't get married without having you, dear. Let me know if you can be here. I thought you might be coming home for the holiday, anyway. There's another problem

*to settle. Judy wants to be my maid of honor. Actually,
it should be you as the oldest daughter, but her heart is
set on it. Would you be hurt if that's what we do? Write
me at once so I know.*

*I'm also working hard on the King Neptune ball. I
would give anything if you could come. It will be held
November seventh. It would be wonderful if you could
come home about November first so you could attend
the ball and then help me with the wedding.*

Just as she was reading the letter, Philip came into her
office. "I have to go into town to buy something. I stopped
to see if I could do any errands for you."

"Yes, you can send a wire to my mother. Here, read her
letter."

When he finished it, he said, "I think you should go to San
Francisco the first of November. You not only have to help
your mother with her wedding, but you must make arrangements for ours as well."

"But I want to keep the Alpine open as long as possible
and get out all the gold I can to pay off my debts. I'd give
anything if I could pay my mother back the fifty thousand
dollars I owe her before her wedding. I couldn't give her a
gift she would appreciate more."

Philip kissed Dorcas and nuzzled her neck. "Darling, in
case you've forgotten, I'm running the Golden Star. Don't
you think I could manage the Alpine as well? Let me take
over at the end of the month and I'll keep it in operation until
sometime in December. We'll get everything out of the drainage tunnel we can, and then close it up for the winter."

"Oh, Philip, could you really do that?"

"Of course. Red and I will manage just fine."

She put her arms around his neck. "It's going to be such a
relief to have your help."

He nodded. "Especially since Andy left you in the lurch
the way he did."

She gave him a quick kiss. "Now I'll write my wire down
so you can go."

Soon she had composed the message: COMING TO S.F. NOV. 1
HAVE JUDY AS MAID OF HONOR. LOVE, DORCAS. She looked up at
him. "I wish you could come to San Francisco in time for
Mother's wedding. We could announce our engagement then."

Philip shook his head. "I can't get away until mid-December. My uncle would fire me if I left early." He laughed. "It'll be bad enough when he finds out that I'm going to marry you."

Dorcas shuddered. "It'll be even worse when I tell Grandfather."

"He ought to forgive you almost anything, since you discovered the lode. Even marrying me." He kissed the tip of her nose and left.

On the way to town, Philip made plans. He would design special sleds to pull the ore out of the drainage tunnel. They could set up a temporary hoist to get it to the top of the cliff and haul it in wagons to the stamp mill. He would make every possible effort to get the maximum return from the lode in the limited time they had. Now was his chance to gain Dorcas's full confidence, to show her how skilled he was. Even if he had to send some of his best men from the Golden Star to help the crew at the Alpine, he would do it and take a chance on old Elliott's finding out about it. If the Golden Star was going to be closed anyway, what difference would it make? With Dorcas's rich mine to manage, who needed to put up with his uncle?

What they would get out of the lode now was a drop in the bucket to what they would realize next year, of course. In the spring he would completely reorganize the Alpine. Sink new shafts to mine the lode, install the right equipment, and completely recondition all the old machinery. He'd hire more engineers and they would have a major operation. Then they would see the real profits roll in.

Philip planned his strategy carefully. The main goal was to get Dorcas out of debt as soon as possible. Think how grateful she would be. How she would admire his ability to manage her mine. Then, slowly but surely, he'd gain control of it. He could afford to bide his time. Next spring was not very far away. First, they would have the wedding during the Christmas holidays. They could take part in all the city's social activities. He could just see them being lionized as the Golden Couple at the balls and dinner parties. Later in the spring, they would return to Alpine Heights and settle down in the Richmond house. By then, perhaps Dorcas would be expecting. Just be patient he told himself. It will all fall into place.

Dorcas wrote a long letter to her mother, telling her how happy she was that Lenore was marrying Dr. Fuller. Of course Judy should be the maid of honor. Hadn't her sister always given so much of herself to their mother? No one deserved the honor as much as she did.

From then on, the weeks flew by. Each day Dorcas was more impressed at how hard Philip worked in her mine. Somehow he also kept things going at the Golden Star.

Not only did he make an all-out effort at the Alpine, but he devoted himself to her as well. They rode horseback together, went on walks through the forest, and often ate their dinner at either her house or his. No one could have paid her more attention.

Yet she often asked herself why she wasn't happier. Why this dull ache at the bottom of her heart? She grieved for Andy, she had to admit. No matter how hard she tried to forget him, she couldn't do it. He seemed to be a special part of her. She often held her little wooden statue to her face and blinked back tears as she remembered how Andy have given it to her in the Easter basket. She hoped he was doing well. Perhaps by now he had found another girl. But even that thought caused pain. How could she be such a dog in the manger?

On the last payday in October, the miners lined up for their envelopes. Dorcas said, "I can't thank you enough for your loyalty and excellent work all these months. From now until the mine is closed for the winter, Mr. Richmond will be in charge. But I look forward to seeing all of you next spring."

They all shook hands with her, and when she spoke to Red, her voice thickened. "You've been just great. I surely hope you'll be back in the spring."

"I'll be here, Miss Hamilton. I wouldn't miss getting into the main part of the lode to see what we have there." He gave her hand an extra shake. "I'll cooperate fully with Mr. Richmond and see that everything is closed snug and tight for the winter."

"I know you will." She smiled at him. "I hope it wasn't too hard working for a woman boss."

He grinned back at her. "Well, there were plenty of times I wanted to quit, but I'm glad I didn't. All of us men sure admire you. You're a real hard-rock miner, ma'am."

"That's the nicest compliment I've ever received."

After the men left, she stayed in the office, waiting for Philip. When he came in she put her arms around his neck. "I'm sorry I can't spend the evening with you, but I have to help Esther pack and close up the house, since we're leaving tomorrow," she said.

"I'll see you in the morning, dearest one." He kissed her for a long time.

Dorcas snuggled against him. "I'll miss you so until you come to San Francisco in December."

"But just think what we have to look forward to." He caressed her hair. "Whatever you plan for the wedding will be fine with me."

"It'll be a relief to finally tell the family about our engagement. I'm sorry we had to keep it quiet, but I want to give the news to my grandfather in person."

"I don't think he'll like it at all."

"I know he won't, but they're our lives and we have to do what's best for us."

He kissed her again and went out to his horse. In a way it would be a relief to be alone for a while, he thought as he rode back to town. At heart he knew he was a loner. He could give just so much of himself to others. The attention he'd paid to Dorcas since their engagement had been a strain. But it would all pay off in the long run.

During the long trip to San Francisco, Esther often saw Dorcas gazing out the window with a pensive, almost sad expression on her face. Why was that? The girl was delighted about her mother's forthcoming marriage, but what about her own? If only Dorcas were marrying Andy instead of Philip, Esther thought with regret. Funny how things work out sometimes.

While they rode the ferryboat across San Francisco Bay, Dorcas put her hand on Esther's arm. "We must stay in touch. I think of you as a dear friend."

"I'll probably find a job as housekeeper with a family here in San Francisco, but if you ever need me again, I'll come running. I'll never forget this summer. And I'll always let you know where I am."

*   *   *

They parted at the ferry building. Dorcas hired a cab to take Esther to a friend's house, and another one to drive her to the Hamilton mansion.

It was wonderful to see her mother, Keith, and Judy again. And late that afternoon, when her grandfather came home from his office, he looked like a different person. Gone was the worried, haunted look of a broken old man. Instead, he strode in with his old confident, commanding presence. *The* Clyde Hamilton, no less.

When Dorcas saw him, she rushed into his arms. "Grandpa, it's so good to see you!" She gave him a hug. "How wonderful you look! Quite the old robber baron again."

"You look tired, young lady." He held her out so he could gaze at her face and then hugged her again.

"I'll soon be rested." She kissed his cheek. "I want to have a long talk with you, Grandpa."

"Later on, when things calm down a bit, you can come to my office and give me a full report." He chuckled. "At the moment we're having so much going on. Your return. That King Neptune ball and Thanksgiving and the wedding. Lots of hullabaloo."

"You'll soon have peace and quiet, when everyone moves out."

"You'll stay right here with me, won't you?" he asked quickly.

"I was going to ask you if I could." She gave him another hug. "And I want you to be my partner at the ball."

His eyes lit with pleasure. "I wasn't even planning to go."

"Oh, you must, Grandpa. We'll go together."

Clyde Hamilton chuckled. "I could go as a pirate. A lot of folks think I'm that anyway."

"And I'll go as your first mate."

Dr. Fuller arrived and they all gathered in the parlor for a toast before dinner. Lenore looked radiant as she sat next to her husband-to-be. Both Keith and Judy seemed to be on excellent terms with the doctor as well. How would Philip fit in with this group? Probably nicely, except for her grandfather. All the others would remember with gratitude his role in helping with the rescue operation during the cave-in.

But as Dorcas looked at Clyde's hawk nose she thought of how severe he could be. Her heart sank at the very thought of telling him that she was going to marry a Richmond.

CHAPTER 25

Clyde Hamilton made a delightful pirate captain in his daughter-in-law's opinion. His tall, thin frame carried the costume with an authoritative air. A black hat folded up in front with the skull and crossbones on the front, along with an eye patch and his hawk nose, would strike terror in any sailor's heart. And there were plenty of sailors at the King Neptune ball. He sat in the front row of the sponsor's box, holding a long sword across his knees and looking proud.

Prescott Fuller, very distinguished in a naval uniform, sat between Clyde and his bride-to-be. He turned to her, saying, "Here you were worrying that we wouldn't sell any tickets. I understand they were all sold out."

She nodded. "We should clear at least a thousand dollars. I think we'll have some donations as well." She looked toward her father-in-law and whispered, "I'm going to approach him one of these days. Now that the lode has been discovered, he can afford to be more generous."

"Well, good luck." He took her hand in his and glanced at her shimmering costume, which resembled fish scales. "You make a very beautiful mermaid, Lenore."

Once again she looked out at the crowd on the ballroom floor. She was still amazed that the ball was such a success. "You wait," Virginia Reston had told her. "The Hamilton name will be a real drawing card. There's been so much publicity over the big lode that was discovered. People will want to come and see you."

In any case, hundreds of people were here, filling the dance floor. Soon the floor show would start, with all the hired singers and dancers. Then would come the lavish buffet in the adjoining dining room.

Dorcas waltzed across the floor with a fisherman in a yellow sou'wester. The broad brim in back that was designed to protect a man's neck in a storm at sea must be awfully warm tonight, she thought in sympathy. She glanced up and saw a tall Polynesian chief in flowing robes; wearing a carved mask over his face. But there was something very familiar about his wide shoulders and the way he carried himself. Could it be Andy? Her heart raced excitedly. How she wanted to see him. If she could only talk to him, perhaps she could heal the awful breach between them. When the dance ended, she worked her way around the edge of the crowd. He was standing near the door. Perhaps they could slip out and visit for a few minutes in the hall.

When she reached his side, she put her hand on his arm. "Andy."

He whirled around, stared at her through his mask, and shook his head. Then he turned and moved away, and she lost him in the throng. But it *was* Andy. She was sure of that. He had deliberately snubbed her. She felt a wrench of hurt and regret. Oh, Andy.

Swearing to himself, Andy made his way to a side door and slipped out. Now that Dorcas had spotted him, he'd have to leave. Why had he ever accepted the ticket that Fred Langley had given him? "You go," his boss said. "I just bought the ticket to help out this society dame."

Andy was sorry that he had ever depended on the mask he had made to hide his identity. Now that Dorcas knew that he was in San Francisco, she would likely track him down. And he couldn't see her. He must forget that she ever existed. He had to admit to himself that he'd come tonight hoping that she might be here, but that had been a mistake. He must make a new life for himself without her.

Clyde helped Dorcas into the carriage two mornings later. "I hope you're prepared to spend the whole day with me. We haven't had a chance to talk about the mine yet," he said.

It was the Monday after the ball. Soon they would be all

caught up in the wedding festivities. They'd better have their talk now, while they had a lull. "Of course I can spend the day with you, Grandpa. There's so much for us to discuss."

"Good." Clyde looked at her and smiled. "We'll go out to lunch."

"To the Hamilton Regency, I hope. By the way, how's it doing?"

"Very well. Booked solid through the holidays. Of course, that's when people want to entertain." He planted his cane between his legs. "I guess I wasn't so foolish to build it after all."

"Of course you weren't." She squeezed his arm. "Just wait until the mine pays off all your debts. Then you'll have nothing at all to worry about."

"I can't imagine being in that state." He tipped his hat to another financier who was passing by in his carriage.

It had all been worthwhile, Dorcas thought as she watched her proud grandfather sit with his shoulders squared and that old imperious expression back on his face. Once more he was Clyde Hamilton, the financier and civic leader.

They arrived at the Hamilton Building and took the elevator to the top floor. Her grandfather's suite of offices overlooked Montgomery Street, the heart of the business world not only in California but all over the West. All the clerks greeted Dorcas, and the accountant, Abel Long, came out of his office to shake her hand.

Finally they were in Clyde's private office. He helped her off with her coat and hung it beside his own in the closet. The old man was not to be hurried. He sat down at his desk and indicated that she was to sit across from him. "I have all your reports right here," he said as he opened a drawer. "I want to review them right from the beginning. Start with the men stealing the gold."

It took all morning to get through the first few reports. They stopped at noon and went to the Hamilton Regency dining room for lunch. Clyde presided at his specially reserved table. It seemed to Dorcas that a constant flow of colleagues and well-wishers came over to greet her grandfather. Some asked favors and others just wanted to court his good will.

When they finished eating, Clyde said, "Now, please excuse me, Dorcas. I must rest. I keep a room here so I can go upstairs and take a nap before I go back to the office. I trust you can amuse yourself.''

"Of course. There's a letter I need to write, anyway. You'll find me in the hotel's writing room when you're ready to go.''

All the time she wrote to Philip about the King Neptune ball, she debated whether she should tell her grandfather about her engagement that afternoon. Clyde seemed to be in such a mellow mood, perhaps she should get it over with. But a feeling of dread gathered in her. Would her news spoil this delightful day they were having together?

By the time she and Clyde were back in his office, it was two o'clock. "We've covered everything up to the earthquake and the hot spring, so I'll tell you about that, Grandpa,'' she began.

"Did Woodard find out how to solve the problem of the hot water?''

Astounded, she asked, "How did you—''

Clyde interrupted. "Now, he's a fine young man. Seems to have a good head on his shoulders.''

"When did you see him?'' This certainly was a surprise.

"When he brought me the check.''

"What check, Grandfather? What are you talking about?''

"The check for a hundred thousand dollars from Elliott Richmond. The one I used to make the October first payment. Of course, what I had left from the gold you sent to the mint made up the rest.''

Dorcas stared at him, unable to believe what she was hearing. "But I don't understand. Andy brought you a check for that much money? From Richmond?''

"Didn't he tell you about it? He was going back to Alpine Heights from here.''

"He came to see me, all right, but it was just after we had discovered the lode. He never had a chance—''

"But didn't he stay in Alpine Heights? He was going to help you with the Alpine.''

"Grandpa, start at the beginning and tell me all about what happened when he came to see you.''

"First, let me get out the report he showed me.'' Clyde opened a drawer and pulled out a folder. "I thought it was strange when I got this by messenger one day. No cover letter or anything. Just this package. I had told him to turn it all over to you so you could file suit against the Richmonds if you wished. We're entitled to a lot more than the hundred thousand dollars.''

Clyde untied the cord that closed the folder and took out a handful of pictures and charts, which he spread out on the desk. ''I told you a long time ago that the Richmonds were a bunch of crooks. When your father was alive, we had a regular feud with that outfit. We were sure that Elliott Richmond, like his father before him, was cheating us, but we had no proof. Well, that young Andy saw through him and gathered this evidence right after the cave-in.'' Gradually the old man told Dorcas the whole story and showed her all the evidence.

''I guess when Woodard faced Richmond in Sacramento, they had a real donnybrook. Nearly come to blows. Andy demanded a payment as compensation for the cave-in, and he got it, too. Here's a copy of the agreement he signed on our behalf. He said he was determined to get the hundred thousand dollars to me in time to make the payment. And he did. Saved me from going under.''

Sick with remorse, Dorcas picked up the photos and studied them. She thought of the hours Andy must have spent gathering this material. He had given up his position and risked repercussions from the Richmonds and from government agencies as well, just to help her. A dull ache formed around her heart. Poor dear Andy. How disappointed he must have felt when he hadn't even had a chance to tell her about it.

''I can't understand why you didn't know all about this. Hasn't Woodard been working for you all this time?'' Clyde demanded.

''No.''

''But he told me that he was going right back to the Alpine. He was going to help you.''

''I know.'' Her throat thickened. She blinked back tears that stung her eyelids. ''But as soon as he got back he left again. I believe he's working here in San Francisco.''

Clyde studied her for a long moment. Finally he said in a low voice, ''Andy thinks the world of you, Dorcas. I hope you didn't hurt him.''

''I'm afraid I did, Grandpa.'' She covered her face with her hands and started to cry. ''I didn't give him a chance to tell me about all this. I was so full of the big strike.''

"Well, I can understand that. However, you'd better see if you can find him and make amends."

"I'll try to."

"Where did you say he's working?"

"I don't know the name of the place. But his former landlady said it was at a company here that makes custom equipment for mines."

"That's likely to be Fred Langley's company. You might try there."

She wiped her eyes. "I will. I feel so terrible after all he did for me and the Alpine."

Her grandfather leaned forward. "Dorcas, if Woodard is here in San Francisco, who is running the mine? Surely not just your manager."

This was the question that she'd dreaded. She took a deep breath. "Philip is helping him."

Clyde's face reddened. "Good lord! Not Philip Richmond!" He thumped his fist on the desk. "I won't have it! Not for a moment!"

"Grandpa, he is a very skilled mining engineer. Andy would tell you that. Philip runs the big Golden Star. Surely he can keep an eye on the Alpine until it closes for the winter."

"I wouldn't trust that man for one minute. You send a wire right up there and close it *now*!"

"What has Philip ever done to you, Grandpa? It's true that Elliott Richmond cheated you, but that was before Philip ever came to Alpine Heights."

"He's a Richmond, isn't he? I won't have him on my property!" He glared at her in fury, his jaw set and his fists clenched.

Tremors of fear shot through her. But she had to stand her ground. She looked straight at him. "The mine is not your property, Grandfather. Not any longer. Have you forgotten that you signed it over to me? Well, you did, and I intend to run it the way I see fit. You're being very prejudiced and unfair!"

Clyde Hamilton sat back in his chair, his jaw dropping in surprise. Finally, he retorted, "You're a naive, too-trusting girl. If you ever see a cent out of that mine while Richmond has control, I'll be surprised!"

"That remains to be seen. I hope to get enough from it to pay mother back before she's married."

"I doubt that you will. Not with that scoundrel in charge. And you'd better go see Angliers and ask him to wait for his money a little longer. You're likely to lose your jewels, yet."

"I have until Christmas to redeem Grandmother's jewels. And I will." She got to her feet shaking with anger. "I'll run along now so you can get back to work. Thank you for the lovely lunch." Without kissing her grandfather or saying anything, she stalked out of the room.

Clyde banged his fist on his desk. Drat that stubborn, pigheaded girl.

Just as Dorcas left, the accountant walked in. "My, your granddaughter certainly resembles you, Mr. Hamilton." His boss glowered at him, Abel dropped a check on the desk. "This came from the mint, sir. I thought if you would sign it, I'd have it deposited."

Clyde glanced down at the check, gasped at the amount, and hastily signed the back. Abel made a hurried retreat. Hamilton got out of his chair and paced the room restlessly. He looked out at Montgomery Street and watched all the horses, delivery wagons, cabs, and carriages below him. He was still seething at Dorcas's stubborn attitude. At least she had spunk, though, he had to admit. And smart as a whip. The only one who had guts enough to stand up to him. Too bad she was a female. Otherwise, she could run the whole damn company, and he'd retire.

As the cable car worked its way up a long hill, Dorcas stared out at the water. The waves, as gray as the cloud-covered sky, dashed against the rocky shores of the islands in the bay. Her heart felt sorrow-laden every time she thought of Andy. As soon as she got home she would look in the telephone directory and see if she could find a Langley company. Then she would telephone and see if Andy was employed there.

At least they were all going to a dinner party tonight in honor of her mother and Dr. Fuller, so she would have no more time to grieve over her dear friend. Nor would she have to face her grandfather. How could she ever tell him about her forthcoming marriage to Philip?

The next morning she dressed carefully in a brown wool suit and wore a fur cape over her shoulders. Before she left her room she wrote a note.

> Dear Andy:
>   I'm outside waiting in my carriage. I am very anxious to see you and thank you for what you did for my grandfather and for all of us. Won't you please come out and speak to me?
>
>   As always, Dorcas

For a long time, Andy held the note in his hand. One of the men had brought it to him. "It's from a lady sitting outside on the street in a swell carriage. Her coachman brought it to the door. She's waiting out there." He whistled and grinned.

Andy recognized the handwriting. It was Dorcas, of course. He longed to run right out and see her. Not an hour during the day passed that he didn't think of her and wasn't conscious of the dull ache in his heart. Would he ever stop seeing her lovely face in his mind or wanting to hold her in his arms?

Angrily, he tore open the note and read the short message. But why go out there? Why be so close and yet so far from her? His heartbreak had begun to heal a little since he'd left Alpine Heights. It was bad enough to have had her approach him at the King Neptune ball. So why set himself back again? Why put himself through all that misery once more? What would be gained?

Andy picked up a pencil and scrawled on the bottom of the note. *I see no point in opening old wounds. Every good wish on your marriage. A.W.* He beckoned to an apprentice and told him where to deliver the note. Then he stood at his drafting board and tried to make sense out of the work in front of him. But the drawing swam in front of his eyes. Angrily he broke his pencil in two. He would love Dorcas with his whole heart until the end of his life.

When she read Andy's note, Dorcas felt she had been slapped in the face. Well, she would never try to contact him again. But how bereft and lost she felt. She leaned forward and instructed Wilson to take her to the Episcopal church where her mother was to be married. She must start making plans for her own wedding. There was so much to do. So many things to decide. But she couldn't tell the rest of her family until she told her grandfather.

What a storm there would be. Clyde had been so upset over Philip's running her mine; what would he do when he heard about the marriage? She'd better postpone her announcement until after her mother's wedding. Nothing should spoil that happy occasion.

When Dorcas arrived at the church, a man was sweeping leaves off the steps. "Is the church unlocked?" she asked. "Is it all right to go in?"

"Yes, ma'am."

She walked into the carved entry, passed through the narthex, and gasped at the beauty of the stained glass windows in the nave and behind the altar. Her intentions had been to look over the chapel and perhaps make a reservation for a wedding near Christmas. But instead she sat down at the end of a pew. She leaned her head against her arm. All she wanted to do was cry. Oh, Andy. She sobbed silently, feeling her body wrench with hurt. Oh, Andy.

Late one afternoon Judy let herself in the front door of the mansion, picked up her mail from the hall table, and walked slowly up the stairs as she read the invitations to more luncheons, parties, and balls to be held before Christmas. With a shock she realized that she was getting very tired of the constant social activities. One saw the same people and listened to the same conversations over and over. And after all the effort and expense, what was accomplished? Nothing, really, she had to admit. Never once had she found the satisfaction that her art had brought her.

Restlessly she walked into her room and threw the mail on top of her bed. She put her hat and purse away and hung up her coat. Then she glanced down at the envelopes again and for the first time noticed a letter from the director of the Northern California Art Institute. Why would he be writing to her? Her heart thumped in excitement as she opened it and read:

Dear Miss Hamilton:

The Acquisitions Committee and I have had the privilege of choosing a collection of paintings for a traveling exhibit to be shown throughout the United States. We are having a special section for the beginning artists of real promise. Your portrait Little Girl and Her Doll, *has been selected for this part of the show. This letter is to ask your permission to exhibit this work.*

Actually we wish to purchase it for our Contemporary Artists Gallery of the musuem when it is completed. Our offer is $100 if it is for sale. Please let me know at your earliest convenience if you accept our offer.

This coming Sunday afternoon from three until five, at the Bayview Gallery, we are holding a reception honoring the artists and showing a preview of the exhibit that will go on tour. We hope you will be there. We all wish to congratulate you on your achievement. I understand that you are a young artist with great potential. I hope to see more of your work in the future.

Yours sincerely,
Walter B. Cathcart

Judy read the letter over and over to convince herself that it was real. Her painting would be exhibited throughout the United States. The museum wanted to buy it for a hundred dollars. She had painted a picture worth that much! It seemed incredible.

She ran into her mother's room. "Mama! I have some wonderful news!"

Tears swam in Lenore's eyes as Judy read the letter aloud. She hugged her daughter. "Oh, darling, I'm so proud. I had no idea that you could paint a picture good enough for a real exhibit. It's wonderful!"

"Imagine, people will see it all across the country. My painting!"

The whole family, including Prescott Fuller, accompanied Judy to the reception for the artists. They made their way through the crowd to the room with the Artists of Promise exhibit and stood in front of Judy's portrait of the little girl.

Tears came to Lenore's eyes once more. "Darling, I'm so impressed. It's wonderful."

Keith spoke up. "Gosh, Sis, I had no idea that you were this good. I thought you were just killing time going to study with that bearded guy."

Dorcas gave her sister a hug. "I'm so proud of you. What talent you have! You must start those lessons again. You owe it to yourself."

Dr. Fuller put his arm across Judy's shoulders. "I agree with Dorcas. And as your future stepfather, I want the privilege of paying for your lessons. I'd like just a little part in furthering your career."

"Thank you, Doc. I'll think about it." Judy gave him a radiant smile.

The others moved on to see the rest of the paintings, but Clyde Hamilton stood staring at her portrait. As Judy looked at her grandfather she asked herself, Does he like it? Does he think it's a lot of foolishness? He's never had much use for me. What is he thinking?

The old man turned to her. "If only your father were alive to see this. That's what I regret." His voice was low and husky.

He reached out and touched her arm. Judy gazed at his gaunt, old face and saw how proud he was. For the first time, she felt he approved of her the way he did Dorcas. It was then she determined to go on with her art.

She started to speak, but a reporter rushed to their side. "Mr. Hamilton, I'm Evans from the *News*. What do you think of your talented granddaughter? You must be very proud that her painting was chosen."

"I am, indeed. She has far more ability than I realized. I thought her interest in art was just a hobby, but I can see it that it's far more than that."

The reporter started to ask him more questions, but Clyde shook his head. "You must ask my granddaughter. Now, if you'll excuse me, I want to see the director and make a donation to the acquisition fund."

The reporter turned to Judy and asked question after question. He wrote the answers down on a folded sheet of paper.

Finally Judy asked, "Aren't you interviewing everyone who has a painting in this exhibit?"

"No, ma'am. Only you, besides the director."

"But why me? This is my first painting. I'm sure there're artists of real note here this afternoon."

"But you're a Hamilton, miss. That makes you newsworthy." He put his pencil and paper in his pocket.

As her face flushed, she looked him up and down. "Mark my words. Someday your newspaper will ask for an interview because of my reputation as an artist, not because I'm Clyde Hamilton's granddaughter!"

The reporter shrugged and walked away.

"Good for you!" someone behind her said.

Judy whirled around and faced Courtland Burke. "You!"

He smiled. "Is that so surprising? I have a picture in this exhibit, too."

"I suppose you were listening."

"That's right. I heard everything you said. It gave me some hope. Perhaps underneath that spoiled, shallow surface of yours there might be the makings of a true artist. Have you been painting?"

She shook her head, ashamed to meet his eyes. "I still have the teachers' names you gave me. I'll get in touch with one of them right away."

"Do you mean you'll actually take the time away from your parties and flirting to do something worthwhile?"

She stamped her foot. "Oh, stop it, Courtland. You don't have to be so sarcastic." She turned away. "You'd better go back in the other room and mingle with the people there. That's what we're supposed to be doing."

He took her arm. "Meet me at the entrance right after five. We'll get something to eat and I'll take you home."

She nodded. "I do have some questions I want to ask you."

For the rest of the afternoon she was the center of attention in the beginners' gallery. How satisfying it was to be accepted as an artist, someone in her own right, and not just as a member of a famous family. But of all the praise she received, it was her grandfather's admiration that touched her the most.

"This is the best Italian restaurant in North Beach," Courtland said as he pushed open the entrance door. "Nothing fancy, but wait until you taste their ravioli."

When they were seated at a corner table, Judy asked, "How did the committee happen to choose my picture?"

"Because I submitted it. Remember when I told you that I was going to have your painting evaluated?" When she nodded, he went on. "I thought it was worthy of consideration by the committee. I wanted it to be part of this touring exhibit, which will raise money for acquisitions for the museum."

"Oh, Courtland. I'll always be grateful."

He leaned forward and took her hand. "Do you have any idea of what this means? Your painting will be shown along with those of great California artists in all the big galleries in America."

"It's wonderful credit. Even for you. What one of yours did they choose?"

"The old man with the boy and his kite."

"I love that picture. It's so poignant. I still feel it inside."

"That's what I want you to do. To paint from your very depths so that the viewer senses something special. A touch of greatness."

Tears came to her eyes. "I'm going to try with my whole heart and soul. Courtland, I want to achieve now. I'm so tired of just going to one social event after another. It's no challenge at all." Her chin trembled. "Seeing my painting hanging there this afternoon was the most thrilling thing that ever happened to me."

Later they rode the cable car and walked along the dark streets to the mansion. Courtland took her in his arms. "Judy," he whispered against her fragrant hair. How beautiful she was. So lovely it almost hurt to look at her in the faint light from the street lamp. "Judy, I want you to come back and study with me."

"Oh, Courtland!" She threw her arms around his neck. "I'll work. I promise I'll work hard, if you'll only take me back."

He gazed into her eyes. "You've grown up a little. I think you're ready to learn from me now."

"Oh, I am. I want to start at once."

He raised her hand to his mouth and kissed it. "You'll have to work harder than you ever have in your life."

"I will."

"I promise that I'll bring out the best in you. Oh, my dearest girl, you have so much talent, there are no limits to what you can accomplish." He kissed her fingers. "We'll do it together." His eyes showed his adoration.

For a long moment she stared at him. Finally she whispered, "Courtland, have you fallen in love with me?"

"Perhaps, but we're not going to let that stand in our way, my lovely Judy."

She looked stricken. "But I couldn't possibly marry you."

"I don't want you to. It would be a disaster for us both. We'd soon hate each other." Tenderly he smiled down at her. "Don't worry about being with me. I'll never take advantage of you. I promise you that."

"I believe you. But I'm sorry you feel this way. It's so awful!"

"But it isn't. Don't you see that the artist I help develop will always be mine? No matter whom you marry or what children you will have someday, there will always be this special bond between us. The artist in you is my Judy. My exquisite, lovely girl. No one else can claim that you. She's mine!"

Judy kissed him. "You'll always be special to me, too." She smiled. "I promise I'll make you very proud of me."

"Even more important is that you're proud of yourself."

A week before Thanksgiving, Dorcas joined her grandfather for a drink of sherry before dinner. They sat in front of the fire. He acted as if he wanted to tell her something but didn't know how to begin.

"What is it, Grandfather?"

"Well, I just want you to know that I've been receiving checks from the mint. I transferred the money to your account so you can pay back your mother. You said you wanted to do it before the wedding."

"How much did you put in my account?"

"Humph. Well, let me see—"

"You know how much it is. You're just reluctant to admit that you were wrong about Philip Richmond."

He glowered at her. "I'm not admitting anything. But you do have fifty-six thousand dollars in your account."

"Fifty-six thousand dollars!" She put her sherry down and ran to him. "That's an enormous sum!" She squeezed his shoulders. "You'll have to admit that Philip has looked after my interests very well."

"This time, perhaps." Clyde slumped down in his big chair, obviously reluctant to admit that he had been wrong.

Dorcas kissed his cheek and wanted to gloat, but she didn't dare push him too far. They heard the dinner chimes, so she helped him out of his chair and they walked arm in arm into the dining room. She was in better spirits than she had been for some time. Although Philip had written that he was using men from the Golden Star to get as much ore out of the Alpine as possible before they had to close for the winter, she hadn't really expected so large a return.

As Dorcas leaned across the luncheon table, she took her mother's hand. They were alone in a small French restaurant noted for its souffles. This afternoon they would meet Judy for the final fitting of the dresses they would wear in the wedding.

"Mama, I have something for you. I can't tell you what it means to me to give you this receipt. I've paid back all I owe you, plus interest, into your account at the bank. The vice-president will replace all the bonds that had to be sold."

Tears flooded her mother's eyes. She took the receipt, folded it carefully, and put it into her handbag. "Thank you, darling. I've been so ashamed of myself for writing that letter. It showed how little faith I had in you. You have no idea how that has worried me ever since you made that big strike. I'm sorry, dear. I truly am."

Dorcas smiled. "Mother, you can be thankful every day for the rest of your life that you sent the letter." She told her all the circumstances leading up to her order to blast as a very last resort. "Because I made that act of desperation against everyone's advice, we discovered the lode."

The rest of the afternoon was a joyous time for them as they had their last fittings, and Dorcas chose a flowered-covered hat to go with her cream-lace afternoon gown.

* * *

The November sun slanted through the stained glass rose window in the church chapel. Baskets of deep pink gladioli and white chrysanthemums stood on each side of the altar. Dorcas and Clyde sat in the front pew and watched Keith and a young intern usher the guests to their seats. Soon Prescott and his son, dressed in formal morning clothes, took their place at the altar. Judy, wearing a turquoise lace gown and carrying a small bouquet of roses with long velvet streamers, came down the aisle first. Lenore, in stunning old-rose lace that enhanced her coloring, followed her daughter. She, too, carried a bouquet of roses and velvet streamers. But her eyes never left those of her groom as she walked toward him and stood by his side to take the marriage vows.

"Dearly beloved, we are gathered here together in the sight of God and in the face of this company to join together this man and this woman in holy matrimony, which is an honorable estate instituted by God. . . ."

As the rector's voice resounded in the small chapel, Dorcas was surprised to hear herself whisper, "Andy."

CHAPTER 26

Dorcas couldn't put off the inevitable any longer. She had to tell her family about her coming marriage and make her wedding arrangements. It was already almost the end of November, and she hadn't said a word to anyone.

Her mother and Prescott were now back from their short honeymoon. Judy and Keith had moved to the Fuller house, so there were no more excuses. When Lenore asked her for lunch and to see her renovated home, Dorcas determined to tell them all her news.

But first she must tell her grandfather. As she was dressing for the day, Clyde telephoned.

"I just received a check for forty-five hundred dollars from the mint. That gives you enough to pay off Angliers' if you want to come and pick it up on the way to your mother's," he said.

"Yes, I'll do that. Will you be in your office all morning?"

When he assured her that he would be, she decided to leave at once and get it over with for once and for all.

On the way to Clyde's office, Dorcas stopped at the church and reserved the chapel for Saturday afternoon after Christmas. It was hard to act eager and happy in front of the assistant rector when she felt so full of dread.

More than once she caught the minister glancing at her with a puzzled expression in his eyes. Dorcas said, "I haven't had a chance to talk this over with my mother yet, but I assume that date will be agreeable to her."

"Well, we'll put the reservation down. We can always make a change, but we're booked very solidly through the holidays. The only reason that Saturday afternoon is available is because we had a cancellation."

Afterward her feet seemed to drag as she walked down the hall toward her grandfather's office. What would he say? What would he do?

When Clyde handed her the check, he said, "This is going to take a great burden off my shoulders. It's almost as big a relief as making the payment to my creditors. I felt heartsick over the possiblity of your losing your grandmother's jewels. They meant so much to her."

"I'll go right away and put this into my account and then stop by Angliers'." She put her hand on his arm. "We should be very grateful to Philip for helping me so much. And you should have seen how hard he worked when he took charge of rescuing Keith and Red Wallace. I think you should change your attitude toward him. You aren't being at all fair."

His eyes seemed to bore right through her. "Why are you telling me this?"

She glanced away, trying to screw up her courage. Finally she took a deep breath and burst out, "Because I'm going to marry Philip."

She looked at her grandfather's shocked, ashen face. He tried to speak. No words came. He just stared at her.

Finally he banged his fist down on his desk. "You can't marry into that bunch of crooks. By God, I won't allow it!"

"But Grandfather—"

Thump! Thump! Thump! His fist banged down. "How long have you been promised to that rat?" He half rose from his chair.

"Just a short while."

"Exactly when did he propose?" Clyde loomed over her, his face purple with rage. "Answer me!"

"I'm not sure."

"Of course you're sure, Dorcas. Don't lie to me!"

"I'll have to think."

"It was after the lode was found, wasn't it?"

She had never seen her grandfather in such a state. She wanted to run and hide. Too frightened to answer, she pulled herself back in the chair and shielded her face with her hands.

"Answer me, Dorcas Hamilton. At once!"

"Yes, I guess so."

His old voice quavered in fury. "Exactly what day?"

"The day the lode was found."

"Did he know that the mine is in your name?"

Dorcas's chin trembled. He was in a rage. What would he do to her? She tried to speak, but the words didn't come.

"Answer me!" Clyde roared.

"Oh, Grandpa! Please—"

"Answer me!"

"Yes." She felt her voice was coming from far away. This all seemed unreal. A nightmare.

Clyde's fist banged down again. "You little fool! Don't you realize he's marrying you just to get his hands on that mine?"

Tears ran down her cheeks. "But we love each other."

"Love? He's not capable of love. All he wants is to look out for himself."

"I don't believe that."

"Have you lost your senses?"

"Grandpa, you don't understand—"

"I understand, all right, young woman. That Richmond's out to feather his nest."

"But I want to marry—"

"If you want a husband, pick Andy Woodard. He's a real man, and he sincerely cares for you."

"I know he does. No one can doubt Andy's devotion."

"Then marry him, you foolish girl."

"But I love Philip. I always have."

Thump! went his fist again. "Then get out of here!"

Grabbing her coat and hat, Dorcas ran out of the room. She ignored the curious stares of the clerks in the outer office. Of course they had heard the shouting and banging.

As soon as she reached the sidewalk, the cold wind hit her. Her hair whipped around her face. She ducked back into the doorway and pulled on her coat and stuck pins in her hat to hold it on her head. She found Wilson and the carriage waiting farther down the street. She instructed him to take her first to her bank and then to Angliers'.

It took all her talent as an actress to face the kindly jeweler with poise and enthusiasm.

"Well, Miss Hamilton, you certainly surprised all of us."

"When I found that lode, it was the happiest day of my life," she said with forced gaiety. "And this is another triumphant one, to be able to buy back my jewels."

"They've been right here in our vault, safe as can be. Now, let me find the papers so I can cancel the bill of sale and write you a receipt."

"I want to thank you for all your help, Mr. Angliers. I couldn't have started my project without your money."

"I'm here to help you anytime," the jeweler told her.

"Do I owe you any interest?"

"Indeed not. Mr. Hamilton will be along one of these days to buy wedding gifts for you and your sister. That will more than repay me."

Just the mention of her grandfather and her wedding almost broke Dorcas's rigid control. Don't think about the awful scene he made, she told herself. Just don't think about it.

At last she was able to get away with all her receipts and papers that proved that she was full owner of the jewels. At least her grandfather couldn't castigate her for that.

What a relief it was to enter the happy atmosphere of her mother's beautiful home. She kissed Lenore. "You look lovelier than ever. I think marriage agrees with you."

"Oh, it does. I haven't been this happy in years. Judy will be home soon. While we wait for her, I'll show you around. All except her room and studio. I'll let her take you there when she comes."

They moved from room to room while Dorcas exclaimed over the wallpaper, the custom-made draperies and spreads, the carpets and refurbished furniture. All the time she basked in her mother's happiness, she wondered if she would ever feel the same complete joy. How could she when she had hurt both her grandfather and Andy so deeply?

When Judy came home she grabbed Dorcas and whirled

her around. "Dori, I love it here! I feel I've been let out of jail. Come see my room."

The pink and white room was the ultimate in luxury and a perfect setting for Judy. "See what our stepfather had built for me. This was a special gift from him," she said. They stepped into an adjoining room that faced north. In it was everything an artist could desire in a studio. A model's platform, easels, cupboards and shelves for supplies, and a drawing table. An attractive linoleum covered the floor. In one corner was a supply of toys for the child models.

"You always accused me of being spoiled rotten, Dori. I don't know what this makes me."

"There's a difference, Judy. Now you have to work very hard to live up to our expectations of you."

"Your expectations are nothing compared to those of Courtland Burke. He's a regular slave driver, Dori. You have no idea what I put up with."

"I know. And you're loving every minute of it. Now let's find Mama, for I have something to tell you both."

When they were all settled in their mother's sitting room next to the master bedroom, Dorcas began. "Philip Richmond has asked me to marry him and I've accepted."

"That's marvelous!" Judy cried as she jumped up to go over and kiss her sister. "You've always been so sweet on him."

"That's right. I have."

Judy rolled her eyes. "He's so handsome. All the girls swoon over him."

Dorcas smiled and turned to her mother. "What do you think?"

Lenore went over to her and kissed her as well. She sat down on the love seat beside Dorcas. "I don't know what to say. I think he's very charming myself. But your father was always so bitter toward the Richmonds. And I shudder to think how your grandfather will react."

"He already knows. I told him this morning. He's absolutely in a rage." She paled as she recalled the scene.

"I'm not surprised." Lenore took her daughter's hand. "You don't seem very happy, dear. Are you sure this is what you want?"

Dorcas leaned her head on her mother's shoulder while tears gathered in her eyes. "I've wanted to marry Philip for years. So of course I accepted him. But I feel terrible about Grandpa. I don't want him so angry at me.''

Judy stamped her foot. "He's an old man. He's had his life. Why should he spoil yours?''

Lenore put her arm around Dorcas and held her close. "Darling, you have my approval, if that will help.''

"Oh, it does.''

Her mother went on. "Philip didn't cause the trouble between the Hamiltons and Richmonds. He wasn't even there at the time. It had nothing to do with him, so he shouldn't be judged because of it.''

"I know; it's all so unfair.''

Judy put in, "I don't understand why you put such store in what Grandpa thinks.''

"Dorcas has always been devoted to Father Hamilton,'' Lenore said. "You're the only one who ever got along with that difficult old tyrant,'' she said to her eldest daughter. "Your father wouldn't live in San Francisco because of him.''

Dorcas wiped her eyes. "Would the Saturday after Christmas be all right for the wedding?''

Lenore frowned. "Yes, but you won't have much time to get ready.''

"But I want a small wedding. Just like yours.''

Judy cried, "Well, I don't when I get married. I love weddings. I want hundreds of people and six bridesmaids and everything.''

Dorcas smiled. "I don't know all the people you do, so just the two families and a few intimate friends will be fine.'' Her voice died away. "I don't know what to do about the reception afterward. I doubt that Grandfather will let me have it in the Hamilton Regency. Yet it wouldn't seem right to go to another hotel.''

Lenore patted her shoulder. "Have it here. I know Prescott would approve. He told me he wants to do lots of entertaining over Christmas. For so many years he didn't do any.''

"Oh, Mother, that would be wonderful! It would solve so many problems. This home is so beautiful, and I'd feel so right about having it here.'' Her voice thickened. "I hope I can persuade Grandfather to give me away.''

Lenore looked at Dorcas with a worried expression. "Darling, I think you'd better consider this step very carefully.

Why not postpone your wedding until spring, so you can think it over carefully?"

"Philip wants to get married as soon as possible. He's coming to San Francisco before Christmas. . . ." Dorcas's voice died away. It was going to be hard being pulled between him and her grandfather. How would they manage all the prenuptial parties and Christmas itself if Clyde refused to take part? Her heart sickened at the thought of Grandpa being alone. Still she said, "We'd better go ahead with that date."

"Then you should move over here when Philip arrives." Lenore waved her hand. "Goodness knows, we have plenty of room."

"Why don't you come right now?" Judy suggested. "I was never so glad in my life to get away from that mansion and Grandfather. I felt I was tiptoeing on eggshells all the time so that he wouldn't get angry at me."

Dorcas shook her head. She couldn't hurt him even more. It was better to stay in the mansion but avoid him as much as possible. Besides, she might have a chance to talk to him again and make him change his mind. The one thing on earth she wanted was his approval.

Dorcas sought out Mrs. Williams when she returned to the mansion. "I'd like just a light super served in my room tonight. I had a big lunch at my mother's."

Back in her room, she changed out of her street clothes and sat at her desk to write a letter to Philip. But tears clouded her eyes. She grieved for her grandfather's love. She could hardly bear his disapproval. He might be an old tyrant, but he had always had such a special place in her heart. If she could only talk her troubles over with Andy. But she'd lost him as well. She put her head down on her arms and sobbed.

At six-thirty, Mrs. Williams knocked on her door. When Dorcas opened it, the older woman said, "Mr. Hamilton wants you to come to the dining room at once. He refuses to have dinner served without you." She lowered her voice. "You'd better come, Miss Dorcas."

Dorcas glanced down at her mussed cotton dress. "Tell him I have to change."

When she took her place across from her grandfather, properly dressed in a blue dinner gown, he looked at her and said, "As long as you are a guest in my home, I expect you to dine with me. You owe me that courtesy, at least."

"Yes, Grandfather."

"How did you find your mother and sister?"

She told him all about the house and Judy's studio. It was a relief to have a safe subject to discuss.

"Did you ever get in touch with Woodard to thank him?" Clyde asked suddenly.

"I went to see him. He works at the Langley Company, just as you thought."

"A fine business. I've used Fred Langley's services in the past. What did Andy have to say?"

"I sent in a note asking him to come out to the carriage, but he refused."

"I don't blame him at all. You treated him shabbily."

"Grandfather! That's not true. We were always good friends. I never—"

"You broke his heart. He cares for you. He told me so."

A maid came in with the main course, so they talked of other things. But it was all Dorcas could do to eat her food. She kept thinking of how she had alienated both her grandfather and Andy.

When they went into the library to sit in front of the fire, Dorcas finally screwed up her courage. She rose from her chair and knelt on the rug beside him.

"Grandpa, you're dearer to my heart than anyone else in the family. As much as I love Mother, Judy, and Keith, I care even more for you. I can't bear it to have you so angry at me. Let's talk over our problem."

He seemed to shrink back in his big leather chair, but he reached out his hand and took hers. "It hurts me to be at odds with you, but I can't stand the fact that you plan to marry that scoundrel."

"Please don't call Philip a scoundrel. He's never done anything to you. Look how he's sent the gold bars down from the Alpine. Just because his uncle—"

"I'm not accusing him of being part of that old trouble. But I can see through this proposal of his. He wants the mine and your future inheritance. Not you—"

"Oh, Grandpa—"

"What if I had gone into bankruptcy? Would he have wanted to marry you then?"

"Of course."

"What if you hadn't discovered the lode? Would he still have proposed?"

"Grandpa, we love each other. It has nothing to do with my inheritance or the lode. Please understand. Don't shut your mind this way. He has many fine qualities that you refuse—"

"Oh, he's handsome. I'll grant you that. He has a fine appearance and sweeps the ladies off their feet. And no doubt he's a well-trained engineer who can always get a job. And much to my surprise, he's been smart enough to ship all the gold from the mine to the mint. He wants to impress us."

"Well, then—"

"He has you mesmerized. You seem absolutely blind to the fact that there's no inner core of character there. I can sense it. He's so wrong for you!"

"Grandpa, it hurts me so to have you talk like this. I want your approval. I want you to be part of my wedding. Please put aside all these prejudices of yours and be happy for me."

Clyde slumped back in his chair. "I'll say no more."

"Grandpa, I want you to give me away. I want to walk down the aisle on your arm."

The old man sat up straight and glared at her. "Never! I refuse even to come to your wedding if you marry Richmond." He banged his fist on his chair arm. "Don't ask me again!"

Dorcas jumped to her feet and ran up to her room.

Dorcas slipped the red taffeta ball gown over her head and straightened it carefully over her hips until each pleated gore hung properly from her waist to the end of the train. The dress was simple but elegant and a perfect setting for her grandmother's ruby necklace and earrings. It was the latest addition to her trousseau.

Philip had arrived that very afternoon and telephoned from his hotel. He had seemed delighted to spend their first evening together at a ball. Had she caught a note of relief in his voice? Strangely enough, she felt a sense of relief as well. A need to postpone making the final plans for their wedding.

When she picked up her fur cape and evening bag to go downstairs to wait for him, she wondered why she wasn't more eager to see him. What was the matter with her? He was still the same Philip she had loved so deeply all of these years. She shrugged off her feeling of dismay. It's only bridal jitters, she told herself.

When she got to the bottom of the stairs, she put her bag and cape on a chair and walked into the library to say good night to her grandfather. He sat in front of the fire, staring into the flames.

"I'm going to be out this evening, Grandfather. I just wanted to say good night." She leaned down and kissed his cheek.

He glanced at her. "You look very beautiful. That's a perfect dress to wear with your rubies."

"I think so, too. That's why I chose it." She touched the necklace, thankful again that she had been able to redeem her grandmother's jewels.

"I suppose Philip Richmond is in town."

"Yes. He arrived this afternoon. He's coming for me soon."

Clyde Hamilton grasped her hand in his thin one. "Dorcas, it breaks my heart to think of you marrying that man."

"Grandpa, let's not go into that again—"

"I'm warning you for the last time that all he wants is to get control of your mine. It's not you that he's after—it's the Alpine. Mark my words. If you marry him, it'll be the biggest mistake you'll ever make."

Fortunately, she heard the sound of doorbell and a maid hurrying to answer it. "I have to go now. Good night, Grandpa."

When Philip signed Dorcas's dance program, he said, "I've saved you a dance for a friend who's coming later on."

"Who is he?" she asked.

"Gene Sibler. He attended mining school with me. I've asked him to be my best man at our wedding."

"I'll be glad to meet him. I take it that he's a mining engineer, too."

"Yes, he manages a big silver mine in southern New Mexico. He's come to spend Christmas with his sister and her husband, who live here."

She started to ask him more, but they were soon surrounded by their friends who wanted to exchange dances.

Philip was by far the most attractive man in their group, Dorcas thought proudly as she slipped her program off her wrist and handed it to him. As he took her arm for the Grand March, Dorcas saw the envious glances of the other girls. She pushed her grandfather's warning to the back of her mind and determined to enjoy herself at this elaborate Christmas ball.

It was after supper when Gene Sibler arrived. "I don't like him," Dorcas told herself in dismay when she met him. He was personable enough, with his light wavy hair and clean-cut features, but there was a cockiness about his manner that rubbed her the wrong way. I'm being unfair, she thought. Give him a chance. Surely she would feel differently as she got to know him better.

When she took his arm to go out onto the dance floor, she gave him her most dazzling smile. "Philip tells me you two are old friends."

"There was a group of us at school that ran around together. Phil and I have kept in touch ever since. But we had a lot of catching up to do last night in Sacramento. I met him there and we stayed in the same hotel. Came down here today on the train."

"He tells me that you're going to be his best man at our wedding."

"That's right. Not only that, but I'm going to work for him when he opens his mine in March."

"You are? Do you mean the Golden Star?"

"No, as I understand it, he just manages that one for his uncle's company. I guess it's going to be closed down permanently next year. No, this one belongs to Phil. It's a real rich mine. Tremendous possibilities, since they just found a lode. We talked most of the night making plans about what we're going to do."

Dorcas stared at Gene in shock. Finally she managed to ask, "What plans did you make?"

"You probably don't know much about mining, so I won't go into them. But I guess we'll be neighbors. Phil said he and you'd be living in town, but the mine is only a couple of miles out. Got a nice furnished house on it where I can stay. With a setup like that, I'll be getting married, too. I never wanted to take my girl to the mine in New Mexico. It's way out in the desert away from civilization, and she wouldn't care for that a bit. Rita likes to be around people, and I don't blame her. But Philip says that Alpine Heights is a nice town, with stores and churches and all.''

"So, I understand," Dorcas murmured, her throat so dry she could hardly talk.

"If I do say so myself, I'm a top-notch engineer. My present boss wants to send me to Guatemala to straighten out a mess in a company mine there, but I'd rather be here in California. So as soon as I get back to New Mexico, I'm going to hand in my resignation and break in a new man. I can be back here by the first of March."

"I imagine you and Philip will have a lot to do in his mine. Isn't it called the Alpine?"

"That's right. Must have been named after the town."

Somehow Dorcas managed to get through the rest of the dance in spite of the fury that boiled within her. When they rejoined Philip, she said, "Please take me home. I'm not feeling at all well."

"Oh, I'm so sorry, Dorcas. You do look pale. Perhaps you're coming down with a bad cold."

"Perhaps. All I know is that I want to get home as soon as possible."

"Of course. I'll get your cape."

Gene spoke up, "While you're doing that, I'll go out and hail a cab."

Dorcas sat between the two men on the way to the Hamilton mansion and said little. When they arrived, Philip helped her out and up the stairs.

After he unlocked the door and handed her the key, she said, "Come inside for a moment. I have something to say."

Philip followed her into the parlor and lifted her cape from her shoulders. "Darling, I'll call you first thing in the morning and see how you are feeling."

She squared her shoulders and looked right at him. "I'm not ill, Philip, except that I am sick at heart. I found out the truth about you tonight. I am not going to marry you."

"Dorcas! What on earth are you saying?"

"Our engagement is broken. My grandfather has been telling me all along that you were marrying me just to get control of the Alpine. I didn't want to believe that, but I do now."

"I don't understand you! What happened?"

"Fortunately I had that dance with your good friend Mr.

Sibler. He told me that you had hired him to work in *your* mine, the Alpine. I wasn't even consulted! Let me remind you that the mine belongs to me, not you.''

''Dorcas, I intended—''

''Nor was I consulted about the house on the property. You told Sibler he could live there. Never mind the fact that the house belongs to me and the furnishings to my mother! We weren't even asked.''

''I was going to—''

''For the first time I can really see the truth. You don't love me at all. You never have. All you've been interested in is what you can get out of me. I was too much of a fool to recognize that fact. But I do now. So I'm not going to marry you. Please leave now. And you are never to set foot on my property again.'' She saw his shocked expression as the color drained from his face.

When Philip closed the front door, Dorcas grabbed her fur cape and ran upstairs. She saw a light under her grandfather's door.

She knocked and asked, ''Grandpa, may I come in?''

''Of course, my dear.'' When she opened the door, she saw that he was sitting up in his easy chair with his glasses on, trying to read.

She knelt beside him and started to sob. ''I'm not going to marry Philip.'' After a few moments she was able to tell him what had happened.

He patted her hair. ''Thank God! My prayers have been answered.'' Tears ran slowly down his cheeks.

CHAPTER 27

Judy poked Dorcas in the ribs. ''Look who's coming in.''

They were sitting behind their mother and Dr. Fuller in a box seat at the concert hall, waiting for the symphony orchestra to begin. She looked down at the concert goers in the main aisle.

"Do you see them?" Judy asked.

"Who?"

"Lila Rondell and her sister. See who's with them."

Dorcas looked for the debutantes and gasped when she recognized their escort. "Andy!"

"That's right. I heard they were going out quite a bit together. Doesn't Lila look smashing?"

A stab of jealousy pierced Dorcas as she looked at Lila, who was wearing a short sable cape over a red taffeta dress. She and her sister were both attractive girls. No wonder Andy had invited them to the concert. It hurt to watch him help the girls with their capes. She followed every move he made as he walked back down the aisle toward the checkroom.

She tried to tell herself that she was acting like a fool. What difference did it make to her if Andy was turning to someone else? Why shouldn't he?

The orchestra members filed in, took their seats, and began to tune their instruments. But Dorcas paid little attention to them. All she was aware of was the wave after wave of envy that washed over her. Oh, Andy, her heart cried. Of course I'm not jealous, she tried to convince herself. She simply felt terrible that she and Andy had parted under such unhappy circumstances.

When the orchestra began to play, she hardly listened. She sat in her seat and stared ahead. Realization slowly came over her. She loved Andy! Not Philip but Andy!

Of course she had been infatuated with Philip. He had dazzled her. He was almost an obsession. But the man she really loved deep in her inner soul was Andy! She had grieved for him ever since they had parted, because she loved him. Now she understood why she felt nothing but relief to be through with Philip. It was Andy she wanted.

Somehow she had to see him. Not this evening, of course. She must make her peace with him as soon as possible, however. But how? Soon the first half of the concert was over. The beautiful music had been entirely wasted on her.

During the intermission, the doctor invited them downstairs to the refreshment stand, but Dorcas said, "I think I'll stay here. You go ahead."

As she waited, another girl she knew slipped into the seat beside her. "Oh, Patty, how nice to see you," Dorcas exclaimed.

"I was talking to Judy downstairs and she said you were here. I wanted to say hello. I'm so glad you're back in San Francisco." Patty had a mop of dark red hair and a sprinkle of freckles over her plump face. She was not a particularly pretty girl, but her friendly disposition and sense of humor made her one of the most popular girls in the city.

They talked a few minutes and Patty went on. "I'm inviting some of my friends over on Friday evening. I'd love to have you come. It'll just be a fun time. I have some new sheet music and I thought we could all sing and dance for a while. Maybe play charades."

"It sounds wonderful. I'd love to come."

"Is there some fellow you'd like to have me invite as your partner?"

Dorcas looked down and saw Andy and the two Rondell sisters returning to their seats. "Do you know Andy Woodard? He's down there with Lila."

"Yes, I've met him several times."

"Could you invite him without Lila?"

"Of course. She and her sister couldn't come anyway. They're going to Monterey to take part in a family wedding and staying down there for Christmas."

Dorcas grabbed Patty's arm. "Good. Maybe you could help me. I want to talk to Andy alone. He worked with me up in Trinity County at my grandfather's mine. Well, we had a misunderstanding. It was all my fault, and I want to apologize."

Patty grinned. "I suppose he got sore and isn't speaking."

"Something like that. Could you have the two of us over a few minutes early?"

Patty nodded. "I've asked everyone else to come at eight-thirty. You come at eight and wait for him in the back parlor. I'll send him in."

"You're a darling. I'll be so grateful if I can make my peace with Andy. It's worried me terribly."

"Leave it to me," Patty told her.

Dorcas took no chances. She arrived at Patty's house well before eight and waited anxiously in the back parlor. It was an attractive, homelike room with a fire burning briskly in the hearth. She looked at herself in the mirror hanging over a Hepplewhite table. Although a big bouquet of holly berries took up much of the room in the glass, she could see that her hair was still in its becoming pompadour and that her red velvet dress exposed her neck. Her ruby pendant on a gold chain was her only jewelry. She turned away from the mirror and paced restlessly around the room. What would Andy say? What would he do?

When she heard Patty and Andy out in the hall, she stepped to one side. "The others will be coming soon. You wait in here, where there's a nice fire going," Patty said.

Andy came into the room and walked toward the fire as their hostess closed the door.

Dorcas stepped toward him. "Andy."

He whirled around and looked at her. The color drained from his face. "What are you doing here?"

"I want to talk to you. I asked Patty to invite you."

Surely he'll be friendly, she told herself, but he crossed the room in long strides and grabbed her by the shoulders. "Why are you doing this to me?" His fingers pinched her flesh. "Don't you know that it tears me apart to be near you?"

"Andy, please listen—"

"All I ask is for you to leave me alone. Let me put my life together again." His voice broke. "I want nothing more to do with you. I'm leaving." He turned and strode toward the door.

"Andy, please. Don't go. I can't bear to live my life without you."

He glanced back at her. She held out her arms. "I love you, Andy."

Hardly believing what he was hearing, he stood in shock for a moment and then ran to her. As he held her close, a dry, tearing sob shook him. "Oh, my darling, is it true? Do you really care for me after all?"

"Yes. I've been heartsick ever since I learned about what you'd done for us and I didn't even have a chance to tell you how grateful I was."

"Oh, Dorcas, my dearest girl," he murmured as he held her against his heart.

"Oh, Andy, I didn't mean to be so cruel when I burst out the news about the lode and my plans to marry Philip." She hugged him as if she could never let him go. "Please forgive me."

He couldn't answer. He buried his face in her hair.

"Then when you wouldn't speak to me at the ball or come out to the carriage at Langley's, I realized that I had lost you. You can't imagine how I grieved for you. I didn't know what was wrong with me. I tried to make wedding arrangements and I couldn't."

"I want out with other girls and tried to forget you," Andy murmured. "But it was impossible. I doubt that I could ever get you out of my system."

"A long time ago you asked me to marry you. You said if I ever changed my mind about Philip, you'd be waiting for me."

"I still want you more than anything in the world."

"Well, I would like to marry you, Andy."

"Oh, my dearest, I've dreamed of this, hoping against hope that you would come to feel toward me the way I do toward you." He lowered his head and kissed her.

Soon the kiss became deep and electrifying, seeming to consume every bit of Dorcas. She heard nothing but the crackling of the fire, the faint moans in his throat.

How could she have thought she was in love with Philip? Her feelings must have been shallow, because they were nothing compared to the way her very inner being was responding to Andy now. A wave of happiness engulfed her. All the tearing grief over losing him was gone. This was so right. So basic and good.

"I love you, Andy," she whispered. "I don't know why it took me so long to realize it."

"I've loved you since that first day I met you when we went to the midwinter fair. But you only had eyes for Philip."

"I know. He had been an obsession with me ever since I was in my teens. I think I truly was in love with him at one time. But you gradually took his place in my heart, although I didn't know it."

He kissed the hollow of her throat and then held her close. Finally he said, "He was after your money, Dorcas. The Alpine. Your inheritance. How I wanted to warn you. But it would have looked as if I were talking against him just to get you for myself."

She laughed and kissed his cheek. "Don't worry about warning me. My grandfather took care of that in no uncertain terms. Then something happened and I saw through Philip at last." She told Andy about her conversation with Gene Sibler. "But I'm marrying you instead, beloved. At least I know you aren't just after my money. You proposed to me when I was sixty thousand in debt and my prospects pretty dim."

"The first thing we'll do is get you out of debt," Andy said.

"But I am out of debt. Every cent has been paid back. Philip took over the mine and has been taking the rich ore out of the drainage tunnel and the rest of the mine. He even used men from the Golden Star to help out. He sent all the gold down to the mint, and Grandpa got the checks. We have to give Philip credit for that."

Andy kissed her again. "I'm glad to hear that. Especially the part about using the Golden Star miners. How Elliott Richmond would blow up over that if he knew." Andy put his cheek against hers. "Let's get married as soon as possible."

"I already have a church reserved for the Saturday after Christmas. We can go look at it together and see if it suits you."

"Any place would do just as long as we can get married in it."

She snuggled against him and laughed. "How surprised the rector will be to learn I've changed grooms."

"Have you made any other arrangements?"

"No. It was so strange. I couldn't bring myself to make them. Something kept holding me back." She put her head on his shoulder. "Let's go tell Grandfather. He'll be so pleased. He's wanted me to marry you all along."

They hunted up their hostess and said they would be back later. As Patty found their wraps, she grinned. "I think I played Cupid."

"Could be," Andy said as he put his arm around Dorcas and led her out the door.

"Let's walk. It's only a few blocks," Dorcas cried happily.

With only the stars above and the faint glow of the gas lamps to light their way through the gentle darkness, they walked back toward the mansion.

* * *

"Andy!" Clyde rose from his chair and put out his hand. "It's good to see you again." He looked from one to the other and sensed their happiness.

"I came to ask your permission to marry your granddaughter." Andy liked and respected this old tyrant. They'd get along just fine.

Clyde shook his hand with vigor. "You've got it! How did you ever get this foolish girl to come to her senses?" He held out his arms to his granddaughter.

For a long moment she stayed in his embrace. Then she explained, "I saw Andy at a concert with another girl and I nearly died of jealousy. I realized I couldn't live without him. So tonight I proposed to him and he accepted."

"Well, for once you used your head." Clyde kissed her and held her to him. His voice thickened as he said, "This calls for a champagne toast. I'll call a servant."

"No, let me go down and find Mrs. Williams. I want to tell her myself," Dorcas said.

"I wish you both every happiness." Clyde lifted his glass a few moments later, after the housekeeper had come up with the champagne. "I couldn't be more pleased."

"That means so much to me. I want your approval more than anything." Dorcas blinked back tears. As difficult as he was, she adored her grandfather.

"Telephone your mother. If they're free tomorrow tell her that I'm taking everyone out to dinner at the Hamilton Regency to celebrate this big event." Clyde's old voice quivered with happiness.

When she told her mother, Lenore said. "Oh, I'm so glad. I can tell by your voice that this is right for you."

After a happy weekend, Andy came over Monday evening to make plans.

"I can work for Fred Langley in the winter when the Alpine is closed," he told Dorcas and Clyde over dinner. "By the way, Fred and I have worked out a way to divert the hot spring. At least I'd like to try it—with your permission, of course, Mr. Hamilton.''

Clyde nodded toward Dorcas. "It's up to her now."

Dorcas spoke up. "We must get the whole mine project set up in a businesslike way. I went at it so haphazardly before, but was lucky in spite of myself."

"After dinner, let's go into the library," Clyde said. "I want to discuss the advantages of setting up a regular mining company. You should get incorporated, Dorcas. And both of you would own equal shares of the stock."

"I'd like that. Wouldn't you, Andy?" Dorcas asked.

"Of course." He smiled at her. "If I'm going to support a family I'll need to be paid a salary."

Clyde spoke up. "Make it a darned good one. If you carry all the responsibility for the Alpine, you'll earn every cent."

"We can build a house for ourselves on the grounds of the mine," Dorcas put in. "Then we can turn the cottage over to Red Wallace. I'm sure he'll come back once he knows he won't have me for a boss."

Andy grinned at her. "I suppose you'll come underground and stick your nose into everything just the same."

"Of course." She turned to her grandfather. "If we incorporate, I could be an officer, couldn't I? An important one, so I'll have some say?"

Her grandfather looked at her over his hawklike nose. "I'll explain everything to you later when we go into the library. Before you make any final decisions, we should hire a lawyer with a background in corporations. He can go over all the responsibilities and complications. It's not simple. But there's plenty of time after your wedding to go into that."

"There's so much to do." Dorcas's eyes glowed with excitement. "Even a small wedding takes some planning, and I should start looking for an apartment here in the city for us during the winter."

"I have a suggestion that you might consider," Clyde put in. "For some time I've been thinking about moving downstairs. I could use the guest bedroom and the back parlor for my living quarters. Then turn the whole upstairs over to you two. You can do anything you want with it. This whole mansion will be yours someday anyway. Thanks to Andy here, we've still got it in the family."

Dorcas looked at Andy and he nodded his approval, so she

said, "We'd love that arrangement for the winter months, Grandpa. And we'll have a special room for you when we build the Alpine house so that you can come visit when you want."

As they walked into the library, Dorcas whispered to Andy, "Grandpa sent Philip a generous check from the Hamilton Company and thanked him for his services at the Alpine. If he's going to be out of work soon, he may need the money."

Andy smiled. "Don't worry about Philip. He'll probably go after Healther La Pointe now. She's wealthy, too."

With her wedding veil floating in a cloud behind her, Dorcas walked down the chapel aisle on Clyde Hamilton's arm. The massive arrangements of red carnations and gladioli on each side of the altar repeated the colors of the magnificent stained glass window above.

Judy, in her green velvet maid-of-honor dress, preceded her. The pews were filled with their friends and the staff from the mansion. Esther wiped her eyes as she stood with Mrs. Williams. Lenore, wearing her own lace wedding dress, clasped Prescott's hand. She looked serene and beautiful.

Best of all, Andy, with his best man, stood by the altar, his shoulders back, so tall and honorable. As Dorcas came toward him, she saw his sweet, endearing smile.

Her heart cried out to him, "Oh, Andy!"

ABOUT THE AUTHOR

"The Gilded Age," a term coined by Mark Twain, is of particular interest to Dorothy Dowdell, as it was during this period between the Civil War and World War I that the innovative entrepreneurs developed the early industries of the West. Her first historical novel was GLORY LAND, about the building of the transcontinental railroad over the Sierra Nevada. A WOMAN'S EMPIRE, which came next, dealt with a timber dynasty in the Northwest. GOLDEN FLAME has a gold-mining background and is set in Trinity County in northern California and San Francisco in 1894. She plans to write more novels inspired by the accomplishments of the dynamic women and ambitious men of this fascinating era in the West.

Mrs. Dowdell was born in Reno, Nevada, but has spent most of her life in California. She is a graduate of the University of California at Berkeley, where she majored in English and history. Besides her historical novels, she has written suspense, gothic, and romance novels, as well as eight nonfiction books for young people in collaboration with her late husband, a college instructor in science. Her main interest outside of writing is traveling. She lives in Los Gatos, near San Jose, and has two grown children and five grandchildren.